CALLED

A HOLLOWAY PACK NOVEL

J.A. BELFIELD

PRAISE FOR CALLED

---

*"This book is fast-paced and engaging from the moment the reader is forced to ask, **Who is Sean?** to the very end when the answers are revealed. I found myself frantically turning pages to find out the secrets embedded in her dreams."* ~ Keri Lake, author of the Sons of Wrath series

"Darkness and Light is an amazing story, and I loved reading it! It has an amazing main character, some fantastic secondary characters, and one remarkable storyline." ~ BurningxImpossiblyxBright

"It draws you in, mesmerizes you, and captures your breath until the very last word." ~ At Random

"J.A. Belfield has successfully made werewolves my favorite paranormal creatures of the night." ~ Lovey Dovey Books

"At the risk of sounding completely cliché...OMG! If you love Paranormal Romance and specifically Werewolves, then you have got to read this book." ~ Nocturne Reads

CALLED
A HOLLOWAY PACK NOVEL

Published by J.A. Belfield
www.jabelfield.com

Previously published as *Darkness & Light* [2011] and *The Wolf Within* [2017]

Cover art by Aimee Laine.

First Printing: July 2011

10 9 8 7 6 5 4 3 2 1

CALLED

For Newlyn, Nevyn, and Bethyn—you know why.

Chapter 1
LIGHT

S*ean!*

I jerked awake, the echo of the name in my head merging with the trilling of the alarm clock. With an inward groan, I slapped my hand on the snooze.

Movement behind told me I'd disturbed Peter. A second later, his arm reached out to draw me back against him, and I lowered my lids, drifting back to thoughts of my dream.

Other than watching myself wandering around some forest, not much had happened in it. Yet, the vividness of the imagery lingering in my mind had me questioning the significance of the dream I'd had for the past four nights. Just as I puzzled over the name I'd been greeted by for the past three mornings, as well as the past three afternoons, and the past three evenings.

At the second call of the clock, I hit the switch again and rolled to face Peter. Inhaling, I detected the lingering odour of the previous night's meal upon his breath, the unintended ejaculated fluid that always escaped during sleep, and each separate fragrance of the toiletries he'd used in his pre-dinner shower the evening before.

His eyes snapped open. "Are you sniffing me again?"

I smiled with my spoken, "No," and slid from the bed.

At the door, I snagged my gown and pulled it over my matching nightdress before heading downstairs. I plodded into the kitchen, switched on the kettle. With a tilt of my head, I tracked Peter's footsteps to the bathroom, where he performed his morning urination at a volume only men are capable of.

By the time I made my way back upstairs, carrying a tray laden with two mugs of cappuccino and a plateful of toast, Peter had slid back beneath the duvet to await our ritual of breakfast in bed.

He smiled when I handed him the tray and climbed in beside him. "Thanks, Jem."

I reached out for a slice of toast and tried to eat without filling the bed with crumbs. Peter made no such effort. As his housewife, I'd be expected to clean it up later.

Peter downed his cappuccino before returning to the bathroom.

When I climbed from the bed, I brushed out the hiding crumbs and straightened the duvet. After ensuring Peter's work clothes were folded neatly on the end of the bed for him, I headed back down with the tray.

As usual, it took Peter only fifteen minutes to get ready for work. He strode into the kitchen in his cement-stained trousers, his close-cropped hair groomed to perfection.

I laughed as he grabbed me, bent me backward like a finale of the Tango, and planted a hard kiss on my lips.

"Have a good day, Jem."

"You, too," I said as he straightened us.

He gave me one final squeeze before ducking into the hall to pull on his work boots. A few seconds later, the click of the front door announced his departure, to supervise what he referred to as his minions at the site where he worked.

Once alone, I took a shower, and with hot water running

over my shoulders, I tried to figure out the dream that refused to leave my mind. Four nights of recurrence meant I could recall it well: the calm expression upon my face as I'd walked amongst nature, trailing my hands across bark as though completely at one with my surroundings. Although I hadn't experienced them directly, I could imagine the scents of the forest, as though I had actually been there.

Sean!

The name exploded inside my mind—a word my mind chose to conjure without warning since the first occurrence of my dream. I could've coped with the incessant invasion of my thoughts, but the accompanying twitch to my body and unexpected shivers of exhilaration that coursed through me each time were something else entirely. I didn't even like the name Sean.

Back in the bedroom, I kneeled to slide out my bottom drawer. Inside were my favourite items of clothing—the ones I only wore when I knew I wouldn't be seen by Peter. Everything else, found in the drawers above and the wardrobe, consisted of skirts, dresses, blouses, sandals—feminine wear, which men like Peter preferred to find their women in on their return from work. I guessed what he couldn't see, couldn't hurt him.

Dressed in knee-length denim shorts and a pink vest, I tackled my blonde hair with the straightener. Given the choice, I'd have left it to its own devices—I much preferred it wild and untamed—but my life wasn't always about what I wanted. As wife, and provider of food and sex to Peter, my life revolved around what he wanted, what he needed me to be.

WITH ONLY TWO minutes to spare, I pulled up outside the four-bedroom detached house of my best, and only, friend. From my little Peugeot, I walked to the front door and knocked.

"One minute." The muffled call came from upstairs some-where, and ten seconds later, the pound of footsteps followed. The door opened to reveal a smiling Poppy.

"Are you ready?" I knew she wouldn't be.

"Come in a mo." She stepped back to grant access. "I just need to find my shoes. Ben must have hidden them again."

Smiling at the mention of Poppy's eight-year-old son, I stepped inside. "So, what did you have on your feet when you went to the school?"

"Trainers," she said. "I want my sandals for shopping."

I rolled my eyes, heading for the huge corner-suite to settle in for the wait. Past experience told me I could be there for as long as twenty minutes. I flopped back as Poppy ran up the stairs, and soon the sounds of spraying and thuds carried down to me. The latter, combined with the occasional grunt, suggested she searched for her missing shoe.

Only ten minutes later—a record for Poppy on a search mission—she reappeared with a pair of sandals and a smile. "Got them."

We reached the supermarket at ten twenty-five. Having shopped with Poppy for the previous four years, the ritual we shared came naturally to us, and the first place we headed was the clothing department.

Poppy paused in her study of a T-shirt sporting a lurid logo, turning as I picked up a pair of jeans in one hand and a skirt in the other. "What are you doing?"

I waved the hung clothes about like she couldn't otherwise see them. "I'm not sure which to get."

Her eyes narrowed. "Well, you're not buying that God-awful skirt. I won't let you."

"But Peter likes me in skirts."

She took a step closer, her finger pointed my way. "Let him take you shopping for the damn things, then." Before I could blink, the flowery chiffon piece landed back on the rail with all the other flimsy garments. "You're thirty-two, not fifty-two." Her eyes flashed for a second. "It's high time that man of yours remembered we're not all nearing forty."

Sean!

I jerked at the suddenness of the name popping into my head.

"Jem?"

My eyes dart left and right. A frown formed on my forehead, and I reached up, surprised by the tremble of my hand. Whether from excitement, fear, some kind of nervous reaction, I felt wrong—again.

"Jem?"

My fingers smudged over a fine coating of sweat upon reaching my brow, the discovery deepening my frown, rather than reducing it.

"Jem?"

Gripping my shoulder, Poppy shook me, and I turned to her.

Consternation filled her eyes. She gave a slow headshake. "I've no idea where you just went to, but you definitely were not inside your head for a minute there."

I gave another wipe across my forehead. "Sorry, Pop. I don't know what came over me."

"Are you okay?"

I nodded, tried to smile. "I think so."

After watching me for a few seconds longer, Poppy loosened her grip and, bending, grabbed something from the floor. "Are you getting these jeans?"

I hadn't noticed them fall. "I shouldn't." I blinked to bring myself back. "I'm running out of space in my bottom drawer."

"For goodness sake, Jem, just buy the damn things. Wear them in front of him. What can he say?"

I shrugged.

"Why do you let him tell you what to wear?"

"It's not like that," I said. "Peter just prefers me to dress nice."

Poppy scowled before making a visible effort to rein it in. "Well, you look nice in jeans. Buy them."

"But I'm running out of space—"

"Okay." She put the jeans in my trolley, herded me along. "I have two spare drawers in my wardrobe—"

I couldn't help but smile. "You haven't got a wardrobe. You've got an entire room dedicated to fashion."

She grinned. "Exactly. It's called a walk-*in* wardrobe, Jem. And I have space. So, if you want to buy more stuff, do so. Just come over earlier to change when you want to wear any of it."

"Thanks, Pop."

As ALWAYS, the shopping trip preceded a trip to the supermarket café, where our regular lunch of fish and chips came with chatter of our week. Poppy was a blissfully happy, unmarried-but-long-term-dating mother of two. I was a happy wife and provider of food and sex. Yet, however many times I tried to tell Poppy I was happy, she never believed me. She told me I was in denial, that I'd never had another relationship to compare with. She argued that I believed Peter made me happy because I didn't know any different. Poppy always had a habit of saying exactly what she thought.

"So," she said, waving her fork about, "that dream—did you have it again?"

"Which one?"

She rolled her eyes before settling them into place to give me *the look*.

I breathed out a laugh and nodded. "Twice more."

"And you're still in the forest?"

"Uh-huh." I popped a piece of battered fish in my mouth.

"Anything else happen?"

"Nuh-huh," I managed through chews.

"Weird."

I nodded, almost said, 'Not as weird as the name that keeps bothering me'.

For some reason, I decided to keep that little detail to myself. I couldn't even recall knowing anyone named Sean.

Chapter 2

Friday evening, Peter's dinner sat on the table growing cold. In eight years of marriage to him, Peter had never been home later than six thirty—never. I glanced at the clock for the fourth time: seven twenty.

Concerned something could have happened at the site, I picked up my phone and called him.

"Hello." Background noise blared over his voice.

"Peter?"

"Hello?"

"Peter, can you hear me?"

The mutterings lessened, and his voice hit my ear with force. "What do you want, Jem?"

"Where are you?"

"I'm out."

"Where, Pete?"

"My name's Peter, not bloody Pete."

I cringed. "Sorry."

"I'm at the pub. The boys invited me out."

I'd never known Peter to drink before. "You didn't say you were going to the pub."

"Because I didn't bloody know, did I?" he asked, his speech slurred.

"But your dinner has gone cold."

"Is that why you rang? To tell me my bloody dinner's cold?"

"I was worried when you weren't home on time, Peter. You're never late."

"Well, I am today."

"What time—"

At the dead connection, I stared at the phone. Peter had never spoken to me like that before.

THE DVD CLOCK flashed twelve forty when Peter's key fumbled against the lock of the front door. I'd only waited up because he preferred for us to go to bed at the same time, but fatigue had kicked in a good hour before.

He staggered to the middle of the living room. His work boots still adorned his feet, and the dried mud they carried broke away onto the cream rug beneath him. From the sofa, I watched as further clumps departed onto the floor.

I'd have to ensure they were cleaned away before morning.

Hands on his hips, Peter swayed, his lids lowering over eyes settled on me. He swayed some more, as though gyrating to a slow song only he could hear. Each movement wafted his unsavoury odour my way.

Unable to stop myself, I inhaled. Peter reeked of the sweat men always gave off after spending a few hours compressed with other males. He also stank of the alcohol he'd consumed— the staleness of many pints of lager and potent whisky fumes. For a man I'd never seen drink alcohol, he'd evidently gone way over his limit.

I inhaled deeper and surmised he had, at some point, come into contact with someone wearing a floral eau de toilette, as well as spent time with the establishment's smokers.

His eyes snapped open, narrowed in a glare. "Were you sniffing me again?"

I shook my head. "No, Pete."

"It's Peter. How many times do I have to tell you? And how many times do I have to tell you to stop fucking sniffing me?"

My shoulders stiffened at his tone. "Sorry, Peter. I couldn't help it."

"Couldn't help it?" He stared at me like he thought me insane. "Of course you can, Jem. You just don't fucking do it."

"Sorry, Peter."

"Sorry, Peter, sorry, Peter," he mimicked.

He waved his hands about. I had no idea why. His body rocked from side to side as a result.

Like an idea had struck, he stopped and lurched forward, wrapping his hand around my arm. "Come on." His tug jerked me to my feet.

I pushed at him. "Peter, what are you doing?"

"Time for bed." He tucked his shoulder into my stomach, folding my body in half as he lifted my feet from the ground.

My head swam in its upside-down state. "What are you doing?"

As he headed for the stairs, his mirthless chuckle sent a chill through me. "I'm going to give it to you good, girl."

I pushed up, tried to straighten my body. "Put me down."

"Shush!" He climbed three steps in succession, the jolted movement flipping my head down low until the carpet beneath danced in a kaleidoscope of colour.

Reaching around, I pried at his fingers clawing into my thigh. "Please, put me down, Peter."

"Quiet!"

The vicious yell of his voice startled me into submission,

and I hung there, breaths short, pulse racing. Somehow, he made it up the rest of the stairs.

My head clunked off the doorframe to our bedroom, and I cried out, pressing my hand to the afflicted spot.

"Stop fucking whining." He strode to the bed and dropped me down.

The springs of the mattress bounced my body back up. Pain shot through my head.

He loomed over me, all humour and softness evaporating from his eyes. As I scrambled backward, he grabbed my ankle and dragged me forward.

I pushed at his hold. "Peter, don't." My voice came out breathy.

"Shh." Pressing a finger against my lips, he shoved me back down before unzipping his trousers and sliding them over his hips.

"This isn't like you, Peter." Clutching at his shirt, I tried to look him in the eye, to make him see me, but he seemed to have lost all focus for anything other than his goal. Fear thudded through my body. "Please, I don't want—"

"I said *quiet*!" His fingers dug into my thighs.

I peeled at them, but determination gave him strength, and with one yank, my head flew back as my rear lifted toward his pointing erection.

Asking him to stop would have been a waste of time—his desperation for sex showed in his rough groping, his heavy breaths. I tried to advise myself to just let him take it, then it would be over, and I could forget about it.

That didn't stop my tears when he lifted me higher and prepared to plunge.

A smile spread his lips as his tip came into contact with me. My breaths stalled, my chest beating to the stress of my heart, as I braced for his entrance into complete dryness.

Peter's face went slack. His eyes rolled to show the whites. In the next instant, his jaw fell, as did his hold.

I barely escaped the full blow when his body hit the mattress and his arm thumped across my chest.

Breaths rapid, I lay staring at him, stale alcohol wafts blasting my face. His features, twisted in sexual resolve mere seconds before, adopted total serenity in sleep.

Unwilling to remain so close, I wormed out from beneath his arm, rolled him away from me onto his back. Grunts burst from me against the effort of hauling his deadweight to his own side of the mattress.

I glanced toward the door, considered going into the spare bedroom, but knew Peter would be upset if I didn't share his bed. Ignoring my tremors, I climbed in beside him.

Sleep, however, had no intention of coming with ease.

Each time I closed my eyes, visions of Peter's face filled my mind—not his usual face, but an ugly mask. More than once, I jerked awake to the stench of his breath. With each awakening, the bruises he'd created hurt a little more.

Chapter 3
DARKNESS

As an observer, I watch my dream-self walk within the forest. The sun glares down, yet the dense canopy of leaves permits it no entry to dapple the ground. Tree limbs hang low, hang high, long, short, thick, thin, entwined, embracing their neighbours. With hands caressing the roughness of bark, her eyes search upward then ahead.

Sean!

Smiling, my dream-self moves deeper into the forest. Strewn leaves sigh a susurrant tune as the hem of her lemon dress teases their crisp edges. The only other sounds are the almost inaudible crunch of the ground beneath her feet, the barest of breaths as they pass her lips, and the faint rustle of foliage, no more than a whisper in the near-absence of wind.

Her tranquil features reflect her mood, as does her relaxed stance, and she moves with a grace I am incapable of when conscious.

Sean!

At a noise to her left, my dream-self turns, her head tilting as she peers ahead. With a new smile coating her lips, her steps become purposeful.

A bush shivers, almost imperceptibly, yet my dream-self spots it. She elevates to the balls of her feet, causing no disturbance to the quiet. Although her expression does little to reveal her emotions, the rise and fall of her chest hastens with each nearing step.

With obvious caution, she reaches the bush and pushes herself higher onto her toes. Whatever she discovers on the other side widens her eyes.

Unable to see through the eyes of my dream-self, I drift closer.

Once alongside, a glance to the left shows me her—my—profile: the small pointed tip of her nose, the deep blue of her irises, the blonde braid curving over her shoulder and tickling the modesty lace covering her small cleavage. Matching my pose to hers, I lean forward for a clearer view.

Upon seeing what she does, I give my attention back to her, study her reaction. There should be terror, fear, horror in her expression, but none of those are present. Her frown and biting of her lower lip portray only intrigue.

A creature claims the ground beyond the bush, its ever-changing appearance rendering it unidentifiable. Four legs are supported by four paws, a hunkered head holds a canine appearance, but in the midst of deformity, it alters as we watch. The body contorts, a low growl rumbles from it, and it moulds to resemble a new form as though shaped by an unseen hand. Fur becomes flesh, bones a new skeleton, the skull redeveloping until what we see is no longer animal ... but human.

The man remains on all fours, head hung, breathing laboured.

My dream-self takes a step back, her stance showing her attempt at stealth, followed by another. A third step brings her foot onto a stray twig.

The crack resonates through the quiet, and the man's shoulders tense. His head whips high.

When his eyes lock with my dream-self, he omits a rumbling growl.

Chapter 4
LIGHT

S *ean!*

I awoke to quiet. My body had curled at some point during the night, and I lay in my usual position, facing away from Peter. At his shallow breathing, confirming his unconsciousness, relief blew from me.

I'd spent hours awake, trying to justify his despicable behaviour from the previous night. Every explanation I conjured pointed to his alcohol consumption. Even that, after ten years of not a drop passing his lips, warranted answers.

Pushing it aside, I allowed my mind to flit to my latest dream but frowned when it dawned on me that the events had altered. Though, thinking back through the happenings in the forest of my mind, the confusion I'd felt during sleep evaporated. Having dreamt of the mythological creatures since the age of seven, I knew, without a shadow of a doubt, the man's original form had been a wolf. Yet again, a werewolf had visited my subconscious.

I couldn't help but wonder how many nights I'd endure the new dream before it subsided or continued to progress, as I knew it followed on from the previous four. Yet, why I thought as such escaped me. There'd been no clapboard announcing 'Jem's latest werewolf dream: scene two'—I just knew.

The mattress dipped and creaked, as Peter stirred behind me.

Fear encompassed me in a way I'd never felt around him before—one that insisted the drinking may not have been responsible for his actions, that I'd be subjected to the same treatment again. For the first time in our marriage, my body stiffened at the thought of him touching me.

"Jem?" he murmured. "Are you awake?"

I considered feigning sleep. Instead, I nodded my head, fuzzing my hair against the pillow beneath it.

His hand slid over my stomach, and he pulled me back against his erection.

Suppressing my shudder took effort.

"Is there anything to get up for today?" He brushed my hair to the side, skimmed his lips across the nape of my neck. "Or shall we have a lie-in?" 'Lie-in', to Peter, meant pre-breakfast sex.

"Actually, Peter, I don't feel too good this morning."

He continued to kiss my downy hairs. "What's up, Jem?" If he recalled his behaviour from the night before, he gave a fine performance in concealing it. Or maybe his drinking had been responsible, after all.

My muscles relaxed a little, yet I kept up the charade. "It's just a little stomach ache."

"I can help with that." With a quiet laugh, he rolled me onto my back.

The second his alcohol-lingering breath encompassed me, I gagged, slapping a hand to my mouth. "I'm going to be sick."

"Quick." He shoved me away. "Don't get it on the bed."

For ten minutes, I retched over the toilet with nothing coming out. Only the memory, which Peter's breath had ignited, nauseated my stomach. With my forehead resting against the toilet seat, I closed my eyes.

"Jem?"

I didn't answer.

"Are you alright?" he called.

My lids lifted. "I don't feel too good."

Footsteps crossed the landing before slapping against the lino at my rear. His hand rubbed my shoulder. "Maybe you should spend the day in bed." His frown gave the appearance of genuine concern, as he helped me to my feet, lending reassurance that his behaviour had been a one-off. With his arm around my waist, he escorted me to the bedroom, tucked me beneath the duvet. "I'll go get breakfast."

I gave him a small smile, offering my lips for the kiss I thought he intended when he leaned forward, but he veered off to peck my cheek like he'd had second thoughts. *God forbid should you risk contracting something contagious from your wife.*

He left me to head downstairs. His curses arrived about five seconds later. "Jem, there's bloody mud all over the floor down here."

My pulse picked up. I'd forgotten about the mess. "It must be off your work boots."

"And you didn't get it up?"

"It must have happened after I'd come upstairs." I winced beneath the lie.

He didn't question me further, but his grumbles carried loud and clear, and I knew he'd leave the mess to me. Stilling my breaths, I closed my eyes. It didn't take long for him to come back up, carrying the breakfast tray, which he set on my lap.

I looked at the singular mug. "Where's yours?"

"I'll eat downstairs," he said. "You might be catching."

My eyebrow lifted before I could stop it.

"Don't worry." He rubbed a hand across my hair. "I'll come back up and see you later."

Left alone, I nibbled on a corner of my toast, lifted my cappuccino for a sip.

Sean!

My hand gave a spasmodic jerk, spattering hot fluid across the tray.

I put my mug down, flexed my scalded fingers before licking them clean. My eyes closed in frustration, as I pinched the bridge of my nose and tried to recall how many times I'd heard the blasted name in my head.

Thirty-three times in six days.

Maybe I was going crazy.

Chapter 5
DARKNESS

My dream-self holds eye contact with the crouched man beyond the bush—yet only for a second. With a spin of her body, a hastening of her breaths, she begins to run.

Through the trees, she races away, her bare feet creating no hindrance to her escape. There is refinement to her movements, each step as fluid as that of a gazelle in slow motion.

She glances back. Her eyes widen. I follow her stare to see the man is mobile. The distance between them is already diminishing.

With fear tightening her features, she turns to face the way she runs and increases the tempo to her racing feet.

The forest ends, opening into a clearing, and she bursts past brush until bathed with light. Her eyes seek assistance, falling on a house ahead—and people. My dream-self must experience relief at their presence—I feel it within myself.

Four male heads turn as she dashes toward them. She holds their interest for moments before they give it to the man who follows close behind. Within a moment, the men's long strides carry their muscular frames forward with a grace unexpected for their build.

Wary of the ones she is running toward, my dream-self stumbles to a halt, toppling in her abruptness. Her eyes, as frantic as an ensnared rabbit, absorb the men approaching her, before her head whips toward the wolf-man at her rear. Left and right, back and forth, she appears to seek escape.

As though aware of her intention, the men separate and surround her. The opportunity to leave evaporates with each passing second. One of the men raises his palms, a gesture of calm, yet the circle they've created around her lessens in size.

With nowhere to go, she remains leery—she knows she is trapped.

The wolf-man reaches her and, grabbing her shoulders, hauls her to her feet from her fallen position.

"What's going on?" one of them asks.

Her pursuer looks to the speaker. "She saw me."

"What?"

"I caught her watching me."

The one who spoke first—who seems to be some kind of leader—runs a hand over his head as a low groan leaves his throat. He looks at my dream-self. "What were you doing in the forest?"

A rough shake of her shoulders by the wolf-man prevents her answer. "We can't let her go."

"Please. Just let me get—"

Her attacker spins her around, cutting off her words.

She squirms in his grasp. "Let me go."

The wolf-man speaks only to the men. "She *saw* me."

Although his tight expression suggests he is unhappy, the apparent leader gives a nod of his head.

My dream-self claws at the hand of her attacker, as he takes her by the throat, her eyes wide with pleading. "No!" The ground disappears from beneath her feet and the kick of her legs swings her hanging body. "No!" She gasps. "You don't understand."

Chapter 6
LIGHT

Tuesday morning blessed me with an empty house. Peter had shown no outward sign of awareness, regarding Friday night. If he remembered, he'd excelled in his covering skills. That didn't stop my body tensing, though, whenever he came near.

I dawdled in my robe before making it into the kitchen. Hot water spurted into the sink when I turned on the tap, and I lifted my eyes to the window, peering out at borders in need of planting.

Sean!

The plate I held slipped from my hands and it hit the water, splashing suds at my chest with a loud glop. "Damn name's driving me crazy." Swiping at my damp front, I heaved out a sigh. "Damn dreams are driving me crazy, too."

Over the course of ten days, three different dreams had plagued my sleep, which, when moved into order, seemed to sketch an entire story in my mind. The night before, I'd finally come close to having contact with the Sean character bugging me. Being mentally invaded by a name could in no way be classed as meeting him, but I felt certain I'd see him in the dreams soon.

I just hadn't a clue who he was.

My khaki shorts, plimsolls, and the purple of my T clashed with the lime green of the sofa as I dropped down on it. At nine fifteen, Poppy would be expecting my phone call—I always called her at that time on Tuesday's. By nine ten, I'd had enough of waiting.

"Jem, I presume," she answered. "Although why I'd presume that is beyond me."

I breathed out a laugh, despite my sombre mood.

"What's up? You're early."

Even though she couldn't see me, I shrugged my shoulders.

"Jem?" The brushing of fabric reached me, like she'd adjusted her position. "What's wrong?"

I realised I didn't want to share my Friday night experience with Poppy. I couldn't bear the thought of listening to her 'I told you so's'. "Everything's fine." The words came out flat.

"Hmm, if you say so."

"What's the plan?" I asked, changing the subject. "Shopping, or caffeine fix in front of your flatscreen?"

"I need new shoes."

I rolled my eyes. "Of course you do."

"I do—white ones."

"You have white ones, Pop."

"They discoloured on me, so I threw them out. You know I need to replace them before I decide I need them again."

I couldn't help but laugh. "Sure you do."

HIGH STREETS SEEMED infinite when I stood at one end and knew I had to work my way to another I couldn't even see.

Poppy dragged me into every shoe shop we passed, and every non shoe shop on the off-chance they had shoes.

In the fourth store, Poppy's eyes focused on the back wall of footwear. "You treating yourself today, Jem?"

I shook my head. "Just along for the ride."

She turned to me. "You should treat yourself, cheer yourself up."

"I'm okay." I shrugged.

She stopped walking to give me *the stare*—the look that had Jase, her partner, squirming on many occasions.

"I'm okay," I said again. "Really."

Although she turned back to the shoes, her face showed she hadn't bought what I'd said. I guessed I hadn't done a very good job of selling it.

We hit twenty stores before Poppy found a pair of white shoes resembling what she sought. She sank into one of the available stools to try them on, and I perused racks of jeans and vests. At maxi dresses in all colours, I found myself wondering what Peter would think if he came home to me wearing one of those.

Sean!

I twitched with a blink. Though, it hadn't so much been the resounding name which startled me that time, but the familiarity of the voice that had verbalised it—my own.

I glanced about. No stupor could be blamed—my mind was alert—but the name had begun to drive me insane, and I needed answers. On tiptoes, I peered over rails, leaning to check around them. I even walked the length of the store, out the doors, and searched the river of pedestrians.

Nothing. People bustled about their business—shopping, eating, drinking, talking—but none looked like they should be called Sean.

"Jem?"

At Poppy's voice, I didn't look back.

"Jem, what are you doing?" she asked.

Whether I looked left, right, over or around people, nobody seemed to be right.

Poppy tugged at my shoulder. "What are you doing?"

I turned to her. "Nothing."

"Were you following someone?"

"No. I just needed fresh air."

Her expression told me she didn't believe me.

"Did you get your shoes?" I asked.

She swung a bag from her finger, even allowed a smile to reach her lips.

I smiled back, trying at the same time to ignore the steady beat drumming away inside my head: *Sean, Sean, Sean, Sean, Sean!* Blinking, I pushed it out, stretched my lips into a grin.

Poppy's smile wavered as she studied me harder.

"Isn't it lunchtime yet?" I asked, my voice a little high.

"Yeah, we'll head to Lorenzo's," she said, slipping her arm through mine, and I nodded, relieved she'd agreed. "And while we eat," she added, "you can tell me what's going on in that head of yours lately."

Busted! I breathed out a laugh. Maybe the time had come to reveal all.

Chapter 7
DARKNESS

Throat held by her attacker, feet dangling below, my dream-self grabs at the hand on her windpipe. Her eyes plead with him for release as the other four men observe. "You don't understand," she gasps.

The one who appears to be some kind of leader steps forward. "Understand what?"

Sean!

My dream-self's eyes dart to the side, frustration within them.

Sean!

"Let ... me down." She struggles to speak past her attacker's compression, but gains no reprieve from the wolf-man. "Please." Her weakened voice is panicked. "He's ... coming."

The leader takes a step forward. "Who's coming?"

"Sean. It's Sean—he's coming."

Although they all look toward the forest, my dream-self is not released.

Her body wriggles to no avail. '*No, no, no,*' forms on her lips as she grips the arms of the wolf-man, and determination fills her eyes as she swings her right foot back.

From the forest, the leader turns toward her, but as his gaze lands upon her braced body, he points just as my dream-self fires her foot forward, right for her attacker's groin. *"Look—"*

The leader's call coincides with contact, and the wolf-man turns toward the warning. In the next moment, an agonised crumbling overtakes his features. His grip loosens, and my dream-self drops to the ground. Breaths gasping from her, her eyes dart toward the forest.

A huge, chocolate-coloured wolf emerges from the trees.

She clambers to her feet, and her sights remain on the wolf as she breaks into a sprint across the lawn.

At a speed much greater, the wolf dashes after her.

"Sean!" the leader shouts.

Her step falters, but the wolf does not cease to run.

As though he intends to head off the wolf, the leader rushes forward. *"Sean!"*

The wolf darts to the side, and as my dream-self takes off again, all of the men begin to run across the lawn—chasing the wolf, as the wolf chases her.

Chapter 8
LIGHT

"I thought we could go shopping today," Peter said on Saturday morning. "You haven't been in a while."

I didn't mention I'd already been three times that week, but merely smiled.

He lifted his brows. "Okay?"

"What time?"

"Now." He headed to the hall for his shoes.

"But—"

"You're ready, right?" he called.

Apart from the dishes and housework, sure, Pete. Returning to an unclean house always put Peter in a foul mood. "Yes, but—"

"I'll wait for you in the car."

*

Peter hated the High Street—'Too many idiots,' he grumbled—so we ended up at his favourite department store. With Peter's salary being our sole household income, what he wanted took priority, making Menswear the first section we visited.

Whenever we shopped together, he'd never ask my opinion. An item would be taken from the rail, he'd hold it up and study it, and then tell me he'd make it look good—just as he told me what I'd look good in, too.

The basket contained an entire outfit for him before we headed for Ladieswear, where he held a knee-length skirt against me. "This is nice."

Jem, you're thirty-two, not fifty-two. Poppy's words bounced inside my head like a ping-pong ball as I stared at the pleats.

"Jem?"

"Huh?"

He frowned like he considered me some kind of miscreant. "Pardon is the word you're looking for."

"Pardon, Peter," I muttered. "What did you say?"

"I said, *this is nice.* What do you think?"

If Poppy were there, she'd have found some place to hide it, to prevent me parting with money for something so awful. "Actually, Peter, I'm not keen on the colour." I cringed once the words left my mouth.

He stared at me as though seeing me clearly for the first time. I'd never disputed anything he wanted to buy me before. "Well, I like it." It went in the basket with the nice, modern clothing he'd chosen for himself. "There are some cardigans on the other side I spotted last time," he continued, walking off. "We'll get one to go with it."

I trotted behind like his good little wife, but managed no more than a handful of steps before annoying tingling dotted the flesh of my arms. I brushed at them, despite seeing nothing there.

Peter paused and turned back, regarding me as I rubbed the length of my arms. "What are you doing?"

I glanced up at him. "My arms feel funny." The tingling grew stronger. I rubbed harder until friction burned my skin and marked it red.

"Will you stop that!" he said. "People are staring."

"I can't help it."

The tingling extended to my legs. I bent to study my shins protruding from beneath my skirt, expected to see a bug infestation crawling across me, but found nothing.

"Stop it, Jem. You're causing a scene."

My hands neglected my arms to rub at my legs.

"Jem, stop it."

"I—"

Intense throbbing bulleted through me, beating against the inner walls of my body, and a gasp burst from me as I doubled over. As though my bones had fractured into a thousand splinters, tiny needle-like stabs jabbed at every inch of my flesh, until a mewled cry took over the gasp.

With the intensity of an inferno, heat shot up my spine and into my skull. My knees collapsed. I threw my arms out, landed hard with a grunt, and swayed on all fours.

I'm changing. I frowned as I panted. *Why on earth would I think that?*

"Jem?"

Spasms raged through every muscle I possessed.

I glanced down. My eyes widened.

Pulsations washed over me, evident where they weren't before. With the elasticity of dough, my skin stretched over my body into impossible contortions. My back snapped down to a low bow, with a crunch crashing through my hearing and agony powerful enough to twist my spine.

I slammed my lids shut. My cry echoed off the high ceilings. Upon opening my eyes, even my hands beneath me had altered form.

How can this be happening?

"Jem?"

Hairs sprouted from my pores as though fed on rapid-result fertiliser. My breaths and pulse increased to a manic rate. Rationality argued otherwise, yet I knew my body to be in the midst of a change. The how and the why were far from my comprehension, but somewhere deep within, my mind told me to wait it out, that it would be over soon.

"Jem?"

Squeezing my lids tight, I attempted to block the torture needling through me. With deep breaths, I imagined a farmer's meadow, with butterflies and bumblebees, buzzing and fluttering amongst the wildflowers. The trick had always worked to calm me as a child, to chase away the unwanted return of nightmares. I threw my concentration into the yellow and black of the flying creatures, the brilliant white of the flickering wings, the swaying of purple petals upon the gentle breeze, until my pain subsided.

I opened my eyes to a dense forest. Fresh foliage coated every inch of higher-based timber. A deep inhalation discovered a musky scent on the air, and I shivered, drawing it in deeper until intoxicated by its allure.

Sean!

The breeze, which carried the beckoning scent, led the way, and my claws scratched at dirt as I took off. Upon rounding a broad trunk, a huge, dark wolf came into view.

Sean!

The wolf's jaw dropped, its tongue hung loose, before it spun on its hind legs and raced away. So near, the wind swirling a whirlpool around my face, the scent of my mate aroused me. I threw my head back and released a howl.

"Jem?"

With feet dancing, I awaited his response. He matched mine with a cry of his own, and I took off, caught him up in his loitering lope. Side by side, we picked up speed.

"Jem?"

The wind whipped at our faces before changing course to batter our coats from the side.

"Jem?"

The forest dissolved. Vanished. I blinked.

"Jem?"

Lifting my head, I squinted beneath the harsh glare of strip-lights hanging in rows along the high ceiling.

"Will you get up?"

Another blink brought Peter's blurred face into view.

"For fuck's sake, get up. You're making a right spectacle of yourself." Peter's irritated features swam into focus.

"What ... what happened?"

"Is she alright?" I couldn't identify the speaker.

"What happened?" I repeated.

"You must have fainted, dear."

I looked toward the owner of the voice to see eyes filled with concern.

The shop assistant frowned as she studied me. "Are you okay?"

I nodded at her, pushed on my left leg to stand. Unsteadiness overtook me, and the assistant grabbed my arm. From status of floor-seeking nutter to composed wife of Peter Short, I stood looking at Peter. His face held nothing but contempt.

When I thanked the assistant, she handed me over. Peter didn't offer help. Instead, he grabbed my bicep and dragged me off around the corner, away from the prying eyes of the congregated crowd.

"What the hell was that all about?" he snapped.

I shrugged my shoulders at Peter's glare. "I don't know. What did it look like?" I almost stopped there, but knew the next question needed asking. "Did I do anything?" I cringed, waiting for him to tell me I'd pranced about the store with howls flying freely.

In front of Saturday shoppers? Too much to bear.

"What do you mean, Jem, did you *do* anything?" The basket swung in an arc with his gesturing arm. "You bloody fell on your knees, closed your eyes, and sniffed the fucking air like a bloodhound." The basket continued to swing. At my offered frown, his free hand fisted before settling on his hip. "What the hell is wrong with you lately?"

"What do you mean?"

"You've been acting off for days." Peter turned to walk away.

Just as he knew I would, I trotted behind. "What do you mean, *off?*"

"Your bloody attitude." He had to be really wound up to persist. Peter never argued in public. He continued to walk away, increasing his pace until I had to almost jog to keep up.

My own irritation kicked in to affect my tone. "What do you mean, Peter?"

We entered the cardigan aisle. He marched to a rail, snatched one up. "This one." He turned to hold it in front of me as though envisioning a personal dress-up doll. "This will look nice with the skirt."

"Peter!"

His head snapped up, his eyes registering shock before narrowing. "I asked you what you think, Jem."

"No, Peter, you never ask me what I think." Though surprised by my response, I continued, "You tell me what *you* think."

"If you feel that strongly,"—he shoved it back—"we won't get it." He walked off to a different rail.

I followed. "I'm trying to talk to you, Peter."

He rounded on me, his eyes dark. "What is *wrong* with you?"

"I don't even know what you're talking about."

"You have anything you want." His hand tugged at his cropped hair. "I give you everything. You don't have to work—"

"You don't want me to work, Peter."

An elderly couple appeared. They took one look at our faces, mumbled something about coming back, and disappeared.

"You've been off with me," he said.

"What do you mean, *off?*"

"You've barely come near me—"

"I'm never away from you, Peter. If you're home, I'm home."

"You've been ill—*twice*. Jem, you're *never* ill."

I frowned. "Twice—when?"

"Sick last Saturday, and then today—*this*."

My head shook. "I'm not ill today."

"Well, you didn't look too good from where I was standing." He paused, took a deep breath, and stared straight at me. "Are you pregnant?"

Peter couldn't father children, thanks to a brain tumour as a child and chemotherapy rendering him infertile, but his insinuation refused to click in my mind. My eyebrows lifted, and my mouth hung for a split-second. "Excuse me?"

"Are you?"

My brows lowered to frown. "How can I be?"

"Last chance." He spoke slowly. "Are you pregnant? Yes, or no?"

"You know I'm not. How can I be?"

Anger pumped out of him as he studied me. His chest rose and fell, as though public control took its toll.

As my brain un-clouded, my eyes narrowed. "You think I'm having an affair?"

He shrugged, his mood bringing jerkiness to the action.

A lump formed in my throat. "How can you?"

"You haven't come near me in a week."

My mouth opened, but closed with no response.

Two young women made the turn into our aisle, halting upon seeing our exchange. They moved away, but the overpowering waft of the one's orange-scented body spray told me they went no farther than the far side of the clothes rack.

"Every time I touch you lately, you flinch." He shrugged his shoulder, raised a palm. "Tell me you haven't."

Unable to argue with the truth, I remained quiet.

"Why do you pull away when I try to hold you?"

My fingers curled as my body trembled. I hadn't been prepared for the change of direction.

His hand dropped to his side. "Tell me who he is, Jem."

Jaw clenched, I shook my head.

"What, you won't give me his name?" His eyes glowered.

I gave another headshake.

"What are you shaking your head at?"

The initial arrival of tears pooled in my lower lids.

"Who is he?" Certain of his own-drawn conclusion, his questions grew monotonous.

"Nobody," I mumbled.

"He must be somebody to make you behave like this toward me."

Because it can't possibly be due to anything you've done, can it? "I'm not having an affair."

"You must be." He nodded as though to add substance to his words.

My lower lip trembled. "I'm not, I swear."

"So, explain your behaviour, then." His hand visited his hip, lowered to his side.

I shook my head.

"Why do you keep avoiding me, Jem?" His voice increased in volume.

Hands clenched tight, fingernails gouging my palms, I gave another headshake.

He took a step forward. "Why?"

I kept my eyes on him as tears blurred my vision. One made its escape, tickling my cheek on its descent. It reached my lip, and my tongue darted out to trap it, absorbing its saltiness.

"Why, Jem?"

My mind followed the trail of the second tear until it came into sampling distance. It, too, held a light salty taste.

"Tell me, Jem." His hand released the basket to clatter onto the floor and came to his side, matching his other in fisted pose. "*Fucking why?*" The depth of his yell shook his body.

"I can't stand you touching me anymore," I said. "You bloody come home pissed-up, drag me upstairs to throw me on the bed ..."

He took a step back, mouth open. Whether from the explanation or my language, I couldn't be sure—Peter considered it unacceptable for ladies to speak crudely.

"You came this close"—I held my thumb and finger together—"to raping me, Peter."

His head shook.

I nodded.

He gave another headshake.

"You were going to *rape* me, Peter!"

His expression darkened with his narrowing eyes. He kicked at the basket he'd dropped, sending it skidding like a spinning top. With one final glare, he strode away.

I took a step. "Peter."

He didn't stop. Instead, he picked up speed with each stride. As soon as he vanished from sight, unfamiliar faces appeared at each end of the clothes rails. Faces filled with disgust or amusement at my public humiliation, or even excitement. One or two took on pitying stares.

The shop assistant who'd helped me from the floor rounded the corner. With a smile of sympathy, she placed her hand on my arm. "Would you like me to find you somewhere private to sit for a while?"

My chest heaved with my sigh. With a half-smile of gratitude, I gave a small nod and allowed her to steer me away.

Beyond a pass-coded door, she led me to an office, where she urged me into one of the seats. "Maybe there's someone you can call?"

POPPY STRODE into the office where I waited. "Isn't this where you bring the shop lifters?"

The shop assistant smiled. "It is."

Poppy looked down at me in my seat. "You got something to tell me, Jem?"

"No." I snorted.

"She hasn't done anything wrong," the assistant said. "She was just a bit upset."

Poppy's eyes appraised me before she gave an abrupt nod. "Let's get you home."

By home, she meant her house. After reassuring the assistant I'd be fine, I trailed behind Poppy through the store. In the cardigan section, all traces of the argument had vanished.

We'd scarcely pulled away in Jase's Tourer when Poppy began her interrogation. "So, are you going to spill what happened?"

I took a deep breath. "We argued."

"You and Peter never argue," she said. "He says jump, and you say how high, but you never argue. Did he piss you off enough to answer him back at last?"

I nodded.

"I bet that went down like a lead balloon." She knocked the indicator up before glancing at me. "I'm proud of you, girl."

I couldn't help but smile. I doubted it reached my eyes, though.

"What started it? For you to have something to say for yourself is odd, but ... What was it?"

"I had a ..." I paused, realising I didn't want to share with Poppy what I'd shared with a heap of strangers. "... funny turn."

"And ..." Her hand waved in prompt.

"Peter was mad because I embarrassed him."

Poppy shook her head. "Arsehole."

Agreeing with her for the first time, I nodded.

"So, you argued about your funny turn?"

I should've known she'd want more. "No, Peter ranted about my behaviour lately. He accused me of being pregnant and having an affair."

She raised an eyebrow. "Are you?"

I glared at her.

"I'm kidding, Jem. And Peter walked out because he thinks you're having a fling?"

I should have told her the truth, but couldn't bring myself to admit it to her. Besides, if Poppy knew about Peter's behaviour, she'd never allow me home again—ever!

I sent her a nod.

A KNOCK at the door disturbed our relaxation after a dinner of chicken salad. With a knowing nod, Poppy left me and Jase in the living room while she went to answer it.

"Is Jem here, Poppy?"

At the sound of Peter's voice, my body stiffened.

Poppy didn't answer him. I imagined her giving him one of her looks.

"I'm worried about her, Poppy."

Still no answer. After years of perfecting the art of *the look*, she could keep it up for a long time.

"Please, can you ask her to at least talk to me?"

Bare feet swished across floorboards, followed by the quiet rap of leather-soled shoes.

"Thanks," he muttered.

Jase gave me a supportive tap on the shoulder before leaving me on the corner-suite to join the kids outside. As he left, Peter entered and hovered in the doorway behind Poppy.

"I'll be in the kitchen if you need me." The expression Poppy sent me was a fraction short of a stern wink-wink, nudge-nudge.

"Jem ..."

I turned to Peter.

"I've come to take you home."

I looked away.

"Is it true, what you said?"

My glance from him to the kitchen, where I suspected Poppy eavesdropped, would have told him all he needed to know.

He released a deep sigh, lowered his voice. "Is it?"

My brow creased. I nodded.

His hands brushed across his hair. He frowned. "I'm sorry."

Biting the inside of my cheek, I gave another nod.

"Will you come home? We should talk about this."

I stared away toward the world passing by outside the window before turning back to him. "Okay."

He smiled.

As though materialising from thin air, Poppy appeared in the kitchen doorway. "You're going home?" Her eyes searched mine.

I nodded. "Thanks, Poppy. I'll see you on Thursday."

When I neared Peter, he reached out and rubbed my arms.

I sidestepped him to make my exit, my body stiffening beneath his touch.

Chapter 9
DARKNESS

The men run across the grass after the wolf, as it chases my dream-self. It gains on her, her lead diminishing with each step. The one who appears to be the leader shouts as he runs. If the wolf hears, he shows no indication of it.

My dream-self stops running and turns to the wolf, her tone full of plea as she shouts, "Don't bite me!"

"*Sean!*" The dominant male grows nearer, also.

The wolf's pace slows from a run as he takes slow, almost tentative steps toward her.

"Don't you dare bite me, Sean!"

"*Sean.*" The leader is no longer shouting, yet there is deep warning within his voice.

The wolf pauses in his stalking, turns to the leader.

"What are you doing?" the leader asks.

The wolf watches him.

"He wants to bite me," my dream-self says. "He wants me to be like him."

"He wouldn't."

"He will." Although speaking to the leader, her eyes do not leave the animal.

"He wouldn't," the leader says again.

She nods, her anxiety shown in the jerked action. "He's done it before."

"So, you are wolf?" His expression is one of disbelief.

"No, not now."

He frowns. "What?"

The wolf moves closer still.

"Please don't, Sean." She takes a step back.

The leader stares at her. "What do you mean, *not now?*"

She tilts her head, her eyes locked with the wolf's. "Not in this life."

It seems like a ridiculous thing to say. The leader's incredulous expression indicates his agreement.

She takes another step backward.

The wolf follows.

"Please don't," she says again.

As though alarmed by the wolf's sudden proximity to my dream-self, the leader jerks forward. "*Sean!*"

The wolf darts to the side, dodging the leader. In one fluid movement, the wolf holds my dream-self's hand in his jaws.

"Sean, *no!*" the leader shouts.

Her face doesn't crumble immediately, despite shifting her stare from the wolf to her hand.

The other men move toward the unfolding scene. "What the hell are you thinking, Sean?" one of them asks.

As though aware they are closing in, the wolf presses down with his teeth.

Pain overwhelms her expression as her brain registers the sensation.

The leader kicks at the wolf as the others run forward, but the wolf releases his hold on my dream-self and darts aside before turning to run back into the forest.

"*Sean!*" The call of his name follows in his wake—not just from the leader, but everybody.

"I can't believe it," she mumbles. "I can't believe he did it again."

They pause in their shouting for Sean, turn their attentions back to her.

Holding her hand before her eyes, she stares at the crimson escaping the wound. It hits the lawn, the contrast garish as it mars the fresh green. The men, too, stare at the blood as it drips.

Clutching her hand tight, she staggers, a groan leaving her.

Almost dancing in their ambiguity, the men go as if to take a step closer, just as quickly stepping back.

The one who grabbed her, who I am certain meant to end her life, peers from the leader to the forest. He appears to be the most unsure of them all.

Her groan becomes a cry before evolving into a scream that echoes through my subconscious.

Quieting, it evaporates to a whisper. "I can't believe you bit me again, Sean."

Arms falling to her sides, face taken over by spasm, her body convulses, once, twice, and then again—an action that should be impossible while standing. As the violent judders come to an end, her rolling eyes offer only blindness. She knows it is all over.

Finally, she drops to the ground.

Chapter 10

LIGHT

Tuesday morning, Peter leaned in to kiss my cheek before leaving for work, just as he had on Monday. He didn't bend me over backward as he used to, hold me close, or tickle me in a gesture of playfulness, and he didn't kiss me on the lips. Maybe it showed consideration for me. Maybe he was no longer sure of the woman he married. His reasons were irrelevant. The damage had been done.

Once alone, I dressed in my bottom drawer clothes. The previous day, I didn't even bother to change from them before Peter returned home. Although he didn't say anything upon seeing me, his covert glances told me he noticed.

Armed with cappuccino, I settled onto the sofa with the phone and dialled one of the few numbers my brain made the effort to store.

"Hello?"

"Jess? How are you?"

"I'm pretty good ..." For some reason, my sister always managed to sound exuberant to hear from me. "... but you've got something on your mind."

I rolled my eyes at thin air. "And you know that how?"

"Because I know you."

I blew out a breath.

"So, squeal," she said.

"Dreams."

She perked up. "Werewolf?"

"Of course."

"Cool."

Despite two years of seniority, and the ability to feed me occasional pearls of wisdom, Jess always managed to portray the mental age of a teenager at the mention of my dreams. She'd also come to expect my dreams to be of werewolves. The first one, at age seven, was in no way my last. Over the following twenty-five years, I'd encountered numerous werewolves in my dreams—some good, some bad. I'd been chased by them, had sex with them—definitely not while in their wolf form—and even changed, myself, into the body of a wolf. They all had my sister convinced I must have been one in a former life.

In no way matching her enthusiasm, I murmured, "Hmm, cool."

"So, what's happened in them, then?"

I gave her a complete rundown of the events from my dreams over the previous seventeen days—everything, including the name Sean constantly invading my thoughts.

"Weird," she said.

"Totally."

"Have you told Peter about these dreams?"

I almost laughed at the idea. "Of course not."

"I'd keep it that way, if I were you. I doubt he'd be too impressed."

I nodded to the empty room. "He knows something's up, though."

"How?"

"Because something happened, Saturday ... Peter was with me."

"Oooohh, I'm intrigued."

Hit by the Jess-bug, I laughed.

"So, what was it?"

"I experienced a change."

Jess choked on her sharp intake of breath. "Holy shit! When? Where?"

"Clothes shopping."

"Why are you only telling me now?" Her voice pitched high. "I knew you were a werewolf. Didn't I tell—"

"Don't be ridiculous. There's no such thing."

"How am I ridiculous? You changed, so you're a werewolf—simple."

I took a deep breath. "Except I didn't actually change."

"But ..." Her pause spoke volumes of her confusion. "You just said you did."

"I'm not sure I was fully conscious when it happened."

"So, you were unconscious in the department store?" She snorted a laugh. "I know shopping with Peter must be tiresome for you, Jem, but—"

"I was awake," I cut in.

"So ... how ... ?"

"I don't know." I shrugged, although she couldn't see. "It was like I experienced the change, but ... not."

"What?"

"I don't know how to describe it."

"*Try.*" I could almost picture Jess bouncing in her seat.

"Okay." I concentrated. "One minute I was talking to Peter, then the next I felt tingling, and ..."

"Yes."

"... it was in my arms, and then my legs, and although I felt certain I should see something happening in them, I couldn't. Then I fell, and it was like some kind of ... vision, I guess."

"Awesome! What happened in the vision?"

"The change went through—it *really* hurt—and I could see it happening. When it finished, I was a wolf. The store had disappeared, I was in a forest, and then an amazing scent wafted—"

"Was it beef stroganoff?"

"Jess, I'm pretty certain it was this Sean character, because when I ran toward the smell, I found another wolf and took off with him. I think the wolf was Sean."

"Cool. What else happened?"

"Then I blinked and was back in the store again."

"Jem, you are, by far, the weirdest person I know."

"I'm the weirdest person I know, too."

She laughed. "What the heck did Peter make of it all?"

"Probably thinks I'm mentally ill, or something."

Another laugh travelled the line. "You want my evaluation?"

"That's why I rang you."

"Okay." I heard the smile in her tone. "You were a werewolf in a former life—"

"They're not real, Jess."

"You don't know that."

I looked to the ceiling as I flopped my head back. "They are a *myth*."

"And every myth emerges from truth. Never forget that. Are you interested in my opinions, or not?"

"Sorry, please continue."

"Okay, from what you told me, if your dream recounts are accurate ..."

"Always," I said.

"Then, obviously, at some point, you have been bitten by

this Sean within a lifetime. You seemed to think he'd done it before, but you weren't a werewolf when it happened … so when he bit you previously, it must have been in yet another lifetime."

My head ached. "Huh?"

Her heavy sigh was audible. "Sean must be your mate, Jem —your *soul* mate. He travels, just like you, from one life to the next, and somehow you find each other."

"How can he be my soul mate? I'm married to Peter."

"Peter's a dick."

"Jess …"

"Sorry, I didn't mean it." Her tone told me she had. "Anyway, hang in there. Sean will show his face. I'm sure of it."

"How can you know something like that?"

"I just do." She ended with such finality, she'd probably have considered it an insult to her personal insight, if I continued to question the absurdity of her ideas. Believing herself a witch in her former life, the act of returning to earth after death seemed perfectly normal to Jess.

"So … what should I do? My dreams are driving me to distraction."

"Because they mean something to you."

I showed the walls another of my eye rolls.

"Write them down," she said.

"Then what?"

"When you've got all your thoughts logged, I'll take a look at them for you. I could even take them to my dream analyser, if you want."

"Dream analyser?"

" Yep."

"And does she know your medium friend, and the spiritualist … and the Wiccan, and—"

"Quit the sarcasm. You asked for my help. This is it."

"You're right. Sorry."

"So," she said, "you'll write them down?"

"If you think it will help."

"It will. If nothing else, it may straighten it all in your own head."

"I'll give it a go, then."

"Good."

"So, how are the kids?" I asked.

With my problems out of the way, we went on for another hour or so, discussing my sister's family, her cranky ex, her job, what she did at the weekend, until my mind and body relaxed into the comfort of listening to tales of somebody else's life.

A LITTLE AFTER ten on Thursday morning, Poppy and I submerged ourselves in the clothes section of the supermarket. "This is nice," I said, lifting a blue strapless summer dress.

Poppy looked over and blinked. "Yes, it is."

My eyebrow shot up. "What, you're not going to criticise?"

"No, Jem, it's really nice. You should get it—you could even wear it with your plimsolls."

With enough items in Poppy's trolley to fill the two-foot gap on her hanging rail she'd discovered two days before, we moved from perusing the clothing to the toiletries.

"What do you think of this?" Poppy waved hair dye at me.

I stared at her before taking the box and setting it back on the shelf. "You can't dye your hair."

"Why not?"

"Because you're hair is beautiful as—"

Sean!

My head snapped up and round.

"Jem, what is it?" Poppy asked.

I glanced left, right.

"Jem?"

Sean!

I marched to the end of the aisle and searched both ways, expecting to see something, yet *not* expecting to see anything at the same time. At a bump against my legs from behind, I gave a low yelp, turning to discover who'd interrupted my thoughts.

An old lady, hair so grey it appeared lilac, stood behind me with her trolley, looking right at me through ridiculously thick glasses. A glance to the left showed plenty of room. She could have gone around if she'd tried. "So sorry," she said.

I smiled—kind of. "No worries." I stepped aside to allow the woman past just as Poppy approached.

"You looked like you wanted to tear her head off," she said.

My attempt to laugh her comment away didn't sound very convincing.

We meandered to stationery, where I found a decent writing pad and popped it in my trolley with a couple of pens.

Poppy glanced up from the celebrity magazine she had her nose in. "What are those for?"

"I spoke to Jess yesterday. She thinks I should write down my dreams."

"Like a story?"

I smiled. "No."

"I think you should make it into a story." She put the magazine back on the rack. "It'll make it interesting if you elaborate, spice it up."

"I want it to be a record, Poppy."

"But writing a story would be a good hobby. You need more stimulation for your mind."

"It needs to be accurate."

She sighed. "Can I read it when you've finished?"

"*If.*"

"Did Jess sound like she believed this wouldn't end?"

I shrugged.

"She has a habit of being right about things. Your sister is even weirder than you."

"Thanks for that."

Sean!

With spasmodic glances, I moved to the end of the aisle and turned right to scour the shoppers. Hands on hips, my narrowed eyes took them all in, one by one. Just about to give up again, my knees jolted forward at a collision from behind.

I grunted an oath, my hands fisting at the annoyance of another assault. When I turned, the same lilac-haired granny peered back. Maybe she had something wrong with her eyesight, or because I'd foregone garish colours for dullness in my attire, she couldn't see me.

"So sorry, dear."

Blowing out a breath, I forced my fists to unclench. "It's okay." I attempted a smile, but the widening of the old lady's eyes behind her bottle-thick glasses told me I hadn't succeeded.

As I moved aside to let the aged nut-job by, Poppy caught me up. She giggled as she whispered, "Breathe, Jem. Deep, slow breaths. If you're not careful, you may lose your temper."

I tried to smile again—yet failed.

No further events interrupted our shopping, and, within no time, we climbed the stairs to the café. Unlike me, Poppy had the bladder of a camel and, at the top, she headed for the food queue while I ducked into the loos. On re-emergence, Poppy already had a table for us, and I waved before joining the seven-long queue, studying the pre-packed sandwiches as I waited.

Sean!

I spun.

Nothing—other than the striding off rear of a man.

I stared at his broad build, at his chocolate-brown hair, and instinct—rather than conscious thought—lifted my nose into the air. An alluring, musky aroma filled my nostrils, prompting deeper inhalations. Before I could stop myself, I followed the scent.

Searching the heads of shoppers on my descent of the stairs, I spotted the flash of dark brown bobbing through the throng. My pulse on overdrive, I jogged down the remaining steps, but a momentary blockage stole the man from my sights. By the time I reached the door, I'd lost him. Even the musky scent had disseminated, but that didn't stop me glancing wildly about.

Frustration kicked in when my search revealed nothing, and I had to grit my teeth and rein in my irritation at yet another knee nudge from behind. I turned to my assaulter, glaring as my gaze settled on the same damn lilac-haired granny.

She nudged me again, like her wrinkled lips were incapable of producing speech. I began to wonder if she had something mentally wrong with her.

At another nudge, I snapped. "Have you not heard of the words excuse me?"

Her head shot up as she took a step back.

"Three times now, three bloody times, you have bashed my legs with your trolley."

She glanced about, probably hoping for rescue, before mumbling, "I'm sorry."

"You bloody will be." I almost toppled her trolley as I shoved it out of my path. Re-entering the store, I walked straight into a frowning Poppy.

"That's some temper you've got in you today." Taking my arm, she ushered me back toward the café. "Is it almost that time of the month, sweetie?"

Being such close friends, Poppy would have known I had weeks to go, but I bit back the growl I felt brewing and allowed her a nod. If believing I was hormonal helped Poppy rationalise my behaviour more comfortably, I could allow her that.

. . .

FRIDAY, I began to write. It was important to me, I realised, to get the details right, so it took a while before my hand sent the pen across the page and produced words. Focusing on my first dream, I detailed every inch of the forest, as though the images had somehow been laser-etched into my memory. Time flew by, and my pen still flowed when I heard Peter's car pull up outside. Engrossed in the importance of my recordings, I'd forgotten everything else normally important to me and hadn't even prepared dinner.

I ran into the kitchen and hid my writing implements in the cupboard beneath the pouches of microwave rice, as Peter came through the front door. While he paused to remove his boots, I slipped back into the living room, my pulse thrumming at the thought of having to tell him dinner wasn't done.

"Good day?" I asked as he entered from the hall.

His eyes narrowed. "Not bad."

I couldn't blame him for being suspicious. I hadn't initiated a conversation since the department store incident. "Good ... Good." I didn't know what else to say, felt out of practice at conversing with my husband.

"What's for dinner? I don't smell anything."

"I fancied a take-away." I smiled, trying to make it convincing.

His eyes narrowed further. "But ... it's Friday," he said. "We have take-away on Monday."

I studied him, as he battled to accept my suggestion.

"But ... it's Friday," he repeated when I didn't speak.

I watched the confusion in his eyes. "Is there any reason why we can't have take-away on a Friday?"

"Yes, because it isn't Monday."

"Not even if it makes better sense to have it on a Friday?"

He stared at me like he thought I'd lost the plot. "You really want take-away on Friday instead of Monday?"

I couldn't believe how long-winded our conversation had become. After years of not answering back, just accepting his ideas, I never had the opportunity to see how obsessive he could be. "Yes, Peter. What's wrong with that?"

"Nothing, I guess." He rubbed at his face. "It's just ... Let me think about it."

I stared at him.

"I'm going for a shower," he mumbled and disappeared upstairs.

On Saturday, Peter worked. Peter didn't work on a Saturday unless saving for home improvements. The last time had been for a conservatory, three years previously.

Peter also worked Sunday. In all our marriage, he'd never worked a Sunday.

It appeared the distance between us had expanded.

Chapter 11
DARKNESS

The room I am in, with its dark patterned walls, holds no familiarity. Upon a bed in the centre, my dream-self writhes. From the way she twists and turns beneath her thin cotton covering, her face contorting, she must be in some kind of agony. I have watched for only seconds, yet the depth of her apparent discomfort leads me to believe she has lain there for hours—maybe days—as though trapped from within.

Her eyes open. Brightness seeps through the unadorned window, lessened only by the branches of a tree, which filters the sun and creates striated patterns across her body. She blinks and, although it appears to take great effort, her hand lifts to cover her face. Her other hand, at her side, clenches and unclenches. Her feet flex—back, forth, back, forth—at the ankles, before her toes do the same.

I hear a low groaning. Although unable to see the face of my dream-self, it appears to have come from her.

Her hand shoots from her side to her stomach, joined by the other to clutch there, exposing the scrunch of her features—a second before her body rolls. Head hanging over the side of the bed, vomit leaves her mouth, pitiful retches joining each heave surging through her. With each deposit upon the carpet, each wet slap of moisture on dryness, her body lurches and panicked growls burst out.

She heaves breaths into her body. "*Sean.*" Her call arrives as a raspy whisper. "*Sean.*"

Running her hand over her head leaves vomit within the strands. She slides her legs to the floor, but falls as soon as she attempts to stand. Her hands reach out, squelching into the soggy mess, though my dream-self doesn't appear to notice.

Head low, she crawls toward the door, her body encased in the twisted bedsheet. Her taut expression shows the effort it takes to pull at the handle. With a grunt and a quiet gasp, she succeeds.

She crawls out, finds herself on a landing. To the right are four other doors. The setting is as unfamiliar as the bedroom—to her, it seems, as well as me. She heads left toward a staircase that leads down. At the top, she attempts to stand, pushing her feet into the carpet, groaning as she straightens. Her legs sport sculpted muscles—evident as she puts them to work—and I become aware of other muscles, ones already present but more pronounced now than before. As she teeters at the head of the stairs, her covering slipping away to expose her rear, they are revealed across her naked flesh.

"*Sean.*" Another call attempt—a little louder but still strained.

Hands clenched at her sides, her shoulder leans against a high banister to the left. The first step down appears to cause her pain, yet she takes another, followed by another. Halfway down, her left foot becomes entwined in the trailing cotton, and her leg gives way. As she flails, her body dips to the side, her head hits the banister. On her fall, her body greets each step. Small cries announce each impact, until she lies in a tangled heap at the bottom. Her low moans tell me she is still alive.

From the right, a man appears. His shoulders are broad—his muscular build evident through the fabric of his shirt and in his forearms released of sleeves. He kneels beside my dream-self. From my spectator position, the features of his lowered face are obscured by thick, dark hair. Voice deep with emotion, he says, "Jem?"

Her eyes flutter open, and she looks up at him.

"Jem, are you all right?"

The tightening of her eyes accompanies her headshake. "How can I be?"

The man doesn't answer at first, as though unsure. When he finally speaks, he says, "I'm sorry, Jem. I panicked."

A small tear trails the cheek of my dream-self. "I can't believe you bit me again, Sean."

Chapter 12

LIGHT

Monday, after pacing the house like a caged animal for forty minutes, I realised I needed to get out. I'd spent a couple of hours trying to get a grip on the recording of my dreams, but hit a wall when I couldn't conjure, with clarity, the facial features of Sean.

I thought long and hard, screwing my face in concentration, until a headache formed at the back of my eyes. All I found in my mind—as some form of description—was the outline of a body, a mess of brown hair the hue of rich dark chocolate, and the rippling of muscles beneath flesh. Everything else was a blur. Maybe that should have been description enough—but it wasn't for me.

In need of a break to clear my head, I grabbed my gear—pen and paper included—and headed out the door. I drove until no longer in Lichfield, no longer familiar with my surroundings. Lost in thought, I barely paid attention—like driving on autopilot, as though my brain took a snooze and allowed my subconscious to take the wheel.

Without conscious effort, I took a left into a large car park and reversed into a free space. Turning off the engine, I blinked at my destination: a burger bar. Maybe my subconscious wanted to tell me I needed food. I decided to listen to it, and climbed from the car.

Pen and paper tucked beneath my arm, keys and cash in pockets, I headed for the doors. Upon entering, the icy blast of the air-conditioning prickled my skin. I'd never really been one for fast-food joints, so I surprised myself when my menu perusal ended with a request for double-bacon cheeseburger and a cappuccino.

The restaurant held very few customers, telling me I'd missed the lunchtime rush. At one table, a pair of girls in fluorescent T-shirts, shorts and leg warmers sat. The second table housed an elderly lady, who clutched the handle of her shopping trolley like her life depended on it. A glance at the final occupant showed a greying gentleman in a navy business suit, peering at the screen of his laptop in front of him and seemingly oblivious to anything else.

Labelling the old lady as the one most likely to talk to strangers, I took the seat farthest from her, near the window to my right.

The burger tasted pretty disgusting as far as burgers went, but the people behind the counter watched me, so I ate it out of politeness. I got up to deposit the empty packaging in the bin and sat back down. After getting as comfortable as the plastic chairs would permit, I began to write.

From the corner of my eye, I spotted movement from the businessman. He checked his watch, folded his laptop, and left. Ignoring him, I wrote some more, my scrawl bordering on ineligible, until the roll of squeaky wheels drew my eye.

The old lady crossed the floor. I paused to watch her, taking a sip on my drink. She reached the exit, heaved open the door to pass through, dragging her trolley behind. As the heavy door swung shut on her precious cargo, it became jammed, her tug of the handle only seeming to make matters worse.

As though her misfortune had made their day, the fluorescent fans giggled behind their milkshake cartons. Not totally unsympathetic, I blew out a breath and pushed up from my seat, but my foot only took one step before assistance arrived from the other side of the door.

Through walls made of glass, the three men approaching the restaurant could be seen clearly. They were all tall, muscular, two blond and one dark, dressed in jeans and T-shirts. One of the blond men held open the door for the woman to pass through before entering himself. I allowed him a brief once-over before slouching back down in my seat and returning my attention to writing the previous night's dream.

My mind conjured sensations I imagined had been present in my body upon awakening. As my limbs twitched along with my thoughts, suppressing them took effort. Brow wrinkled in my concentrated state as the fingers of my free hand tightened, my pen flew across the page as though entranced by a spell. So engrossed I became that, as the opposite chair scraped back, my eyes didn't lift. Only a cursory glance was permitted when a knee nudged mine beneath the table, and I became aware of the seat's new occupant.

Hoping he'd get the message that I didn't want to be disturbed, I ignored him.

He caught on for only a few minutes. "What are you writing?"

His voice held a smooth, velvety texture. As I listened to him, my pen paused mid-sentence. Once he'd stopped, my hand brushed the paper again—detailing my passage to the bedroom door.

"Aren't you going to tell me?"

Again, the sound of his voice faltered my hand. "It's a record," I said, without removing my eyes from the word I'd just written.

"What about?"

"Dreams I've been having." I frowned at my willingness to explain, yet still continued, "It's a record of a story within my dreams."

"So ... are you in your story, then?"

My lips twitched, but my focus didn't waver. "Obviously, if they're my dreams I'm writing about."

He gave a deep chuckle, but I didn't glance up, merely finished my disrupted sentence. "What do you dream about?"

I wrote another line before answering with a shrug. "Werewolves."

He didn't laugh, as I expected him to. "Do you have many dreams about werewolves?"

My head nodded slowly. "They're almost always about werewolves—have been my entire life."

I didn't know why I took the time to answer him while busy. Maybe I liked the sound of his voice and wasn't averse to hearing it a little more.

"So, if the story is about you, what's the name of the heroine?"

"I think *heroine* is a major overstatement," I said. "But if you want to know what *my* name is, maybe you should just ask."

He chuckled again as I wrote another line. By that time, the stairs of doom had been reached. "If I ask your name, will you tell me?"

I took a deep breath but didn't answer.

"Is there a hero in your story?" he asked after a brief silence.

"Sean isn't a hero. He's a pain in the arse." I frowned, surprised by my language, as well as my assessment.

"Sean," he said, his voice full of amusement again. "Sorry, what did you say the heroine's name was?"

"My name's Jem."

"Jem? Not Jemma, or Jemima?"

"Just Jem," I said.

His sigh was audible. "That's because you were born in June, right, after the star sign, Gemini?"

My shoulders stiffened, and my eyes narrowed.

"The twins," he continued. "Two sides to the same person?"

With a slow lift of my head, I studied him properly for the first time.

Deep brown, dangerous-looking eyes sparkled back at me, his full mouth turned up at one corner to reveal a crooked smile. His arm lifted from the table, and he rubbed across hair standing thick and unruly above a face softened by an angular jaw line with cheekbones to match.

I followed the flight of his hand, took in the rich, chocolate brown strands it ruffled, and my heart beat a little faster. As my eyes travelled across his body, took in prominent muscles—evident even beneath his casual attire—I realised he'd come in with the man who'd held open the door for the old lady.

Lowering my feet to the floor, I sat up straighter, glanced around. A few tables back were his two blond friends—staring straight at me.

The fluorescent girls alternated between watching them, and me and my concentration-breaker, as though hoping for the other two for themselves.

I turned back to him. "What did you just say?"

"Gemini," he said. "You're called Jem because of your star sign. You *are* Jem Stonehouse ... aren't you?"

How could he know me? He even used my maiden name. Heartbeat building from timpani to an army of bass drums, I asked, "Do I know you?"

"I really hope you do, otherwise I'm making a complete fool of myself."

"Who are you?"

He smiled, his eyebrow lifting with his slight head tilt. "My name's Sean, Jem. I'm Sean."

Chapter 13

As I stared at the guy across from me, my pen dropped to the floor, while my mouth opened and closed like a guppy in a hurry. I must have stared for a full minute.

He raised both arms, resting them atop the table, a small smile on his lips.

I went to speak, but no sound emerged. My breaths blew past my lips too fast. The leadenness of my arms and hands prevented their gesturing. I didn't know what to do, what to say. Forcing myself into motion, I picked up my pen and stood.

He, the stranger—*Sean*—watched me.

When I went to walk away, my foot tangled with the leg of his chair, almost stumbling my escape. I glanced at him when I reached the door and tugged it open, and again just before I turned away and made a run for my car.

I reached the car at a full-out sprint, almost colliding stunt-style with the side. When I retrieved the keys from my pocket, I dropped them before they could connect with the lock, scooped them up, dropped them again. With the door eventually open, I threw my pad and pen onto the backseat and braced myself at arm's length against the outer frame.

A glance back at the restaurant showed the stranger on his feet. His face pressed so close to the glass, condensation should have concealed him, yet it didn't.

"What the hell is going on?" I mumbled. "This cannot be possible."

Not knowing what else to do, I pulled out my mobile and dialled.

"Hello?"

"Jess, it's Jem."

"Yes, I know—your name is on the caller display, silly."

Breaths still heavy, I pushed away from the car, paced the tarmac.

"Jem?"

Another glance toward the restaurant showed the stranger still there. He ran his hands over his hair, but his gaze stayed on me.

"Jem?"

"Something's happened."

"What's he done?" Her tone sharpened.

"Who?"

"Peter, what's he done?"

"Not Peter." I raked my fingers through my hair, tugged at it. "Peter isn't even here."

"What's wrong, then? You're worrying me, Jem."

"It's Sean."

She perked up. "You had another dream?"

"No." I tugged my fingers free of my tangled strands. "He's found me."

"What do you mean?"

"He's found me. Sean has found me—he's here."

She gasped. "You're with Sean? From your dreams, Sean?"

"Yes ... no ... urgh." I groaned, yanked at my eyebrow. "I don't know."

I didn't much appreciate the laugh which followed. "Calm down, Jem, and tell me."

Taking a deep breath, I began, and told her every happening since leaving the house, right up until I rang her.

"Holy shit!"

"Exactly."

"Where are you now?" she asked.

"By my car."

"And where's he?"

I glanced back, my heart tripping as my eyes met his. "He's still inside."

"What's he doing?"

"Watching me," I said, wondering if he could lip-read.

"Don't leave, Jem. You may never see him again if you blow this chance to get answers."

"What am I supposed to do? This is too weird, even for our family. How do I even know he is who he says he is?"

"I don't know."

"How do I know it isn't some prank?"

"Wait ... I'm thinking."

"How can I go talk to somebody, thinking he's who I think he is, and then finding out he's not?"

"Be quiet a minute," she said. "I'm trying to think."

I shut my mouth but resumed pacing. Usually the most patient person in the world, according to Jess and Poppy, I became less so by the second. "Jess—"

"Shh."

Holding my phone in front of my face, I shook it in frustration before placing it back.

"I've got it," she said at last.

"What?"

"You know what he smells like, right?"

I frowned. "Not exactly."

"You said when you had your vision in the store, you followed your nose and it led you to a wolf, right?"

Sudden wariness moved in. "Yes."

"And you believed the wolf was Sean, so that must be how he smelled to you in your previous life."

I could have argued again about previous lives, the existence of werewolves, but the timing for it pretty much sucked. "How does that help me?"

"You need to sniff him."

"*What?*" I almost choked. "I can't go around sniffing people."

"Jem, you're always sniffing people."

"I—"

"Yes, you are."

"I can't go up to a guy I've just met and start sniffing him."

"If he's who he says he is, he'll understand."

My feet halted. "Huh?"

"If he's *the* Sean, he won't mind—or think it's weird."

"You really want me to sniff him?"

"It's the only way." She said it like she considered me stupid for not realising myself.

I lifted my gaze back to the dark eyes still watching through the glass. "What if he isn't *the* Sean? Won't I look an idiot?"

"Does it matter?"

"I ... guess not." I tore my eyes away, kicked my toes against the asphalt. "So, I have to sniff him?"

"Yes."

I gave a small nod. "I can *do* this."

"Yes, you can." I heard the smile of victory in her tone.

"I'll call you back."

"*No-no-no-no.*"

I paused in hanging up.

"Take me with you. I want to hear."

"Okay ... I'm going in."

With a long release of breath, I headed back to the restaurant. The stranger's expression altered from upset to unsure, then to a smile when I pulled open the door. As I stepped through, the icy air-conditioning urged another shiver through me.

He turned as the door whooshed closed.

I ignored his staring friends. "I'm back in the burger bar," I said to Jess as I moved. "I'm walking back over to him."

"This is *so exciting*," she whispered.

He smiled. "You came back."

"Is that him?" asked Jess.

"Shh. Be quiet a minute." I faced the man before me. "I need to do something."

As his eyebrow cocked, matching the one-sided twitch of his lips, my hands shook and my heart pounded.

"I can't do this, Jess," I whispered into the phone. "He'll think I'm a freak."

"Little sis', if he knows you, he already *knows* you're a freak."

The man's smile stretched into a grin.

"Just do it!"

I jumped at Jess's snapped order. "Okay." I gave my attention back to the tall, dark, handsome man before me.

"What did you want to do?" he asked.

"I ... um ..." I blew out a breath. "I'm going to do something, because I need to be sure. And if you're who you say you are, and who I think you are, then you won't find it weird."

His grin widened. "Okay."

"Jess, I'm just going to put the phone down for—"

"Don't you *dare!*"

"This is private." I sighed. "I'll pick you back up in a minute."

With my mobile on the table beside us, I gave my attention back to the man. "Please, don't move. I just want to ..." I bridged the gap between us until my toes pressed against his. On tiptoes, I closed my eyes, braced my hand against his chest, leaned forward to bring my face to his throat ... and inhaled.

At the overpowering scent of pure, unadulterated, male muskiness, I gasped. My eyes flew open to him smiling down at me, his hands partway lifted, as though to catch me if I fell. I lowered my lids again, inhaled deeper, searching for more in a moment of greed.

The sound of his breathing carried to me as his warm exhalations tickled my cheek.

Somewhere behind, a chair scraped and a male voice said, "I don't believe it."

To my left, a tinny voice escaped my mobile. "Jem? Jem?"

I opened my eyes.

His attention had shifted from me to his friends, his expression filled with smugness. Turning back, he smiled down at me. "I knew it was you, Jem."

I didn't know what to do—again. With a step back, I unclawed the hand clinging to his T-shirt and glanced down toward the voice screeching from the table. My hands shook as I picked up the phone. "I'm back."

"Holy shit, Jem! You were ages. What took you so long?"

"I was doing what you told me to do."

"You sniffed him?"

I nodded. "Yes."

"Shit! You're nuttier than a fruitcake."

"Thanks for that."

"Well?"

"Huh?" The man held me to him with his intense stare and seemed to listen to my every word.

"What happened?" Jess prompted.

"It's him," I said. "It's Sean."

Sean's entire face lit up as he beamed at me.

"Holy shit!" Jess said again, into my ear.

"Exactly," I muttered.

Chapter 14

My shaking knees gave out on me, and Sean nudged a chair behind my legs, lowered me into it. I still held my phone pressed to my ear, but after I'd told her to bloody be quiet, Jess hadn't spoken for at least two minutes. Neither had Sean nor I. We'd simply stood looking at each other, oblivious to the attention we'd gained from Sean's friends, from the restaurant staff and fluorescent girls.

Overwhelmed by it all, I dropped my head into my hand. "I have to go," I said into the phone.

After saying goodbye, I placed the phone on the table and peered up at Sean, as he pulled out a chair to sit opposite. He seemed to be waiting for me to speak, but I didn't know what to say. I could barely think straight, let alone compose a conversation, not while he studied me so closely—nor with his appearing frown, like it dawned on him that all was not well inside my mind.

Pressing my fingers into my eyes, I blocked him out for a second. When I lowered them, he hadn't moved, but his frown had deepened. "I need to go," I said.

He nodded, like he'd already predicted as such.

I pushed up from my seat. "I'm sorry. I should go."

His hand reached out before retracting. "At least take my number."

At his nod to his friends, I turned to see one scribbling on a napkin. When he walked over and handed it to me, I folded it around my mobile.

"Can't you stay?" Sean asked, standing.

Averting my eyes, I shook my head. "I need time to think."

"What's to think about?" His hands rubbed across his hair. "Do you have any idea how long I've been waiting? Why would you need to think about this, at all?"

I looked up at him, but wished I hadn't when I took in his hurt-filled eyes. "It's complicated."

"No, Jem, it isn't. Just come back with me. I've—"

"It's not that simple, Sean."

He frowned. "Why? Why isn't it?"

Hesitating, I took a deep breath before delivering the blow. "I'm married."

Sean staggered backward, his hands lifting to fist in his hair before rubbing across his face. He glanced down at my left hand, searching for confirmation, and his face twisted in torment as he shook his head. "No."

"I need to go." I turned for the door.

He grabbed my arm. "Please, don't."

"I have to. I need to think. I don't ... I don't know what to do." I stared back into his eyes.

"Please, at least give me a chance—promise you'll call me."

Before I could stop myself, I nodded. Why, I didn't know, especially as I hadn't a clue what I intended to do at that particular moment. But, if nothing else, I owed him a call to tell him one way or the other, so I nodded again. His hand loosened its grip.

. . .

Back in my car, it occurred to me I had no idea of my location. After driving out of the car park, I spent at least twenty minutes searching for road signs, to find some indication of the direction back to Lichfield.

Once on the right road, I allowed myself to ponder the improbability—*impossibility* even—of what had happened. Consumed by my thoughts, it didn't register that I'd driven straight to Poppy's until I turned off the engine.

I glanced at the house, peered along the street, and turned to the dashboard clock. Three twenty—school-run time. I decided to wait.

Ten minutes later, Poppy emerged with her two red-haired bambinos—one either side, holding her hands. The second she spotted me, she hastened her step.

She tapped on the car window. "Coming in, Jem?"

I climbed out and trailed behind her up the path.

"Go play upstairs, sweeties," she told the kids once we were inside.

I followed her into the kitchen and pushed up to sit on a stool at the breakfast bar, while she filled the kettle.

She gathered mugs, glancing at me. "Did you and Peter have another argument?" She spooned sugar and coffee into the two cups.

I shook my head.

"Did he do something to upset you, sweetie?"

With another headshake, my eyes prickled.

"If you don't tell me what's wrong, how can I help?"

My right eye leaked its contents onto my cheek.

"Something obviously happened, and you must want to talk about it, or why else would you be here?"

I nodded, the movement flicking my tears away.

"Something happened?"

I gave another nod.

"Something bad?"

A shrug followed my headshake, and my lower lip quivered.

The kettle boiled, and I watched Poppy fill the mugs with steaming water. With that done, she came around, dragged out a second stool to sit beside me. When she rubbed at my shoulder and pulled me into her arms, I began to sob.

Poppy didn't speak, just let me cry myself out. My shoulders continued to judder long after all my tears had departed.

I lifted my head to look at her. "It's Sean."

"More dreams?"

I shook my head.

She frowned. "What, then, Jem?"

Luckily, Poppy had pried my Sean 'occurrences' out of me already, and I tried my best to explain the events of my day in the most believable way possible, though I could hardly believe it myself.

She sighed once I'd finished. "Wow."

I nodded, wiping at my nose and cheeks.

"Maybe that sister of yours isn't as crazy as we all thought."

When I produced a smile, Poppy matched my expression.

"I bet you have no clue what to do," she said.

"Absolutely none."

"You have his number, though?"

I pulled my mobile from my pocket to retrieve the napkin.

"You can't take that home with you," she said.

"I know."

"Let me take care of it for you."

I handed it over. "Thanks, Poppy."

I stayed with her until almost the end of Peter's work day. She didn't hound me with questions, as others may have, nor urge me to immediately try finding my solution. Instead, she called the kids down, took me into the garden, and involved me in a mind-numbing game of badminton. By the time she and the kids had finished with me, I was ready to face Peter and behave like nothing had happened.

Chapter 15

After two sleepless nights and strange looks from Peter, I rang Poppy and asked her to make the call. My nervous rear refused to stay still, squeaking against the leather of the sofa in my impatience. Four minutes and twenty-seven seconds after disconnection, the phone rang.

I snatched it up. "Poppy?"

"It's arranged," she said. "He knows where the supermarket is, said he was there last week. Did you know that, sweetie?"

"I had a feeling, but I didn't know."

"Are you sure about this?" Her tone portrayed concern. "I think he's been stalking you."

"That's what predators do best, Pop."

Obviously unimpressed by my humour attempt, she remained silent.

"Sorry, that wasn't funny."

"No, it wasn't. Are you sure you're doing the right thing?"

"I can't just walk away without talking to him—it isn't fair on him. Besides, I can't live the rest of my life with a huge *what-if* hanging over my head."

"So, you're going to talk to him, and then come home?"

By home, she meant her house. "Yes."

"Do you need me to come along?"

"I'll be okay." My escalating pulse suggested otherwise. "Did he give a time?"

"He said it doesn't matter. He said if he gets there before you, he'll wait—all day, if he has to."

I pushed to my feet. "I'll go now."

"Make him wait, Jem. Keep him on his toes."

"This isn't some kind of date. I'm just going to talk to him."

"I know, but I worry about you."

I smiled at her motherly tone. "I'll be fine."

She seemed to hesitate a moment. "Just remember you're married."

"I thought you hated Peter."

"I do—the man's an arsehole. I'm worried about you."

After about thirty promises to not do anything rash or foolish, I hung up and left the house, running for the car under a heavy rainfall. A check in the rear-view mirror reflected wild hair glued to my brow. *Brilliant.*

Fifteen minutes later, I parked up outside the supermarket, turned off the engine, and glanced around—why, when he'd requested we meet in the café, I didn't know.

While musing over my insanity, I spotted the arrival of a bright yellow Porsche. It hadn't been on the burger bar car park, yet I somehow knew I'd see Sean behind the wheel—confirmed when he spotted me and veered my way.

He peered through the rain-patterned window as he pulled up beside me before climbing from his car.

My eyes followed his walk around to my passenger door. As he opened it and climbed in beside me, I asked, "You're alone?"

"This is private."

I nodded in agreement.

He gestured to the supermarket. "Are we going in?"

"Are you hungry?"

The twitch of his eyebrow matched that of his lips. "I'm always hungry."

"Then, I guess we're going in."

I climbed out into the downpour and considered making a dash for the shelter of the store, except Sean didn't appear at all troubled by the meteoric raindrops bouncing off his head. Hands tucked into the pockets of his jeans, he took long, easy strides, in no apparent hurry. By the time we entered through the automatic doors, my hair and clothes clung to me, as did his. I probably looked a right state, whereas a quick study of his clinging clothes and hair showed him looking ... something else entirely.

"Do they do breakfast here?" he asked on our climb to the mezzanine café.

"You've been here before—did you not look at the menu?"

His dark eyes turned on me. "I was too busy looking at you."

I ignored the tripping of my heart. "Did you know I'd be here, when you came?"

"No. I'd never even been here before, and I didn't believe it *was* you." He shrugged. "I thought I'd made a mistake."

I recalled the other times I'd searched for his presence. "Was that the first time you saw me?"

"Yes."

"You knew I was following you, that I'd spotted you, didn't you?"

He paused before nodding.

"So, why? Why run off when you had the chance to talk to me?"

He shrugged. "I panicked."

We reached the hot food plates, where the scents of bacon, sausage, eggs, beans, tomatoes, mushrooms, fried bread, all wafted out on the rising steam. "Two large breakfasts," Sean said when the server looked up.

My eyebrow lifted. "How hungry are you, Sean?"

"One of them is yours." He smiled.

"I've already eaten."

"You're too skinny. You need to eat more."

"I eat like a horse."

His smile widened. "Then, eat what you can, and I'll finish it for you, lightweight." He turned back to the server observing our exchange and nodded. "Two."

She handed the plated food over, and Sean took them to the register to pay.

I walked off while he finished up. "Over here."

"No, this way." Sean headed in the other direction and led me to the remotest corner of the café. He set his tray down and sat in a chair as he pulled out the one beside it, which he patted for me to take.

I slid out a chair opposite and sat there instead.

He frowned for a moment before his smile returned. With one plate in front of himself, the other in front of me, he handed me a knife and fork. "Eat."

"I'm not hungry."

He nudged the cutlery into my hand. "Eat the food, Jem."

Sighing, I stabbed the fried egg to nibble on, popped a bit of bacon into my mouth. Sean's shoulders relaxed, and he smiled before tucking into his own. As my jaw worked through one bite after another, I watched him eat—just as he watched me—until absorbed by the movements of his hands and the concentration on his face each time he decided what to shovel in next.

Sean scraped the last of his bean sauce from his plate and glanced down at mine, his smile reappearing. "I thought you weren't hungry."

I glanced down, my lips squidging to the side on finding only one item left.

"You didn't save me any."

"You want my fried bread?"

"No, eat it if you want it."

I nudged it toward him. "I already told you I'm not hungry."

"So you say." He chuckled as he reached with his fork to snag the bread, devouring it in two bites. "You want coffee?"

"Cappuccino."

"Cappuccino it is, then. Don't disappear on me, Jem. I don't want to have to drag you with me just to get drinks."

My eyes narrowed.

He laughed. "I'm kidding."

"Liar."

He went alone to fetch the drinks, but his attention didn't leave me once. Even when paying, he handed the money to the server over his shoulder. On his return, he placed mine before me, sat back down opposite. Curiosity had me glancing at his mug—he'd ordered the same for himself—as we both took a sip of our drinks, eyeing each other over the rims.

"So," he said at last, "you're really married?"

Eyes on his, I nodded.

"What's his name?"

"Peter."

"How long have you been married?"

I set my mug down. "Eight years."

"What's he like?"

Watching him place his drink on the table, I didn't answer.

"Does he treat you well?" His hands flexed, and I studied the way it tightened the tendons along his forearms, felt recognition stir from somewhere. "He's not right for you."

I lifted my head to look at him. "You don't even know him."

He nodded. "Maybe not, but I know he's not right for you."

"How can you possibly know that, Sean?"

"Because he's not me."

"How very arrogant of you."

"It's not arrogance, Jem, it's a fact. I'm the only one who's right for you. Always have been, always will be."

I thought he'd said it in jest, but his eyes held no humour. My chair squeaked as I stood. "This was a mistake."

He reached out, snared my wrist. "Please don't go."

I glared at his hand around my arm before lifting my eyes back to his. "You know, I had absolutely no idea what I was going to say to you once I got here today, but I came because I figured I, at least, owed you something." I pointed at him. "You're only interested in talking if we're saying what you want to hear, and if I don't say what you want to hear, you make it up to suit yourself."

His eyes twinkled and a smile spread his mouth, and, for some reason, I drew in a deep breath and sat back down.

"I ..." Frowning, I twirled a finger around a clumped tail of my still-wet hair. "I don't know you well enough to accept you making demands of me."

Hurt filled his eyes, as he brushed a hand across his head, flecks of moisture spraying out. "You're right. I'm sorry."

We both reached for our drinks, took a sip, and went back to watching. For some reason, it seemed enough, like words weren't needed to fill the bubble of silence that had formed around us. With him in my sights, my shoulders un-tensed, my hands un-fisted, and my body relaxed.

After a while, I announced that I needed to leave, but Sean encouraged me to stay with a further cappuccino, despite no conversation passing between us for almost an hour. He'd lounged back in his seat, feet spread wide, and studied me with his crooked smile on his lips. I guessed I should have been somewhat freaked by him, yet he filled me with nothing but calm.

My gaze tracked him as he placed my refill in front of me before taking his seat. He rested his forearms on the table, hands cupped around his own drink, and went back to staring.

"Sean ... you asked me here to talk, but you've barely said a word."

His lips twitched. "If I keep my mouth shut, I can't piss you off."

I took a sip of my drink to hide my smile.

"Can I ask you some ... things?"

I gave a slow nod. "Within reason."

"Okay." He scratched at his head. "You work?"

My head shook.

"So, what do you do?"

"I'm a housewife."

His eyes clouded, and he frowned.

"What about you?" I smiled in the hope of smoothing his brow. "Do you have a job?"

Toying with his cup, he nodded. "Yes, I do."

"So, why aren't you there now?"

His deep chuckle teased somewhere below my navel, and I breathed out a quiet laugh. "I had a better offer." He held me steady as his gaze intensified.

I opened my mouth, but found I couldn't speak. After floundering for seconds under his attention, I downed the rest of my already tepid drink. "It's time I left."

He studied his hands before lifting his eyes back to mine. "Can I see you again? Tomorrow?"

I shook my head, holding up my hand when he went to protest. "Thursday is my day with Poppy."

"The woman who rang me?"

"Yes."

"Is she a good friend?"

"She's my best friend."

"Then, she wouldn't mind if you cancel."

"I'd mind, Sean. Thursday has been my and Poppy's day for the last four years. I'm not cancelling."

His fingers tapped the table. "So, when can I see you again?"

I hesitated, but only for a second. "I'll ring you."

He leaned closer. "Do you promise?"

"I promise. I'll ring and let you know when I can meet you."

"When, not if?"

I nodded.

He smiled. "Okay—okay, that's good."

We were quiet again on the walk to our cars. When Sean leaned in to kiss me, I tilted to offer only my cheek. His lips were warm, his skin smooth, as he lingered for a moment.

I took a step back. "Bye, Sean."

His smile remained burned into my brain on the drive back to Poppy's house.

THURSDAY MORNING, after Poppy had me searching the house for a black cardigan that'd spent so long in the laundry bin mould had set in, we arrived at the supermarket.

"Hey, Jem, what do you think of this?"

I lowered the jeans I held, as Poppy pressed up against a skirt that wouldn't have covered the cheeks of any backside. "For goodness sake, Pop, you're thirty-five, not twenty-five."

She laughed, probably at her own regular comment twisted around and thrown back at her. "You're right, it would look hideous."

"You could always buy it for the bedroom." I wiggled my eyebrows. "I'm sure Jase would love it." As she giggled and put it into her trolley, I went back to studying the jeans in my hands. "Do you like these?"

"They're okay, but ..." She picked up a pair of denim shorts. "... you'd look better in these."

"You think so?"

She smiled. "Sweetie, I know so."

She dropped them in my trolley, and we headed toward the music department.

Sean!

I spun on the spot. Head tilted, I scoured the store behind me—catching the glimpse of dark hair before it disappeared around the corner. "You've got to be kidding me." I took off in that direction.

"Jem?"

I held my finger up to Poppy, strode to the end of the aisle. As I swung round the corner, I almost collided with Sean. "What are you doing here?"

"Jem." He grinned. "What a coincidence."

"Coincidence? Are you following me?"

His grin diminished as he dipped his chin. "Sorry, I couldn't help it."

I glanced back at Poppy, and Sean leaned forward, throwing her an impressive smile. When she waved back at him, I rolled my eyes. "Wait here."

Poppy could barely take her eyes off him as I walked back to her. "Is that him?"

"Yes."

"You didn't say he was hot. Sweetie, he's gorgeous. I'd leave my Jase if that was on offer."

I blew out a breath. "Don't exaggerate, Poppy. You'll never leave Jase."

"I know, but if I was with Pet—"

I glowered. "You're not helping."

She looked at me at last. "Sorry. What's he doing here?"

"In your words, stalking me, I believe."

"Are you going to introduce us?"

I waved Sean over with a sigh. On approach, he smiled his head off, and the wider his lips stretched, the more dangerous he looked. I imagined it had something to do with the flashing of his wide, white teeth. The simple act of watching him tightened my stomach.

I shook the sensation away. "Sean, this is Poppy. Pop—"

"Lovely to meet you." Smiling, she took a step forward with extended hand, which Sean shook.

"Okay, can we go now?" I turned to walk away.

"Can I come?" Sean asked from behind.

I peered back over my shoulder. "I already told you, Thursday is my day with Poppy, and—"

"I don't mind."

Glaring at Poppy's interruption, I whispered, "You changed your tune," through gritted teeth.

"Careful, you may lose your temper again." She tutted. "Twice, two Thursdays running—what is the world coming to?"

"I can't believe you're not backing me up," I hissed. "Yesterday, you tell me to be wary of the *stalker*, and today you invite him to join us."

"Yesterday, I didn't know he was a sweetheart."

My eyebrow lifted. "Sweetheart?"

"Can you not see how he's looking at you?" she whispered. "He's besotted with you. I think you should give him a chance."

"I'm *married*, Poppy."

"I won't interrupt your day, Jem. I promise," Sean said.

I paused in my snake impersonation to glance at him. Dark eyes gazing down at me from beneath lowered long lashes, he slid his hands into the pockets of his jeans.

I melted—a little. "Okay, you can stick, but ..."

"I won't get in your way."

From there, Sean trailed me and Poppy round the super-market, and we tried to behave like he wasn't there. Or rather, I did—I caught Poppy sending him adoring smiles.

As was our routine, the bags were packed into the car before we headed for the café. Sean followed us there, too. Excusing myself to use the bathroom, I told them to go ahead. When I emerged, I found Poppy's head pressed close to Sean's, but they jerked apart, Sean chuckling, as soon as their gazes connected with me.

My eyes narrowed in suspicion, but my deep scrutiny went ignored.

Sean nudged a plate toward me. "Fish and chips."

I stared at him.

"I told him you like it," Poppy said with a shrug.

We ate in silence, mostly because during our grazing sessions, Poppy and I talked about topics uninteresting to men, or griped about the hardships of being born female. Sean's presence seemed to stop Poppy's usual flow of words.

Once we'd all finished, I stood. "I'm going now, Sean."

"We could do something this afternoon." He gazed up at me, hope in his eyes.

"I'm busy."

"Liar," Poppy murmured.

I sent her my best glare.

"When can I see you again, Jem?" Sean asked.

I shrugged. "I'll call you."

"Tomorrow? Can I see you tomorrow—please?"

"Of course," said Poppy.

"I'll think about it," I said.

Back at the car, Sean, as before, leaned in to kiss me. Once again, I offered only my cheek. When he bent to kiss Poppy, telling her how lovely it had been to meet her, Poppy almost swooned as she said goodbye.

Traitor.

"He's hot," she said as soon as we'd pulled away.

"Whose side are you on, Pop?"

She smiled. "Yours, sweetie—always yours."

Chapter 16

Friday, as I sat deciding on the day's agenda, the telephone rang. "Hey, Jess," I answered.

"So, what's been happening?" No beating around the bush for my sister.

"Not much, really."

"What about Sean? Have you seen him again?"

I nodded. "I met him on Wednesday."

"And you didn't tell me this because ..."

"We only met to talk."

"About what?" Her voice held both exasperation and excitement.

"Nothing, really, now I think about it." I pursed my lips. "He asked me about Peter, told me I was with the wrong guy—"

Jess barked out a laugh.

"And we didn't say much after that—just sat awhile."

"Sounds riveting."

I ignored her sardonic tone. "Not really."

"Have you seen him since?"

I smiled. "He stalked me yesterday, when I was shopping with Poppy."

Again, she laughed. "And did you speak to him?"

"Actually, he spoke to Poppy more than me."

"Are you seeing him again?"

"He wants to meet today. I said I'd let him know."

"Think you will?" she asked.

I shrugged. "Haven't decided yet."

"I expect the deets if you do."

"Sure." She made me promise before I hung up.

As I replaced the receiver, it rang again. "What did you forget, Jess?"

"Been fishing for gossip, has she?"

I smiled. "'Morning, Poppy." My frown pushed in as I remembered the day. "Why are you calling me? You never call me on a Friday."

"I am the bearer of messages."

"Huh?"

"Sean rang—"

"How?"

"What do you mean? He picked up his phone and—"

"Very funny." My hand came to rest at my hip. "How has he got your number, Pop?"

"I gave it to him ... yesterday."

I groaned. "Brilliant!"

"You can't have the ball totally in your court, Jem. It's unfair if you're the only one able to make contact."

My blown out breath misted the mouthpiece.

"You still there?" she asked.

My shoulders slumped in submission. "What's the message?"

"He wants to meet—said he has something to show you."

"I bet he has."

Poppy laughed.

"Where?"

"He said meet him at the supermarket again, and he'll take you from there."

"When?"

"He said it doesn't matter. He'll wait however long it takes."

I rolled my eyes. "Yeah, yeah."

"So, are you going?"

"I'm not sure. I don't want to give him false hope when I'm married to Peter."

"Peter's an arse."

"Poppy!"

"Sorry, Jem. But you should go. I think he wants to talk."

"You just said he wants to show me something. Which is it?"

"Probably both. Are you going? You said yourself you didn't want to live with the what-ifs."

She'd backed me in good and proper with that one. I stuck out my lower lip, blew my hair from my eyes. "Tell him I'm on my way."

SEAN's bright yellow Porsche beckoned to me as I pulled into the car park. He grinned as I parked beside him, but faltered when I didn't move. Within seconds, he'd climbed from his car to join me, and my little Peugeot dipped as he settled into the passenger seat. "You came."

"I shouldn't have. I don't even know why I'm here."

"You're here because you wanted to see me."

My eyes narrowed. "Do I detect a hint of arrogance again?"

"No." He smiled. "You detect a hint of truth."

With a sigh, I leaned forward until my head rested against the steering wheel. "I'm married, Sean."

"He's not right for you."

"And you still think you're innocent of being arrogant?" At

the sound of his sigh, I turned to see him watching me. His smile had vanished, his hurt expression lending him an air of vulnerability. Once again, I melted. "Poppy said you had something you wanted to show me."

He nodded. "I want to take you somewhere."

"Where?"

"Come and get in. I'll drive you there."

My eyebrow lifted. "You want me to come in your car with you?"

He grinned. "Yes."

"No, Sean."

His grin faded. "Why not, Jem?"

"If I come with you with no wheels, you'll probably keep me there."

The smile that crept back onto his lips told me the thought had crossed his mind.

My heart skipped a beat, and without intention, I said, "I'll follow you in my car."

He gave a small laugh. "You think this will keep up?"

"Well, if you go too fast, I'll turn around and go home."

Although his laugh wisped away, his smile remained. "You'll follow me, then?"

I nodded.

Back in his car, he drove at the speed of a tortoise across the car park, giving the impression he was mocking me. I followed behind—doubted I could've objected, even if I wanted to, especially as common sense didn't seem to be ruling me very well right then.

On the roads, Sean stayed within the limits. If I failed to make a turn directly after him, he pulled to the kerbside and waited for me to catch up. Each time I lost sight of him, my mood plummeted; each time he reappeared, my pulse increased.

Once we'd crossed the county border into Derbyshire, we drove for ages on windy, tree-lined roads, eventually passing a road sign that informed me we'd entered a place called Wild Woodington. A couple of miles in, Sean slowed and indicated a left turn. I followed his lead, but didn't spot the huge open gateway until almost upon it.

As Sean turned in, I came to a halt outside the gates and peered up through the windshield at a large sandstone house amid a sweeping block-paved drive. My gaze was still glued to it when Sean climbed from his car and walked over to mine.

He tapped on my window. "You need to bring the car *in*, Jem."

I glanced at him before putting the car into gear and pulling forward. Sean opened my door before I'd even turned off the engine.

"What are we doing here?" I asked, stepping out.

"I've brought you home with me. I wanted you to see the house."

As I stood before it, light reflected off the windows. With its interior obscured, it held an air of mystery, as though enticing me to enter if I wanted to see more.

Sean walked to the steps, waving me to follow. When I caught him up, he opened the front door and ushered me inside.

I lifted my gaze to the high-ceiling of the hallway above then dropped it to the tiled floor patterned with traces of dirty foot-prints. A wide staircase stood to the right, and three doors led off —two each side of the hallway faced each other, with another directly ahead, in the wall supporting the head of the stairs.

"You live here?" I asked.

He closed the door at our rear. "Yes. Take a look around."

When I didn't move, he opened the door to the left and placed his hand against the small of my back, nudging me forward.

I scanned the room, absorbed the two huge, navy sofas with matching armchair and footstool, and a large flatscreen in the corner beneath a window overlooking the driveway. "Living room."

Sean followed as I turned to leave the room and crossed the hall to the opposite door. "This must be the dining room." I smiled, tugging down the handle.

When the door swung open, I blinked. No dining furniture sat in the room, only weights and exercise equipment. "Shouldn't this be in the cellar?" I blinked at my own question.

"Not anymore," he said. "We moved it because this room never got eaten in, and it's bigger for storing this stuff."

"What's in the cellar, then?"

His eyes sparkled as they narrowed. "How do you know we even have a cellar?"

"I don't." I frowned. "Do you?"

"Yes."

"So, what's down there, then, a torture chamber?"

His hand lifted to smother his laugh, but my frown didn't shift as I turned for the stairs.

I swept my fingers over the smoothed, carved end of the banister and made my way up with Sean hot on my heels. At the top, I paused, taking in two doors on both sides of the landing and one directly ahead.

I pointed to the latter one. "That's the bathroom."

Nodding, Sean watched me like he'd found a new toy and wanted to see how many tricks I could do.

Intent on confirming my presumption, I marched forward. Opening the door revealed a large space with claw-footed bath in the centre, toilet and wash basin to the right, and shower cubicle in the far left-hand corner.

Nodding to myself, I turned to find Sean still at the top of the stairs. He tracked my walk back to the two doors nearest the bathroom, where I grabbed the handles and pushed both open, one either side. Each swung wide to expose bedrooms. Green decorated the one on the left—on the right a rich coffee colour. I moved to the next two. The first revealed a lilac bedroom. I turned to the right-hand one with warm cream coating its walls.

Eyes narrowed, I walked through the final doorway to study the room further. Besides the cream walls, sapphire blue dominated the space—in the bedding, curtains, black-out blind, the rug. Almost everything besides the walls and furniture came in the deep blue.

I turned to Sean as he stepped in behind me. "You like blue, Sean?"

"It matches your eyes," he said. "How did you know this was my room?"

Lucky guess? I shrugged. "Who else lives here?"

"My dad, my brother, that's all."

"So, who sleeps in the lilac room?"

His eyes flickered to the side. "Nobody, at the moment."

"Where are your dad and brother now?"

"Working." He looked back at me. "They don't know about you, yet." He jerked his chin to the side. "Come on," he said, twisting away.

Downstairs, Sean showed me to the one door I'd yet to go through. On the other side, I discovered a beautiful kitchen, with oak-fronted cupboards, and a huge, matching dining table set in the centre. Beyond the table, large windows sat each side of French doors that led into a conservatory. I shifted my gaze to the nearest window, and a singular glance had me moving for a closer look.

Through the French doors, the conservatory, I kept going until I stood at the rear of the property. The block paving that flanked the front of the house circled the entire building to meet the stretching lawn. A freestanding garage, almost as big as the home I shared with Peter, dominated the area to my right.

None of those had drawn me, though.

Ahead, the garden's perimeter wall sported wide arches that stood evenly spaced along the entire width of the rear stretch of bricks, and through those arches stood a vast forest.

A deep sigh of contentment drifted from me. "You really live by the forest," I whispered.

SEAN TOOK a seat on the opposite side of the table, placing our drinks down before us. I'd declined his offer to take a closer look at the forest—for some reason, my dream, and what happened after entering a forest where I suspected Sean to be, had screamed in my mind.

"Jem, can I ask you something, now we're alone?"

I studied him before nodding.

"Why weren't you surprised when I spoke to you in the restaurant? I mean, obviously you were, but not shocked ... not like—"

"I've been having dreams."

He nodded like that explained everything.

"How did you know who I was?" I asked. "Did you have dreams, too?"

"Dreams, visions ..." He smiled. "They've been driving me crazy."

"I know how you feel." I peered down into the depths of my drink, quiet for a few moments, before I lifted my face. "How did you know it was me?"

He merely shrugged.

"I didn't know it was you until I ... you know ... and even then I didn't really know what I was sniffing for. But you—you knew it was me straight away ... How?"

"I knew how you would look, how you'd smell."

"You didn't get close enough to smell me."

His eyes met mine, held me steady.

"You're saying you could smell me from across the room?"

He scraped his chair back as though to leave but pulled it back under.

My pulse kicked up a dance. "Are you really the same as in my dreams? Are you a ...?" I couldn't bring myself to finish.

He watched me as my hands wrung on the table before me, but didn't answer. I doubted it had anything to do with not understanding my gibbering questions. After an intolerable pause, he asked, "Do you believe in your dreams?"

My brow creased. "How can I?"

"You believed them enough to believe who I was, to run the risk of humiliating yourself by sniffing me in front of strangers."

"How can they be real?"

"You still show some of the traits, Jem. Who else, what else, would confirm my identity by scent?"

"So, are you ..." I swallowed. "Are they real?"

Another few seconds of silence followed before Sean broke it again. "What do you remember from your dreams, Jem? Can you remember how you felt—how any of it felt? What did you mean when you said you didn't know how I was supposed to smell?"

"Because I only remember what I can see, from watching myself, what I do ..."

A knot formed between his brows. "You watch yourself?"

I nodded. "In my dreams."

"You mean, you're not in your body?"

"No. Are you?"

He nodded slowly. "Yes, everybody is, Jem."

"No, normal people see their dreams like watching a movie."

"No, they don't." His frown deepened. "Yours sound more like astral projecting to me."

"Astral what?"

He waved it off. "So, you're not in your body ... at all?"

I shook my head.

"Weird."

"Like I haven't been called *that* before."

His lips twitched. "So, if you're outside your body, how can you feel anything?"

"I can't. I don't really experience the sensations my dream-body does—can't smell anything either. I can only watch and listen."

Curiosity lit his eyes. "Yet, you recognised my scent?"

I gave a reluctant nod.

"Had you smelled it before?"

"I think so."

"Where, if not in your dreams?"

Fidgeting, I tapped my fingers against my mug. "You demand a lot of answers for someone unwilling to answer most of *my* questions."

"Please, Jem." He gripped a clump of his hair like it frustrated him. "I need to know."

I took a deep breath. "I had a kind of vision, but not in a dream."

"What happened?"

"I changed."

He lowered his arm, his eyes attentive. "You watched this happen?"

I shook my head. "No, I was inside my body. I felt the change, watched hairs sprout from my flesh. I smelled ..."

His gaze grew more intense with each word. "What did you smell, Jem?"

"You," I said, meeting his eyes. "I followed your scent, and you were a wolf, just like me. So, are you still going to deny it?"

"I haven't denied anything."

"Your answers haven't been very forthcoming, either."

Quiet fell again, seeming to last even longer with neither of us speaking, neither looking away.

Sean's hand pushed across the table toward me. "Come back to me, Jem."

I glanced away.

"I want you to come back."

"How can I come back when I was never here to begin?" When my attention returned to him, his eyes squinted as though I'd caused him pain.

"You don't really believe that," he said, voice deep.

"I'm married, Sean."

He groaned. "He's not right for you." His outstretched hand slapped the table, making me jump, and my hands fisted. "You belong here, with me."

I shoved up from my seat. "Why do you always have to be so arrogant?"

"I want you to come home, Jem." His hands raked into his hair as he stood.

"I don't belong with you. I'm married to Peter."

"Does he make you happy?"

I stepped away from the table. "I'm leaving."

"You know this is where you belong." His volume rose as his shoulders tensed.

"I'm *married*, Sean. Don't you get it?"

He flinched at each mention of the 'M' word. "You shouldn't be. It's not right."

"I've been married to Peter for eight years. He's my husband."

He lowered his head until his gaze levelled with mine. "He

doesn't. Deserve. You." With his steadily darkening eyes, his deepened voice, and hands curling into balls at his sides, he looked pretty close to snapping.

I didn't feel far off it myself. "I should never have come here," I said, backing up. "And I should've never let you stay yesterday, or agreed to meet you on Wednesday—I shouldn't even have stepped back into that bloody restaurant. Meeting you has been one huge mistake. I should've run while I had the chance." I spun and stormed away.

His footsteps followed me along the hallway, but I yanked open the front door and strode outside. "Jem, I'm sorry."

Blanking him, I climbed into my car with trembling hands.

"Jem, please ... come back."

I slammed my door, started the engine.

He jogged down the steps, his lips already open in apology. Rather than listen to his words, I reversed away from him and drove out of the gates, but his despair, reflecting in my rear-view mirror, stayed with me long after I'd left him behind.

It took me a while to calm myself. Even once Peter returned home, it was clear he thought something to be wrong in the way he kept looking at me. Although he didn't bring it up, he studied me through dinner. We even watched the factual channels in silence. Only once we went up to bed did he speak.

"Good day, Jem?"

Glancing at him from the bedroom doorway, I shrugged. Peter had never asked before.

He stared at me for a few minutes before pulling back the duvet to climb into bed. As I hung up my robe, he lifted back the bedding on my side. "You look nice tonight. I like what you did with your hair."

My hair hadn't been straightened in days. Peter hated my hair that way. Tugging at a strand, I slipped in beside him.

Peter smiled at me. He hadn't smiled since the incident in the department store, and his expression prickled the hairs on the back of my neck. As I went to lie back, he reached out for me, sliding me down the mattress to his side.

We hadn't been intimate since his drunkenness. My heart sped up as I stared at him.

He leaned over me, placed his lips against mine. When I stiffened, he pulled back, but only a little. "I've missed you, Jem." His body half covered mine, his warm breaths tickling my lashes.

As I stared back at him, only thoughts of Sean swirled through my head, and I silently admonished myself. I had no right to think of another man while in the arms of my husband, or to have spent the time with Sean I had.

Peter was a good husband; he wasn't really bad; that night hadn't been him.

Yet, each time I mentally rationalised why I should be in Peter's arms, Sean's face moved into my mind as the opposing reason. For the first time, with Peter's warm hands against my body, I questioned if I was in the right place.

Chapter 17
DARKNESS

My dream-self stands on the peak of an incline. She is not alone, but back-to-back with a man. I watch as eight others form a circle around them. All eight men are armed, some with knives, others with farming tools.

My dream-self and her companion turn, hesitantly rotating, until his face comes into view. The man with her is Sean. They whisper to each other, their voices low, lips barely moving to pass the spoken words.

One of the men screams out. "Witch!" He waves a pitchfork as though prodding at hay.

"What should we do, Sean?" she whispers.

"Be calm."

No buildings are in sight, no houses, shops, pedestrians. The landscape is filled with greens and browns, dips and rises, with nothing else on the horizon for the eye to perceive, as though of another era.

"How many do you count?" she whispers.

"Eight," Sean responds.

"All armed?"

"Yes, Jem."

"What shall we do? My flesh pulsates."

The men take a step closer toward where Sean and my dream-self stand central in their lessening circle.

"Hold on to it, Jem," Sean murmurs. "I am thinking."

"*See!*" screams one of the advancers. "See the way her body contorts? The witch is possessed."

She gasps. The skin across her face tautens, and the muscles beneath her flesh tighten in spasm. "I am changing, Sean. Change with me."

"Can you not reverse it?"

"My body refuses to listen to reason."

"Then you will have to allow it," Sean whispers through almost inert lips.

"But they will see."

"I will join you." Reaching back, he squeezes her hand. "These men will not live to tell the tale."

Her hand grips his and she nods. In the next second, she drops to her knees.

The men halt, their expressions filled with disgust and fear, as her face twists, as cries leave her deforming mouth and her flesh shimmers.

"It's the devil!" one of them cries. "The devil is within her. She should be burned."

The men take another step forward, but halt when her body shudders.

Bones contort, muscles distort, thick hairs lengthen to coat her flesh—until she becomes fully wolf, and a snarl rips past her bared teeth.

"It's the beast!" one cries.

She circles Sean's legs, and as his flesh begins to pulsate, his face reflects the pain bestowed up on him, and he lowers to the ground in preparation for what is to come. Still, my dream-self winds around him, vigilant while he is vulnerable.

"The other is turning," comes a cry. "We must kill them now."

She faces the bearer of the voice. With weapon brandished high, he leans forward, prepares to attack. Sean is not yet ready, and as the man takes his first step, my dream-self leaps. Snarls explode from her during flight.

The man brings back his pitchfork to strike, but he is too slow—or she is too fast. Her teeth snap open. Close. Her head whips to the side with a deep growl.

With his throat torn from him, the man falls to the ground.

The remaining seven men are inanimate, as she returns to Sean's twisting form. Their eyes fixate on the blood pooling beside the dying body on the ground.

Sean snarls through the final stage of his transformation, and one of the men drops his weapon. Sean does not hesitate, but gives chase to the fleeing body and is quickly upon him—tearing at him, mauling him. The screams of pain jolt the other men into action.

Further screams reverberate through the countryside. Any still clutching weapons throw them down, as though to hasten their escape. My dream-self inhales, drinking the atmosphere deep into her lungs. Her eyes close, her expression one of pure rapture, and as they snap back open, they hold a look of frenzied excitement. Lifting her face to the sky, she opens her mouth to release her howl.

As Sean's response echoes back at her, she scans the fleeing men before racing off after one of them. Her bites and tears render him disabled until he no longer moves. She turns to another, Sean mirroring her actions.

The landscape fast turns into a bloodbath, and the presence of blood, the cries of the men, appear to add to their mood. They leap, race, shred until the sounds grow silent, the bodies upon the ground still, and they are certain of their safety.

Sean snorts as he watches her and takes a step forward, loud exhalations blow from his nostrils. She crosses to him, and together they stand on the apex of the hill, their bodies shivering as they admire their kills.

Chapter 18
LIGHT

Chest heaving, I awoke to darkness. My hands clutched at the bed sheet, the pulse points in my wrists throbbing as though the blood surged through them.

Sean!

At his name, the dream I'd been in before waking flashed through my mind. Revulsion filled me as I recounted each stage. Sean, there with me. My change, and then Sean's. The fear that must have driven me to kill, to defend myself.

The way my body beat out a tune of arousal.

Disgust burned through me as it sank in that the memories —every single detail of each kill—had fuelled the desire.

How had I produced such images? How could I enjoy them?

Did I even know myself any longer?

Mind too consumed with everything to relax, I didn't return to slumber for the rest of the night. When Peter climbed out of bed, announcing he was off to work, he didn't wait for breakfast, or to see if I got up with him. He simply kissed my cheek, washed, dressed, and left.

Alone, I dragged myself to the bathroom for a shower. It

didn't matter, though, how hard I scrubbed, my self-distaste refused to be cleansed away. Friction marks and red splotches covered my body by the time I'd finished.

At the trill of the telephone, I plodded downstairs, answering it on the tenth ring. "Hello?"

"It's Poppy."

"It's Saturday."

"I know. Is Peter at work today?"

"Yes."

She sighed. "Okay."

Without knowing why, I frowned. "Why are you ringing me on a Saturday?" Listening to the quiet crackle of the phone line when Poppy didn't answer, it dawned on me the only other time Poppy called me on an irregular day. "What does he want?"

"He said he's really sorry, Jem."

"I don't care how sorry he is. I'm married to Peter, and I need to try and make that work."

"Peter's an arsehole," she said.

"And Sean isn't?"

"Possibly, Jem, but he's a nice arsehole."

I huffed down the phone at her.

"He wants you to meet him again, said he needs to explain."

"He could have done that yesterday. He had me right there with him, and he blew it."

"I think you should give him a second chance."

Another huff answered her.

"I think you'll regret it if you don't."

"You want me to consider the possibility of having an affair, Pop? Sean doesn't want me as a friend. He wants to *be* with me."

"I just don't think you should throw the option away completely."

"Would you consider it, if it were you in my situation?"

"I'm not married to Peter."

"Yes, Poppy, *married*. Neither you, nor Sean, seem to be grasping that."

"Oh, we know, sweetie. We just don't think you should be."

I emitted a long sigh. "I don't know what to do."

"Are you going to let Sean apologise?"

My fingers caught as I raked them through my wet hair. "I'm so confused."

"I know you are, but you wouldn't be feeling that way if you had no feelings for him."

"How can I feel something for someone I don't know?"

"Some people just connect, I guess—like me and my Jase. What did you and Peter have in common when you first met?"

"We both liked food." I gave a half-laugh at the stupidity of my answer, followed by another of sorrow when I realised I'd spoken the truth.

"You should meet Sean today. Let him apologise."

"You really think so?"

"Yes, sweetie, I do."

As HE HAD the day before, Sean led me to his house. He parked his car on the block-paved drive, climbed out, and waved me forward to him. When I stopped, he pulled open my door.

I peered up at the house. "Ever feel like you're running around in circles?"

"I wanted to show you something, Jem. This is the only safe place to do that."

"Why?" I turned to him. "What is it?"

"I'm going to show you the truth." Despite my frown, he continued, "I'm going to head into the forest. Give me five minutes, then come find me."

I opened my mouth to protest, to tell him I had no intention of going anywhere near the forest with him, but he'd already taken off.

From the car, I jogged around the side of the property, spotted Sean nearing the arches. His steps stalled for a moment as his head spun toward the house, and I paused, believing he'd stop. Instead, he picked up speed and raced for the trees.

I broke into run, hoping to catch up before he had the chance to get too far in.

"Hey!" From the left, a huge man approached. "What the hell are you doing?"

I slowed to a stop. Glancing to the forest, I pointed that way and thought about calling Sean, but he'd already vanished.

"I said, *what* are you doing?" As the guy neared, his face stirred a memory, like I'd seen him before but couldn't recall where. "This is private property. You can't come running around in here. Get the hell out."

"I'm not trespassing."

"Yes, you are."

"No, I'm not." Hoping I could spot Sean to come and clear the matter up, I started toward the arches again.

I only managed a few steps before the man grabbed my arm and spun me to face him.

Up close, I studied him hard, and it clicked why he looked familiar. His features and body mirrored Sean's, except he was bigger—all over.

"Ethan, what's going on?" a voice called from the conservatory.

I glanced around him to see a red-haired man.

"Trespasser," said the one still holding my arm. "I'm just getting rid of her."

I frowned at him. "I'm not a trespasser."

"You are, if I haven't invited you."

I wriggled against his tight grip as his fingers dug in.

Opening his hand, he nudged me toward the front of the house. "Get out of here."

Instead of obeying, I swung past him and darted back the other way toward the forest.

"Why, you persistent little ..."

I ran across the lawn, his footfalls falling too close for comfort, but as his hand brushed my arm, pain shot through my skull. My knees gave way, and I slammed into the grass and wrapped my arms around my head as I rolled to my back with low groans and gasps flying from me.

"What the hell did you do to her?" The redhead's voice was nearer.

"I didn't do anything. She just dropped. Maybe she's epileptic, or something."

"What's going on?" called a third voice. That, too, came from the house.

My body curled, before I flipped over against the agony to land on my knees. I gasped again, hands flying out, my eyes opening.

Fine hairs pushed through my pores, jolting panic within me—until I realised they weren't mine. When I had my 'vision' in the store, my hairs had been pale. When I changed in my dream, I was blonde, as I had always been as human. The new hairs lengthening to coat every inch of flesh in thick shagginess arrived far too dark to be mine.

"What's she doing here?" the newcomer asked.

"Trespassing."

"I don't think she is," said the third voice. "What's wrong with her?"

"Who knows," said the second voice. "She just dropped ..."

The longer I stared, the quicker the dots joined. The fur I could see covering my limbs wasn't my colour because it *wasn't* mine. It had to be Sean's—which meant he had to be changing. In the forest.

What if he came for me, like in my dreams?

Move!

I forced my hand up and rubbed at my face. Despite my arm refusing to work properly, I banged at my head, my cheeks—anything to snap me round from my vision.

"What the hell is she doing?" asked the one called Ethan.

I blinked back to the scene in front of me, shaking my head to clear it further. "I need to get up."

"Oh, good. She's back with us."

"Help me up." My voice held desperation.

"Come on." The voice that spoke sounded like the third guy who joined us.

"Get her out of here," Ethan said.

"Yes, that's exactly what I need to do." With the help of hands holding me, I scrambled to my feet. "He's changing already."

The two men in front of me froze, confusion mingled with fury twisting the features of the big one.

"What did you just say?" he growled.

I glanced from him to the redhead, and back again. "I need to get out of here. He's changing. There isn't much time."

He gripped both my arms. "Who the hell are you?"

"Ethan, you don't understand," said the third voice as he moved to my right.

I tried to turn to him, but the big one grabbed my jaw, holding my face in place. My panic escalated at the parallels to my dreams. "Déjà vu."

"What?" His grip tightened, his fingers digging into my throat.

I tried to pull away. "You have to let me go."

"Not until you tell me who you are and what you want."

"I think you should loosen her, buddy," said the same voice as before.

"I'm taking her inside," Ethan said. "She's not leaving until this is sorted out."

"Yes." I attempted a nod. "Take me in the house—*please*."

As he released his grip on my throat, I gasped in air. Before I'd recovered, he snatched my arm and propelled me toward the house.

"We need to move faster." When I lifted my head, I saw a face I remembered. "*You*." I pointed at him. "You know me. Tell them we need to move faster."

"Will you stop rambling," Ethan said at my rear.

The young man who'd been with Sean the day we met gave a small shake of his head.

I ignored the warning. "How long does it take him?"

"What?" snapped Ethan.

"How long does he take to change?" I looked to the only one I could consider an ally. "Ten minutes—fifteen?"

"Actually, he's pretty fast. He's through in five," he said.

My shoulders were jolted from behind. "Be quiet! Do you know her, Danny?"

His gaze sliced to Ethan and he nodded.

"Who is she? Why does she know so much about us?"

"It isn't my place to say. Sean—"

"Sean's got something to do with this?"

"He's got *everything* to do with this." I'd have thrown my hands in the air, if I could've. "He brought me here, and now he's run off to change, so he can bite me. And if you don't move faster, he'll succeed."

"Bite you? Why the hell would he do something like that?"

His grip loosened at last, and I faced him. "Because he wants me to be like him."

He frowned. "That's ... insane."

At the beat of running hitting the lawn, our heads all spun toward the forest.

My eyes widened at the huge brown wolf hurtling our way. "Oh, no!"

Ethan looked from the approaching wolf to me. "Why—"

"Keep him away from me!" I threw myself toward the house.

The sound of paws followed. The three men shouted at him to stop. When I heard heavy footfalls, I presumed they were chasing the wolf chasing me. Flying inside the conservatory, I grabbed the door handle to prevent myself falling and spun around.

The door slammed shut just as Sean reached the edge of the paving.

My hand pressed against the glass, my chest heaved from panic, and I glared at the brown wolf studying me.

Ethan caught up with him and prodded him with his foot, but Sean continued to watch me. "Go and change the hell back!" Another footed shove. "Go and change back, *now*! Dad's going to be furious with you over this."

With his wolf eyebrows knitted together, Sean's attention flickered between me and Ethan, before he turned and ran back toward the forest.

Heaving a sigh of relief, I collapsed into the nearest chair.

Ethan yanked open the door and entered the conservatory. "What the *hell* is going on here?"

"You're Sean's brother, aren't you?" I asked.

"Is someone going to tell me what's going on?" When the other two came in and sat, Ethan pointed to the one he'd called Danny. "You know."

"You should ask Sean."

"So, you *do* know?" asked the redheaded man.

"It's complicated." Danny peered sideways at me. "That's

why you should wait and ask Sean. If he hasn't told you, maybe he didn't want you to know."

"Hasn't told me what, Daniel?"

Daniel's eyes flitted between me and Ethan.

Ethan turned to me. "Do *you* know what's going on?"

I nodded. "I already told you what he was doing."

"Why, though? Why you? If we've never met you, Sean must barely know you."

"Like Daniel said, it's complicated."

Ethan glanced up, as a human-looking Sean emerged from beneath the arches and approached across the lawn. I went to stand, but he pushed me back into my seat and strode out of the conservatory himself.

The redhead stared hard at me. "Who *are* you?"

"I'm Jem."

Outside, Ethan stalled Sean from ducking past by giving him a good shoulder shaking.

"You?" I asked.

"Kyle." His gaze narrowed on the duo. "Danny's brother."

"And Josh's," added Daniel.

I glanced at him.

"The other one you saw with us in the burger bar? He's my other brother."

"You must be pretty important if Sean's willing to take on Ethan to get to you," Kyle said. "Nobody in their right mind takes on Ethan without good reason—sometimes not even *with* good reason."

"I don't believe Sean *is* in his right mind," I said.

Kyle chuckled as we watched the two scrapping brothers. Ethan had Sean in a headlock, with Sean attempting to break free while slowly making his way toward me.

I pressed a hand to the glass. "He's going to hurt him."

"Ethan would never hurt his brother," Kyle said. "He's just teaching him a lesson."

After a few more minutes of grappling, Sean broke free and ran across the lawn.

I turned on him as he flew through the door. "What were you thinking?"

He halted. "I needed you to see."

"By *biting* me?"

"What exactly was on your mind, Sean?" Kyle asked.

"I wasn't going to bite her." Sean turned to me. "I wasn't going to bite you."

"Don't lie to me." My finger tapped my temple. "I've seen it all, remember?"

Ethan shoved Sean farther inside and closed the door behind him.

"I should go." I pushed to my feet.

Ethan grabbed my arm, pulling me back down as he took the seat beside mine. "You're not going anywhere."

Sean took a step forward when I rubbed at my arm. "Don't touch her like that. None of this is her fault."

"I know," growled his brother. "It's yours."

My brow creased as I looked up at Sean. "Why would you bite me?"

"I wasn't—"

"Don't lie to me." I shoved to a stand in front of him. "I know you were going to do it again."

Ethan jerked upright in his seat. "Again?"

"It's not like that," Sean said to him before turning to me. "Jem, that wasn't why I changed."

"I don't believe you."

"It's the truth. I told you I wanted to show you the truth today. That's why I asked you to come."

I went to step around him, but he reached for me, his eyes

pleading. "I shouldn't be here, Sean. I can't keep messing with my head like this. *You* can't keep confusing me, and that's how I feel whenever I see you."

"Please, Jem. Yesterday, you wanted the truth. Today, I showed it to you. I've never been honest with anyone else, not like this ..."

"That's true," murmured Kyle.

"... and now you're going to walk away—again."

"I should never have come in the first place." I tugged my arm free.

"You can't leave," Ethan said from behind. "You've seen too much here today."

"You're going to stop me from leaving?" I glanced over my shoulder, and he shrugged. "Was that your plan, Sean—make it so I couldn't leave?"

"I don't want you here because you have no choice. I want you to stay because it's what you've decided. I don't—"

"Then, I'm leaving." I turned to Ethan. "You can always use force, but I won't make it easy." Opening the door, I sent Sean a hard stare. "You should talk to your family before you come up with some hare-brained scheme and invite me here again."

"Can I drive back with you?"

I strode off. "No, you cannot!"

Sean didn't follow—none of them did. Once in my car, I drove until far away enough to be sure and pulled in to a lay-by. Head back, eyes closed, I attempted to regain control of the shaking threatening to take over my body.

Chapter 19

My heart sank when I pulled up and saw Peter's truck outside our home. That, I could have done without. I went into the house, pausing only to shut the front door and remove my shoes before continuing into the living room. The second I saw him, I stopped.

Peter sat on the sofa, muddy work boots still on his feet, arms resting across his knees. He glared up at me, his eyes conveying a dark depth while appearing arctic.

A cold pit of dread formed in my stomach.

"Where have you been, Jem?" His low voice barely held control.

"Poppy's." The lie didn't sound convincing, even to my ears.

He shook his head once, rubbed his palms the length of his thighs. "No."

"I ... went to Pop—"

"Don't treat me like an idiot, Jem."

"I'm not, Pete, I—"

"It's fucking Peter, not Pete!"

I went to apologise but shut my mouth, afraid of digging myself a bigger hole.

"Where ... have ... you ... been?" He measured each word.

"I—"

"And don't tell me you were at Poppy's, because I know you weren't there."

My hands curled, clamminess forming within. Dampness beaded across my brow and trembling affected my knees as my eyes darted to the side. I didn't know what to do, what to say to him.

"Where were you?" he asked again.

The tremors spread to my shoulders.

"Maybe I can put it in simple terms for you. *Who was he?*"

I stared at him.

"Who were you with today?"

"I don't—"

"You were *seen*, Jem. Man with a yellow Porsche. Ring any bells for you?"

"How—"

"Do you know how humiliated I felt when John strolled in and announced in front of my entire workforce that he saw my wife with another man?"

"I didn't—"

"You didn't what? Fuck him? What?"

I glanced away, stared at the corner where ceiling met with wall.

"Are you going to tell me it isn't true?"

My hands tightened—an unfruitful attempt to control my shaking body.

"Fucking *look* at me, Jem!" He jumped to his feet.

My head whipped back.

"Tell me it isn't true." Leaning forward, his expression furious, he no longer resembled the Peter I knew. "Tell me you weren't with another man today."

Panic clouded my thoughts. "It's not like that, Peter."

"Liar!"

His fist made contact. Blinding pain shot through my head and blackness moved in.

My hair being torn from my scalp brought me to. Screaming out, I reached up, but Peter had my hair wrapped around his fingers, his hand around my throat.

"You are supposed to be my *wife*, Jem, not some fucking whore. How can you do this to me? I knew you were up to no good. I fucking asked and you denied it. You've done nothing but lie to me ..."

Each of his roared words sprayed my face. Every time I shut my eyes against his flying phlegm, he shook my head until they opened again. Within seconds, my breaths evaded me.

I tried for the hand holding my hair, tried to grab the one at my throat.

As I hit the verge of sinking into the blackness, Peter pushed at my face and released me. "You're not worth it, whore!"

He moved away, and I curled into a ball, hugging my knees to my chest. My body trembled as I watched him through half-open eyes.

He went to the windows, locked them. I heard him do the same upstairs. At the front door, he used my key to lock it, slipping it into his pocket once done. He did the same with the back door. Back in the living room, he strode over to me and shoved his hands into my pocket. When I flinched, he shoved harder.

He removed my car keys, followed by my purse, taking all money and cards before discarding the empty container on the carpet before me. With lack of empathy, he rolled me to reach my other pocket, tugged out my mobile. After breaking it apart, he smashed it beneath his foot.

I lay there throughout, head pounding, pain shooting through my face. With the coming bruises making their presence known, tears trailed over my cheeks.

Chapter 20

I spent Saturday night on the living room floor. Peter had gone to bed after kicking me with his dirty boots as he passed, and I made no move to follow. Only once certain he'd fallen asleep did I stir. If not for the need to use the bathroom, I may not have bothered at all.

Peter and I spent the entire Sunday in the house, which turned out to be pretty horrendous, also. At lunchtime, he dragged me into the kitchen, stood me before the cooker, and snapped, "Make my fucking dinner, like a proper wife."

When I moved to the fridge, his hand took my head and shoved. I cried out on collision with the door as pain shot through what I presumed to be a black eye. When I grabbed the pork and turned, he spat at me—for the fifth time since he'd ventured downstairs. I did nothing other than wipe the tears from my cheeks.

With dinner prepared, he insisted I eat with him at the table. My stomach didn't want to deal with food, churning against each offering, but Peter's screams to clear my plate convinced me I should eat.

After dinner, he propelled me back into the kitchen. "Make

me some tea." He went to walk away, came back. "And cake. I want a fucking cake, whore."

When evening arrived, he prodded me into the living room, bent my knees until my rear hit the sofa. His crappy programmes filled the hours until bedtime, and when he hauled me upstairs and threw me onto the floor of the spare bedroom, relief flooded me.

Once certain he'd gone to work Monday morning, I headed straight for the phone. If I could ring Poppy, she'd know what to do.

The cradle stood empty. He'd taken it.

Around the house, I tried every door and window, in the hope he hadn't been as vigilant as I feared. No chance. Well and truly trapped, I had no way out, no way in, no way to call for help.

My face stung as the spray hit it in the shower, my scalp protested when I applied the shampoo. Fifteen painful minutes later, I took my first look in the mirror.

Shameful swelling affected most of my right cheek, closing the eye to a slit. Blackened flesh and my seemingly deformed nose were further evidence of my beating. I ran my fingers across my throat, where the mark of each of Peter's fingers had burned into my skin as a reminder of what he could do. I touched my hair—even a good brushing wouldn't hide the patch of missing strands just forward of my crown.

As I studied the reflected state of me, I recognised all those women who'd adamantly insist they'd walked into a door, tripped, anything other than the truth.

My body slumped to the floor, and the tears, once erupted, refused to stop.

At two-thirty in the afternoon, I made myself move, dressed in a skirt and blouse, and went to prepare dinner.

Peter returned home early. My body stiffened at the sound

of his car, trembled when the key turned in the door. He paused only to remove his boots before entering the living room. I must have looked as though standing to attention.

"What's that smell?"

"It's dinner, Peter," I mumbled.

"What day is it, Jem?"

"It's ..." I couldn't think straight while he stared at me. "It's ... Monday, Peter."

"So, it's ..." He lifted his palms.

My heart pounded when I realised my mistake. "Take-away day."

He nodded slowly before walking away. "Fuck it. I didn't want anyone knocking on the door anyway."

I breathed out a sigh of relief.

Monday night went along the same route as Sunday night. Peter made me eat with him, wouldn't let me leave the table until I'd finished, and he sat me beside him on the sofa to watch TV. Come night, he shoved me into the spare bedroom.

Tuesday became a repeat of Monday, Wednesday of Tuesday—like I'd gotten jammed in a poorly-written rerun, with someone hogging the remote control. Every time my hellish day ended, the buttons were hit as a cruel joke to make me start over —play, stop, rewind.

Thursday morning, as I began to lose hope of life ever being any different, I caught a sound that almost brought tears of joy to my eyes. Head tilted, I followed my hearing until I stood on the landing, peering up at the loft hatch.

Five-foot-seven couldn't be considered small for a woman, but the hatch was out of reach, even for me. Fearing I'd be too late if I went in search of a step-up, I climbed the banister along-side the stairs. My balance wobbled me on the top strip as I reached up to push at the loft cover, and feeling around inside, I grabbed the missing receiver.

Placing it against my ear, I hit the button, but didn't speak for fear it could be Peter checking up on me.

A few seconds of silence passed, then, "Hello?"

Poppy. I sobbed out my relief.

"What is it?"

"Poppy."

"Jem, what's wrong? What's happened?"

I hiccupped into the receiver.

"Jem, calm down and tell me. I knew something was wrong when you didn't call Tuesday."

"I can't ... Poppy, I ... can't come ..." My strained voice didn't sound like my own.

"Did you and Peter argue again, sweetie?"

"He ... hit ... me."

"He hit you?"

I sobbed some more.

"Get yourself over here, Jem. I'll take care of you."

"I ... can't."

"I'm not asking, I'm *telling* you."

"I can't. He's ... locked me ..."

"He's locked you in?"

More tears spilled over.

"Didn't I tell you that man's an arsehole? I ..."

The phone fell from my juddering fingers, and I scrambled to pick it back up.

"... not helping matters. Well, you just wait there. Poppy's coming to get you."

"Can't ... Doors ... windows ... all locked."

"Did you forget, sweetie? You gave Poppy the spare key."

UNABLE TO REMAIN STILL, I paced a diagonal path across the living room. Terror raced through me at the thought that Peter might find reason to leave work early and return to catch Poppy coming to my assistance. My hands switched from clenched beside my hips to full-out wringing at my waist while I waited. When I heard the key in the front door, I'd almost reached breaking point. Even then, I expected Peter to enter instead of my friend.

My feet stopped moving, and I stared wide-eyed. At Poppy's entrance, I nearly collapsed from relief.

Her hand shot to her mouth. "Oh, sweetie, what did he do to you?"

I didn't need to answer—the evidence spoke for itself.

She looked me over. "You're not dressed."

"What's the point?" I mumbled. "I can't go anywhere."

"Actually, you're coming with me."

"I can't, Poppy. If I'm not here when Peter gets—"

"You're coming, Jem. The taxi's waiting outside."

"I can't," I whispered.

"You can, and you are." She turned and headed upstairs, returning a few minutes later with an armful of clothes. "Put this on." She pulled a long cardigan around my shoulders.

"I can't, Poppy."

Ignoring my protests, she fed my arms into the sleeves and produced a huge pair of sunglasses from her bottomless bag. "I thought you might need these."

When I didn't respond, she eased them onto my face before squeezing my clothing into her bag. With her arm around me, she guided me to the front door.

I pushed back, but she nudged me closer to the outside world. I jabbered on about how mad Peter would be if he found out, how she didn't understand, didn't know what he could do. Poppy continued to shepherd, and I found myself on the wrong side of my front door, wearing nothing but my nightdress and a cardigan.

. . .

DURING THE JOURNEY to Poppy's house, dread roiled in my stomach.

On arrival, and after listening to my complaints that I hadn't any money to pay the taxi, Poppy hushed me and coaxed me indoors. From kitchen, to bathroom, to kitchen, she filled the kettle, ran me a bath, made drinks.

With a mug of steaming coffee for me, she took my hand and led me to the bathroom. A swish of her fingers frothed bubbles to the rim of the tub before she told me to get in, because it would '*soothe the tenderness and help me feel better*'.

I disagreed but didn't like to say.

Left alone, I followed Poppy's instruction. Bubbles fizzled across my chin as I closed my eyes. I didn't bother to wash, simply concentrated on the gentle flow of the water against my soreness.

Once the liquid grew cold, I pulled out the plug and climbed from my temporary sanctuary. Poppy must have heard, because I'd only dried my arms when she shouted through the door to use the robe hanging on the hook. After pulling it on, I carried my empty mug downstairs.

"In here, sweetie," called Poppy from the kitchen.

I followed her voice, threw a longing glance toward the over-sized corner-suite in the living room. As I stepped into the kitchen, my eyes fell on Sean, sitting atop one of the stools.

Gaze instantly connecting with my face, he scrambled to his feet, and my fingers lost their grasp of my mug, sending it to the tiled floor with a tinkled crash.

Sean went to take a step but stopped, his hands lifting and dropping then running through his hair like he didn't know what to do with them.

"I'll clean it up." I stepped forward.

"No! Don't move!" Poppy reached out a hand. "You'll cut your feet."

But my brain had already told my foot to move in that direction and my sole met with the broken shards. "Poppy?" I frowned at the sharp pain slicing into my sole. "I cut my foot."

"Take her through to the living room, Sean," she said, leaning down and scooping up some of the larger splinters. "I'll clean this up before she hurts herself further."

"Did you *call* him, Poppy?" How could she?

"He was already on his way. When I called you, he'd rung to ask my address. He thought it the only way to get you to talk to him. I didn't give him a second thought once I'd spoken to you, Jem—forgot he was coming."

Sean came toward me. "I need to lift you, Jem."

I stared at him, into his eyes—searching for what, I didn't know.

"You have porcelain in your foot. I'm going to carry you, Jem, okay?"

A glance down showed my foot still hovering above the floor. Sean's movements were slow as he lifted and carried me through to the corner-suite. His eyes never left mine. Ashamed to be seen in such a state, I turned my face away.

By the time Poppy joined us, Sean had my foot upon his knee, plucking the sharp slivers from my sole. Red stained the pale denim of his jeans.

"I've dripped blood on your carpet," I said to Poppy.

Taking the seat beside me, she handed Sean a first aid kit. "It'll clean."

I flinched, drawing my foot back as a fragment sliced my skin on exit.

"I think that's the last one," Sean said.

He worked with care, causing no further discomfort as he cleansed, padded, and dressed my wound, and I leaned my head against the cushioned back of the sofa, sinking into the corner. Eventually, my breathing began to steady itself again. Having barely slept in days—afraid Peter would pay me back in ways I didn't want to contemplate—and being comfortable, warm, safe, I almost dozed off.

Poppy didn't move, and Sean kept my foot on his leg, made small brushing movements across my bridge. Although they never spoke, I could imagine the eye-rolling, lip tightening and brow-raising passing between them.

Only when I pushed my drying hair from my face did Sean speak. "Why, Jem? Why would he do this to you?"

I lifted my lids to Sean studying my face—his eyes held fierceness when they met with the finger marks on my throat. "Peter thinks I'm having an affair."

Sean looked away, his hand clenching into a fist. "It's because of me, isn't it?"

"We were spotted. One of Peter's work colleagues saw us on Saturday ..." I turned to Poppy. "Peter was already waiting for me when I got home."

"This is my fault." She frowned. "If I hadn't talked you into going—"

"No, Pop. I shouldn't have gone, I know ... but it was my decision. I knew I shouldn't—"

"Will you two quit blaming yourselves? The only one to blame here is her bloody husband. He had no right to do this to you." He rubbed his palms across his face before covering his eyes. His hands lowered to reveal moisture. "Did you know he would do this to you? Did you know this would happen, if you saw me?"

I shrugged.

"Why would you take such a risk for someone you barely know?"

I gave another shrug.

"How could he do this to you?"

"I don't want to talk about this with you. You couldn't understand. You—"

"Please, do not make excuses for him, Jem."

"He didn't mean—"

"Sean's right," Poppy cut in. "Peter had no right to hurt you."

I closed my eyes on them.

"You're exhausted, sweetie. Maybe you should take a rest."

"I can't. I have to make sure I'm back before he returns. If I fall asleep, I won't wake in time. He'll be furious." I heard the hysteria in my words, knew they must have, too.

"Sweetie, I don't think going back is a good idea," Poppy said.

"I have to." My eyes snapped open. "If I'm not there, this is the first place he'll come looking, and then you'll be in trouble, too."

"Then, stay somewhere else." Sean growled. "We've got a spare room. You can have that."

I stared at him. "Being with you got me in this mess in the first place. Do you have any idea what he'd do, if he had even the slightest inkling you're here with me now?"

"I have a pretty good idea, yes—which is why I don't want you going back."

"I have to. Peter's my husband. He had every right to be upset at the thought of me with another man."

"He did not have any right to treat you like this. Look at you, Jem. You're a mess. And I don't mean your bruises. You're a quivering wreck. This isn't the Jem I remember. She'd never let a man treat her this way. Hell, you'd have kicked my arse just for speaking to you like I did on Friday. But this?" He shook his head. "There's no way."

"Maybe I'm not who you think I am."

"I know you are."

"Did you have the dreams, too, Sean?" Poppy asked, diffusing the tension a little.

He seemed surprised as he studied her for a few seconds before nodding.

"What was in your dreams?" she asked, as though to change the subject.

"Everything," he said hoarsely.

"When did they start? Did they start at the same time as Jem's?"

He glanced at me before answering, "Almost eight years ago."

"Lordy!" Poppy's eyes goggled. "Eight *years*? You must have been going round the bend by the time Jem showed up."

He half-smiled.

"How did you know, Sean?" I asked.

Confusion claimed his eyes and wrinkled his brow.

"How did you know I'd be there that day?"

"I didn't. I don't even know how I ended up there." He shrugged. "We were hungry and that was the nearest place to eat."

"But the restaurant is nowhere near where you live."

"It's even farther than where you live," he said. "What were the chances of you being there? Stranger still, what were the chances of us *both* being there, on the same day, at the same time?"

"I don't know."

"I always said you were weird, sweetie."

My lips curved at Poppy's words.

"What were you doing there, Jem?" asked Sean.

I shrugged. "I don't even know the area—almost got lost going home. I didn't even remember the drive there. When the car stopped, I was in the car park. It was weird."

"So," Poppy said, smiling, "you both have dreams about each other. You're both ..." She seemed to consider her words before saying, "... *something else* in your dreams. You both just happen to be in the same place at the same time, and you both knew who the other was? Sweetie, that alone should tell you why you ran around behind Peter's back to see a man you barely know. Just because you hadn't met him yet, doesn't mean you didn't know him, because obviously, you did."

Chapter 21

Despite Sean's and Poppy's protests, I insisted on leaving. Poppy even came with me in the taxi and locked me back in, when I explained I didn't want to risk having my only source of release in the same house as Peter. My threat to walk home and wait outside for him had ended up the major factor in her decision to concede.

I upset Sean, though, refusing his offer of a lift. He begged me not to return home, pleaded with me to stay with Poppy. Other than using physical restraint, he had no choice but to let me go.

After Poppy had turned the key, I stared at the door for several seconds—almost unable to believe I'd subjected myself to going back, despite Poppy's promises to return the next day—before perking myself up.

With the telephone in its exact position, the loft cover replaced, I ensured the house looked tidy enough to convince Peter I'd never left on his return home—so, other than spending a few hours at Poppy's, Thursday turned out just like Wednesday. Beside him on the sofa, I watched TV programmes I detested. Come night, I slept in the spare bedroom.

. . .

AFTER PETER LEFT for work Friday morning, I was on the verge of going for my wash when the key slid into the front door lock. Convinced Peter had returned, I paced back into the living room and sat, listening as the front door opened then closed.

When Sean walked in, I almost had a heart attack. "What are you doing here?" I jumped up, shoved him back out into the hall. "Peter has barely left. If he's seen your car, he'll be back through that door like a shot."

"Jem—"

"You have to leave. *Now!*"

"Jem—"

"He knows your car. He'll know it's you, he'll—"

"I didn't come in *my* car, Jem." He took my wrists, as I grabbed for the door handle. "I came in Ethan's pickup, and I waited until he'd definitely gone before I came in. Please, stop worrying."

"But ..." My eyes narrowed. "Where's Poppy?"

"She asked me to collect you." When I continued to stare, he continued, "Poppy gave me the key," and my stalled breaths resumed.

"Okay ... okay." I loosened my tense arms. "I should dress. I need to get dressed. We're wasting time." I turned and hurried up the stairs.

In the bathroom, I splashed my face clean before brushing my teeth. From there, I headed to the bedroom and pulled on shorts and a vest to keep me cool during what already promised to be a warm day. When I ran back down, Sean stood exactly where I'd left him.

His eyes skimmed over me. "Shoes, Jem."

With my feet in plimsolls, we left the house. Sean held open the truck door, helped me into the passenger seat. As he drove, I leaned back against the headrest, trying to steady my pounding heart. I'd almost succeeded when it occurred to me we'd headed in the wrong direction.

"You missed the turn." I pointed. "Poppy lives that way."

He stared ahead. "We're not going to Poppy's."

"Then, where are we going?"

"I'm taking you home with me."

I straightened. "Did Poppy put you up to this?"

"She couldn't make it this morning—has to watch her kid's school play, or something. She didn't mention it because she knew you'd panic. I didn't mention it because I knew you'd refuse to come."

"How long is she there for?"

"Does it matter?"

"So, Poppy *did* put you up to this?"

"She didn't put me up to anything, Jem. It's not a conspiracy. When she knew she couldn't make it, she asked me to help because she couldn't stand the thought of you being stuck in there again." He paused. "I do think she's hoping I'll talk some sense into you, though."

"Of course she is," I muttered, leaning back and lifting my feet to rest on the dashboard.

He didn't speak again. Probably because I'd finished ranting, and he didn't want to induce a second round. After another restless night, my lids drooped, and my breathing slowed, and I couldn't be bothered to block the heaviness consuming my brain.

My body jostled, despite lying down, and I blinked against harsh sunlight to see Sean's face hovering above me, instantly aware of his arms looped beneath my shoulders and knees.

"I can walk," I said.

He smiled. "I'm sure you can."

"Put me down, then."

"Shit!" he hissed, halting.

My pulse zoomed. "What?"

"Dad's here. He's supposed to be at work."

I followed his gaze to an older, even bigger than Ethan, replica. As Sean set me on my feet, his father watched from the conservatory.

"Does he know about me?"

Sean nodded. "I've told them everything." Taking my arm, he started walking toward our waiting observer, but I tugged back, and he turned to me again. "What's wrong? He won't be mad about you being here. He'll understand."

"My face," I whispered. "He'll see."

"Jem, he already knows."

I glanced at the huge man, then back at Sean.

With a firmer grip, he started walking me again. "It'll be okay. Come on."

Shrugging loose, I positioned myself behind Sean's approach, hoping his dad wouldn't notice the mess of my face.

"I thought you were at work today, Dad," Sean said as he entered.

"Evidently," rumbled a deep bass.

"Is there no job on today?"

"Supplies are delayed until Monday. We're stalled until then."

With the back of his hand, he nudged Sean farther inside, exposing me in the doorway. For minutes, he studied me, but his stare weighed too heavy to deal with, and I looked away, catching Sean's smile before my eyes rested on the garden outside.

At footsteps, I turned back to Ethan's entrance from the kitchen.

"Jem." He didn't sound annoyed to see me—didn't sound particularly pleased, either.

I inclined my chin. "Ethan."

Sean's dad spoke at last, pointing to my face in a circular motion. "Is this what he did to you? That man of yours?"

I sent him a nod.

"Because of Sean?"

My shoulders shrugged, and I brought my gaze up. In contrast to the brothers' dark brown eyes, pale blue peered back from their father, and I couldn't help but stare.

"And yet, you've still agreed to see him today, despite that?"

"Actually, I didn't really have any say in the matter."

His lips twitched. "Sean tells me you went back to that man of yours, yesterday. Even after you got out, you still went back?"

I gave another shrug before nodding.

"That makes you pretty brave in my books."

"She didn't go back out of bravery, Dad, she went back because she was too afraid to do anything else," Sean said, his voice deep.

His dad turned to him, warning in his tone. "Even acts fuelled by fear can be considered brave, Son. Haven't I told you this?" His attention returned to me. "Well, I guess you better come in while I make you a drink." He extended his hand. "I'm Nathan, by the way. Once you've got to know me better, say in about two minutes, you can call me Nate."

"Nice to meet you, Nathan." Accepting his handshake, I allowed him to lead me inside.

"Actually, I'm surprised you came back at all,"—he pulled out a chair at the table, gesturing to me to sit—"after the way this lot treated you last week."

"Again, I wasn't really given a choice, Nathan."

"Nate, Jem. It's Nate to you now."

. . .

As we finished our coffees, the front door swung open and Kyle and Daniel bustled in. Behind them followed the second friend of Sean's from the restaurant, Josh, and an older man I didn't know.

Josh grinned when he spotted me at the table. "Hey, it's the girl who likes to sniff strangers." He jerked back. "Whoa! What happened to your face?"

Daniel shoved him by the shoulder, as I cringed and hid behind my hand. "Nice one, Josh."

"Sorry," he mumbled.

"You can make the drinks for that idiotic greeting," Nathan said.

With his head hung, Josh crossed to the kettle, and the other newcomers pulled out chairs to sit.

"Did your man do that to your face?" Kyle asked from across the table.

"He did it because somebody saw her and Sean together," Nathan said before I could answer, "and they told him."

Seven brows furrowed for a moment, until the one I hadn't met before spoke. "Did you really sniff Sean?"

I studied him—his red hair like Kyle's, green eyes like Daniel and Josh—and turned to Kyle. "Another brother?"

"No." The man grinned. "They're my sons. I'm Connor."

"Jem." My lips curved in response to his impish expression.

"So, did you? Is it true?"

I gave a small nod.

"And you've been having these—what are they—dreams?"

"Kind of, but mine were a bit different to Sean's."

"Different how?" Ethan asked.

One glance at Sean had him stepping in to explain how our perspectives differed, then about the one vision I'd had where mine had been the same as his. The others remained engrossed, even more so when they realised I knew how it felt to experience a change.

Sean turned to me. "You said *were*."

I frowned.

"When asked about your dreams, you said they *were* different. Have they ended?"

"Haven't yours?"

"No. Haven't you had any more at all?"

"Just one since I saw you in the restaurant."

"What was it about?"

"I don't really want to discuss it." I glanced around at the watching faces before dipping my head. "Dreams are private."

"Was it ... personal?" he persisted.

My voice lowered. "It was very ... violent."

The others seemed to hang on our every word.

"Human violent or ... *other* violent?" His expression held determination as he ducked his eyes to mine.

"Other," I whispered, tilting my face so only he could see the reddening of my cheeks.

"Eight of them?" His eyebrows lifted, and he seemed to understand at the same time I did that we'd had the exact same dream.

"Yes, on a hill."

"I had that one, too," he whispered.

"Surely, it occurred to you before now that we may have had some the same if we're both in them," I said, my volume a little louder.

"I'd never really thought about it. We've never talked about them." He twisted his body further toward mine, and I found my own body responding. "How long?"

Our companions faded away as our bodies faced, our eyes locked. "How long what?"

"Poppy was gobsmacked at how long mine had been going on for, so how long have you had yours, if not the same as me?"

"Five weeks."

"Five weeks?" He tossed his hands up. "Five *weeks*?"

I nodded.

"Eight years, Jem." His hands brushed his hair to stand on end. "And you've only been getting them for five weeks? No wonder you aren't up to speed. Where have you even got to?"

I stared at him.

"What's happened in them?"

"You bit me." My eyes narrowed at the memory.

"Is that it?"

"Isn't that enough? You bit me, just like you were going to the other day."

"I wasn't going to bite you."

"You seem to forget I've seen it. I already know what's going to happen."

"Well, it's a pity you didn't get farther in, then you might not be so difficult."

I glared. "What does—"

"And I wasn't going to bite you," he continued.

"So *you* say."

He leaned in closer. "Why—*why* would I bite you, Jem?"

"I don't know. Why did you bite me before?" I lifted my fisted hand to the table. "And don't say you haven't because I know it's true ... somehow."

"I—"

"Was it because you're arrogant enough to believe all would be forgiven because I couldn't bear to live without you, maybe?"

"I didn't want it to be like that this time. I've already told you I don't want you here because you feel you have no choice. I'd rather wait until you realise it's what you want."

"Until I *realise?* You just can't keep that arrogance of yours down, can you?"

A low growl rumbled from him.

"Don't growl at me, Sean. It's not polite. If you can't behave civilised, then you may as well take me home."

"I'm not taking you home."

"So much for not forcing me to stay." My teeth ground. "How long did it take you to change your mind? Thirty, forty seconds?"

His sigh blasted my cheek. "God, you're so beautiful when you're angry."

My mouth opened but froze there. A hush fell upon the room. My eyes flittered around, caught the stares, the barely contained smiles. With a roll of my eyes, I gave an internal groan.

Chapter 22

After harrumphing off with the excuse of needing the bathroom, and staying there until fed up with hiding, I went back downstairs.

Only Ethan remained in the kitchen. He stood at the cooker, frying vast amounts of bacon in one pan, multiple eggs in another, but he didn't turn. "He's in the garden, tantrum girl."

"Tantrum girl?"

"That's some temper in you, Jem. Even if nobody else can see it, I know it's there, bubbling away under the surface."

"You know, it's funny, Ethan, but I never had a temper before Sean entered my head, and I've never gotten as annoyed before as I get at him. Has it never occurred to you that maybe your brother brings out the worst in people?"

"Or the best," he said. "Depending on which way you look at it."

"You're as bad as he is."

"Actually, I'm much worse."

"I can believe that."

His shoulders jiggled with his chuckle.

I crossed to the window. Outside, Nathan and Connor had taken two of the conservatory chairs to sit on, while the three brothers and Sean bounced a basketball around.

"You know, if you don't go out there soon, he'll come looking for you. He doesn't do patience very well. It's a family trait." He moved to the left of the cooker and piled the mountains of food onto two plates. "Can you tell them lunch is ready while you're out there?"

The sweet and greasy aromas pooled saliva in my mouth. "Are you doing toast with that?"

"You want toast?" He spun to me at last, a smile on his lips.

I shrugged. "Toast is nice with eggs."

"Go tell them to come in for lunch, and I'll make you some, then."

"And if I don't?"

"Off you go, Jem."

With a sigh, I headed out. The two older men turned in their seats when my footsteps hit the paving, and the boys paused in their ball game.

Way to make me feel like the day's entertainment.

A glance back over my shoulder showed Ethan watching through the window. He waved his spatula at me, as if to urge me further. When I shrugged my disagreement, he shook his head and waved some more. Scowling, I walked closer to where the men and boys were watching and looked back again. He stuck up his thumb.

Nathan's voice brought my attention to him. "Are you coming to join us, Jem?"

"Come and play." Josh tossed the ball at me.

"Actually ..." I caught the ball with a loud slap, earning an approving look from Josh. "Ethan asked me to tell you lunch is ready."

At the announcement, the ball hit the grass and the boys headed straight for the house, long strides carrying them at a decent speed.

"Are they always like that?" I asked Nathan.

"Pretty much." He took my arm. "Come on. If we don't hurry, there'll be none left."

In the kitchen, we found the boys already sitting, grabbing at the food in some kind of wild feeding frenzy.

"Where are your manners?" Connor's roar seemed to calm them—a little.

Nathan sat where he had earlier, as did Connor. That left only two seats: one beside Sean, one not. Ethan set a plateful of toast in the space next to his brother. "Here you go, Jem." He smiled before walking around to the other side of his dad.

Sending Ethan a glare, I went to my seat.

"How come only Jem has toast?" asked Daniel, eyeing the pile.

"Because she asked for it."

"You want some?" I pushed the plate forward.

Ethan nudged it back. "I made it *for you*."

Sean grinned at our exchange—as much as anyone could grin while chewing on eggs and bacon. Nobody spoke throughout the rest of the meal—too busy chewing, swallowing, reaching out for more to pause for conversation.

Once all food had been eaten, the plates wiped clean, and my leftovers fought over, I turned to Sean. "What time are you taking me home?"

"I think we should take a walk first."

"Where? In the *forest*?"

Ignoring my sarcasm, he pushed back his chair. "In the garden." He didn't wait to see if I followed.

After making him wait for at least a whole minute, I made a big show of huffing before going after him. I found him near the arches, banging the ball against the brick columns, and darting a hand out, I snatched the ball midflight. "Did you ever intend to take me home, when you brought me here this morning?"

"I hoped you wouldn't want to go back."

"I have to go back."

"You say it like you don't have a choice."

"I don't. I'm married to Peter. I belong at home. If I'm not back before he is, I'll be in a heap-load of trouble."

"Then, don't go back."

"I've already told you, I have to."

He gestured to my bruises. "What if he does this again?"

I shrugged, averting my eyes.

"Why would you even let a man treat you like that?"

"Perhaps I don't know any other way to be?" I murmured.

"That's bullshit. You can defend yourself, just as well as the next person."

My gaze swung back. "I'm not like that, Sean. I don't get violent, or lose my temper. I don't argue with people—"

"You manage to argue with me pretty good."

"Yes, and it confuses me like crazy because that isn't *me*."

"You have no idea who you really are, do you?"

"I know who I am. I'm Jem Stonehouse, married to Peter Short, and I need to go home."

"I'm not taking you, Jem."

A bubble of dread arrived in my chest at his words, and images of what Peter might do if he returned to find me gone flashed through my mind. "If I knew you had this planned, I'd never have left with you this morning."

"Wouldn't you?"

I shook my head. "Can you take me home, please?"

"I can't take you back there, knowing what he's done to you, and knowing you're not prepared to defend yourself."

"He'll go mad." I lifted my palm. "He's expecting me to be

there. I'm his wife. I'm supposed to be there in an hour. I have to start dinner—"

"Can you hear yourself, Jem? You're petrified of him. When did you become so subservient?"

"I'm not."

He pointed at me. "Your life isn't supposed to be with a man who doesn't know how to treat you."

"This is my life. You can't change that. I'm married to Peter, and I should be there now."

"You're not even behaving like the Jem in my dreams. The woman I remember is vibrant, passionate, not trembling and afraid of her own shadow."

"Maybe you've got the wrong person."

"I know I haven't. I know you're in there. It's you who hasn't figured it out."

"Can you take me home now, Sean?"

"No, Jem, I won't do that to you."

"It isn't your decision to make. Please take me home. What if Peter comes home early?" My voice hitched at the memory. "What if he's waiting like last time?"

He brushed at his hair. "If only your dreams had continued, this would have been so much simpler."

"How? I would still be married to Peter. You know—Peter, who I'm supposed to be home waiting for?"

His hands balled into fists each time I mentioned Peter's name.

"Take me home, Sean, *please.*"

"And then what? Maybe you'll let me sneak you out another day?"

"I—"

"You say you don't know me. You haven't had the dreams I've had, so I understand you're not on the same page as me. But why, if you don't know me, and all you've experienced is me biting you ... why would you even be here, if you didn't feel something for me?"

He was right, but I'd never admit it. I knew I'd felt something for him, even before we'd met, but denied it like crazy. From my very first dream, Sean had consumed my mind. I shook the thoughts away. "I need to go home. Peter's—"

"I wish he never fucking existed!"

"But he does. I'm married to him."

"And if you weren't?"

I bit down on my trembling lip. "But I am."

"Maybe you're right." He nodded. "This can't work. Maybe you're not who I thought. You're welcome to ask one of the others to take you home, but don't expect me to. I can't." He turned to pace away.

"Are you just going to turn your back on me, now?"

"If I continue this with you, I'll always be in the sidelines. I want more than that. You're not going to give it to me, so I'm wasting my time." He resumed his walk.

"What?" My brows winged up before scrunching. "You bring me here, constantly confusing me, messing with my head ..."

He paused for a second before taking another few steps.

"This is your fault, Sean. You turn up a couple of weeks ago, convince a married woman you're the man of her dreams. Eight years ago, you said you had your first dream. Why couldn't you have looked for me then? Why wait until now?"

"You wouldn't have known me eight years ago. You hadn't had any dreams, remember?"

"How do you know things couldn't have worked out? Eight years ago, I was barely even married to Peter."

"Okay, you're with *Peter*," he spat. "I get it. And we've established this isn't going to work, you're not you anymore, so let's just leave it at that, because I can't take any more of this ..." He looked about to say more, half-turned his body back toward me. Instead, he strode off.

I took a few steps to follow. "Where are you going?"

He didn't answer, just marched away.

"I haven't finished talking to you, yet."

His receding back irked me. Poppy had been right all along. I had wanted the ball completely in my court. "Get back here, Sean! I said I haven't finished." My hands clutched at the ball within them.

He carried on moving.

My nails dug into the hard rubber, shoulders tightened, and my eyes narrowed. "Don't you *dare* walk away from me when I'm talking to you, Goddamnit!" I lifted the basketball to my shoulder and flung it as hard as I could, and the instant I did, my gasp burst out.

I couldn't believe I'd screamed at him. Nor could I believe the ball flying right for its target.

A split-second before the ball met with the bull's-eye, my hands flew to my mouth.

Sean's head jolted forward. His feet slammed to a halt.

My lips stretched into a grimace at the turn of his body.

As his gaze swung round, the hunger oozing from his eyes sang of a deep passion, and despite my seized-up larynx, a small squeak of panic escaped.

Sean stared at me—more than at me, into me. His lips widened into his predatory smile—one that provoked irrational behaviour in my pulse. "See, Jem?" His eyes darkened as he strode back to me. "I knew you were in there, somewhere."

Knees weakening, my heart thudded, betraying my fear of his ability to turn me to mush merely with one look. I took a step back, followed by another, almost stumbling in confused clumsiness.

Sean reached me, grasped my hips, and my feet left the

floor. I lifted my arms to fight him, a pathetic attempt against his strength. They folded against my chest as my back collided with the brick structure, the air whooshing from me beneath the blow of his body and the crush of his lips.

I shoved my hands against his body with no impact. I tried to remove my lips from his, yet failed.

Think!

I closed my eyes. The moment I did, like a neurological switch had flicked inside my brain, I ... remembered.

My mind shut down to everything but scenes dancing behind my lowered lids.

A kiss in a field, upon a hilltop, within the warmth of hay, beneath the stars, in a bed, beside a stream—every one of them with Sean. Like some kind of amphetamine-fuelled slideshow, images flittered—but with feelings, emotions, tastes, all added into the experience.

My nerve endings sprang to life. My heart adopted a rhythm of excitement.

I ceased to struggle.

My constricted body provoked a groan of frustration, and I shoved my arms free and up, brought them to the back of Sean's head to urge him closer.

He shuddered. His hands slid down from my hips to my thighs, and my legs wrapped around to draw him nearer still.

Drinking him in, I realised I'd waited a lifetime for the feel of him so near. For the intoxication of his scent to overwhelm me. For the taste of him upon my tongue. Pausing only long enough to gasp in quivering breaths, my lips melded back to his. His frantic breaths almost matched mine, as did the erratic pace of his heartbeat.

As his body staggered beneath his wavering control, his grip weakened, and he pressed his face to my throat, remaining there for a long moment. At the slide of his hands to my hips, my feet lowered to the ground. With his chest rising and falling against mine, he lifted his face, and his eyes, darker than ever, held crystallised dampness—no doubt reflected back within my own eyes.

With his next breath, a small smile illuminated his face. "Welcome back, Jem," he murmured.

Chapter 23

When I hadn't spoken moments later, Sean's expression faltered. "Are you okay, Jem?"

"I think I may need to sit down," I mumbled. "My legs aren't feeling too good."

They'd trembled when wrapped tightly around him, and they continued to shake once he'd lowered my feet to the ground. If not pinned by Sean to the wall, I doubted I'd still be upright.

"Jem?" He pulled back as though to get a better look at me.

At even the hint of a gap between our bodies, I slid down. My hands left his hair to grope at the wall behind me, and reaching out, he lowered me until I landed on the grass.

Back pressed against the brick structure, I rested my head, closed my eyes. "I ... just need a second." I managed to steady my breathing, my unstable pulse, and opened my eyes.

He knelt in front of me on the grass, his intense eyes studying me.

"I'm okay. It was just so ..."

"Amazing?" He smiled.

I drew my knees up and rested my arms atop them, trying hard to conjure the right words.

His eyebrow arched. "Wonderful?" He reached out, took my hands in his. "Beautiful?"

"Weird," I said, and he frowned, obviously hoping for something different. "One minute I was mad at you," I said, hoping to remove the worry from his eyes, "and then it was as though something clicked."

"Clicked?" His lips twitched.

"I saw things, Sean." I removed my hand to point at my head. "In here."

"Like?"

"Images. But with everything else added in. Feelings, everything, like memories I didn't even know I had because I couldn't remember them. Does this make any sense to you, at all?"

"What sort of images?"

"With you. We were in so many places, places I've never even been."

"You remembered." His smile widened as his eyes warmed. "The kiss helped you remember."

"How can it help me remember something that's never even happened? I don't understand any of this."

"You will, Jem, in time."

"Sean!" Nathan's voice carried from the house.

As Sean glanced over his shoulder, I peered around him. All six men stared in our direction, either from the paving or on the other side of the conservatory glass, and on realising our episode had held an audience, I groaned.

"Your mobile's been ringing," his dad called.

Sean turned back to me. "Wait here, okay? I'll be just a minute."

He jogged off toward the house, slowing to stride past the attention of the others, and disappeared inside. With him out of sight, their attentions turned to me, and I closed my eyes to block them, but knew them to still be watching from the weight of their stares.

When Sean still hadn't returned after about five minutes, I lifted my lids to a deserted garden. As much as I wanted to hide from everybody, I knew I had to face them sooner or later. Later would have worked better, but I climbed to my feet, forced them to carry me to the house.

Following Sean's voice, I found him in the living room. Everyone but Sean sat, and the sofas and armchair, which had looked huge to me previously, appeared minuscule beneath the bulk of their forms. The others watched him as though silently participating in the one-sided conversation he held with his mobile phone, but turned like they'd sensed my presence.

Spotting me in the doorway, Sean paused midsentence, and I allowed him a small smile, a slight shrug. "She's just walked in," he said into the mouthpiece. "You want to talk to her?"

My eyebrow lifted when he took a step forward and held out the phone.

"Poppy," he said.

I held the phone to my ear, my eyes taking in the seven pairs still trained upon me. "Hey."

"Jem, are you okay?"

"I'm fine."

"Are you mad with me, sweetie?"

"Furious."

"I didn't see any other way to get you out ..."

"I know."

"... I knew you wouldn't agree if I forewarned you ..."

"I know."

"... It was the only way."

"Yes, Poppy, I know why you did it. I'm not really mad at you."

"You're not?" Surprise tinged her tone.

"Not now. I've had time to calm down." I glanced at Sean. "And to see things differently."

"Oh ... well, that's good."

"You've been on the line too long for just this, though." When she didn't respond, I said, "You didn't call to ask Sean how mad I was, did you?"

She paused—for too long.

"He knows I'm not there, doesn't he?"

"He rang here, asking if I knew where you were. He said he came home because he'd forgotten something, and he didn't know where you were. The lying bastard tried to tell me he was worried about you."

"His orange," I said.

"What?"

"He left his orange this morning."

"He came back for an orange?"

"He probably left it on purpose."

"If you knew he'd forgotten it, why didn't you take it out to him, Jem?"

I shrugged. "I didn't want to speak to him."

"You do realise, if you go back now, he's really going to hurt you, don't you?"

"He'll probably kill me."

"You can't go back, Jem ..."

"I know."

"I won't let you. There's absolutely no way ..."

"I know, Poppy. You win."

" ... I can let you go back into that house with that ..."

"I know. I said you win."

"... arsehole. And if you think Sean will let ..."

"I know, Poppy. You both win."

She continued as if she hadn't heard me at all. "... you go back, then you're mistaken. If you think ..."

"Poppy, will you listen to me for ..."

"... he'll ever let Peter anywhere ..."

"... one second?"

"... near you—he'll kill Peter before he allows him ..."

I held the phone away from my ear. "She's not listening to me."

Taking it from me, Sean hit the loudspeaker, and Poppy's ranting filled the room.

"I've made up the spare bed for you. You've no need to go home. You don't even need clothes. I have more than enough, some even in your size ..."

"Poppy?" Sean said.

"You're not going back, Jem," she continued, "and that is final. Do you hear me? You are not going. We won't let you." She paused, her breaths heavy down the line. "Are you still there? Have you even listened to a word I've said?"

"For goodness sake, Poppy, be quiet," Sean said, and I half-smiled at the ease with which he got her to pay attention. "I think Jem was trying to tell you something, if you'd paused long enough to listen."

"Well, what is it?" she asked.

I blew out a breath. "You win. You and Sean can have it your way. I won't go back."

"Thank God." She sounded relieved. "He finally got through to you."

"Yes." The worry evaporated from Sean's expression, also, as I kept my eyes on his.

"What changed your mind?"

"Does it matter?"

"Did he talk some sense into you?"

"Sean doesn't know how to talk sense, Pop."

Low chuckles rumbled round the room.

"He must have said something right."

"I've just seen things differently," I said.

"So, you're definitely not going back?"

I rolled my eyes. "That's what I said."

"And Sean didn't say anything to change your mind?"

"*No*, Poppy." I lowered my voice, hoping she'd get the hint to let it drop.

"He must have said something. You know that boy's in love with you, don't you, Jem?"

I glanced around at everyone taking a bigger interest. "Poppy, stop!"

Sean merely stared down at the phone in his hand.

"And don't tell me you haven't feelings for him, because I know you do."

"Will you please be *quiet*?" I held my hand out to Sean for the phone, but he shook his head and smiled.

"I've never seen you so confused. You've hardly known if you're coming or going ... your face lighting up without you even being aware when you spot him in the supermarket ..."

"Poppy, *please*." My cheeks heated, and I tried to reach for the mobile. I glared at Sean when he lifted it out of my grasp.

"Spending years moping around, cleaning up after that arsehole, too afraid to say boo ..."

"Poppy," I pleaded, before hissing, "*Give it to me, Sean.*"

He took a step back, his smile widening.

"... for the first time ever, you actually looked like you were alive. Even before you met him, there was something there, and don't tell me there wasn't, because you were somebody else that day you told me you'd seen him at that restaurant, so don't—"

"Will you please shut up, you are on loudspeaker!"

Her silence at my outburst lasted all of a second. "Who else is there with you? Sean said nobody would be home today."

"Well, the house went from supposedly empty to completely full. Everybody is here. And you just announced my feelings on the matter to the entire room. So, thanks for that."

"Sorry, Jem."

"It's too late. They already heard you."

"Well, at least you're being sensible at last and listening to us," she said. "I was afraid we'd have to kidnap you, handcuff you to the bed ..."

The beginnings of a headache drummed at my temples. "What time do you want me, Poppy?"

"I've made enough Irish stew for you and Sean. We'll be eating at six."

"Did you even ask Sean if he wants to stay for dinner?"

"If you're here, he'll come. Besides, he'll stay tonight, just in case there's trouble."

I looked across at him, lifted an eyebrow. "Sean is staying at yours tonight?"

"Yes, we'll find room for him."

"Did you even ask him, Poppy?"

Sean nodded. "I'll come."

"See?" I heard the smile of triumph in her tone. "I'll expect you home before six."

BEFORE LEAVING, I received a gentle kiss from Nathan, while Sean was given strict instructions to look after me and stay out of trouble. He made me promise to return the following day with an unhindered Sean—meaning not arrested for assault.

With the loan of Ethan's pickup, we arrived at Poppy's shortly after five thirty. On the drive, we hadn't discussed what happened in the garden, or what it meant for us. We'd just sat quietly, glancing sideways at one another, throwing the occasional smile.

However, when I entered through Poppy's front door, she took one look at me, and then at Sean, and a quiet '*hmmmm*' vibrated past her lips before she beamed at us both and waved us in. She even nudged us toward the stairs to use the bathroom *together*.

During dinner, Poppy allowed Ben and six-year-old Lily to eat at the breakfast bar, while the adults took the table in the dining room. The bambino's excitement at being allowed to eat without adult supervision lasted only until their curiosity about the stranger in the house won out. From that point on, they climbed on and off their barstools to take a look at Sean, until instructed by their mother to go back and eat.

Jase—as laid back as ever—showed no concern over us turning up. He didn't even seem surprised that I'd come to stay with a man who wasn't Peter, so I guessed Poppy must have filled him in. Besides, they weren't a couple who held secrets from one another.

Refusing our offers to help tidy away after dinner, Poppy prodded me and Sean into the living room and sent Jase along to keep us company. As one of those people who didn't have to chatter to make you comfortable, he didn't speak much. Instead, he passed me the remote control and told me to find something to watch. I couldn't recall the last time I'd been given a choice. I flicked through the channels until I found a stupid, non-factual programme.

Poppy joined us, trading places with Jase as he headed off to bathe the bambinos before bed, and her scrutiny probed my mind, even without turning to her. I imagined her watching us closely, trying to figure out what exactly had altered between me and Sean.

When I leaned back to discover Sean's arm resting along the sofa behind me, I understood her increased sideways glances. Sean didn't move his arm as I pressed into it, nor did I ask him to, adding more theories for her overactive mind to work through.

By eight o'clock, the children had settled down, presenting us with a strange hush throughout the house and the arrival of my yawns.

"Tired, sweetie?" asked Poppy.

"A little." I gave another yawn.

"Your bed's made up if you need to get in it."

"Where are you putting us?"

"The guest bed's pulled down in the wardrobe for you."

"In the wardrobe?" Sean asked.

"Poppy's wardrobe is an entire bedroom," I said with a smile. "What about Sean?"

If my stepping in before assumptions could be made bothered her, she didn't show it. "I'm afraid the only offer I have for him is the sofa."

"The sofa feels comfortable enough," Sean said, like he sensed the tension in my shoulders.

"You know, I've had your sister on the phone, asking if you're okay," Poppy said. "I didn't know what to tell her."

I groaned, lifting my gaze to the ceiling. I'd completely forgotten about calling her—she'd be going crazy at not being kept up to speed about Sean. "If she rings again, tell her I'll call after the weekend."

"Okay, sweetie. Now, did you want Jase to pull back the covers?"

"Not just yet. I'm good here."

As I watched more TV with Poppy and Sean, and Jase when he rejoined us, the soft tickling sensation of Sean's fingers across my shoulder incited me to lean into him. With my head threatening to dip, my body to slump, I turned to half lie. Poppy chucked a cushion, which Sean placed against his thigh for me. After about twenty minutes of watching old reruns of American sitcoms, with Sean tracing his fingers along the length of my arm, I relaxed enough for my eyes to droop.

At the harsh ring of the doorbell, I jolted and my eyes flew open. I twisted toward Poppy.

Meeting my stare, she nodded before standing to answer it.

I clambered up, as Poppy pulled the living room door closed to shield us from view, positioning myself behind the barrier to listen. Jase stayed on the sofa, his eyes turned toward Poppy's position, as did Sean. Whereas Jase looked quite calm about everything, darkness returned to Sean's eyes, filling them with deep fury.

"Where is she?" Peter slurred through the wood.

"He's been drinking," I murmured to Jase.

Straightening, he whispered, "I thought Peter didn't drink."

"He doesn't ... except once," I said, "and it ended badly."

"She isn't here, Peter." The lie slipped from Poppy.

"Now, come *on*. I bloody know she's here. Where else has she got to go?"

"How badly?" whispered Jase.

"He tried ..." A glance at Sean's tightened shoulders stopped the words. "Badly."

"I've just told you, Peter, she isn't here," Poppy said.

"You're fucking lying." A slight thud sifted through, like he'd banged into the doorframe.

"You're not coming in, Peter. You're drunk."

Following my gaze, Jase leaned in closer. "How badly, Jem?"

"I want my wife," Peter slurred. "I fucking know you've got her in there, and I'm coming to get her. The whore is coming home."

Scuffles followed. "I told you, you are *not* coming inside my house while you're drunk." Strain filled Poppy's voice like she had to hold him back.

My fists clenched at my sides.

"Do you want me to get rid of him, Jem?" asked Sean in a low voice.

One look at him—the muscles bulging along his arms, those in his face taut from the clench of his jaw—and I shook my head. "I don't think it's a good idea for you to go out there."

"There!" shouted Peter. "I just heard her."

The vibrating bang of the front door blasted out. I spun to the living room door and grabbed the handle, as the fist of my other hand tightened.

"If you don't take your foot out of my house, I will call the police," Poppy snapped, her calm façade fading. "You're not welcome here. I know what you did to Jem, you arsehole, and if you think for one minute I would let you anywhere near her, you don't know me very well at all."

"Why you fucking—"

My hand whipped the door open before I'd even heard Poppy's grunt. I swung around it so fast, Peter didn't have time to blink before I barrelled into his chest and knocked him out of the hallway. "Don't you dare touch her!"

Peter's expression altered from surprise to twisted anger. "Why, you ..." He clambered up. "I knew you were in there— fucking knew it."

"Go home, Peter. I don't want you here."

"I'm not going anywhere without my wife." He lurched forward and grabbed my upper arm hard enough to bruise.

"Let go of me."

He dragged me toward the road, as I pried at his vice fingers. "You're coming home."

I dug my heels into the path, yet he still jerked me along behind him. "Let go of me, Peter." My pulse accelerated with each step that took me nearer to the car.

A yank swung me around, and Peter's fingers dug into my cheeks as he grabbed my face. His alcohol breath hit me full force, and I blinked against the white spots flashing behind my eyes. "You are fucking coming home with me."

He hauled me forward, bending as though to sling me over his shoulder, but a roaring growl erupted beside me.

"Keep your fucking hands off her." Sean's arm snaked around my waist. Dragging me to him, he shoved a hand in Peter's chest that sent him hurtling through the air.

Peter landed with a thud.

I stared at his unmoving body. "You've killed him."

"No." Sean's voice arrived deep. "He's not dead."

Peter's head shook, and he pushed himself up. As soon as he spotted Sean standing at my side, his face screwed up in rage. "You think you have a right to take my wife from me?" He clambered to his feet. "She's nothing but a whore. *My* fucking whore! I'm taking her home, and you cannot stop me." He staggered forward. "You are fucking dead, Jem, do you hear me? Get in the car." Halting, he glanced between me and Sean, before he spun and headed for his car.

I almost relaxed when he reached it and pulled open the door, believing he'd leave—until the car door slammed shut and he started back toward us, armed with a baseball bat.

He pointed the bat at me and slung it to balance over his shoulder. "*Now*, Jem, you are fucking dead."

Sean stiffened at my side, his muscles contracting against my arm. Tautness coiling through his body, his knees bent.

I threw myself in front of him, as he sprang. "Sean, *no!*"

His feet left the floor—mine, too—and the forward leap of his body took me with him—toward Peter with his batting hold ready. Sean's downward glance held only confusion, before his arms wove around to encase me and his feet hit ground. I barely had time to recover from the jolt of our landing when he tensed for another dive.

I clutched at his clothing. "Sean, this isn't what I want."

Low growls left his throat, ripples ran beneath his flesh. No way could I allow him to fight Peter—not like that.

"Please, Sean. Don't do this. If you do, I'll lose you, and that isn't what I want."

An inner battle claimed his eyes, while his fury pumped out of him in waves.

"Sean, listen to me. We'll go now, I won't come back. I'll stay with you—anywhere. Just name the place, and I'll come."

His gaze lowered to mine as his jaw un-clenched enough to speak. "Do you mean that, Jem?" Feral gruffness affected his tone.

I nodded up at him.

Though he returned his attention to Peter, he pulled me to my feet and nudged me behind him. With his body shielding mine, he backed away.

My chest rose and fell with my deep inhalations. The evening air around us held fresh moistness, as well as the strong perfume of lavender lining Poppy's front garden. As the under-lying aroma of wolf overtook both of those, I clung onto Sean's T-shirt, the waist of his jeans, and herded him backward toward the house.

Peter laughed. "What are you—a coward?"

Sean stiffened, a low growl rumbling out.

"Ignore him. He's goading you." Tugging, I took a step back, and then another, until my heel hit the doorstep. A hand touched my back, and I glanced over my shoulder at Poppy. "We can't stay here. It's not fair on you. You have your family to think of, and as long as he knows I'm here, he'll keep coming back."

"Where will you go?" she asked.

"I'm not sure yet." A rapid check of her face revealed no injuries from Peter's attack. "Did he hurt you?"

"No, I just stumbled."

I studied her again to be certain she told the truth, nodding when I found no evidence to the contrary. "Sean, can you drive if we leave now?"

"You're asking me to walk away, Jem, from the man who assaulted you?"

Peter alternated between pointing at me with the bat and calling expletives, and telling Sean he would never have his *fucking whore.*

"Yes."

"What if I can't?"

"I need you to, Sean. I need you to do this for me."

"I'm not so sure I can." His fists clenched at his sides, his muscles bulged so fiercely the exterior of his body appeared to be made of multiple segments—even his voice barely sounded human.

"We need to leave before you really can't. If you can't drive us away from here, then I will."

"You're asking me to go against my nature."

Peter continued toward us, one slow doddery step at a time. The bat waved about to point at us before settling back into his shoulder. Mumbled taunts and insults still rolled past his lips.

"Tell him, Poppy. If I don't get him out of here, any second he might lose control."

Thanks to her awareness of my dream relationship with Sean, I didn't need to spell it out for her. "Jase, go and fetch Sean's keys," she said.

Less than a minute later, Poppy grabbed Sean's hand, forced his fingers open and placed the keys inside them. "Jem needs to leave, Sean. You need to get her out of here."

Lifting his hand, he studied the keys, as though having something to focus on helped.

"Okay, we're going to the car," I told him. "As soon as we

reach it, Poppy, I want you to lock your door, and phone the police if Peter doesn't leave, okay?"

"Yes, sweetie."

"Okay, Sean, move."

He stood riveted, his gaze once again on Peter.

"*Move!*" I shoved him forward.

Heading for the truck took an interminably long time. We circled around, so as not to turn our backs on Peter. Too many times, Sean tried to take a step toward Peter until a tug from me drew him back into line.

I'd no idea what stopped Peter from charging forward and attacking us. Maybe he saw something in me he hadn't seen before, in my determination to get Sean to respond. Maybe he saw something within Sean to cause him to reconsider his intentions—anybody watching would've seen *something*. Whatever his reasons for keeping his distance, they may have saved his life. By the time we reached Ethan's pickup, Peter had lowered his bat and stood watching us.

With Sean's inability to regain self-control, I figured I'd have to take the wheel. I pulled open the passenger door, shoved him in—no easy feat when he still wouldn't take his eyes off Peter. After running around to the other side, I climbed behind the wheel and started the engine. As the truck left the kerbside, the last thing I saw in the rear-view mirror was Peter sinking to his knees upon the damp grass.

Chapter 24

Finding Sean's home in the dark didn't come easily, but I didn't know where else to take him. Even after driving for forty minutes, Sean still looked like he wanted to rip Peter's head off. I went to pull in, hitting the brakes before colliding with the closed gates.

A glance at Sean showed him staring straight ahead, eyes unfocussed—he hadn't spoken the entire journey. With no other option, I flashed the headlights and leaned on the horn.

Within seconds, Ethan opened the front door and headed down the driveway toward us. He bent to unleash the catch and swung the gates wide.

I parked in front of the house and turned off the engine before jumping out the truck.

"Why are you behind the wheel of my truck?" Ethan asked, striding over.

"He couldn't drive."

"Because ...?"

"There was trouble. Peter showed up, and Sean lost it. I had to get him away before ..." I raised my palms.

Ethan glanced toward Sean, who hadn't moved from his seat. "What do you mean by *lost it*?"

"He was rippling, Ethan. He was so mad. I had to haul him out of there, and that was pretty damn hard. Do you have any idea how heavy he is to move? And now he's mad at me because he wanted to hurt Peter and I stopped him. He hasn't spoken to me ... I'm not even sure he's back in control."

"Okay." He nodded to me. "Go inside and tell Dad I may need his help."

When I didn't move, he nudged me in the direction of the house and stepped toward his vehicle. I glanced one last time over my shoulder and, disappearing indoors, called for Nathan.

"I'm here." He came in from the conservatory. "What's up?"

"Sean's outside in the truck. I think Ethan might need your help."

"What happened?"

"It's a long story. He sent me in to find you."

Nodding, he told me to put the kettle on and made his way outside. I did as asked, preparing four mugs with coffee.

A few minutes later, the men came into the house, headed into the living room. I finished making the drinks, searched until I found a tray to put them on, and made my way to them.

"... to rip his throat out," Sean said. "But *she* stopped me."

"I stopped you because you were going to kill him." I put the tray on the table and took a sip from one of the mugs.

"He was fucking mauling you, Jem." He snarled as he stood to face me. "How can you remain so calm about that?"

"One of us needed to be."

"And why would you make me leave like that? He didn't deserve to walk away."

"You were out of control." Lowering my cup, I pointed at him. "If I hadn't shoved you out of there, you'd have killed him. What good are you to anyone, arrested?"

"Arrested?" He threw his hands up. "How fucking stupid."

"Don't you dare call me stupid, you bloody arse. And, yes, you would have been arrested. How long do you think you had before the neighbours investigated the disturbance? People don't brawl in Poppy's neighbourhood, Sean. If I didn't move you when I did, how long do you think you had before there was no turning back? Do you think the neighbours wouldn't shit themselves if they glanced out and saw a bloody great wolf tearing a man to chunks? Do you think nothing would have been done?"

His eyes glared as he leaned toward me. "You knew what I was, who I was, from the beginning."

"And *you* knew who and what Poppy was before you agreed to stay there. She has *children*."

"This is all bullshit!"

"You know, I couldn't agree more." I turned to Nathan. "I need somewhere to stay tonight. Would you mind if I took the spare room?"

"No, Jem, that's fine."

"Then, I'm going to bed."

Sean took a step forward. "No, you're not."

I glared back at him. "I have barely slept for a week and I'm exhausted. Just when I think I might actually get some rest, Peter shows up, and I have just used whatever energy I had left dragging your arse backward and forward across Poppy's lawn. I *need* sleep."

"You can sleep when we're done talking."

"I'm not talking to you when you're like this. You're not even attempting to be civil. I'm going to bed until morning, whether you like it, or not. Why don't you just haul your back-side out to the forest, bloody change, and go eat some foxes, or something—whatever it is you do to calm down. Just do ... *some-*

thing, because I am *not* talking to you again until you do." I walked away, but paused at the door. "I have nothing to wear."

"You'll find something in Sean's drawers," Ethan said.

"Get back here, Jem," Sean called as I walked away.

Ignoring him, I climbed the stairs, heading directly to the bathroom. After washing with the limited men's toiletries, I wandered back across the landing.

Ethan's voice drifted up. "She's right, Sean. Come for a hunt, it'll make you feel better. Everything seems better ..."

I pushed open Sean's bedroom door and rummaged around in his drawers until I found a big T-shirt and pair of shorts. In the lilac bedroom, I stripped off, glad to be free of the day's clothing. After pulling on the borrowed items, I climbed beneath the duvet, but it took a long time, possibly hours, for my brain to give in. I couldn't relax, not while I believed Sean paced downstairs with his temper still lit.

Only once I heard what sounded like wolf calls from the rear of the property did I allow my lids to droop and my mind to switch off.

I DIDN'T KNOW how much sleep I'd had, but it didn't feel like enough. The temptation to close my eyes again and pull the duvet over my head overwhelmed, but after one failed attempt, I kicked the cover aside.

From the bed, I crossed to the door and placed my ear against it. I had no idea how late the others had gone to bed, but I hadn't heard them come in before I'd dozed off. At no sounds whispering through the thick wood, I pulled down the handle.

On the landing, I turned left and almost walked into a sleeping Sean.

Slouched upon the top step and fast asleep, his shoulder and left cheek pressed against the wall, his chest rising and falling with each breath.

I tiptoed past, put my weight onto the step beside him, and lowered my other foot down on to the next, where I couldn't resist taking a proper peek. With his face squished where the wall distorted it, it looked like he'd fallen asleep sitting up, and his body had squeaked down and failed to take the loose flesh along for the ride. Any frustration from the night before faded at the flutters trembling through the lips of his partly open mouth.

"He's been there all morning."

At Ethan's unexpected voice, my body jerked backward, my arms flinging out.

Sean's eyes shot open, and he grabbed my wrist as he bulleted to his feet. "Are you alright, Jem?"

I blew out a breath, my heart pounding. "I would be if your brother didn't go around sneaking up on people."

"How did I know you'd jump?" Ethan said, walking off.

Sean tugged back on my arm, as I took hold of the banister to continue my descent. "Jem, wait." When I hesitated, he continued, "I'm sorry—for the way I behaved toward you. I shouldn't have spoken to you that way."

I met his eyes for a few seconds. "I know you are. But don't ask me to be sorry for doing what I thought best."

"I won't," he said. "You were right. I should've listened to you, and I'm sorry."

"Is this why you slept out here on the floor?"

"I was worried about you."

"You should have gone to bed." I turned and plodded down the stairs. "I'd still have been here when you got up."

"That's good to hear," he said as he followed.

In the kitchen, I headed straight for the kettle in the hope of refreshing myself with a hot drink.

"I can do that." Sean took mugs from the cupboard. "You're supposed to be a guest."

Peering through the window showed the others had already arrived. I watched the men, carrying chairs out, lighting briquettes in the portable barbeque, though I hadn't thought the barbeque was until the afternoon.

Warm hands took my shoulders from behind. For a moment, I almost moved away, but instead, I leaned back until the firmness of his chest met my shoulder blades. As his hands slid around me, his sigh hitting the side of my head, I brought my fingers up to his forearms, accepting his support.

"You needn't think you're making drinks for only yourself, Sean," came Nathan's voice from outside.

"How did he know—?"

"He hears all," Sean murmured against my hair. "Go on out. I'll finish these. Dad won't believe I haven't scared you away until he's seen you for himself."

Leaving the warmth of his arms, I made myself walk outside, to what I was certain was a pack of werewolves. They seemed too close, too close-knit, to be anything but. It didn't seem to matter to me right then, though—because I realised, as I stepped out, I felt safer amongst them all than I had in a long time.

"You're up, at last," said Josh. "I thought we'd be eating without you at this rate."

"Well, most people don't have burgers at this time in the morning."

"Morning?" He snorted. "Jem, it's almost one in the afternoon."

"You slept right through." Nathan patted an empty chair beside him. "I wouldn't let them wake you. I thought you needed it."

I took the cushioned willow seat beside Nathan. Despite the

warm sun shining down from the clear blue sky, the wind held a chill that perked certain body parts to attention. Conscious of my lack of attire, I wrapped my arms around my drawn-up knees.

Sean joined us, carrying a tray of drinks and a blanket over his arm. Once the tray had been cleared, he wrapped the blanket around my shoulders.

"We should phone Poppy," I said as I sipped my drink. "She'll be going out of her mind by now. We should find out if they were okay after we left."

Sean worked his mobile out of his pocket and, after pressing a few buttons, handed it to me already dialling.

"Sean?" she answered.

"It's Jem. Are you okay?"

"Never mind about me, sweetie. Is Sean okay?" Poppy always worried about everyone but herself.

"He's fine."

"Did you take him home? Did you get him back in time?"

"Yes ... to both."

"And you?"

"I'm okay. Did Peter give you any more trouble after we'd left?"

"No, sweetie, but he was still on our lawn an hour later, so we called the police in the end. I wouldn't allow Jase to go out and talk to him."

"That was probably wise," I said. "So, you're okay?"

"Of course I am. I wasn't the one who jumped in the path of a charging bull. What the hell were you thinking?"

"I just didn't want any trouble. You saw how he was, he'd have—"

"Killed him in an instant," she finished. "I know, Jem. I was there. It's just ..." She sighed before continuing. "Will you try and think things through a little better before you act in the future?"

"I wasn't in any danger."

"You went flying, Jem."

"And he caught me before I hit the ground."

"I know, but—"

My brows knitted. "He would never hurt me, Poppy."

"I know that, sweetie. If he's listening at all, tell him I'm sorry for thinking it. I just worry about you."

"I know you do."

"So, do you need to come back? Try again, get some clothes?"

"I doubt that's a good idea for a few days. Even if the police held him, he'll be out today. I know he'll be back."

"Then, where are you going to stay? You haven't any money."

"Or car," I said.

"Or clothes."

"No home."

"Sweetie, you've always got a home," she said, "but you haven't got a mobile for me to contact you on."

"Could my life *be* any better than this?"

She started to laugh, drawing me in with her.

"I'll figure something out," I said. "Don't worry about me."

"Do you need me to flash the cash?"

"Maybe, for a room."

"You want me to book you somewhere?"

"That won't be necessary," said Nathan.

I twisted to face him.

"Anybody willing to throw themselves in the path of danger to protect my son is worthy of a bed in my home. You can stay here until you're ready."

My lips curved. "I won't need that room after all," I said into the phone.

Taking over the phone call with Poppy, Sean walked off into the house. When he emerged ten minutes later, his damp hair gave away the rapid shower he'd taken. "I need to go out for a while."

I climbed to my feet. "Where?"

"Just out. I won't be long. You should stay here."

"Are you going back to see Peter?"

He sighed. "No."

"I don't believe you."

"Peter's probably still in custody."

"You've just come off the phone to Poppy. How do I know what she's told you?"

"I'm not going to see him."

I studied him, searching for honesty, or dishonesty.

"Would I have showered if that's where I was going?" Smiling, he gestured to himself.

"I ... guess not."

"Right then, I shouldn't be long. I'll try and be back before the food is ready. If not, I'm counting on you to rescue me some. They won't dare take it from you."

I glanced over my shoulder at the others before looking back to him. "Are you sure about that? I've seen how you all eat."

He chuckled, leaning in to kiss my cheek. "You'll be fine."

The burgers, sausages, steaks, all went on to cook shortly after he left, and the glorious scent of smoked meat floated around the garden. Having not eaten since Poppy's stew the night before, my mouth watered as I breathed them in.

"You want a burger, Jem?" called Daniel.

"You'd better give me two."

He raised an eyebrow but didn't question it—just put two burgers onto a plate and handed it to me. I headed for the kitchen, found a tub in one of the cupboards, and placed one of the burgers inside to save for Sean—but where to put it? My eyes fell on the only door I'd yet to go through. I opened it and placed the stash inside.

Pulling away from the handle, I glanced down. The gold band still resided upon the third finger of my left hand. Without even thinking about whether or not I was making the right choice, I slid it off and threw it in the bin.

Throughout the meal, I requested two of everything. Each time they served me, they watched in amusement when I headed indoors to place the new item with the hoard. By the end of the barbeque, Sean had three burgers, four sausages, two pieces of rib-eye, and a whole corn. It looked like a lot of food to me, yet I wasn't sure there'd be enough for him.

Back outside, the younger generation of men prepared for a game of basketball, and once again, Nathan and Connor settled into chairs to watch. Curling back into my seat, I glanced up in time to see the ball hurtling toward me and caught it before it bounced off my chest.

"Want to play, Jem?" asked Josh.

"With you lot?"

Grinning, he nodded.

"You'd slaughter me." I returned the ball to him.

He threw it back. "We'll be good. I promise."

"I can't even play." I chucked it to him again. "I'm useless at throwing."

Six bass laughs echoed back.

"Now, we know that isn't true," Nathan said. "We all saw the look on Sean's face when you bounced that off his head yesterday."

"You haven't even got any hoops." A poor excuse.

"Actually ..." Kyle pointed to the opposite walls each side of the lawn.

I followed his fingers across the garden, which was ridiculously wide for a basketball game, and located hoops about four feet too high. "I won't be able to reach those."

"I'll help you." Ethan strolled over, tugged my arm. "We'll team up: Holloways versus Larsens."

I frowned. "Who?"

"Us against them, Jem." He chuckled. "Come on, let's play."

I trotted behind Ethan. "So, what are the rules?"

Deep chuckles filled the air.

"We don't play by any rules, Jem." Josh threw the ball to me with a smile. "You start."

"No way," I said, hurling it back. "Every time the weakling starts with the ball, they get charged by the much bigger opposition and ground to a fine powder. You start."

"Sure." He laughed. "But go easy on us, okay?"

I DID TURN out to be pretty useless, had expected no different. Ethan attempted to include me in the game, but each time I caught the ball, I didn't move fast enough before one of the others whizzed past and took it. A couple of times, I even ducked when I spotted the ball coming from above, and Kyle and Josh, or Daniel, coming at me from either side. Within minutes, my groans of frustration leaked out, and my hair stood on end from all the tugging.

Ethan threw the ball to me for the fiftieth time, shouting to alert me of its approach. My feet were moving before I'd even caught it. Kyle, the nearest, attempted to snatch the ball from the easy target.

Laughing, I darted around him with a speed I didn't know I could achieve and ran flat-out, the full width of the garden, with the prize in my hands. Shouts that I was supposed to bounce the ball went ignored, as did the feet pounding the grass behind me.

I reached the far wall with metres to spare, peered up at the stupid height of the hoop, and jumped. The second I did, hands grasped my hips. My body soared higher, and I let out a squeal as I rose high enough to shove the ball through the goal, laughing out loud when I swooped back down to the ground with the rush of air flinging my hair up.

My bare feet hit the grass, and my uncontrolled giggles almost sent me sprawling, until the hands at my hips steadied my balance. I turned to Ethan's wide grin and raised my hands above my head. "Yes!"

"You cheated," Daniel said.

I laughed. "How did I?"

"You're supposed to bounce the ball."

"I can play any way I please," I said with a smug smile.

The game resumed. Ethan threw the ball to me more often once he realised I could get away from the others. As temperatures rose, they one by one pulled off their tops, and my eyes absorbed the four fine specimens parading the garden in only shorts.

"Distraction techniques." I wagged my finger. "Who's cheating now, huh?"

Their laughter responded. In no time, nobody but me remained fully clothed—not that Sean's T-shirt and boxers could be considered as such.

After a full sprint of the garden in one direction, followed by a second in the other, my panting breaths got the better of me, and I flopped down onto my back.

"Come on, Jem," shouted Ethan. "We only need two more hoops to catch up. Get up."

With a groan, I rolled over and climbed to my feet. Hands on knees, I bent at the waist to study the state of play before pushing off into another run.

I jogged over, darted through the scramble of bodies,

squeezing between Kyle and Josh. When I snatched the ball from under their noses, they halted.

I grinned. "If you want it, come and get it."

I took off, but fatigue slowed my steps, and Josh's lanky legs darted him ahead. He skidded onto my path, a smug grin across his face. With an inner smile, I raised my arm to brace myself and ran straight into him. A faux grunt burst out. I staggered back, my hand pressed to my head.

"Shit, Jem." Concern creasing his features, Josh reached out a hand.

With a step back, and another, a roll of convincing groans flew from my lips.

The garden grew silent. Everyone came to a standstill.

I waited a beat before I lowered my hand and giggled. "Sucker!" I feinted past Josh and dashed across the lawn toward my goal.

Nathan's and Connor's roaring laughter almost drowned out the pounding feet that chased me as I neared the brick wall.

I went to dive upward—should have fallen far too short of the target without Ethan's help—when hands I hadn't been expecting gripped me. For the second time, I rocketed through the air, giggling like mad as I flung the ball through the ring. As the supporting hands released and spun me mid-drop, my giggle pitched into a squeal.

Grinning, I fell back down to discover Sean, not Ethan, waiting there to catch me. "You're back."

Humour sparkled within his dark eyes. "Having fun?"

"Lots."

"Well ..." He tucked a sweat-soaked strand of hair behind my ear. "I thought you looked amazing when really mad at me, Jem. But laughing?" His lips curved. "Laughing, you're something else."

Still smiling, I danced backward, snatched up the ball. I

gestured to Sean to throw me up a second time, and the ball flew through metal before the other team even realised my intention. "We'll call it a draw, then, shall we?" I turned to walk off.

"No way," said Josh. "Come back, Jem, we haven't finished."

I waved my hand over my shoulder. "I have."

Reaching Nathan and Connor, I sank into an empty chair, drawing my knees up as I closed my eyes. The soft cushion moulded to my head when I leaned back and took a minute to regain my breath. "So, where did you go?" I asked Sean, lids still lowered.

"Shopping."

"For what?"

"For these."

I perked up at the sound of rustling, opening my eyes as Sean placed four large bags at my feet. Intrigued, I dipped my hand in and pulled out a pair of shorts. I reached in some more. Emptying the first bag produced jeans, shorts, vests.

I stared at him. "Clothes?"

Sean shrugged. "You hadn't got any."

A rummage in the second bag produced further items. My eyebrows lifted at the almost entire wardrobe across my lap. I reached into the third bag, found toiletries, including a toothbrush, which I held up like a prized possession. From the bottom, I tugged out a new mobile phone and a pair of trainers.

Glancing up again, I found Sean's gaze on me. "What's in this one? A new car?"

He smiled. "No."

I pulled the bag wide and peered inside to see underwear: bras, knickers, a few pairs of socks. "You worried I might ask to borrow more of yours?"

"Actually, I thought you'd find these more comfortable."

With a nod, I drew out one of the bras—simple pale lemon with ribbon edging—nothing fancy. When I glanced at the label, my eyes narrowed. "How do you know my size?" Before he could answer, I asked, "And you couldn't ask before you went out buying things, spending money on me?"

"I didn't buy all the clothes."

I lifted my eyebrow, awaited an explanation.

He sighed. "I met Poppy, and she picked everything out. I was going to pay for it, but she said it would probably make you mad, so after arguing about which of us were going to fund them, she won."

My lips twitched. "Poppy never backs down."

"Is everything okay for you?"

"Yes." His dark eyes held mine as I looked into them, and I leaned across, brushed my lips across his. "Thank you. It was very thoughtful."

"You're welcome."

"Are you hungry?"

His smile reappeared. "Did you save me some food?"

"It's in the torture chamber."

Ethan laughed. "In the *what*?"

"You went into the cellar, Jem?" Sean's frown creased his brow.

"Don't look so worried. I didn't go down—your food's just inside the door. I figured they wouldn't expect me to put it in there."

He pushed up and headed for the house.

"What?" I called after him. "Did you think I'd left it on the stretching rack, or the electric chair, maybe? You know, I did consider playing with the thumbscrews while I was in there." I turned back to everyone's eyes on me. "I'm just kidding."

Sean came back out with his food and placed it on the warm barbeque before rejoining me.

"Are you going to tell me what's really in the cellar? I was only kidding when I said it was a torture chamber, but ..."

His lips lifted at one corner. "There's nothing down there."

I studied him and everybody else. "Well, then ..." Standing, I placed my new items on the seat. "You won't mind if I take a look, will you?"

Mumbles started up behind me, but nobody followed my strides to the house. Through the kitchen to the far wall, I pulled open the cellar door and groped around inside for the light switch to illuminate the stairs. I went a few steps before pausing, almost reconsidering if I really wanted to see what was at the bottom, but, taking a deep breath, I descended.

At the bottom, I found nothing but a white-walled, low-ceilinged space. Empty, apart from a small wooden table and singular chair—yet, my suspicious mind nagged at me to move around, and my hands swept the walls. The cold, painted smoothness slid beneath my fingers without sound. About to give up and declare myself foolish, the sound quality of my hand brushing altered. I ran my hands across it again, tested the entire rear wall, and tapped on it. Its hollowed quality didn't match the other three.

Corner to corner, from ceiling to floor, no joins suggested the wall to be removable. I knew it was, though—just as I somehow knew to check the walls in the first place.

All eyes followed my emergence from the house, as though awaiting my return.

"Well?" asked Sean around eating his warmed food.

"Absolutely nothing." I gathered up my new clothing before walking away.

"See? I told you it was empty."

"You did. Not too sure about what's behind that hidden panel, though." I glanced over my shoulder to see their high eyebrows. "Did you not tell them, Sean, that I knew what was in every room before you showed me?"

Their busy murmurs pursued me through the conservatory doors.

In the lilac bedroom, I folded my clothing away into the drawers, wondering how much input Sean had offered into the choices—especially for the underwear. From there, I straightened the still-crumpled bedcovers. In the eight years with Peter, I'd never left the bed unmade after evacuating.

Peter's not here, Jem.

Hesitating only a moment, I crumpled them back up, laughing to myself as I piled the duvet into a heap.

"What's so funny?"

I spun to find Sean leaning against the doorframe. My shrug and smirk brought a smile to his lips.

"You can mess all the beds up, if it keeps you this happy."

"I've never got up in the morning before and left the bed in a mess. It just occurred to me I can do whatever I want."

He held his hand out to me. "Come on, then." I followed him out, and my lips twitched when he opened his bedroom door and gestured me inside. "Knock yourself out."

"Are you going to make me tidy it afterward?"

He chuckled. "No."

With a grin, I stepped over to the bed. I sent him a backward glance before I leapt on and wrapped myself in the duvet. One roll took me to the left edge of the mattress, a second to the right. Even once I'd tumbled off and landed with a thud on the thick cream carpet, I continued to roll about.

From the doorway, Sean's laughter matched my own. I plucked up his blue rug and chucked it across the room at him with a snort. "Want to play?"

"There's only one duvet."

"I just gave you the rug."

"How about if I lie on the floor while you roll over me?" His eyebrow lifted. "Or, better still, how about I share your duvet? There's room in a king-size for two."

I pretended to ponder before smiling. "Only if you can get in."

"You're on." He grinned as he pulled off his shoes and stepped over the rug.

Expecting him to try and drag the duvet off me, I twisted my hands in the top, clutched it ready. When he knelt by my feet, I considered pushing them against him, but didn't.

He cocked his eyebrow. "Think you can win?"

"Absolutely. They thought I wouldn't score a basket, but I showed them. You should be easy."

As he laughed, I braced, but grabbing the foot of the duvet, as though to pull it from me, he surprised me by flicking it over his head.

I wriggled when he grabbed my legs. "Cheat!"

My body skidded across the floor with his tug, and my arms shot over my head, taking the duvet with them. We struggled, twisted—I kicked. By the time the fight for the upper hand ceased, the crisp fabric of the cover coated our bodies.

Our breaths heavy, the laughter died away. His dark eyes grew serious as he watched me, entrancing me with their depth. I released the cover, brought my hands to his cheeks, encouraging him closer until my lips pressed against his. When I pulled back, our eyes locked for a second, and his mouth came back down.

The deepening kiss hitched my breath, and my fingers slid around into his hair. As his tongue swept against mine, a tremor rolled through him, and my body arched up in greeting. Grasping my hips, he rolled onto his back, took me with him. When a small laugh escaped me, he paused, cupping my face in his hands.

"What?" he whispered.

"This is a bit different to the rolling around in duvets I had in mind."

With a chuckle, he returned to the kiss. My body met his as I rolled us onto our sides. Sliding down, his hand explored my thigh, before he gripped my leg to hook over his.

"Sean?" The voice arrived from the doorway. "Oh—shit, sorry."

We paused in our path to getting carried away. "What is it, Josh?" Sean asked.

"The next batch of food is almost ready," he said.

"We'll be out in a minute."

His retreat arrived at a higher volume than his approach.

"Hungry?" Sean planted a kiss on my nose.

My breathing had yet to steady. "Not really."

"You should eat."

"Can't I shower first? I smell pretty bad." Especially compared to his sweet and heady musk.

"You smell just fine to me."

"We could do a little more rolling first—make sure it's out of my system." I was only half-kidding.

His eyes darkened. "If I roll with you anymore, I'd never want to do anything else."

A quiet laugh escaped me. "Well, I suppose we'd better go down, then."

I unwrapped myself from him, and we attempted to extricate ourselves from the duvet. Running my hands over my bed-hair reminded me I hadn't brushed it.

Sean smiled. "You look great."

I rolled my eyes. "Of course I do."

"You always look amazing," he said, pulling my hand away.

"How?" I asked. "I haven't washed, dressed, or brushed my teeth. I've run around in the garden with a bunch of werewolves until coated in sweat, I rolled around beneath the duvet until my hair stood on end ..." I paused for breath. "... and I've had the best day for as long as I can remember."

"Good." He pulled me to my feet, maintaining the contact when we made our way back out to the others.

They all turned to grin as we followed our noses to the aromas of steaming salmon, roasting vegetables, and chicken legs.

Kyle handed me a plate already laden with food. "I saved you some, in case you came down late."

"Thanks." I sent Sean a smug smile before going to sit in one of the willow seats at the edge of the lawn.

Joining me with his, Sean finished off what I couldn't manage. Unlike them, I didn't have the appetite of a bear just out of hibernation.

The slight breeze, present all day, picked up to blow my hair about with a cold wind. If the others were aware of the lowered temperatures, they didn't show it—T-shirts still lay strewn across the grass. Wrapping up in my discarded blanket, I listened to the men mumbling in low voices about supplies they were waiting on for a job and where we would all be eating the next day.

Sean brought his chair closer to mine and lifted my feet across his lap. As the rub of his hands warmed them, I snuggled lower beneath the thick fleece and closed my eyes. Before long, after too many days of sleep deprivation and not enough hours the previous night to compensate, I fell into an embrace of darkness.

____

Chapter 25
DARKNESS
____

My dream-self's laughter is infectious as she runs across grass, her face aglow with joy. She appears not to be attempting escape from the man following, but merely to entice. The grass swaying around her feet glistens with droplets of dew, creating crystallised prisms as they refract the energy of the full moon. Branches, beneath which she darts, dip and bow against the pressure of the wind.

Her dress and waist-length hair billow out, as she turns to glance over her shoulder. Seeing her pursuer falling behind, she veers around the trunk of a silver birch, her hands sweeping across the bark. With a final glance at him, she continues back onto her path, a lesser distance between. An illuminate glow highlights her cheeks, but it does not appear to be from exertion. Her excitement is visible within the sparkling of her eyes.

Halting, she turns to smile at the man, pausing long enough for him to come nearer, before taking flight once more. The music of her victorious glee fills the land—harmonising with the man's, as his excitement matches hers.

It is evident from his apparent strength that he could catch my dream-self, if he wishes, and I'm certain she is aware of this.

It appears to be a game, a ritual of sorts—the preceding event to something greater.

I glance to see where they are heading. A structure stands ahead, one of wood. Her pace increases as her laughter grows. Behind her, the man's speed almost matches that of my dream-self, as though both are eager for the end in sight.

She fumbles with the doors of the building, her excitement causing clumsiness that was, before, absent. With one final backward look, my dream-self is inside.

Chapter 26
LIGHT

I opened my eyes to everyone staring at me, their outlines silhouetted by the darkening sky. Lifting my head, I found myself still upon the willow seat in the garden.

Sean watched me with a smile on his lips, curiosity in his eyes. "You were dreaming."

"Was I?" I asked, even though every second of it had etched into my brain.

He smiled. "You know you were."

Snorting quietly, I attempted to sit, but couldn't, thanks to the restrictions of the blanket tangled around my shoulders.

Sean gently tugged it away, his smile a little wider. "Was it a good one?"

"How long did I sleep for?" I asked, avoiding his question.

"About an hour, or so. We've been waiting for you to go inside."

I lowered my feet to the ground, but lifted them back up when they hit the cold, damp grass. "You should have woken me, then."

"Why would we do that when you seemed to be enjoying yourself so much?"

As the others made their way indoors, carrying furniture in with them, I pushed to my feet, ignoring the moisture assaulting my soles, and lifted my chair. "How do you know I was enjoying myself?"

"Because people don't usually laugh in their sleep if they're not."

I deposited my borrowed piece of furniture back in the conservatory and took my blanket through to the kitchen. "Do you have any drinking chocolate?"

"We should have," Sean said, coming in behind. "You want some?"

"Tiredness always makes me cold."

He leaned in to kiss my cheek. "Go snuggle up, then, and I'll make you something."

I got as far as the living door when the first yawn broke free. I reached up my arms, stretched the muscles either side of my spine, and finished the expulsion on a body-shaking judder before joining everyone else.

The single armchair supported Nathan. Connor sat on one sofa with Kyle and Daniel, while Josh lounged on the footstool, leaving Ethan with the second sofa to himself.

He layered his lap with cushions. "Come on, sleepy Jem. Come put your head down."

Looking down at him, I considered his offer, before rearranging the pads to settle down and tucking the blanket high beneath my chin. "Do you normally stay this late?" I asked Connor.

"It's only just turned nine," said Josh.

"You know, it's an unusual name: Jem," Nathan said before I could respond.

I shrugged. "I guess."

"Where did the name come from?"

"I don't know. My mum chose it because she wanted

another name beginning with J. My sister's called Jessica, so she kept the theme going ... I think, anyway."

"There can't be many Jems out there."

"None that I've heard of."

"I did hear of another Jem, once."

My lips curved. "You did?"

He nodded. "Many years ago—part of our pack history."

Sean came in with my drink. I turned to lean on my elbow as I took it from him, and he lifted my legs to sit.

"She was the first recorded female werewolf," Nathan continued.

"Hang on." My eyebrows lifted. "You have a history for your species?"

"*Race*, not species."

"Sorry, no offence intended."

"None taken." He smiled. "And yes, we do have history—stories passed down through generations."

"This Jem, was she bitten by any chance?"

"As a matter of fact, she was. Most werewolves are hereditary, some bitten. But there are no records of hereditary females."

I took a sip of my drink, smiling at Sean once the warm chocolaty liquid washed down my throat.

"The Jem in our history records was bitten by a pack member." Nathan starting up again drew my attention back to him.

"Why did he bite her?" I placed my mug on the floor, nestled my head against the cushions.

"Within the pack, relationships were discouraged. So he bit her for that reason. He couldn't bear the thought of them being parted, which is what the pack leader at the time urged for. He thought, if he bit her, the Alpha would agree to her staying and becoming an integrated pack member."

"And did she have any say in the matter?"

"If you mean, did he ask her before doing it, the answer's no."

I lifted my head. "Are there females now?"

"A few, here and there. But back then, Jem was the only one."

"Did she ever forgive him?"

"Of course she did. They were in love. Plus, the wolf's ploy was successful, because she was accepted within the pack as a member. When the wolf went on to take over the responsibility of Alpha, he took his Jem along with him for the ride. But their biggest problem was, once she'd forgiven him and their relationship made public, she was in danger from other packs. It was never heard of, a female werewolf, you see."

"Did something happen to her?" I asked, watching him.

"Not because of that." He smiled. "Jem and this wolf were never separated once she'd forgiven him—he never left her side. The wolf taught Jem to fight, to protect herself, and they always ended up defending their territory together, side by side."

At his description, my dream on the hill sprang to mind. I glanced to my right, to Sean's studying gaze, before looking back to Nathan.

"Also, because they were in love, and he was the one who bit her, they had a connection like no two werewolves ever before. They were almost able to communicate without speaking, without eye contact. They seemed to know what the other was thinking, feeling. Jem and this Alpha died many years later, each in a bid to protect the other, but Jem's mother had placed some kind of spell—"

"Spell?"

"Jem's name came from the star sign Gemini because of her birth date. Her mother was a big believer in astrology, astronomy, fate and destiny, but in those days it was misconstrued as witchcraft."

"My sister claims she used to be a witch in a previous life," I said.

Nathan allowed me a smile before continuing. "Well, Jem's mother placed a spell that bound the two wolves for eternity, tying their love for one another with the promise, that if one were to return to this earth, the other would closely follow behind for fate to reunite them."

Wary of the story's direction, I pushed up and stared at him. "But these are just stories, right?"

"Actually, Jem, we take our histories very seriously."

My pulse picked up speed. "But they're still just stories."

"The wolf who bit Jem is a far descendant of our bloodline. The history of our family is so important to us, I named my son after the Alpha considered to be of the greatest influence."

Like I already knew what he'd say, I turned toward Sean.

"I named Sean after him."

My head whipped back fast enough to blur the room. "You're kidding me, right?"

"Not at all."

"What are you trying to say, Nathan?"

"You know the connection is there," he said. "Look at the dreams."

"Exactly, they're just *dreams*, Nathan." I heard the tightness in my voice, yet couldn't help it.

"We don't believe they're dreams," he said. "We think they're memories."

Swallowing, I stared at him.

"Think about it, Jem. You were led to one another, as predicted to happen. You have the connection they were said to share."

"Connection?" My jaw tightened. "I've just *met* him."

"The dreams you've had are the same, I believe, as ones Sean has experienced. And what bigger connection is there than being aware he was changing?"

"What the hell are you talking about?"

"The day you thought Sean was going to bite you, did you not already know he'd changed before he emerged?"

"I .... Yes, but ..." I surged to my feet.

"How did you know?"

"What?"

"How did you know he'd changed, Jem?"

"I ..." I looked to Sean. "I *felt* it," I told him. "But that doesn't mean anyth—"

"And throwing yourself in front of a charging werewolf, with no regard for yourself, just to protect him? I know it was Sean you were protecting last night, and not Peter."

"I ..." I glanced around, hoping someone would say something rational, but nobody other than Nathan and I seemed to have an opinion on the matter. "There was no time to think about what I was doing."

"But in our history, Jem and Sean would often risk themselves rather than have the other one become injured or in danger."

"I wasn't at risk. Sean wouldn't hurt me."

For moments, only my escalating breaths filled the room, and I shrank beneath the stares of them all.

"You accepted who he was the first day you met him," Nathan said, breaking into the quiet. "You never once questioned if he was the one you'd dreamed about."

"That's because he ..." My eyes flitted between Sean and Nathan, panic drumming through my skull.

"Because he *smelled* right to you? Who else could confirm identity by scent? And that day Sean first brought you here?"

"I ... That doesn't mean—"

"This house has been in my family for generations."

"Well, if that's the case, the garden is wrong." I thrust my hand toward the rear of the house. "There was no barrier to the forest in my dreams."

"The garden perimeter wasn't added until fifty-two years ago."

"I'm not a werewolf." I pumped my fist. "They don't—"

"Exist?" He half-smiled.

I glanced away. After so many years with it as my natural response, that was exactly what I'd been about to say. "They're just dreams."

"But nearly all your dreams, your whole life, have been about werewolves. Isn't that what you told Sean before you even knew who he was?"

I couldn't take any more. "I'm going for a shower." As I darted for the door, Sean stood, also, his hand reaching out.

"You can't hide from it, Jem," Nathan said from behind.

I paused in the doorway, glanced at Sean.

"You still show signs of being a wolf," Nathan said. "It's still in you. It may be buried deep within, but it's there. Every time you come near, I know there's still a hint of the werewolf gene inside you, because I can smell it—we all can."

"You're crazy, Nathan." I strode from the room, climbed the stairs two at a time.

"I'm telling you to alert you, Jem."

Reaching the top step, I spun at Nathan's voice.

He peered up from the hallway. "You need to know. Years ago, Jem was in danger for being the first female werewolf. Every pack knows of your history. You need to be aware that if they find out about this, they may come here, looking for you."

"Is this your very unsubtle way of telling me my life is now in danger, Nathan?"

"You've been in danger since the day you walked into that restaurant."

I closed my eyes against him. "I need a shower."

"You can shower all you like, Jem. The scent will still be there."

I almost ran down the landing to the bathroom, Sean's, "Nicely done, Dad," the last thing I heard before I shut myself in.

Chapter 27

Pressed against the bathroom door, I tried for composure. It took mere seconds to admit miserable failure before I tugged off Sean's clothes and ducked into the shower.

After having a small fit, whereupon I deep-screamed a few times, stamped my feet, and banged my fists against the tiled interior wall of the shower cubicle, my frustration faded enough for me to function. Whatever Sean said to the contrary, the stench clinging to my body needed to go.

Beginning with a good scalp massage, I lathered in the shampoo, but couldn't help thinking about everything Nathan said. Even if the histories were accurate, it didn't mean they had to be true. Right? Yet, the way Nathan had remained so calm throughout the discussion told me he believed every word. Nobody else disputed the story either, or his attempts to convince me—not even Sean. Did Sean believe his father's words, too?

Smoothing thick conditioner over my locks, I thought of the way Nathan tried to tie in my recent life happenings to the story he seemed so familiar with—the way he'd come back at each of my arguments with a counter-argument.

After removing the conditioner, I reached for the shower gel, bubbled it up within a bath-rose. I ran the foamy liquid across my flesh, scrubbed away the day's dirt, thinking back through my dreams.

My sister had insisted there was more to the latest ones than usual. Poppy even admitted Jess was right about those sorts of things, and Poppy was as far from an off-the-wall sort of person as you could find. Even without speaking to Jess, from the very first dream, had I not felt an overwhelming urge to meet the man invading them? Had he not consumed my thoughts, awake and asleep? Hadn't Jess convinced me my dreams may be some kind of precognitive images, a premonition? I'd wanted to believe her, even if I didn't realise it at the time.

Were Nathan's ideas so much more ridiculous than what *I'd* wanted to be true?

Switching the bath-rose for facial wash, I squeezed some into my hands and cleansed my face, closing my eyes as my hands ran over them.

Had I been wrong to get so mad at him, I wondered, over something he obviously believed in? I supposed he had a point, when he referred to my dreams matching those of Sean's. What were the odds of two people having dreams that matched, and even being aware of which dreams we were discussing, if no connection existed?

I braced my hands against the tiles, water beating down on my upturned face, and silent-screamed at myself for not bothering to decipher the meaning of the dreams, or our chance meeting, sooner.

What sort of person wouldn't have questioned it further before becoming involved?

When I'd driven from the restaurant, I knew deep inside I wouldn't allow that to be my last sighting of him. If I'd intended to walk away, I would have done so without phoning Jess or walking back inside.

On top of everything else swirling inside my head, I couldn't help but prioritise how Sean made me feel—feelings I hadn't given myself chance to think about.

Wasn't the saying: ignorance is bliss?

I shut off the spray, stepped out, and moved to the sink. Piping a line of toothpaste along the bristles of my new brush, I glanced at my reflection in the cabinet mirror above the basin, but my thoughts still wouldn't shut off.

Had not the happiest moments of my life so far occurred within Sean's company? Had I not risked my life, as I'd known it for the past eight years, simply to spend a few hours with a man I barely knew? Sean had just seemed too important to me—obviously more important than anything else. Though, my obsession with my recordings should've told me that.

I shoved in my toothbrush and began to scrub.

I'm in love with him.

My hand stopped moving, and I stared at the mirror—at the face whose mind had voiced that thought. Though, the more I thought about it, the more I decided it was the most honest I'd ever been with myself.

I should talk to Sean, not Nathan, I decided. It was something *we* needed to discuss, not everyone else. Maybe, if I truly was in love, I could deal with the other stuff. So long as I could talk to Sean, be certain he felt the same way, everything else would fall into place. I hoped.

I spat out the toothpaste, rinsed my brush and my mouth, gargled, spat, and repeated the process—for as long as I could to put it all off for a little longer. Finally, with a towel wrapped around my body, I peered back in the mirror, my face set in determination.

"You can deal with this," I told myself. "If you've managed to live with an O.C.D. of a control freak for eight years, this should be a walk in the park."

Throwing myself a huge smile, I ignored that it looked a little manic and, a few seconds later, pulled open the bathroom door.

I half expected to see Nathan, maybe the whole bloody pack, standing on the other side of the door. Thankfully, they weren't. After pausing to listen with a tilt of my head, I scurried the length of the landing and flung myself inside the lilac room.

Propped against the window sill, Sean stared back at me, and I almost toppled with my abrupt halt. His eyes held nothing but concern, as he pushed up. "Jem?"

Having hoped for a little more time to compose myself, I managed only a pathetic fish impersonation in response.

He took a step forward. "Jem, are you okay?"

My mouth continued to open and close, until I ordered myself to get a grip and sealed it. I nodded.

Another step brought him nearer. "You don't really look okay."

"It's a ... lot to, you know ..." I shrugged.

"He could have handled it better, too."

I gave a small nod before shrugging. "So could I."

"Are you staying tonight, still?"

My brow creased. "Where else would I go?"

"If you felt the need to leave, I could—"

"I meant, where else would I *want* to go?"

He blinked, and a smile emerged. "You want to stay?"

"Why would I shower if I planned to high-tail it out of here?"

"I thought, maybe—"

"Besides, what would I do? If I head out to the road, you'd

only follow, and I can't outrun a car, especially not the Porsche, because everyone knows the yellow ones are fastest. Or ..." I half smiled, lifting my gaze to the ceiling as though allowing serious consideration. "Or maybe I could make a break through the forest. Goodness *knows* that's a brilliant idea as far as escape plans go, don't you think? It's not like you lot could catch me in there."

He stepped forward and took my arms, which gestured about like a disjointed windmill, before hooking a finger under my chin and lifting my face. "So, you don't want to leave?"

"No."

He breathed out a sigh and smiled. The glint in his eyes and the flashing of his teeth made my stomach tighten, but when I tried to look away, he held me there, his smile fading. "I love you, Jem."

"I know you do, Sean. Why else do you think I'm still here?"

With a fresh smile, he leaned in closer. His lips met mine, and I allowed him to take the lead, but he surprised me by keeping it gentle, drawing it out to a sensual conclusion. When he went to step back, my feet followed, and pressing my face to his chest, I sighed as I inhaled his rich musk.

As his warm palms found the bare flesh of my shoulders, my hands swept around his back, smoothing across the muscles there, until they came to rest against his waist beneath the hem of his T.

"I should leave now," he whispered.

I surprised myself by saying, "Stay."

"Jem?"

"I don't ... want you to go, Sean." Gently nudging him toward the bed, I reached behind to flick off the light switch. He pushed back against me, and as illumination once again filled the room, I quickly switched it back off.

"What's wrong?"

"You can't see me ... naked."

"Jem?" Confusion bled through his tone.

"No man has ever seen me naked before."

"I have." He knocked the light back on. "Every time I close my eyes, all I see is you."

I hit the switch again. "I can't."

"Jem, please. Do you have any idea how long I've been waiting for this? Eight years of dreams have turned into a lifetime of frustration. I've been totally in love with a woman I didn't even know for sure would walk into my life. Now you're here—am I not allowed to revel in that a little?"

"How much have you had to endure in your dreams?"

"*Everything*," he said deeply. "I've known for years what you would look like, how you'd smell and taste. I've already seen every inch of your body. I've seen you laugh, cry, smile. I know where you like to be touched, and how. I know how being able to touch, see, and taste you makes *me* feel. I know everything, Jem—have for years. I have *waited for you*, for years."

"It must have driven you crazy," I murmured.

"You have no idea."

I turned the light back on, his eyes dilating at the brightness. "I didn't know."

"How could you?"

Quiet fell as I studied him. From the broad expanse of chest pressing against the underside of his shirt, to his equally broad shoulders, all the way up to the soft yet strong lines of his jaw. Higher still, and my eyes locked with his. The irises appeared almost black as they shone beneath the artificial light, and the way he stared back reminded me how underdressed I was compared to him. The way his gaze flickered over me also made me want to change that—like, really want to.

With my hand still pressed against his chest, I attempted to make the first move, despite the flush heating my cheeks in my sudden overwhelming urge to see him. "I-I ..." Forgetting useless words, I grabbed handfuls of his T-shirt and tugged it over his head.

Arms lifting, he pulled it off and looked back to me. When I nodded, he unleashed my towel. As it dropped to the floor, I glanced up at him, lashes lowered, waiting while his darkened eyes swept over my flesh. The appraisal probably should have made me uncomfortable, yet it only seemed natural to stand before him that way.

In return, my eyes roamed the sculpted hills and valleys of his chest, his shoulders, the tightness of his stomach. I hooked a finger over his waistband and tugged, and he slipped his shorts down, kicking them aside.

Until we both stood before one another. Both naked.

Minutes passed, the room filled with only the sounds of our breathing, as I allowed my gaze to skim over his hips, stopping just short of dipping further, before tilting my face back to his. On seeing the excitement dancing within the darkness of his eyes, my lips curved—as did my body when his arms reached out and pulled me close.

His lips melded to mine, and he lifted me, his hand firm against my backside as he carried me to the bed. On lowering me, his muscles flexed beneath my palms, and with his face hovering over mine, he stared deep into my eyes, as though awaiting some kind of permission.

Wanting to give that to him, I slid a hand to his hair, tugged him down. "Show me," I whispered, my lips brushing across his. "Show me how it feels."

With delicate precision, he skimmed across my jaw and his tongue teased at the pulse below my ear. His teeth grazed as he travelled the length of my neck to my shoulder, and toes curling, head tilting, I shivered as my nerve endings sprang to life. Nibbling at skin, he worked his way back along my collarbone, his lips suckling at the dip of my throat, until I gave a soft moan.

His face lifted, his eyes looking into me again, every emotion within myself reflected back me in that singular glance. Each of my deepened breaths raised my breasts into contact with his chest. Peering toward where my nipples all but begged for attention, he kissed a path downward, caressed his way over each fleshy mound. As he drew each tight bud into his mouth, the fingertips of his right hand massaged down to my hip, and when his mouth headed south, heated sighs fluttered my lips. Tremors teased through my stomach, as his lips visited every inch of skin around my navel, and my breaths shook with each dart of his tongue, the way it played over skin like he needed to taste all of me at once. My fingers entwined with his hair, and as though of its own will, my body urged closer to the caresses he planted across my hip, chasing the warmth of his mouth as he rolled his tongue across my pubis.

However, when his hands nudged in to part my thighs, my brain froze, and my body tightened into a rigid bed of stone.

Releasing his grip, he pushed back up over me and took my cheek. His eyes verged on blackness as he leaned close, his breaths drifting through my parted lips. "Trust me, Jem," he murmured.

His nearness coated me in his scent, the richness of it even more potent than before, as the length of his erection beat out his arousal against my stomach. With the warmth of his body embracing me, softness seeped back into my muscles. "I trust you," I whispered.

After staring into me for seconds, he slid his arms around, taking me with him as he swung up to sit. In one fluid move, he drew my legs each side of his lap. "I won't push you, so ... reins're yours." Smiling, he dropped his hands to his sides. "*I'm yours.*"

Forehead resting against his, I breathed out a small laugh before ordering my nerves aside. I reached for his fallen hands, brought them to my hips. When I lifted up onto my knees, his face tilted to follow, and I found his mouth with mine, his hair with my fingers. Our eyes remained watching as my tongue darted out for a taste.

The feathering of his palms across my back left a trail of hairs standing to attention, as my lips moved to his neck, from where I laid tiny kisses across his shoulder and back up. As my teeth gave a gentle tug of his lobe, the tips of his fingers pressed into my flesh and vibrations hit my chest as a low rumble emanated from him.

One hand entwined in my hair, his other brushed over my rear, stroked the back of my thigh. For a long moment, his face nudged into the fallen strands at my neck while he whispered my name, before his strong arms enveloped me. Laying back, he drew me down over him, and our mouths reconnected once more.

A low moan escaped when his tip located me, flooding him with my desire, and he joined me with a quiet growl. His hands took my hips, urging them down as his pushed up, until my body trembled out its response and the unsteadiness of his breaths revealed his slipping control. When he pressed against me a second time, breath hitching, I caught his lower lip between my teeth.

For seconds, neither of us moved, savouring the contact, as I studied him from beneath my lashes. Releasing his lip, I licked at any tenderness I may have caused, and as his tongue darted out in greeting, our mouths merged once more. From there, it took only a clutch of my fingers to his shoulders, a slight tilt of my hips to create more moisture, for his control to waver.

Hands hooking my thighs, he rolled us, switching our positions, and nestled within the folds of my limbs. His erection teased at my entrance, and a blossom of heat shot fireworks in every direction.

My gasp erupted when he entered me, and my lids fluttered low over my eyes as my head tilted back. His slow thrusts produced tremors throughout my body, every movement of his controlled, deliberate, as if to enhance every second.

Reopening my eyes brought me a new show of his emotions glistening down at me in his gaze, and as his rhythm increased, I pulled his lips back to mine. Eye contact maintained, our sighs left together, and our hastened hearts matched as though of one body, an infusion of souls. With each caress of his hands, the embrace of his arms, the warmth pumping from him to enfold me, with each powerful yet measured drive of his hips, Sean brought me to life.

Showed me sensations I didn't know I could feel.

Filled me with understanding of what making love *should* be like.

Throughout it all, I became aware of *everything*. His breaths consuming my throat. The heady perfume of his scent. Every place our bodies united. The soft thickness of his hair tangled between my fingers.

More than all of those, the slightly erratic beat of his heart knocked outward to greet each beat of my own. His bodily vibrations matched the tremulous tightening of mine—while the rolling thunder within his chest demanded escape, alongside the gasps breaking free of my own throat.

From the throb at my core, one created by him, a storming heat climbed upward.

My back arched into it, and his arm slipped beneath, moulding my body to his. As my legs rose, encouraging him to move deeper, his muscles tensed beneath my calves.

With each urge of his hips, our gasps evolved into quiet moans, into humming growls and low cries, and our fingers clutched at each other as though afraid to let go. The fire intensified, burning through limbs, licking its flames along my fingertips, raging through every inch of me. On the verge of climax, his name left my throat on a whisper—a heartbeat before the consuming ebb of orgasm left me blind.

Light attempted to reach out to my vision moments later, but still my eyes refused to see. Despite my muscles floating on a blanket of happiness, my clutching hands refused to un-tense, my breaths refused to steady.

Above me, Sean's chest heaved out his own ragged breaths as his arms tightened around me. "I love you, Jem," his said, his soft voice hoarse.

"I love you, too, Sean," I whispered, and my eyes finally cleared to find his filled with shining moistness.

"I've missed you so much."

"Not anymore, never again."

"Can I stay here with you tonight?" he murmured.

I tugged his mouth to mine as I answered, "You'd better."

With a chuckle, he snagged the duvet to cover me, and rolling to his side, he took me with him, grabbing a pillow for us to share. Waiting until we'd settled, side by side, faces no more than an inch apart, he asked, "So, are you going to tell me what you dreamed about earlier?"

My smile snuck out, despite my body still feeling too languid to take orders. "You chased me to a barn."

"That one *is* enjoyable," he said, his lips twitching.

"I have a feeling it would've been even better if I hadn't woken up."

"Poor Jem. You finally get a decent dream, and it's cut short."

I shrugged. "It's not as though I experience it, anyway. Don't forget, I only get to watch."

"Like a home movie." His eyebrow shot up. "That's ... kind of kinky."

A small snort broke out. "Perv."

We lay for a while longer, until Sean said we should sleep, and he stepped out to flick the light switch. Back beneath the covers, his hand reached out in search of mine. As his thumb brushed over where my ring should have been, he nestled in closer and gave a deep sigh.

Chapter 28
DARKNESS

My dream-self appears to be in a barn. She glances around, before climbing to a hayloft that casts her face into shadow. Upon reaching the top, she shifts to lie on her stomach, discarded strands of straw gathering upon her white dress.

Below, the doors fly wide. She edges forward to watch the man who enters. As he glances around, she smothers her mouth over the laughter threatening to expose her.

His head tilts, his nostrils flare with his inhalation, and as his eyes fall upon her position, he smiles.

She shuffles back, out of sight, but he must hear her because he laughs.

His foot takes the first rung. "I don't know why you think I won't find you, Jem."

While he climbs to her hiding place, my dream-self rolls onto her back. Her dress rises to reveal slender legs, as she pushes onto her elbows and begins to kick backward.

When he reaches the top, he stands over her, laughing at her smiling face, at the straw caught in her hair, and the disarray of her attire. Dropping to his knees, his fingers stretch out, and he encases her calf, pulling her to him.

She resists with a push, a feeble attempt against his hold, yet the opposite intention is written into her expression. Her radiance shows it is all part of their mating dance—a sequence of events offering almost as much pleasure as the act to which they are leading.

Jaw set in determination, he draws her to him, as her fingers wrap within his dark hair and bring him to her. No laughter remains in their locked eyes, just hunger, a deep desire for one another.

"Sean," she whispers.

His lips meet hers, and only the sounds of their sighs fill the barn. Her fingers work to unfasten his clothing before her hands push down his trousers, her breathing catching at the release of his erection. As she relaxes back, his hands travel her legs, sliding her dress high until she lies exposed before him. Gaze all but consuming her, he tugs off his shirt, kicks his trousers away in impatience. Naked, but for an unusual wreath about his neck, he leans low to place his lips against her thigh.

A smile adds radiance to the face of my dream-self, and she relocates his hair as he grips her hips. His hands press her into the kisses he plants along her skin, his lips moving higher.

As though he has passed over a sensitive spot, a small giggle escapes with the slight wiggle of her body. His face lifts, before his mouth returns to her flesh.

She watches his every movement, her fingers always reaching, as he skims across her abdomen, her body trembling with the obvious pleasure.

Eyes lifting until they reconnect with hers, he pulls her body to him and with one thrust ...

Chapter 29
LIGHT

I gasped my way to a sense of awareness, arousal from the dream searing heat through my groin. As my mind scrambled to keep the image alive, the unmistakable sensation of soft kisses feathered my inner thighs.

With a sigh of pleasure, I stretched my fingers in search of him.

He lifted to look at me, his voice husky. "I thought I'd recreate the dream for you, as you missed out on the best bit."

My lips curved as I kicked back with my legs. "Well, if we take it back farther, and we're doing this right, my memory tells me I didn't make it quite so easy for you."

He chuckled. "Is that right?"

"In fact ..." My eyebrow lifted. "Didn't you have to catch me first?"

"You want to run around the garden a little?"

"No." I snorted. "But the dream suggests I should at least give a bit of a fight. And my favourite look on your face was when you laughed at the straw in my hair."

"So, now you want straw in your hair?"

"I just thought it set the scene."

He studied me for a few seconds, eyes dancing, before he nodded with a grin. "Wait here, then. I'll be right back." He jumped from the bed and fled the room.

Ethan appeared in the open doorway. "Where did he run off to?"

"You probably don't want to know." I pulled the blanket over my head as a giggle burst out.

Moments later, running footsteps mounted the stairs.

"What the hell are you doing with that?" Ethan asked.

"Can't you disappear?" Sean laughed, and the following bang suggested the bedroom door slammed.

His footsteps brushed the carpet. The duvet disappeared. I blinked up to two handfuls of dried grass cuttings raining down on me and burst out laughing as Sean dove back on the bed.

"Now, where were we?"

"I believe I'm about to feign resistance before you show me what I've missed out on."

"That's right." He knelt and gripped my thighs, pulling me to him.

Laughing, I pushed back, faux fighting to release my legs.

We played at the game for a few minutes, him grasping and tugging, me wriggling and pushing, until the laughter died down long enough for us to study the hunger, evident in our eyes and flushed cheeks.

Sean's mouth pressed to mine with a fierceness that knocked the breath from me before his lips returned to where they were when I woke. His hands lifted my hips to bring me closer to his caressing kisses, and I entwined my fingers within his hair. Sliding higher, his teeth gently nipped. As he hit the sensitive spot where my thigh and pelvis united, I squirmed, and giggled. He glanced up, warmth in his eyes as he smiled, before his lips set back to inducing my tremors.

A lick of his tongue over my stomach tightened my muscles,

a nibble to each breast released my sighs, a grasp of my hips tugged me to him, and one thrust drove him inside me.

DRAGGING ourselves in search of a different form of nourishment, well after eleven, we found Ethan at the kitchen table. He did a double-take when I entered, and I had to suppress my snigger at his expression.

In another set of Sean's underwear, I peered out the kitchen window, while he filled the kettle.

Spotting Nathan outside, I headed out, stopping a few feet behind when he didn't turn. "Nathan?"

"Good morning, Jem."

"I'm sorry I was so rude to you last night."

He glanced over his shoulder. "You weren't rude."

"I wasn't very polite, either," I said, walking around to face him.

"I never expected you to be made of stone, Jem. I knew I'd get a reaction."

"Whatever made you think that? I mean, it's not every day a girl gets told—" Cutting off the rant, I blew out a breath. *Some apology.*

"You're pissed off with me," he said. "I can understand that."

I combed my fingers into my hair, lowering them when they snagged. "No."

"You're not pissed off with me?" His eyebrow lifted.

"No."

"So, you accept I'm right?"

"It's not as simple as that. It's just ..." I peered off toward where Sean watched through the window. "Sean and I crossed a barrier last night, and quite frankly, that's all I'm interested in right now. *Sean* ... is all that matters to me right now."

He nodded.

"I'm going for some breakfast." I began to walk around him. "That's all I wanted to say. I know how I feel about Sean. I don't need to know any more than that."

He nodded as I passed.

"Jem?"

I glanced back from the conservatory door.

He smiled. "Welcome to the family."

I returned the expression before disappearing inside to the welcoming scent of toast.

Sean pointed at the table. "Sit."

Obeying, I pulled out a chair opposite Ethan and sank into it. While Sean took toast slices out and buttered them, Ethan watched me with his nose twitching.

Sean brought the food to the table with a hot mug of coffee. "Eat. I'll make more."

By the time he'd joined me, I'd eaten my toast and had started my coffee beneath the heavy stare of Ethan with his still-wrinkling nose.

"Do I smell funny to you?" I asked.

He smiled. "Not funny, Jem, no."

As I stared at him, trying to figure out why I had his obvious attention, Nathan came in from the garden.

"We'll be eating at Connor's today."

"Do they all live together?" I asked, turning to him.

Nathan nodded.

"Are they far from here?"

"They're also on the forest outskirts," he said, "but on the south side."

"Is that the way you usually go, through the forest?"

"Mostly, yes." He smiled. "But Sean will take you by road. The five mile run might be a bit much for you."

"But you and Ethan will go through the forest?"

He nodded.

"As wolves?"

Another nod.

I glanced from him to Ethan, whose eyes remained glued to me. "But ... won't you be ... naked when you get there?"

That earned me a trio of laughs. "We have clothes belonging to everyone at each other's houses, just for days like this," Nathan said.

"Oh. I knew that."

Ethan chuckled. "Of course you did, Jem."

"I said we'd be there about twelve," Nathan said. "So, if you and Jem would be good enough to get ready, Sean, it might be best if you left first."

"Why?" I asked. "Does it take that much longer by road?"

"No, Jem. I just don't think we'll see you today, if we leave you two here alone."

"Well, if you do get there first, maybe you could tell them I won't appreciate being stared at like an exhibit." I sent an exaggerated gawp to Ethan.

"Certainly."

"Thanks. I'll go and wash, then."

Sean pushed up. "I'll come, too."

"Sit down," Nathan said. "You can wait until Jem has finished."

Though he grumbled beneath his breath, Sean complied, and alone, I left the room under the watchful eye of Ethan. Although I'd only taken a shower the evening before, something told me Sean's family could scent exactly how we'd connected overnight.

I called down once the bathroom was free and ducked into the lilac room. Amongst my new clothing, I found matching underwear in deep, midnight blue, and over them wore grey utility shorts and a blue T-shirt, teamed with my new trainers.

By quarter to twelve, Sean and I were in the Porsche. It didn't take long, with Sean's rapid speed, to reach the other house, and it surprised me to see how much like the Holloway home it was. Sending Sean alone through the front door, I went around the side of the property to investigate.

A generous carport had been attached to the side of the building, as opposed to the free-standing garage at Nathan's. Circling to the rear, I discovered they lacked the conservatory, also. Aside from those details, though, and the ivy creeping along the far corner onto the roof, the two properties could've been made by the same hand. On the upside, the smaller garden didn't have any restrictions, leaving the forest exposed.

I wandered toward the trees, my head tilting as I peered through their thick clusters, the beauty of the scenery drawing me closer.

Hesitation to enter kicked in at the first line of trees, and a few moments passed before I took a tentative step. As though seeking support, I touched the bark of the nearest trunk, my eyes travelling upward to take in the strength of the branches, the vibrant leaves. With my face lifted, one step followed another and I allowed my eyes to close.

I knew when I was no longer beneath sunlight by the cool shadow hitting my face, and I came to a halt. A deep inhalation discovered dampness upon the ground where it had broken through the sparse breaks in greenery, mustiness on the air, leafy freshness, and the woody aroma of the surrounding timber. Listening brought the soft rustle of the weaving wind weaving, crackling dried bracken as small animals went about their day, the flap of wings, the chirps of birds, and *footsteps*.

They drew nearer, and my eyes shot open—to a naked Nathan and Ethan.

"Oh!" I flipped my hands over my eyes, and their laughter erupted.

"You shouldn't be in the forest, if you don't want to risk seeing us with no clothes on," Ethan said.

"I thought you'd be in the house already," I said, my eyes still covered.

"We got sidetracked. Besides, what exactly are you doing in here alone, Jem?"

"I'm hardly *in* here. Two steps in doesn't count as being inside, does it?"

"You're not only two steps in," Nathan said.

Careful not to look at them, I twisted to glance behind. At least five lines of trees separated me from the garden.

"Jem?" The shout came from the direction of the house, followed by running footsteps. "Jem?"

As I turned around and headed back, Sean raced across the garden, with Daniel and Kyle in tow.

His panicked face relaxed when our gazes met. "What are you doing in here? I couldn't bloody see you. I thought you'd—"

"I think she had an overwhelming urge to come greet us," Ethan said, as he and his dad rounded me for the house.

It took real effort not to stare at their retreating backsides.

"You should've said if you wanted to take a look," said Sean. "I'd have taken you in. It would've been—"

I gave him my full attention. "Safer?" At his nod, I continued, "You think going into the forest with a werewolf is safer than if I don't?" He nodded again, and I half-laughed before frowning. "The last time you asked me to join you in the forest, you bit me."

"I'm not going to bite you."

"How can I ..." About to ask how I could possibly believe him, I stemmed the sentence, averted my eyes.

"Don't you trust me, Jem?" Hurt deepened his tone.

I shrugged before I could stop the action.

"So, you trust me not to harm you when my body's threatening to change and I have every chance of losing control, and you trust me enough to give yourself over to me,"—behind him, Daniel and Kyle slunk off toward the house—"but you still don't trust me not to bite you." As I evaded his stare, he sighed out his frustration and tugged me round until our eyes met. His held so much pain, I ached for him. I bit my lower lip to prevent the tremble, but he released it with his thumb before tracing a path along my jaw. "At least get one of us to go in with you next time," he said. "Please don't go in alone."

"Okay," I said, needing to eradicate the worry lining his face.

"Please will you try and trust me?"

"I do trust you, Sean. If I didn't, there's no way I'd be here now. It's just ... when you've been through, and learned, what I have and .... I just need you to be patient with me, okay?"

"Sure," he said slowly. "I can do patience. If it means you stay, I can do it."

"Liar." I almost laughed. "You haven't a patient bone in your body."

"Jem, if I had no patience, we'd have made love long before last night."

With a sigh, he drew me close, his arms coming around to lift me. My hand slid into his hair, and as I devoured his lips, my legs enfolded him, as did my arms, until the kiss deepened further.

The vibrations of his lips ran along mine as he made our way back. When he pulled away and looked at me, my frustration at the interruption must have shown, because he chuckled. "We're back at the house." He lifted a brow. "It wouldn't be polite to borrow a room."

I hadn't noticed the distance *or* speed we'd travelled, and the best response I mustered was, "Huh?"

. . .

After chipping in with a little vegetable peeling, I ducked outside alone and called Poppy. I confided about my relationship progress with Sean, then asked her if Peter had returned—he had, but left when Poppy threatened to call the police, for which I apologised profusely. She let slip the mobile phone and the blue underwear I sported had been gifts from Sean, before her parting words told me I really owed my sister a phone call.

The call to Jess took longer than necessary, mostly due to the amount of times she stopped me mid-sentence to tell me how she always knew Peter was an arsehole, and a dick, and a whole other heap of colourful adjectives. Of course, she wanted to know exactly what I'd done since leaving. I told her everything, including Nathan's history lesson with a solemn pledge to never repeat it to anyone. In return, I had to listen to how she'd been right, hadn't she told me something like that all along, why hadn't I listened to her, yada, yada, yada. Finally, with a promise to keep her updated, we said our goodbyes.

I re-entered the house to food on the table and the pack snatching at it as though they hadn't eaten in weeks. Once they'd finished squabbling over who got the last slice of roast beef, they filled their mouths with enough food to prevent sounds passing through.

Obliterated food preceded the men's venture into the garden, until only I remained at the table. They soon called me to join them, though, and I headed out to where Sean sat chatting with his dad.

"We need you back tomorrow," Nathan was saying to Sean, as I drew near.

Sean patted his lap, and I curled onto him, snuggling into the security of his arms.

"We've already been held up, waiting on this delivery," his dad continued. "We can't afford to fall behind any further."

Sean glanced at me. "I don't think that's a good idea, Dad."

"What's wrong?" I asked.

"It's nothing for you to worry about, Jem," Nathan said.

"Do you all work together?"

He nodded before turning back to his son. "I need you back in."

"You already knew how I'd feel about this," Sean said.

"What do you do?" I asked.

"Property development," said Nathan.

"And you've been held up because of Sean?"

"Not just because of Sean," he said. "Waiting on these supplies has been the biggest problem, but working with six instead of seven of us has had its setbacks, as well."

"You all work together?" I indicated Connor's family, too.

"Yes."

"Sean, how long has it been since you went to work?" I asked.

When Sean shrugged, Nathan said, "We haven't seen him there for almost two weeks."

"You haven't been to work because of me?" I asked.

"You shouldn't be left alone," he said. "It isn't ..."

"You can't put your life on hold because of me." I stood to face him. "Go back to work. You can't spend every waking hour watching my every move. It's ridiculous."

He pushed to his feet, also. "It may not be safe."

"Are you telling me that, now you've walked into my life and—in your dad's words—put me in danger, I'm not even safe at your house?"

"Of course you are." He took my shoulders. "Why do you think I wanted you there? It's the safest place for you."

"Then, there's no reason for you to not go to work." To Nathan I said, "He'll be back tomorrow, but can I speak to you in private for a moment?"

"Sure, Jem." Nathan took my elbow as he stood before walking me to the house.

In the kitchen, I closed the door at our backs, and Nathan and I took neighbouring chairs.

"There's no point talking to Sean, because I don't believe he'll tell me the truth," I said, jumping straight in.

Although he looked intrigued, he didn't respond.

"And you certainly don't seem to have trouble telling me things, even if it may not be what I want to hear." Though he smiled, he remained silent, so I came right out with my concerns. "Okay, give it to me straight. Exactly how much danger am I in by being with Sean?"

"I told you the truth when I said your life has been in danger from the moment you reconnected. And I wasn't exaggerating when I told you, if other packs find out about your return,"—I cringed, but he continued—"they will come looking, if only out of curiosity. Even if they're merely curious, it won't be good. The second one of them finds out, they could tell others. Then even more could come. You were, *are*, such a strong part of our history, they won't be able to resist."

"Do you think Sean's overreacting about wanting to stay close?"

"Of course not. He has every right to be terrified. But what kind of life will it be for either of you, if you stay indoors, too afraid to go outside? And the longer he leaves it to take that first step, the harder it will be. I know him well enough to understand how much he cares for you, and I understand your situation well enough to know why it's difficult for him."

"What can I do?"

"About what?"

"To reduce the risks." I shrugged. "Maybe if we come up with a plan, lay down some ground rules—"

Nathan surprised me by patting my cheek like I'd been a

good student. "I knew I wouldn't have to explain too much to you, Jem. That boy of mine didn't give you enough credit when he said it was too soon to bring it all up. I knew you'd accept everything sooner rather than later."

I stared at him. "I didn't say I believed your bedtime story."

"You're still listening to me, though, aren't you?"

"Are we going to have another argument about what you think I am and what I know I'm not, or are you going to give me advice on taking precautions?"

"We can argue, if that's what you want, but it won't change a thing."

"People don't get ... *reborn*," I said.

"Just like there's no such thing as werewolves." He smiled. "But now you know different."

"That's because I've no choice but to believe when I've been living with three for a weekend."

"You're going on your own beliefs, though, Jem. How many times have you seen any of us change?"

"I ..." I frowned when I realised I hadn't.

"Exactly. Still, you're willing to believe."

"Because I already—"

"Knew? Well, I already know what I told you last night is the truth. How long are we going to debate the possibilities of reincarnation?"

"You're as bad as my sister. All she goes on about is how my dreams are about reincarnated werewolves and bloody reunions."

"Your sister—the reincarnated witch?"

I rolled my eyes. "So *she* says."

"Did it never occur to you that your sister may actually know what she's talking about? Don't forget you've had witches in your history before, so why not again?"

"Now you sound like Poppy," I grumbled. "She tells me how Jess is usually right about these things."

His lips twitched. "So, we're on the same page, then."

"I'm never going to win a discussion with you, am I?"

"Probably not." He chuckled. "Now, those precautions, are you ready to talk about them?"

I lifted my palms but dropped them again. "Sure."

"Good. You should be safe if you stay at the house. But, as I don't expect you to live the rest of your life as a hermit—"

"The rest of my life?"

"Yes, Jem. You can't seriously believe Sean will allow you to walk away now he has you."

"Allow? *If* I stay, it will because it's *my* choice, not Sean's."

"Are you planning to leave?"

"*Can* I stay? I'd never thought things out past the weekend, but—"

"That's settled, then." At the upward curl of his lips, I opened my mouth to speak, but he beat me to it. "As I was saying, we don't expect you to live the rest of your life as a hermit, and you may wish to leave the house at some point in the future, so I have requests regarding that."

I blew out a breath. "Go on."

"We'll want to know exactly where you're going and who with, what time you're going, and when you'll be returning. I don't want you using public transport—"

"But I haven't got a car."

"I'll expect you to use one of the vehicles at home," he continued. "We very rarely take them all, and if you let us know you wish to go out, then I'll make sure you have transport. Does this sound fair to you so far?"

My eyes rolled, but I nodded.

"Okay, I also want you to carry your mobile phone with you everywhere. And I *mean* everywhere. That way, if Sean feels the need to check up on you, he can. I don't want him panicking unnecessarily because you're not answering your phone. If you see, hear, *or* smell anything which gives you cause for concern, or something just doesn't seem right, you ring one of us immediately, and we'll tell you what to do until we get to you."

"Is that everything?"

He nodded.

"Oh," he said as though in afterthought. "And every vehicle will have a baseball bat stored behind the driver seat ... just in case you need to defend yourself."

"In case I need to *defend* myself?" I threw up my hands. "My future sounds more promising by the second."

His chuckle sounded like grated thunder.

"Will you explain all of this to Sean?"

"He already knows. He just doesn't think you'll agree." Smiling, he stood and walked to the door. "I told him you would."

"Hang on, Nathan, I haven't—"

"Of course you have, Jem." Another of his chuckles followed him out the door.

Chapter 30

As soon as I headed back outside after my 'chat' with Nathan, Josh called, "Come and play, Jem," from where he raced around with the others, scrapping over a rugby ball.

I waved my mobile at him. "Need to make a call." Crossing to the other side of the garden, where I hoped they wouldn't overhear my conversation, I rang my sister.

"Jess, can you do me a favour?" I asked when she answered.

"What is it?" Jess's rule number one: if someone asks for a favour, always ask what it is before you agree.

"I need you to look into something for me."

"What's that, then?" Jess's rule number two: get more information before a commitment is made.

"I want you to look into your witchy books and see if you can find any records of spells used to bind people in death, or afterlife."

"You're taking his dad's story seriously?"

"I just need to know."

"Well, I already looked it up, being the anally curious person I am."

"And ...?"

"There was a report about a witch once placing such an enchantment upon her daughter and her lover to allow them to be together for eternity ... and *they were both believed to be werewolves.*"

The theatrical whisper of her words sent a chill down my spine. "You're joking, aren't you?"

"Nope."

"Shit!"

"Jem, *you* don't swear—ever."

"Now seems like a good time to start."

She giggled down the phone.

"What are you laughing at? This isn't funny."

"Because I was only kidding about the werewolf part." She snorted. "But you're hilarious. I can't believe you didn't know I was joking."

"None of this is funny to me. What about the rest of it?"

"What, the spell? Yep, according to my books, and Internet research, it's definitely been done before, because there's history of it."

"Shit!"

"Twice in one day. I'm impressed. Did you want me to research the rest of the story?"

"You won't find it. It's records that are passed down through each family generation."

"I'll look anyway, Jem."

"Okay." I sighed. "But if you find something you think I'd prefer not to know, maybe you should keep it to yourself."

She laughed before promising to get on it.

After hanging up, I strode over to Sean, darted in front of him, and snatched up the ball. "Your dad and I had a chat."

Sean glanced at Nathan before looking back at me.

"You could try talking to me yourself," I said. "I have to find out from your dad that being around you has put me in danger.

And now I have to find out from him that *you* want me to take precautions. Why aren't *you* telling me these things, Sean?"

"You wouldn't have listened if they came from me." When I didn't respond, he asked, "Would you?"

"No," I said, tucking the ball beneath my elbow, "but that's beside the point. If you want me to stick around, I expect you to try. Then, even if your dad has to come along and make me see sense, at least I'll have heard it from you first."

"Okay, I'm sorry." He ran his hands over his head. "Okay, now?"

"No."

His hands rested on his hips as he frowned at me.

I'd had time to think while on the phone to Jess. "You want me to adhere to rules, take precautions? Well, I have some of my own."

He looked over at his dad as if to say, 'you never mentioned this'. When Nathan shrugged, he turned back to me. "Go on."

"Okay, when you leave the house, I want to know exactly where you're going and who with, and I want to know the time you'll be leaving and when I should expect you back." He held up his hand, went to speak, but I talked over him. "Whenever you leave the house, I expect you to have your mobile with you at all times, so I never have to worry because I can't get hold of you, and if you're in any kind of trouble, I expect you to call me immediately."

The laughter built in Nathan's chest as I repeated the demands he'd spoken to me earlier.

Sean's face screwed up in confusion. "What?"

"Because ..." I threw the ball back to him, which he dropped. "... if I'm a potential target, then so are you. There is just as much chance of people going through you to get to me. You're not the only one scared of what could happen if any of this gets out."

"I'm not afraid for me, Jem. I'm afraid for you."

"Then, you're an idiot. Don't dismiss the possibility of my words, because it could happen just as easily as what you're afraid of. Plus, if you don't agree, neither will I."

He glanced around at everyone, frustration at my demands showing in the rubbing of his hair and scrunched brow.

"You know, she may actually have a point, Sean," Ethan said. "You've as much chance of being a target."

"They wouldn't get to me that easily," Sean snapped.

"Doesn't mean they wouldn't try."

"Take it or leave it." I turned to walk away. "But it's my only offer."

It took only three steps for him to agree. "Okay, I'll do it."

I spun back. "Do you promise?"

"I promise."

"Are you coming to play ball, now, Jem?" Kyle asked.

I scoffed out a laugh. "Basketball is one thing. If I play rugby with you lot, you'll flatten me."

"Come on, we promise to play nice."

WHILE RUNNING AROUND THE GARDEN, with five men big enough to break bones if they fell on me, I laughed my head off. If any of them were on the ground, I leaped over; if they got in my way, I ran around them, or, at one point, crawled through their legs; and if I looked in danger of being landed on, Sean or Ethan dragged me out of the way. I had easily as much fun as the basketball game, maybe even more so, thanks to Sean's presence.

Out of breath from a full sprint, I dropped to the grass, the cool tendrils tickling the back of my calves as I slapped them down. My chest heaved in its ragged rise and fall. Within the space of two days, I'd surprised myself with my ability to even remotely keep up with everyone else.

"Get up, Jem," Daniel called. "If you stay there, you'll get crushed."

"Yeah, like this." With a roar, Sean threw himself on top of me.

My scream quickly turned to laughter when his thrown-out arms saved me from his weight. Rolling onto my stomach, feet pressing into the grass, I pushed myself from under him. He didn't allow me to go far before pulling me back. Trying again while laughing, I scrambled away. Once more, his hands grasped my hips, drew my body back beneath his.

I grinned up at him. "More reconstructions, Sean?"

He chuckled, his excitement lending lightness to his darkening eyes.

In a last, half-hearted attempt, I wriggled my body backward, watching him as my hips shimmied from side to side. I thought I'd succeeded—until he yanked me down by my thighs, leaving my legs no choice but to go either side of his.

When he pressed his lips to mine, my eyes remained on his, my body instantly responding. He went to pull away, but my hands darted up to prevent him. As his sweet breaths filled me, my eyes closed, and my legs hooked around to ensnare. The purity of his scent so near sent a shot of arousal coursing through me. Never before had I smelled such strong muskiness —it oozed from his every pore—and my body shuddered beneath the greed of my inhalation.

"Jem." His whispered voice arrived deeper than ever, and I half-opened my eyes to the darkness of his. "You're frustrating the hell out of me." When I stared at him, my own frustration bubbling to the surface, he added, "We can't continue this here."

He glanced over his shoulder, and I followed his gaze. It had taken less than a moment for Sean to render me oblivious to our surroundings—as well as our captive audience. Each one of the pack held expression in their eyes that could only be construed as hunger.

I pulled Sean's head down, placed my lips to his ear. "Why are they all staring at me like that?"

"They can smell you." At my frown, he smiled. "They smell your arousal."

My eyes widened. My cheeks heated.

"Any fluids secreted from your body reach our senses," he whispered.

"Maybe we should leave."

"That's exactly what I was thinking."

On our feet, he took my hand and tugged me toward the Porsche under the scrutiny of the others. "We'll see you at home. Don't rush back," he called before we climbed in, and as he started the engine and spun us away, the tyres kicked up a cloud of dust like a final slap in the face.

THE DELAY of the journey increased our frustration. As soon as the car stopped, we leaped out, Sean locking it with the remote as we jogged. Kissing me at the door, he fumbled blindly, dropping the keys twice and cursing between laughter, until we were inside. We fell over as we reached the stairs, our hands already attempting to undress each other. In the end, Sean lifted me and raced up the steps.

"Bathroom," I breathed.

He ran with me down the landing, threw open the bathroom door, and strode over to switch on the shower. Less than a minute later, my clothes lay in a heap on the floor. As soon as his had joined them, his hands grasped my rear, and he took us inside beneath the warm spray.

Setting me back on my feet, Sean foamed up the shower gel

before trailing the bath-rose across my body, his lips meeting mine whenever close. His tongue tasted the willing flesh of my breast, as his hands washed my thighs, slipping around to my bottom. With the sensual therapy of his mouth over my nipple, shivers clenched at my stomach, shooting downward, until the tremble claiming my legs forced me to grip tight to his shoulders. Even once he switched to washing himself, his tongue continued to dance over me, before his hands reclaimed their grasp and he lifted me once more.

My back hit the cool smoothness of tiles, and I shuddered as the chill marked me with goose bumps. Letting the heat of the spray wash them away, I wove my fingers into his dark hair and led his mouth to my own. As he lowered my body, his hips pushing up as he slid me over his length, my lips opened on a cry. A tilt of my face exposed my throat, and soft gasps filled the air with each thrust.

Our pulses throbbed as he swelled within me. Bringing his face to mine, our hungered mouths searched for more, until, soul completely consumed by him, everything else around me no longer existed. As heat washed through me, as spikes of pleasure pierced through every part of me, all I saw was him: deep passion burning from his eyes, drowning me in their blackness. All I *felt* was him: hands that grasped me with urgency, lips that caressed with contrasting tenderness. With the swell of him bringing me closer to our destination, all I tasted, smelled, was *him*.

My body contracted, and he rocked faster, my head thrown back to free my heightening cries. Arching into him, my orgasm soaring higher, heat licked through my limbs, my stomach, through every inch of my body—until my moan of release filled the small space.

His body trembled against mine, as he drove harder. With each demanding thrust, his low growls and deep guttural grunts echoed off glass. After one final, shuddering drive of his hips, he sank us to his knees, bodies entwined.

His face burrowed into the sodden hair around my neck. Water flowed freely, pooling around us, and our hearts beat out a tune so frantic, I wondered if they could ever return to normal. A few minutes passed with our bodies' music the only sound, before Sean's voice vibrated against my flesh. "That one was *not* in the dreams." He chuckled, the deep sound rumbling along my spine, and I let out a small laugh.

Leaving my throat, he stared so deeply into me he could have been searching for my soul. My lips, cheeks, nose, jaw, were feathered with his delicate affection before he returned his gaze to mine. "I love you so much, Jem," he murmured. "Promise me you'll stay safe."

"I promise," I whispered.

When he finally carried me from the bathroom, he turned into his bedroom. I didn't say anything about his choice of room, didn't care so long as we weren't apart. Wrapped tightly around one another, we remained until too exhausted to stay awake.

Chapter 31

Although I'd encouraged Sean to return to his responsibilities, my chest ached as I stood on the doorstep Monday morning. His arms held me close, my feet hovering above the tiles, his nose burrowed into my hair, while Ethan's truck rumbled upon the driveway where they sat waiting for him.

The honking of the horn finally had him pulling away. After a drawn-out kiss as my goodbye, I watched his slow steps to the other pickup, the reluctant climb in, the rough rub of his head before the engine growled to life. With a satisfied nod, Ethan rolled his vehicle down the driveway and disappeared out the gates.

Sean should have followed, yet eyes fixed on mine, his rigid arms stretched to the steering wheel, he didn't move.

After five minutes of neither of us looking away, the return of Ethan and his dad came as no surprise. Nathan shook his head as he switched trucks. He urged Sean to the passenger seat and climbed behind the wheel to take control, steering him away out of sight.

Alone, I closed the door, locking it like Nathan commanded, and the first tears dampened my cheeks.

A chastisement along the lines of *bloody fool* echoed in my head. He'd only be gone for the day—and Nathan had even made noise about allowing him earlier finishes for the first few days, until accustomed to being away from me.

Still, my tears didn't stop, and I considered curling beneath Sean's duvet to sniff his scent lingering there. Instead, I went into the lilac room. Although certain the room had been decorated in preparation for my arrival, and intentionally mine, I could no longer think of it that way, not since sharing Sean's bed. I smiled at the mess in there—a result of our antics the morning before. Deciding to do something constructive with my day, I went in search of a vacuum.

After clearing the mattress, I shook off the duvet, cleaned the sprinkling of dead grass from the floor, and made the bed. In Sean's room, I did the same—though rather than straighten the bedding, in memory of our duvet rolling, I left it in a crumpled heap in the middle of the bed.

Being occupied seemed to hold my tears at bay, so I pushed opened the doors to Ethan's and Nathan's rooms and gave theirs the same treatment. By lunchtime, upstairs was spotless, and I lifted the vacuum to haul it downstairs—but at footsteps in the kitchen, I jolted, and the vacuum slipped from my grasp, tumbling to the hallway with a blast that shouted 'Here I am'.

I froze in place.

"*Shit!*" Scuffling feet came my way. "Jem?"

When Sean and Ethan came into view, I breathed out my relief. "I'm here."

"Are you okay?" Sean asked.

"I didn't expect you back ... you"—I felt an idiot—"startled me."

"I told you we should ring first," Sean growled at his brother. "'*No*,' you said, '*she'll like the surprise.*'"

"Sorry." Ethan shrugged. "I wasn't thinking."

"It's okay. I just ... it's a nice surprise."

Completing my descent, I righted the fallen vacuum. Reaching to correct it at the same time, Sean looked at it for a few seconds before turning to me.

"Are you doing housework?"

I opted to nod and shrug rather than say, '*Well, duh!*'

"You're not here to clean up after us."

"There was still grass all over the bedroom, so I vacuumed."

"Oh."

"But then I did the other rooms, too." I shrugged again.

"You shouldn't feel the need—"

"I needed something to do, Sean. I'll go out of my mind if I just sit here all day. I did it because I wanted to, not because I had to." When I he didn't argue further, I asked, "So, are you all coming back for lunch?"

"Nope, just the two of us."

Ethan grinned. "I got the decent end of the stick by being sent on chaperone duty."

"Chaperone duty?"

"Because something told us, if we allowed Sean home alone, we wouldn't see him for the rest of the day. I'm here to ensure he doesn't get sidetracked."

I couldn't help but smile.

WE ATE in the kitchen until the time came for them to head back to work. Ethan allowed us an extremely tame kiss before shoving Sean out the door and into the cab of the pickup.

Once again, the house became too quiet, so the vacuum went back on, and I cleaned up the living room. Moving onto the kitchen, I unloaded the dishwasher, cleaned the already spotless work surfaces. Still unwilling to face more time spent uselessly, I hunted in the fridge for something to cook.

I took a painstakingly slow time to peel and chop vegetables, slice steak into cubes, and throw it all into the biggest pot I'd ever laid eyes on. Then I over-cleansed everything I'd used, every surface touched.

Back at the sink, I stood at the window and peered up toward the sky, where the clouds approached at a brisk pace. I didn't last long before my gaze dropped to the basketball. As it beckoned me from the centre of the lawn, I could almost hear the spoken plea of the weekend: '*Come and play, Jem.*'

Before doing anything hasty, I went back over Nathan's ground rules. Had he said I should stay *at* the house, or *in* the house? Once certain the garden wasn't out of bounds—that the rules had only been made for if I went out somewhere—I raced upstairs to tug on my trainers.

Excited by the pull of the ball on my return, I ran halfway down the stairs and jumped the rest, laughing as I landed on all fours. Finding the back door unlocked after the boy's departure only convinced me further that going out would be okay, and, yanking it open, I jogged out.

Closing in on the heavy ball, I scooped it up, bouncing it as I continued to move, the stippled surface sliding easily against my palm. My need for physical activity since arriving with the pack —almost a want—still eluded me, but while I had the ball in my hand, and my feet kept moving, I didn't care about the sheen of sweat bubbling to the surface of my skin, or that my breathing arrived loud enough to block all other sounds, or that each pounding step sent small jolts shooting through my dormant muscles. I didn't care because I'd never been so free. Since arriving, the outside world could cease to exist, and I'd be none the wiser.

I raced the width of the garden toward the far wall, bouncing and scooping. When near enough, I bent at the knees, dived up. My feet departed the ground, and I brought the ball to my shoulder, thrust it upward, eyes on the hoop above. The ball left the security of my fingers to fly high before swooping back down through the goal.

My knees dipped to absorb my landing, and I jumped in the air, clapping at my first independent score. With the prize back in my clutches, I raced toward the other goal, picking up speed the nearer I got. As I flung my body up, I released the ball in an upward shove, and as I landed back on the grass with a grunt, I flung out my hands for the ball.

Except, it didn't arrive. With a singular bounce upon the wall, it disappeared over the other side.

I stared at the spot I'd last seen the sphere like I expected it to reappear. When it didn't, I glanced behind like it should materialise upon the grass. Hands on hips, I stood for minutes, before it sank in that I'd just have to fetch the darn thing.

With a huff, I walked to the end of the garden until I reached the archway and passed beneath. My eyes took a quick scan of the forest, and as I turned the corner to walk along the far side of the brick structure, I spotted the ball ahead, tangled within the confines of a thick bramble. Striding toward it, I tried to retain eye contact with what I'd been so desperate to retrieve, yet my eyes insisted on flickering to the shelter of the trees.

Each time I glanced that way, the forest became darker with clouds shifting overhead. As I reached the ball and plucked it from its captor, the first drops fell. I barely retreated more than a few steps before the heavens opened to shower me in a torrent of rain, and I darted beneath the leafy shelter, using the cover to make my way back. When I reached the section visible through the arches, the rain hadn't lessened, and the glances I shot behind me to the forest increased.

Until I could resist no longer.

For reasons unknown to anything but my subconscious, I removed my shoes, placed them on the ground beside the ball, and a second later, I entered the forest.

Branches and leaves trembled beneath the weighted pummels of the downpour, masking all other sounds. As though enfolded within my own personal bubble of calm, I swept my gaze over my surroundings, and allowing the alluring pull to call me forth, I walked on without pause.

As though content with the depth to which I'd submerged, I halted beside an oak. Knotted bark scratched at my fingers as I traced the etched outlines created by time and elements. In an urge to connect, I pressed my cheek to it, coarseness grazing my flesh as I lowered my lids and inhaled.

The natural aromas of the forest filtered through the rain-cleansed air, and a deeper inhalation brought an olfactory delight of earthy, woody, pure, fruity scents, all of them filling me to the core.

As though entranced by a higher power, my eyes flew open, and I pushed from the safety of my embrace, breaking into a run. My legs pumped as my feet flew forward. The pace seemed out of my control as I weaved, ducked, leaped, coursing my way through like a powerful force—until a quiet gasp brought my flight to a stop.

My feet slewed to the side, the sudden halt flinging my body forward, and I slid along the ground through un-dried patches of mud and fallen bark. My breaths came heavy, their distortion of my hearing an irritation. Slowing them, I took one deep breath, and on an inhalation, a beautiful muskiness consumed me.

Drawn to my feet, I pushed forward to follow my nose, then my hearing at the rustle of a bush. I tiptoed ahead and peered around it. Beyond, hairs pushed through pores, until a thick, chocolate brown coat claimed stake to a body crouched low.

"Sean," I whispered.

Tingling spread through my limbs, and a smile coated my lips. Rather than fearing the pain I knew would follow, my body embraced an imminent change of its own.

I HAD no idea how long I chased the darting brown tail through the trees. As I ran, in my wolf form, laughter rolled through my mind at the thrill of the chase, though no such sounds escaped. With Sean, I raced, dashed, played, tumbled for what seemed like hours before I collapsed to the forest floor, where I lay with moist soil and twigs pressed against my stomach, excitement pulsing through my body.

"Jem!"

Closing my eyes, I drank in the music of the forest.

"Jem!"

The outstretch of my paws left track marks through the soil.

"Jem!"

I blinked at the alien voice. It hadn't been Sean's, yet nobody besides the two of us had been present.

"Jem!"

"Jem!"

The forest filled with shouts and pounding footsteps. My paws sheltered my head against the intrusion.

"Jem?"

The voice appeared closer. As a shadow cloaked me, the vast outline of a man blocked my unfocussed sight.

"She's here!" The shout rang out from the shadow, as it knelt beside me. Gently nudging, hands slid beneath my body.

Turning to the shadow, I let out a growl, and the hands released me.

I recognised Josh's voice, as he called out, "Sean!"

When more running feet fast approached, I considered plotting an escape route but stood my ground. Though, as more shadows appeared to steal my light, I backed up—before falling with a loud gasp onto my face.

"Shit." Though I recognised Sean's voice, I couldn't see him. "Jem?"

Hands rolled my body over, releasing my mouth from the suction of mud, and I drank in air as I lifted my lids. Dark images swam before my eyes until blinking cleared them into bodies. I frowned in confusion, more so when I looked down to discover myself human and fully clothed. How could that be?

Pushing up, I raised my face to the panicked features before me. "Sean?"

He pulled me to my knees, his hands, his eyes skimming over my body. "What happened?"

"We went for a run." A smile formed at the memory.

He frowned. "We ... who?"

"We did."

Confusion clouded his eyes. "What are you doing in the forest?"

I shrugged. "My head wanted to come in, so my body followed, I guess. But then I saw you changing, so I changed and went for a run with you." My lips tugged into a grin.

"What's she talking about?"

I glanced up at Daniel's voice, but blinked on finding the entire pack staring at me like I was a weirdo—which, according to Jess, pretty much summed me up.

Not Sean, though. "Did you have some kind of vision again?"

Vision? I shook my head, but it held little force as I gave his words credence. Had none of it been real? As I pushed up to stand, Sean reached out to help, and the eyes of the pack followed my every move.

Josh took a step forward. "But, you bloody growled at me."

When my frown moved back in, he added, "When I tried to lift you, you growled at me, Jem."

"Maybe I didn't want to be disturbed," was all I could think of to say.

"What the hell were you doing in the forest in the first place?" Nathan said, pointing at me. "You promised to stay in the house."

"Not true. You never told me I had to stay indoors. And I only went out to play ball, anyway, but it went too high and bounced over the wall, and then I was upset because I was enjoying myself, so I went to fetch it." I paused for breath. "But when I got the ball, it started to pour, so I stepped into the trees, just for a second, and—"

"You went inside the forest," Nathan finished.

"Yes." I smiled, though nobody gave one in return.

"You promised to stay safe," Nathan said in a low voice.

"Yes, I know."

"Coming into the forest, and getting lost so deeply in, does not qualify as staying safe."

"But ... that wasn't my fault."

Nathan's voice grew deeper, his eyes darker. "Do you have any idea how we felt when we got back to find you gone?"

I thought they were making a big fuss over nothing. My frown must have told them as such.

Nathan snapped first. "We get back and you're not there ..."

"... when Nathan calls to say you're missing ..."

"Your mobile on the floor outside ..."

"Thought we were too late ..."

One shout merged into another. Faces, mingled with fear and relieved anger, crowded me, until I backed away, one step, two, three.

My hands formed fists at my sides. "Stop shouting at me."

The yelling continued. "... shoes in the forest ... just left ..."

"... searching for ages ..."

Lifting my fisted hands, I held them in front of me, but the pack seemed to move closer and closer with each shout. I covered my ears, closing my eyes as the pounding of my heart beat out my escalating frustration.

"Do you have any idea how terrified I was?" Sean growled.

"Stop *shouting* at me!" My arms swung wide, jerking my body forward with the outburst.

Ears ringing in the sudden silence, I looked up, with ragged breaths, to seven wide-eyed stares.

Sean took a small step. "Jem?"

Focusing on him relaxed me. "I ... I'm sorry," I whispered.

Taking another step, Sean reached out. Did he mean to comfort or restrain?

Confusion at my surfacing fury, and frustration with my inability to control my dreams or visions, crept back in, while my outburst, the amount of fuel in it, and the unexpected violence brewing beneath the surface left me unnerved. My shaking hands lifted to cover my face as I dropped to my knees. "I'm sorry. It's just ... you were all ... please, don't shout at me like that ..."

"Jem, I'm sorry." Sean knelt before me, and his arms scooped beneath my body. "It's okay. Let's get you home." As he lifted me from the ground, I curled into his chest and closed my eyes against the aftermath of my eruption.

Sean carried me most of the way back before I insisted I could walk. Even once he'd lowered me, his arms held me secure, like he suspected I'd break down again any moment. Only when we parted with Connor and his sons did I realise just how far into the forest I'd gone, and it seemed like forever before we dipped beneath the arches.

By the time I trod over lawn, my confusion, my frustration had all dissipated to be replaced by shame—because I couldn't believe the way I'd spoken to them all, or my inconsideration for a game of ball.

Upon entering the house, the smell of forgotten stew hit me. Luckily, it hadn't spoiled, and as I hunted for stock to add, the three men took seats at the table, quietly watched me. Once satisfied with the taste, I gave them a bowl each, allowing them all a brief glance. "Dinner," I said, bringing the stew to the table.

I pulled out my chair and sat, waiting for one of them to say or do something. When none moved, I reached for the ladle. "I'm sorry," I said.

Following my cue, the men helped themselves to the food.

"I was going stir-crazy in the house," I added.

They spooned up one mouthful after another, but none of them spoke.

"You didn't say I couldn't go outside, Nathan."

I pushed back from the table and went in search of bread. Bringing the packet back to the table with me, I helped myself to a slice, placing the rest down for the others. My gaze flicked to Sean. "How long did you think it would be before I'd want to go in there? You must have considered intrigue would get the better of me, sooner or later."

"You should have taken your phone, Jem. I panicked when you didn't answer."

"I had it in my pocket. It must have fallen out."

He nodded. "How did the vision come on?"

"It just ... I was walking, and then it was like I wasn't controlling it anymore—like *it* controlled *me*." I shrugged.

"This is the second time you've had one like this."

"I know."

"Maybe you should stay out of the forest."

My hand paused mid-lift. "But I liked it in the forest. I *want* to go back in."

Sighing, he put his spoon down and rubbed at his face, like everything about my behaviour had left him weary.

"Can't we make ground rules where the forest is concerned?" I asked. "I want to go back, Sean. You have no idea how it felt being in there."

His lips curved in a half-smile. "Actually, I do. But ... if other wolves visit, through the forest is the route they usually arrive by, Jem."

Ignoring the thud in my chest, I glanced at Nathan and Ethan. "How can I expect to learn to take care of myself if I'm never allowed to do anything?"

Nathan stared at me for a long moment. "Leave it with me." He gave a small nod. "I'll think of something, Jem."

Chapter 32

The next morning, before work, the three men called me to follow them out to the forest, where Nathan brought us to a halt just within the border. "Okay, Jem, this is my offer of compromise. Sean isn't ecstatic over it, but it's better than leaving you to your own devices."

I glanced at Sean before gesturing Nathan to go on.

"You are not to go into the forest ..." As I stiffened to protest, he held up a finger. "You are not to go into the forest *without* first calling one of us, to ensure we're on our way home. So, you can only go in at the end of the day, or if we're returning for lunch. That way, you won't be in here long, and we'll come and find you. You with me so far?"

My lips curved. "Yes."

"You must take your mobile with you and double check you still have it before entering." He drew it from his pocket and handed it to me. "Miraculously, it still works."

"Okay." I tucked it into my shorts.

"You'll see I've marked a path on the trees. If you lose your way, all you need to do is look for the trunks with blue chalk marks. Their path, the safest one, leads from our garden to Connor's. It doesn't matter which way you follow it, you'll end up somewhere safe. Still following?"

I almost grinned. "Yes."

"This," he said, handing me a key, "is to Connor's house. If you reach there, I expect you to let one of us know."

"Okay." I placed it in the pocket with my phone.

"Lastly,"—he smiled—"you're now on hourly check-ups. If we call, and you don't answer, this arrangement is off."

"I'll answer."

After assuring me someone would be home at lunchtime to check on me, they escorted me indoors and left for work. I pulled my phone from my pocket, intent on calling Poppy, but started when it rang in my hand.

I frowned as I answered. "Sean, you've been gone ten minutes."

"Where are you, Jem?"

I half-laughed. "I'm in the house."

"Okay." He sighed.

"Were you trying to catch me out?"

"Maybe," he said. "But you know these precautions are only because I love you so much, don't you?"

"Yes, I know."

"What are you doing now?"

I smiled. "I'm talking to you on the phone."

"I mean, afterward."

"I'm going to call Poppy. I haven't called her since Sunday. She might be worried."

"Okay ... well, I'll try and come home at lunchtime."

"That would be good."

After bidding farewell, I rang Poppy.

"Hey, sweetie," she said.

"Poppy, are we still shopping on Thursday?"

"I'd love to. I haven't seen you in so long, I've almost forgotten how you look."

I laughed. "Don't exaggerate. You saw me Friday."

"I know, but it seems longer. So, how are we going to get there with no wheels—because you know Jase uses ours for work in the week. I take it you have a plan?"

"Not yet, but I'm working on it. Nathan said he'd loan me a car if I need to go out."

"Nathan?"

"Sean's dad. He ... they don't want me using public transport."

"Why ever not?"

I'd forgotten I hadn't told Poppy anything of Nathan's words from the weekend. Not wishing to frighten her, I skirted around the truth a little and came up with a plausible story involving being able to get away from Peter. After promising to call before leaving on Thursday, I hung up, and with my feet dangling over the arm, I lounged back on the generous sofa, staring up at the ceiling.

Other than shooting hoops in the garden, which had led to trouble the day before, I hadn't anything to do. For minutes, my feet twirled to the sound of silence, until oblivion crept into my mind—so I didn't hear the invasion of arrivals at first.

Opening my eyes to Daniel and Kyle staring down at me, I almost jumped out of my skin. "Two days, now, I have been snuck up on by you goons coming home and creeping up on me," I grumbled, my voice thick and sluggy.

"How can we approach you otherwise when you're asleep?" Kyle asked. "Anyway, we're only here because you didn't answer your phone again."

"Huh?"

"Sean called like mad, and when there was no answer, he had us all fly back here to hunt for you."

"Way to make me sound like food," I muttered. "Besides, I never even heard the phone ringing."

"Well, I called, and called, and called," came Sean's voice from the other sofa.

I pushed up, peering around the standing men to where he sat on the other sofa.

Sean held his head in his hands. "This isn't going to work. It's driving me insane."

"She's got to have a life, Son," Nathan said from the kitchen.

Sean pushed to his feet. "I should quit."

"We've been through this, and you're not quitting. You and Jem will just have to get used to the routine of you working ..."

The discussion spilled over into lunch. Sean vocalised his unhappiness at leaving me. I agreed, but what other choice did we have? With the argument, discussion—whatever—unresolved, they went back to work, once again dragging Sean along with them.

Other than that, Tuesday continued without further problem. I didn't go into the forest. For some reason, that particular day, I didn't feel the urge. When Sean returned home to find me waiting for him where I should be, the relief in his eyes made me want to ensure I obeyed more often.

On Wednesday, I attempted to stay awake in order to receive Sean's calls. They were supposed to arrive every hour—however, his struggles to wait brought them sooner, with each call following the lines of:

"Hey, Jem, what you doing?"

"I'm in the house, awaiting the return of your handsome face."

Sean would chuckle, I'd giggle, and he'd ask if I'd had any more urges to go into the forest, to which I told him no. Then the phone calls concluded with pledges of love.

Over dinner that evening, I broached the topic of my proposed shopping trip with Poppy.

Sean chewed through his mouthful of chicken and potato, seemed to be mulling it over. "Tomorrow?" he asked, finally looking at me.

"You know Poppy and I get together on Thursdays."

"You want to go shopping?" More deliberated words.

"Yes. Can I? I could always get your groceries."

He peered away. "We get our shopping delivered."

"Okay, I won't get it, then, but can I go?"

"Let her get the shopping, if that's what she wants," Nathan said.

"So, I can go?"

Sean glared at his dad and turned back to me.

"Do you want me to tell Poppy I'm not allowed," I said, "so she asks for an explanation as to why?"

"No," he murmured. "You can go. Just ... be careful, okay?"

An hour after love making that night, our bodies remained close. Sean always seemed unwilling to let go, even once we settled in for the night.

"Can I ask you a question?" I whispered through the shadows.

His heavy lids half-covered his eyes but he nodded.

"Where's your mother? I mean, Kyle, and Daniel, Josh— their mother isn't around, either. I've been wondering about it."

His eyes fully opened. "It's complicated," he said after a couple of beats.

"So, you won't tell me?"

"It just means it's complicated. I'll tell you, if you're certain you want to know, but you won't like it."

My own fatigue stripped away in a flash. "I think I *should* know now you've said that."

He stared into me for moments. "My mother lives far enough away for her to be safe."

I tried to evaluate what that meant. Coming up empty, I asked, "Do you see her?"

Pain filled his eyes as he shook his head. "Dad sees her occasionally, but with heavy caution. He said it's too risky for anything more than that. She calls a few times each year—that's … all we get."

I brushed my lips over his. "Can I ask why?"

"Up until ten years ago, she lived here with us, as did Connor's wife with them." At the emotion in Sean's eyes, a chill spread through me. "Another pack, unable to get to us, waited until we weren't home. Our mum's were, though." He drew in a shuddering breath. "They went to Connor's first, mauled his wife. But she saw them coming and called here to send warning."

"So, they both knew what you all were?"

His head swished the pillow with his slow nod. "Dad always considered it better for them to be aware." He swept a loose hair back from my cheek before continuing. "Josh was only thirteen when they killed his mother. The next day, Dad sent Mum away. He's never told anyone where she is—not us, not even Connor."

"I'm so sorry, Sean."

"That's why we're all so cautious with you. We've already had someone important taken. We … *I* can't let that happen with you. So, go easy on me if I make you feel claustrophobic. Okay?"

"I'll try," I whispered.

"What about you?" he asked. "I know about Jess. But your mother? Where ... ?"

I shook my head as grief pained my chest. "Eighteen months ago. An aneurism."

"Jem, I'm—"

I touched a finger to his lips. "At least we have each other."

"We'll always have each other," he murmured.

DURING MY SECOND coffee the next morning, Sean slid his car keys across the table, along with a shopping list and money. I picked up the keys, turning them over in my hand. "These are the Porsche keys."

"I know."

"I can't drive the Porsche."

"Why not?" asked Ethan. "You managed my truck okay."

"I didn't have a choice. Besides, I wouldn't have hurt your truck if I crashed into something."

Nathan chuckled.

"You won't crash," Sean said. "You don't drive fast enough."

I scrunched my nose up at him before looking through the vast shopping list. "This won't all fit in the Porsche."

"Of course it will." Sean took the list and folded it, handing it back. "What time are you meeting Poppy?"

"I'm picking her up at ten."

"How long to the supermarket?"

"No longer than twenty minutes."

"What time will you be finished?"

"How would I know? Can I have some money for lunch?"

"Take it out of that." He indicated the roll in my hand. "I want you to call when you leave, and again after you've dropped Poppy off, okay?"

"What makes you think I'll get round the supermarket without *you* ringing *me*?"

"Jem?"

I rolled my eyes. "Yes, I'll call you."

As I PULLED up outside Poppy's house in Sean's sporty car, she danced out to me like an eager teenager. "Sweetie, we're shopping in style this week," she said, climbing in. "Now, show me what this baby can do."

I snorted out a laugh. "It does exactly the same speed as the Peugeot."

"Liar. I know it can go faster."

I slipped into gear. "Not with me behind the wheel."

HEADING for the supermarket doors with Poppy beside me, a reflection flashed past in the polished glass that had my feet jamming to a halt. Eyes narrowed, I rapid-peered behind.

Poppy stopped, too. "What's up?"

"Nothing." Pushing it aside with a roll of my shoulders, I carried on in.

List in hand, I shopped for the biggest eaters in the world—if the quantities were anything to go by—yet, I couldn't help but throw backward glances each time I turned a corner.

Poppy, ever observant, scrunched her eyes up as she studied me. "Jem, what's wrong?"

I shook my head—again. "It's nothing."

"Is Peter here?"

"Why would Peter be here, Pop? It's not like he'd follow."

She turned away, but I grabbed her arm and swung her back, and she sighed. "He followed me a couple times. Just to see if I'm visiting you, I think."

I stared at her. "Is he still calling at your house?"

She shrugged. "It's nothing to worry over."

I disagreed, but with her urge for us to continue, we tackled the rest of the aisles. By the time we reached the checkout, my trolley was so full, Poppy and I had to lean over to prevent the contents spilling out. Earlier concerns fast forgotten, we laughed like a couple of goons at how much food I had.

When we struggled with the weight of the trolley to the Porsche, Poppy laughed even harder. "You are *not* going to fit all this in that little thing."

"Don't worry about it, Pop." At the front of the car, I opened the boot lid.

Poppy laughed even louder when she saw the size of it, drawing attention with the racket as she pointed from the trolley of food to the tiny storage space. "Sweetie, really, that is *not* going in there."

Infected by her, I giggled. "Give me your bags."

"I'll get a taxi. You haven't even got room for yours."

Smiling, I took her bags to deposit in the Porsche's storage space, ignoring the amused and incredulous glances from anyone who passed. Finished, I gave her the empty trolley and pulled out my mobile.

It took two rings for Sean to answer, his voice sweet as honey. "Jem, are you having a good morning?"

"Listen, I know you're watching us make complete fools of ourselves, so get over here and make yourself useful."

Seconds later, as Poppy returned from the trolley bay, the black pickup drove to a stop beside the Porsche, with Sean laughing behind the wheel.

"You knew he was here, didn't you?" Poppy said.

"My personal stalker," I muttered, turning to Sean as he hopped from the cab. "You knew I'd have this problem with the

Porsche but made me take it so I couldn't be mad when you showed up with the pretence of helping out, didn't you?"

"I'm sorry, Jem."

"You could have just told me you'd be here."

"You would have been mad at me." He hoisted my bags into the back of the truck.

"No, I wouldn't. I would've understood perfectly."

"Sweetie, if you'd known he was coming, none of this would have been so funny to me." Poppy chuckled as she offered Sean some of the Poppy-love she reserved purely for people she adored.

With all the bags loaded, I started back for the store, until Poppy stalled me. "I forgot to say, I can't do lunch. Sorry, Jem, I meant to call you back the other day."

"I'll make you something at home," said Sean.

"Shouldn't you get to work?" I asked.

"I got out of it this morning by agreeing to feed everyone when they break at twelve. I'll have something ready for when you get back, okay?" He came in for a kiss, smiling as he pulled away. "Look after my car, Jem."

Back on Poppy's road, as though on alert, she scanned the street before relaxing back in her seat with a sigh.

I glanced her way. "What's up?"

"It's nothing, sweetie."

Drawing up to the kerb, I turned in my seat. "You were looking for someone while, at the same time, looking like you hoped not to see them."

"It's nothing."

"Has this got something to do with how quickly you came out? And, now I think of it, you telling me to drive fast?" I gave her my best 'Poppy look'.

"Really, it's nothing for you to worry about."

My eyes narrowed as it dawned. "You were looking for Peter." She didn't respond, but I continued, "How many times has he been here since the weekend—has he been upsetting you?"

She shrugged. "He's just Peter."

"Please tell me."

When she climbed from the car, I followed and helped her with her bags.

"He's been around a few times," she said. "Sometimes when Jase is here, sometimes not. He's resorting to threats, now, wants to know where you're staying. He doesn't believe me when I tell him I don't know."

Fury spread through me. "Has he hurt you, Pop?"

"No." She gave a small head shake. "He wouldn't dare."

"Has he been frightening you?"

Her unusual-for-Poppy demeanour told me he had. "He ... it's just intimidation tactics. Please don't—"

"That's it." I handed her bags over and stormed off. "Enough is enough."

"What are you doing?" she called.

I peered back as I opened my door. "I'm going to put a stop to this nonsense."

RACING Sean's GT3 around streets at a speed I'd never before achieved, my anger fired up. How dare Peter bully my friend that way? It'd been bad enough that I'd endured being beaten by him, but for my friend to be affected to the point of scanning her street on her way home was something else.

At the turning for the construction site, I squealed through the gate posts, flew over the speed bumps, and skidded to a stop. Everyone in the vicinity turned to stare, as I jumped from the car. "Peter!" I took a few steps farther in. "Peter! Get out here! Now!"

Within seconds, he appeared, marching over to me. Grabbing my arm, he went to tug me away, but I pulled loose.

"How dare you harass Poppy?"

He glanced around. "Keep your voice down, Jem."

The eyes of his workforce remained glued to us, their expressions seeming to fill with understanding as they glanced from me to the bright yellow Porsche.

"What is your problem?" I asked.

"My wife screwing around behind my back, *that's* my problem."

"I wasn't sleeping with him."

His eyes filled with rage as his gaze finally locked onto the Porsche.

"I was *not* sleeping with him." I took a step away.

He snatched at my arm, swung me round. "You do not walk away from me, Jem."

"Let ... go ... of my arm!"

He yanked me to him, jerking my body forward. If aware of everybody watching, he no longer seemed to care.

"I'm leaving now," I said. "But if you don't stay away from Poppy, I will make you so sorry."

"Why, Jem, what can you do?" he hissed into my face. "You're nothing but a dirty little whore."

I wrenched my arm free, but he grabbed for my throat. I didn't move, just stood with my temper pulsing through me.

"You're coming home, and you're coming home now," he said, his voice lowered.

"Actually, Peter, I left you, in case you hadn't noticed."

His hand shook me, bashing my teeth together, and my fists formed at my sides. "You *can't* leave me, Jem."

"If you ever go near Poppy again," I said, ignoring his threat,

"I'll put an injunction on you." Ringing trilled from my mobile inside the car. As I turned toward the sound, Peter whipped my head back to face him. "If you don't let go of me, Peter—"

"You'll what?" His lip curled.

One of his colleagues approached from his rear. "Hey, Peter, do you think this is wise?"

"Fuck off!" he snapped at him, before looking back at me.

Two more men stepped from the cabin. Though they paused when they saw us, they didn't intervene.

"I'm not coming back to you, Peter," I said, voice strained by his tightening grip.

"Why else would you be here, Jem?"

"Because I want a divorce."

His eyes widened at my words before narrowing. With a thrust of his arm, I flew backward and hit the gravelled ground, skidding to a halt a few feet from the car. Peter strode toward me with fire in his eyes.

Scrambling upright, I raced for the driver's door, where I reached inside to retrieve the steel bat. Turning back, I pointed to him with it. "You shouldn't come any closer."

He laughed, coming a few paces nearer. "You won't use that."

"Try me. I'm not coming home. I *want* a divorce."

"You'll get *nothing*, if you walk away."

"When I left last week, all I went with was disrespect and bruises. What could you possibly have that I'd want?"

My mobile began another tune. Neither of us moved.

"You'll get nothing, Jem. If I file, you'll be marked as an adulterer, and you won't get a penny. I'll prove you've never worked, never contributed. You won't even be entitled to half the house."

"Do it! I don't want a *thing* from you."

He took a step toward me, but a raise of the bat to my

shoulder halted him. "You're lying. You'll be sorry. You're *nothing* without me, Jem."

"I'm *everything* without you." My mobile rang again, but I didn't dare take my eyes from him.

"You're nothing but a cheating slut."

"And you're a wife-beating wanker. If you don't set the ball rolling within ten days, I will, and I'll make things difficult for you. I've got witnesses who'll testify what you did to me."

He seemed to absorb my words, and his eyes narrowed. "I need an address for you, then."

"Nice try." I almost laughed. "You can mail my letters, through the post, to Poppy's address." Backing away, I headed toward the car and my still-ringing mobile.

"What if I won't do it?" His voice carried only malice.

"Ten days, Peter." I rounded the door. "And stay the hell away from Poppy." I climbed in, started the engine, engaged reverse. At the sound of pattering across the paintwork, my head whipped up.

"Your fucking psycho boyfriend can have you!" Peter's screaming face held such ugliness, I wondered how I'd never spotted it sooner.

Bending, he scooped up more gravel, and as a new round of stones rained down over the car, red clouded my vision.

My hand shifted the gear into first, and I shot the car forward.

Eyes wide, Peter leaped aside.

I slammed my foot on the brake pedal, and as he pushed to his feet, I glared at him before changing gear and reversing out like a lunatic.

"Get the fuck back to work!" he shouted as I left the site.

. . .

Temper aflame, my chest heaved in my struggle to remain calm enough to drive through the incessant ringing of my mobile. After the fifth bout of trilling, I snatched it up. "I'm driving."

"Where the hell are you, Jem? You were meant to be back ages—"

I cut him off, unable to cope with the ranting of another man—even Sean. As the phone rang again, a twitch flickered beneath my right eye, and with barely controlled breaths, I hit the connect button. "I can't talk right now. I'm driving."

"What's happened?"

"I'll be home in ten minutes. I'll explain then."

He released a deep breath. "Ten minutes, Jem."

I hung up, but I'd heard his tone and knew he'd been going out of his mind.

As a result, the rest of the journey passed at stupid speeds. I looked to the radio, considered turning it on but feared it would only further agitate me. Goal in sight at last, I slowed the car, swung left through the gates, and finding myself confronted by everyone standing on the driveway, I hit the brakes and cut the engine.

Their eyes travelled over the vehicle, their expressions speaking volumes, as I climbed from the car. Expecting another round of shouting, I braced myself when Sean strode over, but instead he hugged me, squeezing so tight I could scarcely breathe.

"I'm okay." I cupped his face. "Nothing bad happened. I'm okay."

"Jesus, Jem, you're filthy. Not to mention you sounded about ready to beat the crap out of someone and my car looks like you took it off-roading ..."

I turned to the Porsche once Sean set me back on my feet. As well as the dirt and clay spattering it, scratches and chips covered the boot front. "Bastard!" I ran a finger over a scratch. "I'm sorry, Sean, about the car. I didn't think."

"Where have you been, Jem? I called and called."

"The phone was in the car. I heard it, but couldn't get to it, and then I daren't turn away, in case—"

"Where were you?" His eyes took on a deep ferocity as he studied my neck. "And who the hell did that to you?"

I pressed my fingers against where Peter had grabbed me. "I couldn't let it go on any longer."

"What are you talking about?"

"Bloody harassing Poppy. I won't have him treat my friends that way."

"What? Who?"

"Peter," I said. "He's been there every day, frightening her. I won't stand by and let that happen."

He frowned at me. "You went to see him."

"I had to."

He ran his fingers across the spot Peter must have marked. "Why would you go alone?"

"Because he needed to be told."

"About Poppy? I could have done that for you."

"No—well, yes, but ... I told him I wanted a divorce."

His eyes softened. "You asked Peter for a divorce?"

"No. I told him I *wanted* a divorce, and gave him ten days to contact his solicitor, or ..." I shrugged. "Then he got mad and threw stones at your car."

"No wonder," said Nathan.

"I'm sorry about the Porsche. I didn't know it'd get so dirty at the site, and I didn't know he'd throw stones at it."

"Site?"

"Where he works. It's a construction site."

"I'm surprised he didn't try flattening you," Sean said.

"Well, I think it did cross his mind, but ..." I pulled open the door and brought out the bat. "He changed his mind when he saw this. Nathan, this was an ingenious idea."

"You threatened Peter with a bat?" Ethan asked.

"He bloody pushed me over," I told them.

"Come on, Jem." Ethan slung his arm around my shoulder. "We've all been waiting for you to eat. You can tell us the details over lunch."

Chapter 33

Friday morning brought sunshine so intense the brightness woke me through the closed curtains at Sean's bedroom window. Swishing my arm across the bed, I found his spot vacant. "Sean?"

The house's soundless response suggested emptiness, and frowning, I pushed up. On spotting a note propped against the lamp on the side dresser, I peered at the words.

YOU LOOKED TOO GORGEOUS TO WAKE JEM
BACK FOR LUNCH AT 12
LOVE YOU
X

I smiled, glancing at the clock: ten thirty.

After wasting some minutes showering and dressing, I cleared the laundry and made sandwiches for lunch. Drawn by the brilliance of the day, I went out into the garden to wait, my face tilted and warmed by the sun's rays. Tugging out my mobile, I glanced at the time: eleven forty.

Sighing, I strolled toward the arches until stood at the far side, and leaning back against the brickwork, I peered into the trees. The almost magical appeal they'd held for me when I'd entered on Monday set up an immediate buzz through my veins.

Lifting out my phone, I hit the dial button.

"Jem?"

"Are you definitely coming home for lunch?"

"Yes."

"What time will you be here?"

"Maybe twenty minutes. We're running a little late, but should be leaving any minute. Why? What's up?"

"The forest is calling to me, Sean."

A moment of silence, then, "Can't you wait until I get back? I'll skip out this afternoon, come with you."

"Your dad wouldn't be happy." My head tilted to follow the whip of wings from deep within the trees. "If I go now, you'll be back before I go far. Then you can come search for me, pretend you can't find me, and we'll have some rough and tumble time before your dad yells at you to get back to work." His chuckle travelled down the phone line and sent tremors through my stomach. "Please ..."

"Jem ..." Uncertainty softened his tone.

"I'll make it up to you when you catch me."

His quiet laugh blew through. "Okay. But don't wander off the path, and don't go too far."

"Thank you, baby. I'll see you when you get here."

With a grin on my face, I stepped into the forest. Though the strong pull from within encouraged me to run as fast as possible, I ignored it, forcing myself to amble instead.

The forest allowed the light through only in dappled splotches, and, palms held up, I studied abstractive light and shade and the sequinned patterns they created across my fingers. The breeze swirling through to sway the ceiling of branches teased at my hair, and I reached out, feathered my fingers across every surface, my outstretched arms enabling me to take in the textures around me. With the occasional glimpse ascertaining my path, I closed my eyes and allowed my senses to guide me.

How long I walked, I didn't know. Time seemed irrelevant when enclosed by such natural beauty. However, when Sean still hadn't arrived, I re-checked the time: almost twelve twenty.

Positive he must be within the forest somewhere, I continued moving with ease along the path Nathan had marked. Tempted, once more, to give myself over to the enchantment, my lids verged on lowering, but I snapped them back open at a groan to my left.

Veering to follow the twist of my head, I crept over the dusty earth, faltering a step when a second groan, followed by another, came from the right of the first. On tip-toe, I went even closer—halting as a crouched body came into view, and a second, almost identical, to the right. Beneath the pulsing flesh, limbs twisted, and quiet grunts burst out, and I knew instantly they were in the beginnings of a change.

I took a half-step back, my mind working overtime as I considered if I could be in another vision, but rapid blinks producing the same visual told me otherwise. As I watched in fascination, both bodies pushed forth hairs of dark blond. *Josh and Daniel*—had to be.

Backing away until far enough to disguise my spying, I dialled Sean's number.

"I'm so sorry, Jem. There was a hold up, but I'm on my way now."

"Change of plan, anyway," I whispered.

"No, wait for me, Jem. I'll be there, ten minutes tops."

"We can't, the forest has already been claimed."

Silence, then, "What are you talking about?"

"Daniel and Josh have beaten us to it."

"No, they—"

"I've just seen them changing. It can't be anyone else with that colouring."

"Get out of there, Jem," he said over the roar of an engine, like he'd floored the accelerator.

"Sean, they won't hurt me."

"It's not them. They've only just left us to head home. They can't possibly have reached there." A second, mumbled voice cut through the increased pulse beneath my ear. "Yes, call them, double check," Sean said to whoever had spoken. "Jem, please tell me your legs are moving already."

I urged them into action. "If it's not them, then who?"

More background mumbling, then, "Jem, run!"

"But ..."

"It's not one of us in the forest. Get out of there!"

Snarls echoed around me, and I spun. The dark blond coat of a werewolf ruffled as the animal shook out of its change.

"Oh, no," I whispered.

"Jem?"

"He's through."

"We're back. Dad's taking over the phone while I come for you. I'll need to change, though, so please don't be afraid, okay?"

"Okay." I picked up speed.

"Jem?" Nathan voice replaced Sean's. "How fast can you run?"

"I ... don't know." My breaths already came shorter.

"How *fast*?" he said.

"Fast ... fast."

"Then do it!"

Kicking off, I pumped my legs and flung my arms into motion at my sides. My heart pounded against my chest as I flew through the trees, my frustration mounting at how far I'd come. Unable to resist, I twisted to the right to glance behind.

Two—no three wolves shared my path.

My body jerked, faltering my footing. I grunted when my knees hit dirt, threw out my hands to break my fall, sending my phone bouncing across the ground. Nathan's shouts cut through the earpiece, and I swiped it back up on my leap back to my feet, pushing off into another run as I pinned it to my ear.

"Jem?"

"Three ..." I gasped down frantic gulps of air. My throat burned. "Coming." Pain spread to my chest. Perspiration coated my face, trickling downwards to sting my eyes.

"Keep going, Jem," Nathan urged. "Don't stop."

My breaths, what little energy I had, couldn't be wasted on speech. I couldn't risk not having enough because the pursuing steps hit dirt at my rear—coming closer.

"Keep coming, Jem. You can't be far."

The forest edge entered my sights, lending me a surge of hope—but at two wolves cutting into my path ahead, bounding toward me, hope switched to alarm. My feet skidded, until I studied the advancing wolves—both dark; Sean and Ethan—and optimism returned. I headed for them, feet kicking up dust with each pummel, though, at the same time, I knew the ones at my rear were almost upon me.

With still metres to bridge, something clicked, penetrating the pounding of pulsing blood: a faint alteration in the breathing of the intruding wolves. Somehow realising they were about to be airborne, I dived forward and hit the ground in a skewed roll, landing with a slap on my back. A tilt back of my head showed one dark, one light wolf flying toward me, at the same time as my brain registered Sean and Ethan soaring above from the other direction. I scrambled to my feet, as snarls and roars filled the air, and spotted Nathan ahead by the arches. Terrified by what the battle crashes signified, but refusing to look behind, I lurched forward.

One raced step, followed by another then another, took me

nearer to Nathan—until a powerful force thudded between my shoulder blades.

The air whooshed from me in a loud gasp, as I flew forward, my face crashing into the dried soil and almost stealing my consciousness.

Shaking my head, I pushed up, freezing when a snarl vibrated against the back of my head. Hot breaths hit my shoulder, and my body stiffened further, like I believed remaining still would conceal me from him.

"Sean!" Nathan's yell broke through the din.

A howl broke out at my rear, piercing my ears with its nearness. My feet scrambled for traction, but I managed no more than a few feet before the weight of the wolf took me back down. My heart almost ceased to beat, until Sean smashed against my attacker and the burden disappeared. The wolf landed on his hide with a yelp.

Sean leaped back and, growling, pushed against me with his muzzle. My body wanted to react to the plea in his stare, but my brain struggled to signal the correct coordination. As each shift created another stumble, Sean raced to my other side and took my arm between his jaws. With each of his tugs, distress and despair conquered the beauty of his eyes.

Overcome by his need, I managed a slow crawl, guided by his cautious guiding. Behind me, Ethan's struggle to hold the other two wolves off arrived in the form of growls and clashes. I went to glance that way, but a snort from Sean drew me on—though at the arrival of new snarls, anxiety had me spinning anyway.

Four new wolves flanked Ethan, creating a barrier no wolf with common sense would cross. *The Larsens.* My withheld breath gushed out.

"Sean!"

My focus whipped back to Nathan. As he broke into a run

toward us, my limbs trembled in relief—short lived when movement behind Sean's head widened my eyes. I opened my mouth to blend my warning with those flying from Nathan, but Sean didn't stand a chance.

The blond wolf he'd knocked from me sprinted for him and smacked into his side. With a thunderous roar, he lifted Sean's body over mine.

My arm, still within Sean's insistent jaws, took me with them. The ground jolted up to meet me, as the wrenching of my arm hauled me forth. Upon release, I landed hard with a grunt upon the dirt, my gaze instantly following the path of the two fighting wolves.

Instinct kicking in, I crouched to leap forward, but with less than a metre covered, strong hands grasped my hips and dragged me back across the forest floor.

Ignorant to the scratches and scrapes marking my arms, I kicked back with my foot. "No!"

The flashing of fur and teeth filled my vision, as Sean and the wolf wrestled for dominance. Rips, tears and snarls buffeted my hearing.

As the wolf's jaws snapped at Sean's throat, I booted back again, propelling myself closer by only inches. "No!" Tears pooled in my eyes.

"Jem, come *on*!" Nathan snapped behind me.

I tried to thrust my weakened body forward. No matter how hard I kicked, or tried to scramble away, Nathan's strength expanded the gap between us and Sean. After one final attempt, the ground left me, as Nathan's arms circled my waist to haul me away again.

"Sean." The word hiccupped out on a sob.

"Jem, come on. He'll be alright. We need to get you out of here."

Tears blinded me, yet I knew when we reached the garden.

Nathan lowered us, and as my knees sank into the grass, I dropped forward. As soon as I did, burning coursed through my arm.

Jaw clenched against my gasps, I tried to ignore the pain, hoping it wasn't there—but the burning intensified.

Pulsations evolved into throbs, and my gasps increased into low mewling, as my flesh smarted until it stung. Blood, merged with thick yellow mucus, seeped out in a trail across my skin, and as a wave of agony blasted through me, my cry broke out.

"Jem." Nathan's distorted voice rattled around in my hearing.

Running paws thudded in time with the beat of my pulse.

The unfocused outlines of approaching wolves hit my blurred vision.

My hand tightened around my arm in the hope that constriction would alleviate the agony, but still, unbearable pain surged through me with the force of an inferno.

No longer able to fight off the inevitable, my mouth opened wide to allow passage to my scream as my body convulsed through the release of a tortured howl.

Chapter 34
DARKNESS

For an interminable length of time, my body flickered through fluctuating phases of consciousness and pain. From sleep to awake. From awareness to denial. From terror to peace. Alertness became suppression before soothing overcame burning. Uproar evaporated, to be replaced by serenity.

No light arrived during my hellish nightmare, only varying degrees of darkness.

When awake, I heard the muted voices as they soothed. Even though they appeared near, I could make no sense of the sounds, nor find meaning behind the words. Worse than that, my lips refused to respond. The only answers they received were my screams of agony and terror, my body's response to its undergoing alterations.

When asleep, I heard nothing. No voices. Nor did I hear my screams, my cries, my whimpers.

Awake, the unwelcome sensations ripped through me, as my body endured change after change—until I believed that to die would surely be a blessing, if only as a means of escape.

Asleep, my body repaired itself.

I'd no idea how long I lay there, trapped within a form I held no control over.

Awake, my tortured self writhed, twisted, contorted, deformed.

Only during sleep was I permitted to relax.

Each time I woke, I hoped for unconsciousness, for the blackness of oblivion to wash over me. After endless prayers for a way out of the darkness, at long last, there was only light.

Chapter 35
LIGHT

I pried my eyes open, despite the light stabbing my retinas, and attempted to lift my hand. As every muscle ached with intensity, a soft groan murmured past my lips, and before I'd even moved a few inches, the temptation to sink back under beckoned to me. When tested, my legs refused to move. In the hope of coaxing a more encouraging response, I clenched my toes, thankful for their compliance, before flexing my feet at the ankles.

Reaching up a hand to block the light, I tried to relax my body while tuning into sounds around me. My breaths puffed out a shallow tune. At the softness of other breaths, I listened for heartbeats, detecting two additional rhythms. One beat slow and steady, no anxiety to the pace, whereas the second slowly increased.

I inhaled, but wished I hadn't when assaulted by the unmistakable stenches of vomit and urine—odours I suspected I'd produced. Trying to sniff past the foulness, I gagged at the intake.

"Jem?" The soft swish of footsteps crossed the carpet, and the heartbeat increased further.

I didn't need a visual to confirm who approached. "Jo—"
Throat raw, my cracked lips couldn't form the sound.

Fingers took my arm in a gentle encouragement. As Josh
lifted it, I forced my eyes open, but closed them again at the
penetrating ache before opening them a second time.

"Sss—"

"He's sleeping just over there in the chair."

"Shh—" Needing to see him for myself, I tried to lift my
head.

"It's okay, Jem. He's fine," he said. "Nathan put sedatives in
his drink. He hasn't slept the whole time you've been ..."

Over-exposure to the light blurred my vision, and I rapid-
blinked, unwilling to lose sight of Josh—though the effort
seemed only to bring a new blast of acrid stench. "Smell." If I
didn't move soon, I'd be sick.

"We tried to clean it, get rid of it, but ..." He shrugged.

"Car ... nee ... was ..." My eyes filled in frustration.

"I can't, Jem," he said, like he understood. "You're naked. It
isn't right." He glanced at Sean as though hoping he'd ping
awake.

"Please."

"I'll, um ... Ethan's downstairs. I'll grab Ethan for you,
okay?"

He left the room, and I tracked his footsteps to the bathroom. The sound of washers releasing liquid emerged, followed
by the loud splashes of running water. His feet made their way
back across the landing, down the stairs, and disappeared
outside.

Seconds later, a heavier set ascended, and Ethan rounded
the doorframe. He crossed to me upon seeing my open eyes
focused on him. "Okay, Jem, let me get some things for you, and
we'll get you cleaned up." He left the room, returning with a
large bath sheet. "I just need to get this around you." He

reached under to cover me with it before pulling the duvet back and slipping his arms beneath me. "Okay, I've got you." He lifted me close to his body.

I tried to turn toward Sean, but Ethan angled to fit us through the doorway, blocking my view.

My brow creased as I twisted. "Sean."

"He's fine, Jem."

"Please."

Ethan backed up and turned.

Sean sat—slumped—so low in the chair, he held the danger of sliding to the floor. His head, bent at an uncomfortable angle, tucked his chin into his chest, and his slack mouth hung open. He'd spread his legs wide—likely the only reason he hadn't departed the seat—and planted his feet into the carpet's pile. His breaths and heartbeat had already informed me he was alive, but at the visual confirmation, and in finding barely a scratch upon him, I relaxed.

At my nod, Ethan carried me through to the bathroom. A potent odour hit me on entrance, stinging my eyes until my nose wrinkled. "Breathe through your mouth for a minute, Jem. It's just bath salts. They'll help with your muscle aches." After depositing me in the tub, he turned off the taps.

I'd never taken note before of the depth of the bath. From within, my eyes peered over the high sides while the water lapped my shoulders.

"You should get cleaned up, I guess." He took a step back, eyes on mine as though afraid to look elsewhere.

I forced my knees up to my chest, hoping he'd stay if I covered more of me—I didn't want to be alone.

Moving to the sink, Ethan filled one of the tumblers with water. I took it from him when offered and sipped, choking at the initial shock of cool liquid. The following sips came easier.

When I'd finished, I laid my cheek atop my raised knees. "Is he mad, Ethan?" It was a relief to find my voice returned, even if only a low raspy whisper.

Ethan's eyes darkened, as I'd seen Sean's do many times, and his teeth ground within his tightened jaw, as he gave a stiff nod.

"How angry is he?"

"He's bloody furious, Jem. We all are."

I'd known he'd be angry, had expected it, but having my suspicions confirmed hardened the blow. My lip trembled as my eyes pricked, and I turned my face down, leaving my tears to trickle between my compressed knees. Ethan didn't speak. Maybe he didn't know what to do with an emotional woman.

My body had been too numb to feel the ripples upon entering, but the longer I sat, the more feeling I regained. The water swished around me at the slightest movement, bringing comfort and soothing the aches throughout my body. Lifting my head, I raised my hand and rubbed at my tear-streaked face before stretching out my arms. The straightening of my legs encouraged those muscles to comply.

Ethan sat beside the bath the entire time, his head dipped low, hands between his knees.

"Can you get me some soap, please?" I asked.

He retrieved my own from the shower cubicle, turning away as he passed it to me. The fragrant shower gel smelled so much stronger than it had, inciting me to use as little as possible. At least my resulting odour outdid the stale stench of bodily fluids. Sliding down beneath the water, I allowed it to wash over my head. Emerged, I soaped up my hair before ducking low enough to coat my face with the tender flow. My lips parted as I surged up, drawing in oxygen.

"Can you get out?" Ethan asked.

I shrugged. How could I know without trying?

"I'll get more towels."

On his return, he stood to the side, a bath sheet spread wide in front of him, as he leaned in to grip my shoulders. He helped me to sit on the rim before lifting the towel in front of his face.

I frowned. "You get embarrassed around naked women often?"

"Only when the naked woman is someone I've come to think of as a sister, Jem." He wrapped the towel around me, and despite my situation, I smiled.

Feet planted on the floor, I pushed up and blew out a breath. My legs still shook, but I'd achieved an upright position on my own. Along the landing, I glanced in at a still sleeping Sean before turning into his room.

Ethan waited in the doorway while I rooted through Sean's drawers for T-shirt and shorts to pull on. Once decent enough to engage with others, I turned to him. "Food."

He chuckled for the first time since I'd woken. "Hungry, Jem?"

"You have no idea."

THE FRONT DOOR swung open as the egg-bearing fork journeyed toward my mouth, and I raised my eyes to Ethan, and to Josh, who'd studied my every move.

"I called them when you woke," Josh said. "Nathan wanted to come back and check on you."

Completing the eggs' transition, I aimed my eyes at the doorway to the hall.

"Jem!"

At Sean's cry from upstairs, I jerked, clattering the fork on my plate, and the footsteps inside the front door halted. My heart pounded as I glanced back at Ethan and Josh.

"Jem!" Footsteps raced through the house above me, thudding into every room.

Shaking my head at his furious shouts, I surged to my feet. As my chair crashed to the floor, Josh and Ethan stood, also.

"Jem!"

On awkward legs, I dived for the back door, but my mind baulked at resurfacing memories of the attack.

Clambering footsteps descended the stairs.

"Jem?" said Ethan behind me.

"Sean, calm down," Nathan said from the hall.

I spun, eyes darting for somewhere to hide. Only one avenue remained other than the garden, and I staggered across the room, yanked open the cellar door. My chest heaved as I sank down behind it, just as Sean entered the kitchen.

"Where is she?" I'd never heard him so angry, other than the day he met Peter. "Jem! Where is she?"

"You're frightening her," Josh said.

The room outside grew quiet, and I pressed my ear against the wood. Soft footsteps approached, a scuffle of feet.

"Jem?"

At the closeness of his voice, an urge to touch him overtook me, and I tugged at the handle to create a sliver through which to see him.

He sighed. "Jem."

"Sean, please don't be mad at me," I whispered. "I don't want—"

"What?" He frowned.

"I can't bear it if you shout at me ..."

"Jem, what? I'm not—"

"I'm so sorry." Tears dampened my cheeks, and his fingers slid around the gap of the door as though to prevent me closing it. "I shouldn't have gone in the forest. I knew you didn't want me to, but I wouldn't listen. And I knew you were trying to make me move, and my stupid, *stupid* legs wouldn't—"

"I'm not—"

"Please, don't be angry with me. Let *me* be angry with me."

He frowned, his eyes unreadable as he tugged at his hair. His hand pushed at the door, but I leaned against it. "Jem, please open the door."

I shook my head. "Not until you promise not to be mad."

"I'm not mad with you."

My head nodded.

"No, Jem ..."

I nodded again. "You are. I asked Ethan. He said you're all furious with me."

Sean's head snapped round to his brother.

"I never said that," Ethan said. "Jem, I never told you that."

"You did. I asked you upstairs. You said you were all bloody furious."

"I didn't mean *with you*." He stepped into view. "We're furious with *them* for doing this. And Sean's furious with himself for biting you ..."

"For biting me?"

Sean brushed a hand over his hair and nodded. "After promising I wouldn't, I went and did it, anyway."

"No." I shook my head. "No, you were protecting me. It was an accident."

"I should've been more careful."

"It wasn't your fault." I opened the door. "You saved me, Sean. If it wasn't for you, I'd be ..." I didn't finish the sentence, didn't want to imagine what could have happened, if they hadn't come when they did.

Sean reached for my hand as we stood to face each other. The grief and turmoil, which had claimed him seconds before, evaporated with his softening expression.

"I thought …" My voice threatened to break. "When he attacked you … I thought … aren't you …"

"I'm okay."

"You're not hurt?"

He shrugged. "One bite,"—he pointed to his shoulder—"couple scratches. They're healed now."

"How?" I tugged up his T-shirt to check. "How can they be healed already?"

"Jem, it's been a week."

I halted in my mauling and stared at him.

"You've been unconscious for a week." He watched me as he spoke.

My fingers reached up to trace the dark circles beneath his eyes. "No wonder you look so exhausted."

A small chuckle arrived from an angle invisible to me, and I peeked around the doorframe.

"You get chased and attacked by werewolves. You get bitten, and then try to leap back into harm's way just to save him"—Nathan pointed at Sean—"and now, after you've been through hell, all you're concerned about is how tired *he* looks? Jem, you're unbelievable, do you know that?"

Shrugging, I turned back to Sean. "Exactly what were you thinking, leaving your dad no choice but to sedate you?"

He aimed a glare at Josh and Ethan. "I didn't want to leave you, Jem."

"In case you hadn't noticed, I wasn't going anywhere."

"You might have needed me."

"And what good would you have been to me, dead on your feet?"

"Will you quit worrying about me? You're the important one right now."

"Come out of the cellar, Jem," Nathan said.

I didn't move—not for minutes. I knew everyone was there, heard the exact amount of heartbeats, smelled the seven separate scents. None of them overwhelmed me as Sean's did, but they were all there. Whether through curiosity or concern, it didn't matter. They were waiting—for me. The werewolf me. The one thing they'd tried to prevent happening, despite maybe a deeply buried yearning for it *to* happen—it had occurred anyway.

Sucking in a deep breath, I stepped out. To my left, Nathan's backside rested against the table, and Connor's bulky frame almost filled the hall doorway, where he leaned against the coving. Kyle stood behind Ethan's vacated seat, Josh sat back in his, Daniel to the right of the table, but Ethan hadn't moved from his spot.

My gaze travelled round the room until it fell back on Sean. *My* Sean.

Concern returned to his eyes, and his amazing musky scent embraced me as he held my hand.

I glanced down, my attention falling on the mark still visible from the bite. Without intent, he'd done a pretty good number on it. Even after a week, I could see where the flesh had torn as the pull of his flying body ripped me from his clutches.

At Sean's tightening hand, I removed my stare from the wound. "Fate and destiny go hand in hand." I sought his eyes as unfamiliar, yet familiar, words entered my mind. "It is impossible to change our destiny. Only the path upon which we walk to reach our destination alters. If we should stray from that path, fate will take control and guide us in the right direction." I blinked when my unusual speech drew to a close.

Everyone stared, even more so than before. Nathan's face held an expression of absolute smugness.

"Where did that come from?" Sean asked.

I shrugged before my smile curved my lips, and one step—just one—led me into his arms. Reaching up, my fingers found his hair, and I buried my face into his neck to inhale, as he nuzzled mine, my lids lowering as I shuddered. "You smell so good," I whispered.

"So do you, Jem," he said. "So do you."

Upon Sean's lap, with his arms holding me near, I ate a fresh plate of eggs with bacon. The biggest contrast between a usual mealtime and that one was that the speed at which I shoved in each mouthful almost matched everyone else's.

"Why a week?" I asked after minutes of quiet.

They all paused in their munching.

"Four days last time." I frowned as soon as the words came out.

Sean sat up straighter behind me. "Did you dream that?"

"No."

"Then, how—?"

"I've no idea."

"We think it took that long because of the hint of it you already had in your system," Nathan said. I opened my mouth to argue, but he cut in. "We know it was there—I've already told you we could smell it. Plus, your body reacted like you'd overdosed."

A frown crept across my brow.

"It was touch and go for the first few days."

I waited for further explanation, but none came. Maybe they thought it better for me not to know every detail.

When the plates were empty, everyone who'd left work to check on me headed back out—though not before I'd been squeezed, kissed, and—as though unable to resist—sniffed by each of them. In all fairness, I did plenty sniffing of my own. It seemed strange, after never noticing, how individual they smelled. Each held a distinctive aroma redolent of nature—woody, earthy—and definitely *wolfy*.

With the house quieted, my second attempt to study the garden came easier than my first, more so with Sean's chest supporting my back.

"You want to go out there?" he asked.

Shaking my head, I gazed for a few seconds more before the distinct ring of my mobile called out.

"That'll be Poppy," he murmured. "When you didn't call her, she rang. She's convinced something's going on."

"What did you tell her?"

"That you were ill in bed—didn't seem too far from the truth." The phone continued its shrill tune. "You should speak to her, Jem, convince her you're okay."

With a small nod, I headed into the living room and scooped up my phone from the coffee table. Flopping into the large armchair, I hit the answer button. "Hello?" My voice still held some of the earlier hoarseness.

"So, Poppy was told the truth. You *are* ill."

I frowned. "Jess?"

"Of course it's me. Who else?"

I opened my mouth, yet produced no sound.

"You sound wrong. Are you okay? Poppy's tried to call you for days, and then Sean wouldn't let her speak to you, said you were ill. Obviously, knowing what we both know, she went into panic mode. But her panic's unnecessary ... isn't it?"

My brain tried, and failed, to compose a response—like I wasn't yet alert enough to think on my feet. I glanced around the room, at Josh and Ethan lounging across the far sofa, at Sean with his eyes fixed on me.

"Isn't it?" Jess said.

Ethan straightened, leaning forward over his knees. Tapping his thigh, Josh gestured to me to say something.

"Flu," I managed, just as Sean looked about ready to take the phone away. "I had the flu, Jess."

The tension seemed to drain from three men.

"Flu does *not* make you bedbound for that many days," Jess snapped. "Who the hell are you trying to kid? This is *me* you're talking to. And, anyway, when was the last time you were ill? Can you tell me that? And since when did flu stop your mouth working?"

"I, um ..."

"He bit you, didn't he?"

"Don't be—"

"What? Stupid? Don't forget I know everything, Jem. I predicted most of what already happened to you, remember? Did you honestly think you could buy me off with some pathetic flu story?"

"I—"

"You've been bitten, haven't you?"

"Please don't, Jess."

"Tell me the *truth*!"

"I can't!" My chest heaved as I rose to face Sean. Fabric whispered as Ethan and Josh pushed to the edge of the sofa. The phone line fell silent. "Jess?"

"Did Sean do this to you?" Fury coated her quiet voice.

"It was an accident."

"How? He accidentally put his teeth around your body and just happened to accidentally press down at the same time?"

"It wasn't like that." My eyes never left Sean's. "He'd never hurt me. Sean was trying to protect me."

"With his *teeth*?"

I rubbed my hand across my face.

Jess sighed. "Protect you from what, Jem?"

Sean gave a slow headshake, but Jess had already figured out a lot on her own, and I didn't want her thinking it happened because Sean had a selfish urge to tie me more strongly to him.

I nodded to him before I spoke into the phone. "Other wolves knew I was here."

"Oh, shit!" she said. "What are you going to do?"

"I don't know. I need to get my head straight first."

"And the bite?"

"He was trying to move me, but he was attacked. It was an *accident*. Not his fault, Jess, do you understand? I wouldn't even be alive if it wasn't for Sean."

"Okay ... are you okay?"

"I'm fine—now."

"How long did it take?"

I knew what she referred to. We'd talked a lot about how long such a transformation might take for a body to process. "A week."

"Were you unconscious? For the whole week? Or ..."

"Not awake. More ... aware."

"Did it hurt?"

"Yes." Pain bled into Sean's eyes at my admittance.

"How much did it hurt?"

I stared at the phone. "Are you for real, Jess? I was in—" I clamped my lips shut.

The clench of Sean's hand, the frown that claimed his forehead told me he knew I'd been about to say 'agony'.

"You should call Poppy," Jess said. "She's really worried."

"What am I supposed to tell her?"

"Figure something out. She needs reassurance. Speak to her, let her know you're okay. Maybe it will be enough."

"Okay," I said.

We said goodbye, and I watched Sean as he watched me. His fingers reached out, tugged at my mess of hair.

"You weren't unconscious?"

"Not the whole time."

"Jem, I'm so sorry."

"It wasn't your fault," I told him.

I could see, though, it would take more than one day and a few words to convince him of that.

I DID CALL POPPY—HOWEVER, I didn't believe she accepted my flu story even though she let the subject drop. Like Jess, she came straight out and asked had Sean bitten me. I couldn't let Poppy know the truth. She'd have exploded with panic at the idea of other werewolves posing a threat. Although I knew she knew, I knew she didn't really want to admit what Sean and his family were—she wouldn't be prepared for the truth. Around dodging her questions, I persuaded her to believe I was okay— that Sean only ever wanted to protect me, so why would he hurt me? Begrudgingly, she let it drop and pretended she'd bought it.

That night, Sean promoted me back into the sapphire room, where I entertained him with a sweet enough reunion to convince him I didn't hold him responsible. "What happened to them?" I asked as we lay entwined in the dark. "The ones who came, Sean, what happened? If you're alive, then I—"

He sighed as though he knew the question was inevitable but would have preferred otherwise. "No, he's gone."

"Did you kill him?" I whispered.

"Yes."

His body tensed like he awaited my response. I didn't know what to say about it, though. Would it be wrong of me to be glad the other werewolf died, and not Sean, or me? "And the other two?" I asked, skimming over the subject.

"They bolted when the others arrived."

"Did you know them?"

"They weren't familiar to us, no."

"Others will come now."

"We don't know that. They might be selfish enough to keep this to themselves." I tried to suppress my shudder, yet failed, and Sean's arms tightened around me. "Don't worry, Jem. I'll never let you out of my sight. As long as I'm with you, you'll be safe."

Chapter 36

Not wishing to allow me out in public until ready, Connor's family came to us on Saturday. What they failed to tell me, though, was that 'ready' translated to 'after I'd had my first controlled change'.

Despite the light spitting of raindrops, which had fallen since before dawn, the boys intermittently went out into the garden to throw the ball around. If forced to stay indoors for too long, they paced the rooms as though caged. I knew how they felt—being trapped by the four walls drove me crazy, too.

Since awakening, my view of outside had consisted only of appraisals through windows. About two in the afternoon, after sending Sean out to bounce some rubber and free me from his shadowing, I urged my feet toward the French doors. On a deep breath, I tugged one open and stepped into the conservatory.

Following me, Nathan took a chair in the corner.

In the willow seat by the window, nose almost squished against the glass, I watched the men play. Even with my reluctance to go outside, and despite muscles which had cramped for most of the morning, the pull of excitement I'd experienced each time I played with them still enticed.

Kyle spotted me first, skidding to a halt with the ball. When a pursuing Connor almost collided into his back, I laughed, and they all turned, a smile spreading wide across Sean's face.

As if understanding they were the reason I'd gone out, they continued to play, even as the light pattering turned into heavier rain. I snorted when Daniel slipped and skidded across the wet grass, creating a pathway of exposed mud. The louder I laughed, the more idiotic they behaved. Within half an hour, I'd kicked my chair aside to stand, my hands pressed flat against the glass as my body leaned toward the fun.

I smiled over my shoulder at Nathan. "You'll end up with a mud bath at this rate."

"Grass grows back, Jem." He chuckled, but movement beneath the flesh of my shoulder snagged my attention.

Frowning at the rippling visible below the surface, I lifted my arms. Finding those rippled, also, my pulse lurched. "Nathan?"

He crossed to me and massaged my arms. "Your body will want to change soon."

"How can I change when I can't even bring myself to step outside?"

"Do it indoors, if you have to. It's not the end of the world."

My eyes narrowed beneath my frown. "Do you really think my body will be happy with that?"

He shrugged. "If it's all you have to offer, it will have to be enough."

Relaxing beneath Nathan's magic touch, I turned back to the garden to see a concerned Sean heading for us. I smiled to let him know I was okay. He paused for a second, seemed to debate coming anyway, but I gestured for him to go back and play.

"He's worried about you," Nathan said beside me. "He was heartbroken when he saw what he'd done."

"Not him, Nathan. *Them.*"

"That's what I tried to tell him. He wouldn't believe me, though."

"I'm not altogether sure he believes me, either."

"He will." He drew me to his side. "He'll forgive himself, eventually."

Drizzle coated the glass panes boxing us in. "How long do you think I have before I'll have no choice but to change?"

"Three days, maybe four. You should try and do it before then, or it may turn into an uncontrolled one. It will be harder for you that way."

I blew out a breath. "Three days to get my arse back out to the forest."

"You don't—"

I squeezed his hand. "I can do that."

"I'm certain you can."

"Do you fancy some fresh air?"

He smiled. "You know, Jem, I believe I do."

"Let's do it, then." I stepped to the door, placed my fingers around the handle.

The game outside almost came to a standstill, but I sensed Nathan's headshake encouraging them to return to their actions.

With Nathan's hand still in mine, I swung open the door and stepped outside for the first time in over a week. The increasing rain spatters refreshed my skin. My nostrils flared as I sucked in the cleanliness of the air. Dragging Nathan along like a child's security blanket, I reached the paving edge and sat, tucking my knees beneath my chin.

Nobody made a fuss about my presence, as I sat watching the boys in silence. They all behaved as though it were normal— me, sitting with Nathan, getting wetter by the second. By three thirty, my eyes settled upon the archway I knew Nathan had dragged me through. From there, they moved farther out, toward the edge of the forest.

At least I'd achieved step one: looking.

The ball sailed toward me, snapping me alert, and my hands shot up to protect my face. "Want to play, Jem?" Josh called.

Catching the ball, I rolled backward to land in a crouch. As I lifted my head, eyes darting as I tried to process how I'd so smoothly gone from one place to the next, seven broad smiles aimed my way. For a half-beat, I thought about playing. Despite my ever-increasing spasms and the occasional flesh shimmer, I really want to go—my body, my heart, screamed at me to play. I took a step forward, very nearly raced across the lawn. My feet even bounced on the balls to prepare for flight—but my gaze flicked to the forest, killing my desire.

Sunday brought the promise of a brighter day with the warmth blasting through the bedroom window. I'd spent most of the night twisted by cramps—my fidgeting legs had disturbed Sean, too—and I woke with determination to ease his concerns.

When he turned left toward the bathroom, I headed for the stairs.

If I didn't do it right then, after spending hours feeding my will power with words of encouragement, it might have been days before I got around to it. I didn't have that long. The harder I appeared to adjust, the more Sean would blame himself, so I needed to do it for him—and for the others so they could go back to their lives. I also needed to do it for myself. My first conscious change would be difficult enough—if my visions proved correct. I didn't want one I couldn't control, or to be stuck in the damn house. Subconsciously, I already knew how it felt to run free outdoors as a wolf, how it felt to run with Sean. I may not have chosen to become werewolf, but I refused to shut myself away when I could make the most of a bad situation.

I jogged through the house, past the lounge where Nathan had the news on low, around Ethan at the kitchen table. Through the French doors, I strode to the conservatory door and tugged it wide, marched across to the edge of the paving ... and halted.

"Shit!"

With eyes glued to my intended destination, I stalked along the lip of the lawn, right, then left, and back again. On my fourth width, I spotted my audience inside the conservatory and went a few more paces without breaking stride.

Mumbling from within the glass enclosure informed me Sean had arrived.

I stopped pacing, breaths fast, heart pounding, and faced the way I needed to go. "You can do this."

Fists clenched at my sides, I strode across the lawn—but only made it about halfway before halting again. The air carried moistness with the still saturated grass, though the sun's ascent would cure that by noon, and the dew slathered my soles as I leaned forward and peered through the trees.

Everything within me wanted me to go in there. It was my forest. I'd claimed it that first day I entered. *My* forest. They would not take that away from me.

"Do it," I hissed.

A glance over my shoulder showed Sean outside. I nodded to him once, gestured with my head, 'coming?', before I turned back, bobbed on the balls of my feet, and threw myself into a sprint.

The archways blurred past first, followed by the short gap between brickwork and greenery. I pushed my legs to keep moving, but at the strong scent of blood, my head whipped left and right in search of the source.

Sean came up behind, urged me to keep going, and I picked up my speed again, racing forth until the travelling breeze carried the smell from my detection.

My legs pumped, as did my arms. I whizzed between trees, around, under, over branches. A dart left, right, left again.

Sean ran on my heels—I smelled him, heard his footfalls.

My head tilted at a third set of feet, and an inhalation identified Ethan. With the urge to laugh at the insaneness of us running like lunatics through the shade, I skidded to a stop, spun around. Unable to slow, Sean ploughed into me, and we both went tumbling, our bodies sliding through mud created by the heavy rainfall.

Still laughing, I rolled onto all fours, my neck extended as my nose pushed forward. Every luring scent of the forest enveloped me, new flavours, too—ones I hadn't known of.

Ethan met us, slipping in his abrupt halt to join us on the ground. I turned to look at him, then at Sean. My building excitement rippled the length of my body, beginning at my crown. I shivered as it danced down to depart through the tips of my toes.

The boys' grins matched my own mood, as Sean tugged me back against his chest. "Ready to change, Jem?"

I tried to wriggle free, to run again, but he held tight. Yes, I wanted to change—at least my body did—but was I mentally ready for it? Could I encourage something which would cause so much pain?

"I'll try," I whispered.

Released, I pushed to my feet and checked out potential changing sites. Drawn by a broad bush, I headed around to the far side, where I dropped.

Footsteps neared, followed by Sean's scuffles beyond the thick leaves, and on hands and knees, I willed my right frame of mind to appear. A glance down revealed my clothing.

Rolling my eyes, I tugged them off and draped them across the bush.

As soon as I resumed my position, a tingle spread through me—familiar, thanks to my visions—and, eyes closing, I tucked my chin into my chest, concentrated on bringing forth the next step. All my brain seemed capable of focusing on, though, were my mental taunts that arrived loud and clear.

You know this is really going to hurt.

A few quiet minutes of waning focus passed, then, "Jem?"

Letting out a growl of frustration, I pushed up and stalked away.

Ethan leaned against a wide trunk ahead, and I stalled, but his eyes remained on mine, never once roaming over my naked body. His lips curved as he sent me a small nod.

Fists clenched, I spun and headed back, crouching down again behind the bush Sean sat beyond. "Okay, I'm ready," I murmured, half to Sean, half to myself.

Palms flat against the wet soil, I once more dipped my head, closed my eyes. Within seconds, the ripples returned, slowly at first, before pulsating through me.

My brain hesitated at the next stage: the strenuous, body alterations, and poised, my flesh shimmered like crazy while my mind refused to move on.

Sean's voice sifted through to me. "Bumblebees and butter-flies, Jem."

"How do—"

Pain shot through me. I gasped as it tore at muscles. Tendons burned as they throbbed with their restructure, and I groaned against the stabbing of deforming bones, the tearing of flesh as it rearranged to accommodate my new form pushing through.

My eyes flew open. Against the soil below, fingers thickened as palms swelled. Pale hairs sprouted to coat me, lengthening with speed. Vertebral muscles contracted before expanding, bowing my spine, and my head whipped back to twist in agony at the broadening of my neck.

The splitting of bone widened my skull. My face elongated. My ears shifted.

I dived from the change with a ripping snarl, only just catching my balance before tumbling face-first into the mud.

Confused by colour-blindness I hadn't noticed in my visions, I snorted. A shake of my body ruffled my fur, sweeping through my length to leave with a flick of my tail.

Nose lifting, I sniffed the air. Finding Sean's sweet aroma, my front paws danced, before I threw back my head to release my howl.

Sean's change had begun already. I sensed, heard, scented him. I paced beside the bush as I listened and inhaled, detecting Ethan mid-change, too. At a low growl, I folded my forelegs, tail teasing the air.

Sean stepped around the bush with head dipped, eyes studying me. When I pushed up, he sniffed along my body, his lids lowering in what seemed like delight. I went to dart away, but his low rapid growl held me in place, and he brushed the length of my body, circling around to sweep my other side. When he reached my front, I pushed under his muzzle, ran my spine beneath his throat, his shudder sending a tremor through me.

We turned at Ethan's approach. I waited while he also followed the ritual of sniffing, inspecting and brushing, then, with a small giggle tinkling within my head, I dashed away.

The forest rushed past on either side of me, as Sean and Ethan chased my rear—confirmed by their strong scents and their breaths upon my rump. I dropped back, invited Ethan to take the lead, and ran alongside Sean until Ethan dropped back, offering Sean the lead.

Beside Sean, my eyes darted sideways to him. When beside Ethan, he glanced at me. Within our tight, triangular formation, each stuck close to the others, our pace remaining steady as we leaped and dashed our way through.

We broke into a clearing I recognised as the Larsen grounds. Ethan lifted his head in greeting, and seconds later, Josh and Daniel appeared in the back doorway and set out at a sprint, pulling at clothing as they moved. Kyle came out behind them, racing to keep up. Waiting until they neared, we dashed off into the forest, leaving behind their frantic attempts to catch us.

Soon hearing the three chasing wolves, we delayed to enable the greeting ritual. For a third, fourth and fifth time, I was sniffed, brushed, licked, but when Josh located my rear and took more interest than he should, both Sean and I dived to pin him to the ground. Growling up at us in indignation, he wriggled free, and a glance of amusement passed between Sean and me before we took off again.

Our actions held less uniformity the second time through. We weaved left, right, intersecting each other, our paths crossing enough to enlist in rough and tumble. After being taken advantage of during ball games, to get my own back on them was empowering. With each roll, growl, charge and attack—each of them too cautious to retaliate—I snorted in glee before bolting away, leaving them standing for seconds before they snapped out of it.

If I'd said I didn't have an amazing time, I'd have been lying.

FOLLOWING A MORE direct route meant it didn't take long to return to our changing spot. I whimpered at Sean when it dawned on me I'd have to reverse what I'd done, but he nudged me around the bush, licking my muzzle until he'd caressed me into a calm enough state of mind to try.

Changing from wolf to human brought no less pain, but I didn't struggle, and for some reason, it came easier. Possibly because I knew what to expect, knew when it had reached its agonising peak and wouldn't get any worse. Poppy told me childbirth was easier after the first time, that knowing what she had coming prepared her. Maybe changing was no different.

My chest heaved on completion. Perspiration beaded my brow. I swayed on my knees, my arms rigid to support me, and searched for my breath. With my head hung low, I didn't move, not even at the soft steps when they circled the bush.

"Jem?" Sean sank to his knees before me.

I lifted my head a little, raised my eyes to his. His expression altered from excitement to concern and uncertainty, returning to excitement as though he recognised the light still dancing within me.

Our bodies still thrummed as we stared at each other. "How did you know?" I asked.

"About what?"

"Bumblebees and butterflies."

"I've already told you, Jem. I know you better than anyone."

I crawled across to him, pushed up onto my knees. Sliding a hand into his hair, I drew him to me, and his lips parted, allowing me to explore, as his hands ran across my back in soft, tender sweeps. With the closeness of our bodies, the still-strong vibrations, sending a thrill of anticipation through me, I leaned closer in search of more.

One arm enfolded my waist, and he wove his other into my hair, tilting back my head to expose my throat. As his lips and tongue travelled my flesh, my eyes closed, and I lowered my arms to hang limp, offering myself to him.

The footsteps of the others travelled toward the house, yet I didn't look up, knowing they wouldn't encroach on our privacy. Sean paid them no notice, either. His tongue continued its darting movements, his teeth grazed over me. I trembled, as he moved lower, his welcomed breaths warming the coolness of my breasts before he made his way back up. At a tilt of my head, he nuzzled my lobe, the tender spot surrounding my pulse. My breath caught when his teeth skimmed down to my collar bone.

"Sean! Jem!"

My lids shot up.

"Dad said you're not to be out here alone," Ethan called.

Sean's lips ceased to caress, but he didn't pull away. "We're not alone, Ethan. You're here."

"Well, I don't want to sit out here and listen to the two of you. Show some consideration."

Sean remained there for seconds, seemed to be considering ignoring the order, until, with a low groan, he brought his face to mine. "We'll finish this later."

When we ducked back beneath the arches a few minutes later, only Nathan waited in the garden to greet us. He smiled at our approach. "Feeling better, Jem?"

"Much better. Is that bacon I smell?"

"It is, and if you don't hurry, it will be all gone."

"They wouldn't dare." I laughed as I jogged off to the kitchen.

Breakfast ended up a short affair, mostly because we all ate like we hadn't in weeks—and when Connor showed up too late to join us, he bore clothes for his boys. I hadn't even noticed that naked legs trailed beneath the oak tabletop, though I certainly got an eyeful when I slunk off for a shower.

Beneath the spray, my high refused to leave, as I soaped and lathered and rinsed, every speck of my body still sensitive to the buzz. Even once I stepped from the cubicle, drying myself down seemed to remind me of the thrill.

With a towel as cover, I streaked down the landing to what I'd come to think of as 'our' room. Rubbing the towel over my hair, I nudged the door closed behind me and headed over to select clothing from my accumulated pile.

Bending at the waist, I went to feed my foot into a pair of green knickers ... and froze. My head ducked forward, as I stared at my reflection in the mirror before me. Each of the muscles that had been evident in my awakening dream swelled across my body—but for real.

The door opened, and Sean's head poked round the frame. I allowed him a glance before looking straight back at myself, and he smiled as he came in and closed the door. "Is this the first time you've looked?"

I nodded.

He sat on the bed behind me, bringing his reflection to the side of my own. I caught his eye, held it for a second, and returned my attention to myself.

A lift of my arms and a bend of my knees preceded a run of my hands across my abdomen. I spun and peered over each shoulder, over each hip, searching every inch. When my eyes met with Sean's again, his smile widened.

"I don't know why I'm so surprised." I shrugged. "I saw myself like this in my dream, knew it would happen. It's just ..."

"It's just that it's a bit different when it happens for real instead of only inside your head," he finished.

I nodded. "It's okay. I'll get used to it.

"So,"—he tugged my hand until I faced him—"did you enjoy your run?"

My lips began their upward curve. "Yes."

"They're hoping you'll join us outside today. Think you will?"

My smile widened. "Without a doubt."

I did play ball with the others and found myself able to knock them from my path. Priceless barely described their facial expressions. The first time, I almost stumbled in disbelief, but laughing at Kyle, who I'd sent to the ground, I picked my pace back up and shocked myself again with my jump for the hoop. It took all my effort not to glance down at the lawn as I neared my goal. When I landed, I spun to find everyone staring—until my laughter snapped them back round.

Over dinner, a discussion took place about our next plan of action. Nathan announced that they'd be returning to work the next morning. As I'd proven to be okay, they were taking me along with them. Under no circumstances would he risk leaving me alone.

Chapter 37

As ordered by Nathan, I left with them for work. I wasn't happy about spending a mind-numbing day pacing and twiddling my thumbs, yet Sean showed such relief to have me in his sights, it seemed wrong to argue. I'd almost suggested the two of us stay at home for a few more days, before Sean beat me to the idea, but Nathan insisted that would concern him no less.

Arrival at the site of their latest job brought surprise. By property development, I'd imagined dilapidated houses bought in auctions, plaster thrown up and a few licks of paint on the walls, and the pack selling them on for a nice profit. I had no idea how grand-scale a business they owned. Nathan's company built their own properties from scratch—mostly by themselves, but occasionally, they took on a few extra men.

The few extra men—four, to be precise—paused in their tea drinking to stare at the new arrival. They goggled even harder when Sean strode over, placed a hard-hat on my head, and insisted I wear it at all times outside the cabin—where I'd, apparently, be spending most of my time.

Obeying, I stayed in the office and, between pacing, spent my day swivelling about on the desk chair and drinking coffee.

With my feet propped on the desktop, I attempted to doze through the noise yet didn't succeed. When Sean finally stuck his head in to announce we were leaving, my flight toward the door almost created a whirlwind.

Tuesday arrived, and Nathan growled at me to *get my act together*, when my reluctance threatened to make us all late. Tail between my legs, I left for my second day at the site.

After being given my hard-hat and nudged toward the cuboid-shaped prison, I stropped over, yanked open the door, and deposited my rear in the swivelling seat.

Nathan entered to me spinning at the velocity of a rotor blade. I planted my feet down, eyes whizzing as they refused to focus on him.

"I know this is hard on you," he said. "But this way it's easier on Sean."

"I'm bored, Nate."

"I know you are, Jem. Give me time. I'll figure out a way around it. Maybe ... once the threat has died down."

By lunchtime, I'd had enough. With hard-hat donned, I went outside in search of distraction and decided to take at look at exactly what they were doing with the building. From the structure of the brickwork, it appeared as though it might end up as an apartment complex, despite the lack of windows and roof.

I strolled round to the rear, to see if I'd get a clearer idea from that angle, and turned the corner to the contracted workers on their break. They nodded in greeting, obviously still curious as to my identity, *and* my presence. I considered ignoring them, but fast changed my mind when one waved a sandwich from his lunchbox at me.

I strode over. "What's on it?"

"Chicken, cucumber, mayo ... 'you hungry?"

"I'm always hungry." I smiled as I took it. "Thanks." I pushed up to sit beside him on the scaffolding and tucked in.

Once the braver of the four had enticed me over, the other three aimed their inquisitive looks my way. "So, 'you family, then?" asked the sandwich offerer.

"Yes," I said around bites. "I'm with Sean."

He nodded as though he'd already figured that out.

"You're his girlfriend?" asked a younger one to my left.

Strangely, I felt the need to contemplate the question. Although girlfriend didn't seem an apt description for my relationship for Sean, it sufficed for them, so I nodded.

"I've got roast beef."

I peered round at a dark-haired man beside the young one, his skin severely weathered by years of working outdoors, and smiled as I reached over for the proffered food. "Thanks."

"Jack," said the initial sandwich offerer.

I took the hand he held out, shook it. "Jem."

"I'm Darren," said the young one, drawing my attention, "and this is David, and Andrew." He indicated the weathered man, and another on the end with dust in his hair.

Smiling, I shook each of their hands.

When they rummaged in their lunch boxes, my tongue licked across my lips. I'd known I was pretty hungry, probably the reason I'd needed to get out, to take my mind off it, except watching them ignited my hunger even more.

I laughed as each of them held out a hand, an offering of sustainable substance within. I took them all, placed them in my lap. "Thanks." My accumulated food consisted of sausage rolls, a packet of crisps, a banana, a whole chicken thigh—which I smiled really widely at—and a caramel bar. Oddly, my mood rocketed.

As I tore chicken from bone with my teeth, the first shouts arrived. "Jem!"

I tried to answer, but my full mouth rendered it an impossible action.

Of course, more shouts arrived, followed by footsteps, and calls to each other. Ethan jogged around the corner, took one look at me, and laughed. "She's round here!"

The others all appeared, and Sean strode over with a smile. "Jem, why didn't you say, if you were this hungry?" Lifting my hard-hat, he kissed me. "You can't nick food off this lot."

"I didn't." I peeled my banana. "They offered it to me. What was I supposed to do?"

Once everyone had got over their amusement, and I'd finished eating and been given the promise of lunch within the hour, I was ushered back to the cell—cabin.

WEDNESDAY BROUGHT another dose of guaranteed boredom. I sighed as I climbed from the pickup and lifted my face to the strong, refreshing breeze before scowling around at the site, of which I'd already tired. When Nathan shook his head at me to stop, indicating Sean had also spotted my mood, I smiled— sort of.

By eleven thirty, I was extraordinarily hungry, enough to play name-that-tune from my stomach rumblings—one had sounded close to the National Anthem. Unfortunately, once hunger set in, I couldn't sit still, however much I tried. I harrumphed in the spinning chair, even did some rotations, paced a few lengths of the rectangular floor and peered unsuccessfully through the filthy windows.

Frustrated, I went in search of Sean and found him near the archway they'd built that led into the courtyard parking. The wind whipped through from within, blowing my hair about my face as I strode over. "What time are you breaking?"

He smiled up at me. "What's up?"

"I'm hungry."

"Already?"

I indicated my stomach growls. "Yes. Listen."

He lifted his hat and rubbed a hand across his hair, sending clouds of dust into the air. "We're going to be at least an hour, I think."

"I can't wait that long."

His eyes searched about, probably for his Dad. I wasn't sure if he intended to ask permission for time-out to fetch lunch, or if he hoped Nathan would take over dealing with me.

"I'll go find him," I said, and he nodded in response.

I located Nathan peeking inside the hut. Turning at my approach, he smiled. "There you are, Jem."

"What time are you breaking?"

"Why?" His lips twitched. "Are you hungry already?"

"Hungry is an understatement."

"Can you wait? We'll be breaking in about an hour."

"*No,*" I almost hissed.

"Okay, I'll try and get you something sooner."

"No, Nate. I need something *now.*"

"We're in the middle of something, Jem." His shoulders lifted. "We can't just up and go."

"Then, I'll go myself."

"No." He walked away.

Following, I grabbed for his arm. "I need to eat, Nathan. Please let me go and get something."

Sean headed over as soon as he realised my behaviour attracted attention from the outside workers. "What's going on?" he asked as he reached us.

I turned to him. "I really need food."

"She wants to go and get it herself," Nathan said.

"No." Sean shook his head as though to emphasise his point.

Josh, Connor and Ethan headed over, probably to find out what was wrong with the dancing female.

I spun back to Nathan. "Please."

"No, Jem."

He went to walk away again, but I chased after him and gripped his sleeve. "Please. I'll take the truck, go through a drive-thru. I won't even have to leave the vehicle. If there's a queue at the drive-thru, I won't go, I'll come back." He paused, seeming to waver, so I added, "If I don't eat soon, I'll die of starvation."

"She wants to go for food?" Ethan asked.

"Tell them. How much trouble can I get into at a drive-thru?"

He glanced at Nathan, then Sean, and shrugged slightly, like he agreed but didn't want me to know.

"No," Sean said.

"I want something to eat."

When nobody responded, I marched off and into the cabin. My slam of the door vibrated through the walls so hard, I thought, for a second, the whole box would collapse.

A knock carried through the door. "Jem?"

"Go away, Sean!"

The door pushed open, and he stepped inside.

"I'm hungry," I said. "All I want is to go and get some food, and I'm not allowed."

"I'm afraid, Jem." His voice came low.

"Afraid of a drive-thru?"

"Afraid to let you out of my sight."

"How can I possibly run into trouble? I've been out the house with you since Monday, now. How many times have you seen, or felt, something to concern you?"

"Three days is nothing. I waited eight years for you to show up, and you're asking me to relax because we've had a few quiet days?"

"I'll go directly to the drive-thru. I won't even step out of the truck. If there's a queue, I won't enter. Once I have something to eat, I'll drive straight back. Then none of us will be hungry, and you can all feel silly at your overreaction."

His hands fisted at his sides as he let out a growl. I almost growled back, but as a more civilised person, I merely showed him my teeth. "You're being unreasonable," he said through gritted jaw.

"Whatever happened to your complaints, Sean? *Oh, the Jem I know would never let anyone push her around*," I mimicked. "*The Jem I know would kick my arse for speaking to her that way. You shouldn't have told me to stick up for myself more if you didn't mean it.*"

"I didn't—"

"You only want me to stick up for myself so long as it isn't against you."

"I ... urgh!" He stormed out, slamming the door behind him. "Let her go for the damn burgers!"

My mouth opened as I scratched at my head. We'd had, what I was certain was, our first proper argument.

Nathan came in a few minutes later. "Keys, money." He handed them to me.

"Thanks."

"Where's your phone, Jem?"

I took it from my pocket to show him before sliding it back in.

"Straight there, straight back. Do you understand?"

"Yes. What does everyone want?"

"You can grab them the same as yourself."

I headed for the door but turned back. "Can you tell Sean I'm sorry for yelling at him?"

"He'll want to hear it from you, not me."

Cash and keys pocketed, I went in search of Sean, found him pacing around the far side. "I'm sorry I shouted at you," I said. "But you can't keep me locked away forever. It won't work."

"I know," he muttered.

"I'll be careful."

"I know, just ... don't be long, okay?"

"I'm not going far enough to be a long time. I promise I'll be back soon."

UNHAPPY WITH MYSELF, I bordered on sulking as I drove. I didn't like that I'd lost my temper to get my own way. However, reaching the drive-thru without incident brought a smile—a smug one, yes, but at least my mood improved. The promise of food could have been responsible for that, too.

Ethan's bulky truck barely fit through the stupidly-narrow, winding lane for kiosk sales. I did consider parking and going in, until Nathan's stern voice resounded in my head. At the first window, I gave an order large enough to raise eyebrows. Once the order had been taken, the reseal of the glass panes sucked away the smells from within while those that should have lingered carried away on the gale. My fingers drummed the steering wheel in impatience for my food. A few minutes later, the windows reopened, and the scents of cholesterol-nourishing food engulfed me. Each brown paper bag the male server handed went into the passenger foot-well.

I pulled away, covering only a few feet before my mobile rang. After swinging the pickup into a parking space, I wriggled it free from my pocket and answered.

"Jem?"

"I'm at the drive-thru. Nothing bad has happened to me. I'm fine, Sean."

His release of breath hit my ear. "Okay."

My eyes rolled. "I'll be back soon."

"Hurry back, Jem. Okay?"

I hung up, put the truck into first gear, but as I went to pull off, my phone rang again.

"I said *I'm coming*," I answered.

"Jem?"

"Oh, Poppy." I half-laughed. "Everything okay?"

"Peter's outside."

My hackles rose. "I told him to stay away. What does he want?"

"He's blathering on about needing your address and not mine to file divorce."

"What an absolute crock."

Poppy gave a quiet laugh.

"Have you told him to disappear?"

"Of course. But now he's sitting in his car, watching the house."

I blew out a breath. "I'll sort this out."

"What are you going to do, Jem?"

"Hang on." I pulled open the glove box and rummaged around inside. When my hand fell on some papers, I pulled them out, flicked through: tax receipts, supply receipts, vehicle insurance. I studied the insurance document. "Are you okay to go out and speak to him?"

"What do you want me to tell him?"

"Tell him, if he wants my address, he'd better be at the site when I get there. I'm on my way."

"I'll tell him."

"Thanks, Pop. I'm sorry about this."

"No worries, sweetie. Be careful, okay?"

After promising I would, I pulled away.

I didn't have much time—if Sean knew my intention, he'd have made me wait until he could come. Swinging around roads, islands, junctions, I wished I had the Porsche to get me there quicker. Instead, I had a monster of a vehicle that threatened to take the corners on two wheels if I didn't check my speed.

At the site, I pulled up close to the office and jumped out. Even without making a scene, I managed to attract attention. Ignoring the stares, I pushed open the office door and found Peter leaning over his desk, shoulder to shoulder with some guy.

They both looked up, and the stranger's eyes widened, beside Peter's narrowing ones.

As I backed out, a scent crept into my olfactory and wrinkled my nose. I shook my head. *No, it can't be.* Another uncertain glance to the cabin, and I headed for the pickup.

The door opened behind me, footsteps followed. I tugged open the truck door, reached across for the document, and turned to Peter's smirk. "You want my address?" I reined in my gag at the alcohol fumes wafting from him.

"And you're going to give it to me? Just like that?"

I nodded. "If it will stop you pestering Poppy."

"About time." Smugness coated his expression.

I stared at him, gestured with my hand. "Pen and paper, Peter."

With a scowl, he strode off to the office, and I glanced around through my haloing hair. Despite my alternative transportation, everyone seemed to know it was me. When Peter reemerged, the man who'd been in there followed him out and stood on the top step. As his eyes fixed on me, a sense of familiarity settled in, yet I couldn't pinpoint from where.

"No Porsche today?" Peter sneered.

My gaze remained on the watchful one near the cabin.

"I bet he wasn't happy when you returned it scratched."

I turned to Peter. "Actually, I just thought this would hurt more if I felt the urge to run you over again."

He took a step toward me, fists clenched. Feigning indifference, I slid the pen and paper from his hand and leaned on the bonnet to write, but at movement at the corner of my eye, I lifted my head.

A second man had joined the one on the steps, and both seemed to hold a deep interest in my exchange with Peter.

Turning from their appraisal, I caught Peter checking over my body—I'd forgotten how muscular I would seem to him. Blanking his stares, I concentrated on writing the address and handed it to him. "Will you leave Poppy alone now?"

"I no longer need Poppy."

I studied him, his self-satisfied expression, his nasty little smirk. "I hope you're not thinking of paying me a visit, Peter." His smile widened, yet his eyes held only malice, and leaning forward, I forced frosty coolness into my stare and growled. "Come then. I dare you."

He took a step back, the smile vanishing from his lips. His falter brought immense satisfaction. The moron needed taking down a peg or two.

As I straightened into a more dignified pose, the breeze whipped around my head until I gasped in a lungful of air—air that carried scents to power my pulse into overdrive.

My eyes made a frantic search, falling on the two men on the steps.

They studied me so closely I couldn't help but scrutinise them—their physique, their smiles, the colour of their hair.

My foot stumbled back as I shook my head.

One had blond hair, the other's so dark it bordered on black —the two hair colours of the surviving wolves from the forest. More than that, they smelled like wolves, appeared strong enough to be wolves, and they definitely looked like they fancied me as a tasty snack.

Peter caught my sudden wide-eyed expression. He smiled like he thought he'd caused my uncalled-for alarm.

I allowed him only a brief glance before returning to the two men and forcing my feet into action.

As I shuffled back, they approached. My fingers groped for the door handle, flicking it with a loud snap before I yanked open the door. I clambered in, fumbling with the keys.

They veered off across the gravel and climbed into a Range Rover.

My engine and theirs roared to life in unison. Of course they'd follow, lure me somewhere quieter. Only a fool would take me with so many witnesses—especially when they appeared to be their own workforce.

I shot backward down the pebbled road and reversed straight out without a care for traffic. A glance to the left showed the rear doors of the Range Rover being pulled open and more passengers climbing in.

Four against one.

I let out a groan. *Brilliant, absolutely brilliant!*

Chapter 38

I grabbed for my mobile. *Sean's going to be so mad. Really mad.* My thumb hovered over the buttons, yet I didn't dial.

In my rear-view mirror, the following werewolves reflected back at me. The driver watched the road, while the front passenger met my attention in the mirror. He no doubt saw the fear in my eyes. It had to be there—my heart beat like a bass drum, my breaths arrived high-pitched. My predicament did not look good.

Twenty minutes to reach Sean. If I didn't call him, he'd ring to find out why I hadn't returned—then he'd be even more annoyed at me for not calling when in trouble, after I'd promised I would.

Damn. Poised over the buttons again, I stared at my phone.

The red light hit the corner of my eye at the same time as I spotted the woman step out into the road.

I slammed a foot on the brake, waved a shaking hand of apology at the glaring road-crosser.

My heart pounded harder.

Twisting in my seat, I peered behind. Even the ones in the rear of the Range Rover watched me—and they were huge, all of them. Like bloody sardines in a tin. Driver guy waved, smiling at me. The one to his left grasped the door handle like he considered jumping out.

At the flash of amber, I booted down on the accelerator. With one eye on the road, one on my mobile, I rang Sean. "Pick up, pick up."

The trill sounded out, again, and again, and again.

"Jem?"

Switching to loudspeaker, I placed it down to drive. "Baby, you're going to be so mad."

"Jem, are you in trouble?"

"Oh, yes."

"What's happened?"

Rapid footsteps suggested he was on the move. "I went to Peter's worksite."

A growl, then, "Why?"

"Poppy rang. He was at her house again, nagging for my address. I thought if I just gave it to him, he'd leave her alone."

"So, you went to give him your address."

I took a sharp left with a screech of the wheels. "Yes."

"But you're coming back now?"

"Yes, but ..."

"What's going on, Jem?"

"I've got a tail. They were there, at the site."

"Who?"

"The bloody werewolves. They were there, and now they're following me."

"Shit! Where are you? I'm coming to get you."

"No point. I'm almost there. Just be ready, okay?"

"Tell me where you are."

"Five minutes, tops," I said.

"It's too long, Jem."

Another slam on the brakes. "Shit!" I braced the jerk of my body against the wheel.

"What happened? Jem?"

"Lights. Traffic lights." I glanced behind again. They all leaned forward, watching with smiles. The driver sent another wave, and I turned away. "Come on, come on."

"Please, Jem. Tell me where you are." Sean's tinny voice arrived more and more desperate with each word. The others' voices carried through in the background—he probably had me on speaker, too.

A glance in the mirror showed their passenger door swinging open. "Uh-oh!"

"What? What, Jem?"

"I think one of them is getting out."

"Move, then."

"Come on! How long do these lights take?" I checked the gears, pressed my right foot on the accelerator, my other lifting on the clutch until I caught the bite. My hands left the wheel, one at a time, and I wiped sweat across my jeans before returning them. I peered in my wing mirror. The blond had left their vehicle, his discreet steps bringing him closer to mine. "He's coming."

"Jem, will you get your arse out of there?"

The amber light blinked. I shot off, leaving the blond a few feet short of his intended destination. Fists clenched, he glared at me. The Range Rover paused for him to jump in and resumed pursuit before he'd even shut his door.

"Okay." I blew out a breath. "I'm moving again."

"How far, Jem?"

"Nearly there. Don't worry."

Only a few minutes passed before I turned onto the road where the site stood. The Range Rover tailed me so close I expected a nudge on my bumper, but the site was ahead, I was home free—until a moment of madness overcame me.

I slowed for the turning, checked for approaching traffic. A right then sharp left spin of the wheel swung the truck in a wide arc, and I hit the brakes as the nose of the vehicle hovered above the ramp into Nathan's premises.

The pack stood just inside the gateway. They waved at me to pull forward.

I glanced left, to the smiling faces of the other pack behind their windscreen. They'd had no choice but to stop—my manoeuvre had blocked the entire side of the road.

"What the hell are you doing, Jem?" Sean's voice through my mobile snapped my attention back to him.

"There. Right beside me." I inclined my chin. "Take a look."

Car, after car, after car braked behind the Range Rover—my own build-up of witnesses. With the engine left running, I climbed from the cab.

Sean took a step forward. My heart thudded as I turned away and headed toward the black vehicle, ignoring the following footsteps and calls of the others. At the rear of the Range Rover, I waved to the traffic in a hope to placate before stepping back to tap on the driver's window. It lowered, and I inhaled as I studied him.

"Jem." He smiled. "How good to see you looking so well."

"As opposed to dead, you mean?"

"We weren't trying to kill you."

"Really?" I absorbed his black hair, his hazel eyes. "I guess being chased by the three of you was a mere misunderstanding, then."

His smile widened. "We were ... curious. We wanted to meet you."

My eyebrow lifted. "I must have missed your introductions."

"So rude of me." Releasing a small laugh, he extended his hand. "Jonathon. Jonathon Richards."

Blanking his hand, I nodded to the front passenger, took in his blond hair, brown eyes, his crooked smirk as though he knew something I didn't. "And you?"

"This is Matthew Harrison."

'Matthew' lifted a hand.

"The two in the back are my brother, Thomas ..." Jonathon pointed behind. "... and Stuart Cunningham."

"Do they usually greet people through closed windows?"

The glass slid down, and I stepped to the left. Once again, I clocked their appearance—one brown, one mousy blond—and sampled the scents within the car while breaking them down into four individual ones.

"Okay." I took a step back. "I'm going to walk away, now. You should consider staying away from me, though."

"You should consider coming with us," Jonathon said. "We may be able to offer you more."

"I doubt it." I turned to walk away.

Sean and the pack stood poised on the pavement. At my rear, the driver's door opened and feet hit the road. Cars bibbed in impatience.

"What was this all about, then, Jem?" he called.

I turned to see him smiling. "Because I now know how you all look, and exactly how you all smell. If you're stupid enough to come back, I'll be ready."

The passenger window wound down and a blond head leaned out with a sneer. "Oh, we *will* come for you."

"You must have a death wish."

"No, Jem. We *will* return, and we *will* take you."

A low, long growl rumbled from Sean.

"You can die trying, I suppose," I said.

He shook his head. "Nah."

My lips curved in a cold smile. "Tell that to your dead brother."

His loud snarls hit my back, as I rounded the pickup. I heard Jonathon telling him to calm, their car door open and Jonathon climbing in before engaging first gear. Back in the truck, I sent them a sarcastic salute before pulling out of their way.

Inside the site, I hit the brakes. My arms dropped to my sides, and I leaned forward until my head pressed against the steering wheel. Shaking overcame my legs, the tremble of my hands vibrated against the rough seat fabric, and my heart drummed within my chest.

I didn't know what terrified me more. That I knew for definite werewolves were after me, or the calm manner in which I acted so recklessly. I believed my behaviour won the toss.

The door swung open, and Sean tugged me to him. "What the hell are you playing at?" His tightening arms buried my face into his chest. My fists found folds of his clothing, and we stood for minutes.

Nobody spoke. I could sense they wanted to, that they all had plenty to say. Perhaps my visible shaking caused them to hold their tongues.

I finally lifted my head to look up at Sean. "I'm sorry. I don't know what came over me."

"In the office, Jem," Nathan said. "We'll talk about this in there."

I glanced around to find the contract workers paused in their work and observing the spectacle I'd caused. I pulled away from Sean, removed the bags of cooling food from the truck, and handed some of them to Josh and Daniel before heading across to Jack.

"I got these for you." I handed him four burgers. "To make up for yesterday."

"'You alright, Jem?"

"Just some idiot riding my bumper. Nothing to worry about."

He nodded. "Thanks for these."

The two families waited for me to catch up before trailing inside the cabin. Claustrophobia kicked in when they all turned to me. I took the swivel chair, withdrew a burger, and, depositing the bag on the desk, chomped down on it.

An angry Nathan leaned his fists on the desktop as he peered down at me. "Jem?"

"I know you're mad with me, Nathan, but I don't think I'm entirely to blame."

"How'd you work that out?"

"I didn't intend to go and see Peter, it just—"

"Why didn't you wait for Sean to go with you?"

"I didn't want a repeat performance."

"One of us, then? You should have waited."

Sean pushed forward. "Why didn't you tell me when I called you, Jem? Why tell me everything was fine?"

"Poppy rang *after* you'd called. I wasn't to know I'd get into trouble by going. Besides, at least we know more about them, now."

"Which is?" Nathan said.

"Well, I know their names, what they look and smell like, and I also know where we can find them." I gave a small smile.

Ethan chuckled from the door. Josh joined him, until Nathan swung round and silenced them with a glare. He turned back to me. "How do you know where to find them, Jem?"

"If you sit down and eat, and stop growling at me, I'll tell you."

He pulled food from the bags, indicating to the others to do the same, and rested on the desk.

I chewed around my explanation. "I think the werewolves are Peter's boss."

"Why would you come to that conclusion?"

"The dark-haired one—who is called Jonathon Richards, by the way—was in the office with Peter when I got there. Looked like they were going over plans. I thought I smelled the scent when I first saw him, but dismissed it because I didn't expect it there. Then, when I was talking to Peter, he came out to watch, and the blond one showed up, whose name is Matthew ..." I looked to the ceiling. "Harrison. It wasn't until the wind blew over that I realised who they were. So, I bolted, but two others came over and jumped in with them, and I was left with four bloody werewolves on my tail."

"Weren't you scared, Jem?" asked Daniel.

I stared at him, brows lifted. "Of course. I was terrified."

"If there were werewolves on our territory, we'd know," said Nathan.

"They're over the county border, in Staffordshire. Does that class as your territory?"

Nathan glanced at Connor, who tilted his head.

"Besides, consider this," I continued. "I go to Peter's site and they're there. The last time I showed up, we had trespassers in the forest less than twenty-four hours later. Think about it, Nathan. It makes sense."

Connor gave a small shrug, when Nathan turned from me back to him.

"Plus," I added, my mouth full, "they knew who I was."

"That's irrelevant, Jem. They would have picked up your scent easily."

"But why go over to talk to them?" asked Kyle. "Are you out of your mind? Do you have any idea how much will power it took for us to not intervene?"

"I wanted to find out who they were." I shrugged. "I knew they wouldn't do anything, not with so many witnesses. They introduced themselves when I asked. The two in the back are

Stuart Cunningham and Thomas—Jonathon's brother—so we have their names. I asked them to open the windows, got all their scents."

"Okay, Jem. I'll buy that you might be right about this. I'll even admit you have, once again, been incredibly brave and gathered more information than any of us could have. But if you *ever* do anything like this again, I will lock you in the cellar until this is over. Do you understand me?"

"Yes, Nate."

"You have blown any chance you had of ever leaving without an escort. From now on, if you're hungry, you'll wait until one of us is free. Is that clear?"

I sighed. "Yes, Nate."

After our group 'chat', Nathan sent everyone but me from the hut—at which point I knew a roasting was forthcoming.

From a lot of growls, promises to lock me up, a couple of stresses on how stupid he thought I'd acted, he went on to tell me exactly how Sean looked when I told him who I had on my tail—which was a low blow because that part hurt the most.

He mumbled on and on about how, if I hadn't gone gallivanting again, I wouldn't have been in trouble in the first place.

I apologised, again and again, over and over, and he ended his almost whispered rant with: 'If you pull a stunt like this again, I'll have your ass in a sling, Jem,' whatever *that* meant.

As if the roasting hadn't been enough, he went and locked me inside the blasted box, and I had to yell if I wanted something. Did I think he'd overreacted? Not really, I guessed.

Chapter 39

Thursday morning produced a downpour to induce the return of Noah. With mug in hand, I stared out over the sodden garden. "Can you build in this weather, Nate?"

"No," he said from the table behind me, "but it will stop before lunch, so we'll pick back up then."

"That mean we have the morning off?" I sipped my coffee.

"No, we're all going shopping before we head in."

I turned to face the men. "Shopping?"

"Yes, Jem, shopping."

"All of us?"

"The four of us," Nathan said with a nod.

"What for?"

"I've thought of something to keep you out of trouble."

I studied him. "What is it?"

"Can you decorate?"

"Like paint, paper?"

"Yes, finishing touches, like a woman brings to a home."

My eyebrow lifted. "You forget I was a bored housewife for eight years. Of course I know how to decorate."

"Good." He nodded. "Welcome to your new job."

"You want me to paint the house?"

He sighed, shook his head. "I want you to come up with ideas for the new apartments. I need colour schemes, furnishings, that sort of thing."

I put my mug down. "You're giving me a proper job?"

"Yes. What's it called …?"

"Interior designer," mumbled Ethan beside him.

"You want me to be interior designer for the apartments?"

Nathan nodded as they all watched me. Amusement twinkled in Sean's eyes.

I smiled. "Cool."

AFTER BREAKFAST, I skipped from the house and bounced into the car. I hadn't had a job since before I married Peter. He'd made me believe I was unemployable.

We arrived at an electronics superstore, where the three men ushered me inside, Sean never once letting go of my hand, and found a consultant only too happy to deal with us. Nathan bought me a laptop, so I could find what I needed without leaving the house or site, and the assistant spent a while setting the whole thing up using some little gadget with a weird name that would give me the Internet if plugged into some hole at the side. Technicalities weren't important. He showed me how to turn it on, how to get email, where to plug everything in. By the time we left, it was ready for use.

From there, we drove until Nathan parked outside a huge DIY depot. Once again, we stuck together, trailing around like some sort of posse. It got a bit much, though, when, at one point, all three of them had contact with me. On the verge of suffocation, I opened my mouth to complain, but closed it at one warning glower from Nathan. After collecting every brochure the store had on kitchens, bathrooms, taps, lighting, and every paint colour chart, Nathan told me I'd find anything else I needed on my new laptop and we headed for work.

Once at the site, the three men escorted me to the cabin with a cool box of food. They settled me down for the first day at my new job with one command: stay.

An hour later, Nathan returned to check up on me, to talk me through how many apartments there would be, and he gave me floor plans of each one, with the layout clearly labelled. He instructed me only to consider design for the ground floor apartments as they would be replicated on the other floors. After checking I knew how to use my new laptop, he left me to it.

I still didn't get very far. Not an hour went by without one of the pack sticking their head in the door, pretending they'd come for a drink. By my seventh visit, I realised they really didn't trust me to be left alone at all.

Friday morning, we pulled over at a newsagent and bought handfuls of magazines full of ideas, pictures, yin and yang, feng shui, all that sort of stuff. I was so busy all day, I didn't even notice the time pass and never growled once at the interruptions.

Instead, excitement took over—an eagerness to show them the boards Nathan and Ethan had instructed me on putting together the evening before.

Sean looked relaxed, happy, like he considered his dad to be the smartest man on the face of the planet. Obviously, he didn't say as such, but his face pretty much told that story.

As a result, I reached the weekend without any incidents whatsoever, without making everyone mad, and for the first time, reluctant to leave the site.

· · ·

Saturday morning, I flung the duvet into its accustomed heap, tugged something on, and danced out the bedroom in the best of moods. Even Sean's absence on waking didn't bother me. Nothing, I believed, could spoil my demeanour.

"Sean!"

"In here," he called from the kitchen.

I skipped down the stairs and headed in to kiss him. My body almost shivered on straightening, and I smiled at Nathan and Ethan as gentle vibrations ran through me.

The chair beside Sean screeched across the tiles when I pulled it out to sit. My knees wobbled up and down, slapping the soles of my feet against the cold floor.

The three men merely watched. Although they also appeared to be excited about something, they did a much better job than me of containing themselves.

After more smiles, I pushed up, filled the kettle to switch on. Back to my seat, my knees took up their jerking act again. For some reason, I could *not* sit still.

I returned to making coffee, jigged on the spot. My body even refused to remain stationary long enough for me to sip without spillage. Reaching across, I opened the window. My face pushed forward, and I drew in as much of the natural scents as my lungs could hold before exhaling. Another inhalation, eyes closed, lips still spread wide.

"It's a full moon tonight." Behind me, Sean's voice held a brimful of hidden promises.

Ethan chuckled. "Yeah, I think Jem's already figured that one out."

I opened my eyes and turned to them, snorted out a giggle. A ripple washed over me, creating a wave the length of my body, which my eyes followed. It brought no alarm. I welcomed it.

My feet took to pacing the kitchen. I glanced out as I passed the door, the window, the door again, and then turned back for more deep breaths at the open window. I *really* wanted to go out there. If I went out, though, I'd want to change, and something told me to wait, that patience would pay off.

With another glance toward the forest, an unwelcome thought arose. I turned to Nathan. "We *are* hunting tonight, aren't we?" My tone arrived calm, yet my body language dared him to deny me.

He chuckled. "Yes, Jem."

"All of us?"

"Safety in numbers."

"We discussed going farther away, to be on the safe side," Sean said.

"No." My hair whipped with my headshake. "This is our forest. We can't let them chase us out of it."

Ethan nodded. "That's what we said."

"Besides," I continued, "if we go somewhere else, it won't be familiar. If we stay here, and they're idiotic enough to come, we'll know the area better. We know the smells of the forest. If there are trespassers, we'll know sooner."

"Yes, we've already said all of this. We're staying put," Nathan said.

Grins and pacing resumed. At the sink, I downed more coffee before pacing again. I'd be exhausted by evening if I didn't stop. "How many hours have I got to wait?" I asked, without breaking stride.

"Almost twelve."

I stared at Sean. How the heck could they expect me to wait that long?'

Three smiles responded.

The day ahead seemed infinite. I spent most of my time pacing and jigging, in between drinking and fuelling up, as well as making love—because Sean thought it the only way to keep me still, or still*er*. After dinner, I could restrain myself no longer, and my pacing progressed from kitchen to paving, my eyes glued to my craved destination as I stalked.

With each passing hour, the sun sank lower in the sky, its glow altering from blinding white, to orange, to red on its final descent. Every left pivot revealed Sean watching patiently from the conservatory. He smiled at each eye contact, held up his fingers in countdown to the hunt. At each reduction of appendages, my anticipation increased. Like a slow-release drug intravenously catheterised into my vein, the effects built. If I didn't reach climax soon, I'd explode.

A phone rang indoors. I halted, head tilted. My hands clenched, unclenched, my teeth ground with the effort to stay put.

Doors and windows were locked before the men appeared and Nathan nodded. "Let's go."

I clambered to get to the forest but Sean fast caught up, and we tugged and grappled, both attempting to get there first. In a much more reserved manner, Ethan and Nathan strolled behind.

Inhalations drew me to *my* bush, the one I'd used as concealment previously. Sean disrobed himself, as my clothes were yanked off. We each chucked them onto the other, an effort to hinder, laughing when a clothing war almost broke out. With a leap, Sean sailed over the bush to send me bowling, but we ceased to gambol when it dawned on us that his dad and brother were changing without us.

Back on his own side, he folded down behind the bush, and I mimicked him on mine. Despite the agony I knew would come, I dragged forth the change. The outcome would be worth every second.

I heard Sean's change, felt it, smelled it. Even during that act, our breaths released in sync, our hearts matched in beat, yet when we growled from the change at the same time, my head whipped round in shock.

To my right, I caught a flash of movement, a second before Sean collided with my flank and sent us tumbling through the dirt. Rolling right over, I scrabbled for purchase until I steadied myself upright. With hind legs pushed high, head low, my tail wagged like a wild tease, as he matched my position, nose to nose, paws to paws.

Our eyes flicked to the side at the approach of new arrivals. We inhaled, eyes locking once we'd identified Nathan and Ethan. Excitement, amusement, and enthusiasm reflected in our stares.

With a snort, the two arrivals nudged us to our feet. Nathan's face lifted to the sky. The sweet musical sound of his howl reverberated inside my skull and incited me to unite with him. At the answering song from somewhere to the west, we clouded up dirt and took off.

Exhilaration accompanied running through the forest. The others pounced on me the second I reached them, received low warning growls, yips, snaps of my jaw. Sean did little to assist, merely stood with his tongue lolling out the side of his mouth.

I dived forward, snorted my sarcastic thanks, but forgave him when the brushing of our bodies produced shudders through us both.

The whip round of my head coincided with the flare of my nostrils. I stepped forward, ears flattened as I sniffed and snorted, sniffed and snorted. Eyes closing, my nose lifted into the air, as the feast of flavours accosted me from every direction, and my head bobbed as short, fast inhalations drew them in. It was confusing, frustrating—which way to turn, which to choose. I whimpered, body straining forward until Sean reached my side.

He nudged me, licked at my face.

Another glance back toward the scents, and I sought reassurance before taking off. He urged me forward, shoved at me. The approval was enough.

Sean ran so closely beside me, his body heat, the rub of fur on fur, and his warm breath all reassured as he maintained contact. Unsure, yet elated, I ran one way, caught a new smell, whirled. A fresh one, and I changed direction again.

At a wondrous aroma drifting across on the breeze, my feet skidded to a halt. In an instant, my nose located the route it travelled, and I changed path.

Every surrounding sound, scent, movement infiltrated my mind. The soft wind through the leaves, creaking branches swaying beneath the effort. Paws and claws scurrying as wildlife became alerted to our presence. My own paws, the pack's, heavily yet nimbly placed, made scarcely a sound in their graceful motion.

An owl's hoot followed by another. A squeak—probably a mouse or other small rodent. Farther sounds travelled to me: the roll of tyres, the rumble of an engine.

I blocked them. They weren't welcome.

Bark, wood, leaves, earth, wildflowers, pine, moisture, Sean, the pack—all of them floated to me as an offering of flavours. As well as a whole medley of fresh meat.

Despite pushing myself hard, my heart beat a steady rhythm —Sean's as regular beside me. With each leap, I felt the workout within my muscles, the stretching of tendons, the jolt of each landing, the gentle quakes of the cool ground against my pads beneath each of my attacks.

A gust of wind rustled my coat, battered it flat against my body. Its travelled direction pinpointed the location of my prize —near, so near.

I trembled, the sensation flowing through me, continuing through to affect Sean.

The prey appeared. Scurrying away, darting low to the ground. The scent of fear emanated from its every pore, driving me to distraction.

I had to have it. I *wanted* it. Plunging ahead, I almost tasted it.

Sean ducked to the side. With snapping jaws, he herded it to me, chasing it until within reach. I snarled out my hunger and snatched for it.

The squirming, screeching animal was heavier than expected as I tossed it up. My jaws widened to catch it before locking down. I slowed to a stop, yet the creature continued to fight.

Sean shook his head at me. When I just stared at him, he shook his head again, his eyes hungry, yet twinkling with amusement.

Mirrored flicks of my head to the sides swung the animal back and forth. It squealed its protest. I ignored its plea, snapped left, right, left ...

The creature stilled.

With a shiver, I lapped up the fresh blood—it consumed my senses as it trickled along my tongue, pooled in my mouth, the warm fluid thrilling my taste buds.

When Sean took a step forward, I growled but took notice of his gentle shove. The fox cub hung limp from my jaws as I followed him to a small clearing. Josh and Daniel lay grazing within. Sean nudged me to join them, waited until I lowered to the ground, and then took off.

By the time he returned with a gift to himself, I had the torn creature held between my forepaws, its flesh unrecognisable. My canine purr announced my pleasure as Sean padded over and lay beside me and tucked into his meal. Curious about the different flavour oozing from the meat at his mouth, I shuffled closer. Lifting his head, he allowed me to tear a small chunk, waiting as I sampled it, but preferring my own, I retracted.

Once he'd finished, we lazily washed each other until too sated to move. Even as wolves, we managed to entwine, and my eyes closed in contented satisfaction.

A LOW WHISPER and gentle shake woke me. My lids fluttered before closing, and I rolled over, wrapped my arms around my head.

"Jem, you need to wake up," Nathan said.

I shook my head. "No." Surprised to hear the sound of my voice, I looked up to the glow of breaking dawn.

Nathan stood over me, fully dressed and smiling. The others were up, too, but they averted their eyes as soon as I glanced over.

To my right, Sean rolled to his knees and stretched, rubbing at his thick hair. He leaned down to kiss me with a smile. "You should get dressed." As he stood to pull on his clothing that somehow materialised on the ground, I peered down at my naked body.

"My clothes ..."

"I've fetched them." Nathan turned his back and slung them over his shoulder.

I tugged them on and brought myself to a satisfactory level of decency. As I reached up with my fingertips and bowed my back, working out muscle kinks, they all slowly turned to me. Straightening, I smiled at them, and like a cue to pounce, Daniel grabbed me up. My legs swung, as he laughed and tossed me after a few strides to Kyle. I giggled and squealed as we darted and dashed, and rough and tumbled, the entire walk.

We didn't head home, but followed the Larsen's to theirs, where the day was spent with Connor and his boys. After dinner, we ran around getting muddy in rain, which fell constantly from lunchtime onward, and played ball in the garden. It was absolute bliss but did nothing to reduce my excitement. That remained even once we'd returned home, my body thrumming so hard, I guessed it would take days to descend from my high.

I could live with that.

My LINGERING tiredness made us late for work on Monday. When we pulled up on site, Kyle, Connor and Daniel already worked in their hard-hats, as did Jack and two of his workforce.

After sending them a wave, I reached into the pickup for my laptop and tucked it under my arm before grabbing my sketchpad to stick under there, too. When I went to lift the cool box, Sean stretched around for it. He carried it as he walked me to the hut.

With something to do in the cube—something I enjoyed—I thought of it less as a prison and more like an office. Rather than drag my feet over to it, I waltzed with a smile.

"You'd better get to work," I told Sean when we reached the door. "I've already made everybody late."

Smiling, he lowered the cool box to the ground. "Do I get a kiss before I go?"

"Baby, you can have a kiss anytime."

I giggled when he pulled me close, his ravenous mouth catching my breath and unsteadying me. His chuckle was deep as he danced backward before turning to walk away. From the office step, I enjoyed the swing of his hips, the movement of his exposed muscles, the tightening of his rear with each stride.

He glanced over his shoulder. "I'll come see you in an hour, Jem."

"You'd better."

A tug and nudge opened the door a crack. With laptop and pad secure beneath my arm, I hefted up the cool-box and backed up the steps as the site came to life with mixers, machinery, the bang of brick hammers, and scrapes of trowels.

Before I'd fully opened the door, the stench hit me. My head tilted. My nostrils flared. Alcoholic antiseptic-ness dominated the small space.

Another push widened the door farther, and nose twitching like a crazed rabbit, I swung around to face the interior.

At a flash of movement behind the door, I spun—but not before the door slammed shut.

I opened my mouth to shout, half-lifted my laden arms in defence.

Fingers grabbed for my larynx, asserted pressure captured my words, and my feet lost ground as a face pushed into mine. "Remember me?"

"Matthew." The word arrived on a wheeze as my eyes darted toward the door.

"They're not coming, Jem." He smiled, yet it held no warmth. "Not this soon. If you try anything, I *will* crush your windpipe. Do you understand?"

Beneath his tightening hand, my throat threatened to narrow beyond breaths, but that didn't stop my optimistic gasps for air. Pulse raging the blood beneath my ears, terror lessened my hold on the items I carried.

The cool-box created a loud *thunk* on landing, followed by the roll of spilled contents. Paper fluttered in a downward sail. My laptop hit with a clatter before ricocheting to the far wall.

"I'm going to put this over your mouth," he murmured. "Struggle, and I *will* hurt you."

He lifted a white dust mask, clearly the source of the foreign smell. My eyes widened as the cup fit over my face.

Fumes instantly filled my mouth and nostrils. He held it

there while snapping the elastics around the back of my head, and my eyes stung until the arrival of liquid blurred my vision.

As my balance faltered, his hands grasped me. Before me, one Matthew became two, then three, dancing left and right, in and out.

My arms dropped to my sides like the bones had evaporated.

My legs collapsed.

My back slid down the wall, and the room tilted.

His lips moved. Only a jumble reached my ears like my head was underwater and I couldn't surface. When he tucked his shoulder into my hip, my brain screamed, '*Noooooooooooo!*' Though, all I succeeded in producing was, "Wha ... wha ... wha," past a tongue that had thickened beyond cohesive use.

A whoosh of air whizzed past my ears as he slung my body over his shoulder. I tried to focus beyond my hanging arms but my head spun. He'd got me into my most feared position, and there was nothing I could do about it.

He spoke again, yet I couldn't push past the *Whum! Whum! Whum!* filling my hearing beyond capacity.

A draft of cool air encompassed my limp form. Each swing of my body matched the jolt of pounding feet. My brain told me we moved in slow motion, yet I knew he was running—fast. Beneath me, the swaying ground spiralled, distorted. Nausea arrived. Still, I couldn't move, could not make sound. My mind really wanted me to do something, but the descending weight was too heavy a burden for it to operate—it struggled to carry a load of such magnitude.

Muted cries came from somewhere, as my body flopped backward. Numbness crept through me. Bangs, slams, voices, all sounded as though a million miles away. I'd have sworn I rocked with the sensation of movement, yet I hadn't shifted.

Colours, shapes, light flashed. My eyes rolled in an effort to just *see*. Another roll, followed by another—like I'd lost all control. I tried one last time to see, speak, to hear before my body gave up the fight and I saw, spoke, and heard no more.

My stomach heaved. A roll to the left sent me to the floor in an undignified heap. Carpet greeted my palms, and I blinked my eyes open to roiling and waving—a mad psychedelic pattern of greens below me. Just looking at it fuzzed my brain.

My body lurched as a retch forced past my throat. At the stench of the vomit, my stomach heaved and churned. Further retches followed, each one weakening my limbs until they barely held the strength to support me.

"Ah, good, she's awake."

Arms bent at the elbows, my hair hung in my pool of vomit. No matter the effort, my head wouldn't lift to the owner of the voice.

Hands gripped my armpits, and I left the floor to swing in a wide arc. Springiness greeted my rear. A shock of pain coursed through me.

My hands lifted to the *boom, boom, boom* inside my head, and a groan, hindered by my too-thick tongue, escaped.

Breaths hit the skin of my arms.

I kicked out, ignoring my pounding head that screamed at me to stop.

"Shit!" A chuckle. "Open your eyes."

I shook my head. My brain rattled at the effort. I rubbed at my temples, kneaded my lids.

"Jem, open your eyes."

I pressed the balls of my hands into my sockets, holding them shut against whoever was there. Fingers gripped my wrists, tugged. I blinked hard, and a face, inches before me, swam into focus. Another blink. I reopened my eyes, and my breath lodged in my throat.

Werewolves filled the room around me.

Jonathon Richards took a step back when my eyes remained open, and I glanced around. Other than him, I counted five. My throat dried, as my pulse went into erratic, dramatic mode.

Jonathon smiled. "We've been waiting for you to wake, Jem."

I looked back at him and then down at my hands pressed into a mattress beneath me. A bed? My gaze returned to Jonathon.

"Obviously, you've already met me." He grinned. "And my brother Thomas, and Stuart. Matthew, who I'm sure you're now more than familiar with." His hand gestured to each of them. "However, you haven't met Luke Cunningham—Stuart's little brother—and my father, Hugh. Everybody, this is Jem." His smile was bright enough to warn ships from a rocky peak during a storm, his behaviour suggestive of a social function. Did that make me the guest of honour? Maybe to them, but they seriously needed to work on their people skills.

I didn't speak, didn't smile—just offered them my best scowl. I'd been practicing them, so I probably gave a good one.

"Don't be alarmed." Jonathon grabbed my arm and hauled me to my feet. "They just want to take a sniff."

What the—? My eyes narrowed—which hurt. Surely, he couldn't be for real—except his smile, the way he held onto my hand like we were old friends, told me he very much was. My scowl altered to a frown, and I swayed.

Coming behind, Jonathon took my hips. "It's okay, Jem. I've got you."

I tugged at his fingers, but his vice-like grip became the least of my worries when the four men stepped forward. One leaned in closer with his nostrils flared. I twisted away, and breaths hit my cheek, invading my olfactory. From the scent, I recognised Stuart.

Places were switched, and I was sniffed by Thomas.

I didn't look at any of them when they approached. Neck strained to the side, fists tightly clenched, a low rumble vibrated through my chest—more so when Matthew shifted into my line of sight and sent a leering grin.

The two unfamiliar ones stepped forward and sniffed—Luke, then Hugh. Fingers took my chin, and Hugh forced me to face him before inhaling, another too strong for me to resist. His eyes sought mine, stared into them.

I gritted my teeth and fought against the squirm affecting my body.

Smiling, he took a step back, yet I didn't relax. "You know, I couldn't quite believe it when my boy brought your journal home."

My frown deepened. I wanted to ask, 'What bloody journal?'

"It was just pure luck that it happened to fall into his possession at all. Of course, we'd heard the stories, but you never really know something's true, or expect something like this to happen unless it actually does."

I almost said, 'Sorry, you're making no sense whatsoever,' but kept my mouth shut as my frown returned to a scowl.

"I mean, what were the chances of that husband of yours bringing it to work with him?"

Husband? What?

"You've only yourself to blame. If you didn't fool around with that bloody idiot behind his back, he'd never have taken notice of it."

"What are you talking about?" I finally said.

"Your journal, Jem. Your dream journal. Peter brought it in to work with him, left it lying around on his desk. Jonathon spotted it and scanned through, saw Sean's name. He asked Peter about it and then your name cropped up." His smile bordered on smugness. "Obviously, he couldn't help but borrow it for a little bedtime reading."

"That was *private*."

The sharp swing of my face, tears springing to my eyes, and the 'O' of my gasping mouth were the initial indication he'd hit me. Seconds later, the sting of assaulted flesh travelled to my brain.

"When you speak to me, you will do so with respect," he said.

Teeth grinding in temper, I went to tell him respect had to be earned, but something told me to keep my mouth shut.

"As I was saying," he continued, "Jonathon brought it home. We all read it—very interesting, by the way—and we were intrigued about its owner. Matthew grilled Peter and the other workers. We got the picture eventually, understood what happened, who you were with. And then ..." He gave a small laugh. "We were just planning how to find you when you showed up. How lucky was that? From there it was easy." Straightening, he crossed his arms and smiled down at me like he thought my own stupidity had paved the path to them. For five long seconds I endured his stare—I know; I counted—before he turned and headed for the door. Everyone but Jonathon and Matthew followed, and his words carried back as he strode across the landing. "Boy's, it will be nice to have a lady in the house, don't you think?"

Chapter 40

Jonathon took a step back and sat on the bed, tugging me down beside him, but my attention remained on Matthew —he hadn't moved from his casual stance.

"How's your face?" Jonathon tilted me toward him. "I'm sorry he hit you, but you should try not to antagonise him. Dad can be ... strict."

My lips stayed shut. I had nothing to say to any of them. Just as I had no interest in anything *they* had to say. Unless, of course, it pertained to escape routes.

"I understand you're upset," he continued, "maybe even a little frightened."

When I still didn't answer, he sighed and went to join Matthew across the room. Side by side, they both stared my way.

I glared back—from one to the other, then back again. When their stares didn't waver, and I grew too exhausted to continue, I turned my back on them.

After what seemed an eternity, they pushed up to leave.

Jonathon paused at the door. "We're going to leave your door open, so you won't feel enclosed. But tonight, we'll lock it, for you as much as anything else. Don't worry, though, only Matthew and I will take care of the key."

Time held no meaning as I endured one visitor after another. Each time, I heard their approach and identified them by scent without turning. Mostly, they entered, stayed a while. Sometimes, I only received a pause in steps or inhalation at the doorway. Once or twice, they tried to talk to me. I didn't respond.

When food was brought and left, I didn't look at it, didn't eat it. The only time I spoke was to ask to use the bathroom, mostly to get an untainted drink of water from the tap. My throat had begun to shut down, and I knew if I didn't drink I'd be in trouble, so my pride had to be swallowed for that one.

On his later return, Jonathon *tutted* at my uneaten food. When asked why I hadn't eaten, I remained mute. I figured he was smart enough to figure that one out on his own.

With the enveloping darkness came the locking of the door. Unwilling to risk falling asleep, I remained upright, legs crossed, hands in lap. Only my head moved, tilting from side to side to follow sounds downstairs. Absorbing the difference in footsteps, hesitations and pauses as turns were made, I attempted to gain a mental map of the rooms. Stair climbing helped me estimate my distance from the head of the stairs. I wished I'd taken more notice during my bathroom visits but hadn't wanted to alert them to my scrutiny. After a few hours of dedicated concentration, I had a good idea where the living room and kitchen were situated. I recognised I would have to go a full length of the landing before reaching the staircase and was pretty certain a U-turn would be required to descend them. Other than that, I knew nothing—but it was a start.

The night dragged for hours. I didn't mind. Better to be left alone and not have to deal with their leers, evident hunger and bloody sniffing—the sniffing drove me crazy.

When the key clanked and the door opened the following morning, I stiffened. Without turning, I inhaled—Jonathon—and listened as he neared. The sweet aroma of bacon preceded its appearance, and my stomach cried out for it, yet I pretended I hadn't noticed as he offered the grub.

Jonathon sat beside me on the bed, toyed with a strand of my hair. I stiffened further but ignored him. He gave up within minutes, leaving the door open on his departure.

The open door brought a repeat of visits. Upon waking, the first place they came to was me. I began to feel like a priceless artefact—like they were scared to remove their attention, in case they turned back and found me gone.

That was my plan. I just hadn't figured out how to do it.

The day seemed to take even longer than the night to pass. My body swayed with the effort of staying awake and upright. Again, I requested a bathroom break to drink from the tap—again, I refused to eat. How much longer I'd hold out for, I couldn't be sure. I'd already weakened.

Each meal arrived with an encouragement to eat. They offered more than four square meals, as though to tempt me with something different. Each smelled delicious, yet I didn't look at them, afraid I'd be unable to resist shovelling it in if it came into view. My stubbornness earned me irritation, huffing and puffing, a couple of growls.

I ignored the lot.

THE DRAWING of evening bought the promise of darkness and another visitor. Although I didn't turn, the swishing of the door over carpet with him on the inside offered suspicion of trouble.

Matthew's stares terrified me the most—and I was alone with him.

The mattress depressed beside me. He leaned back to look at me. I stared ahead. His lips moved. I blocked his voice. Whatever he had to say, it couldn't be good.

A tug of my arm to haul me closer got my attention. The growl that left me did so of its own accord. Eyes darkening, he tugged me again. I looked down at his fingers wrapped around my upper arm. As my gaze lifted to his, my lips pulled back.

His hand released me and rose for the swing. I threw my body back. When I hit the edge of the bed, my feet flew over my head, and I came to land in a crouch, lips already vibrating. Before the snarl could be expelled, his back-handed slap bounced off the rawness caused by Hugh.

I gasped, my hands flinging up to protect against further attack, but he grasped my thighs and strode with me. Raising me to his waist, he shoved me hard against the bedroom wall, his crushing body forcing out my grunt.

I turned away as he pushed his face into mine. Trembles swept through me, as his words vibrated through my mind. Although I tried to drown him out, too many penetrated, until heavy dread settled in the pit of my stomach. Hands fisted, I willed myself not to respond.

"... your fight, Jem?" he whispered. "... better when they fight, like the challenge ..."

Closing my eyes, I twisted my face farther away, but when he slid me lower until his groin pressed into me, waves of panic pushed through. With my chest heaving, my heart pounding, dizziness arrived.

Rigid against me, he placed his lips to my ear, giving me no choice but to hear. "... they struggle ... teaching a lesson ... desperately ... you to ... fighter, Jem ... so badly ..."

My entire body shook. Tears trickled down my cheeks. I

tried to focus on the route they took to my lips, to focus on anything but him.

"... when I come for you, Jem, I'm going ..."

I concentrated so hard on the image of the bumblebee fabricated by my mind, followed its whizzing and buzzing from one flower head to the next. I brought forth the white fluttering of butterfly wings, flapping delicately, so beautiful. Purple flowers danced, their narrow stems bending with the breeze. An entire army of grass leaned, trained to mirror its neighbours movements, until my head filled with the show.

Bumblebees and butterflies, Jem. The conjuring of Sean's voice created an ache within my chest, the pain sharp enough to snap me back—to Matthew's fingers digging into my thighs, his breath on my ear, the smell of his body, the rough arousal in his voice as he whispered his sick version of sweet nothings.

"... time I've finished with you ... wish ... here for you, Jem, at first light. My face will be the first thing you see when you open your eyes and the last thing you see just as you start to wish you'd never been reborn ..."

Through my terror came the swish of the door.

"... brother is dead because ..."

"What the hell are you doing to her?"

Footsteps preceded a low snarl. When my slumping body hit carpet, I realised Matthew had been dragged away.

"You've bloody scared her half to death. What the fuck is wrong with you?"

Jonathon's voice registered, yet I couldn't see him through my tears. My legs, twisted awkwardly beneath me, gave pain, but I didn't move. Uncontrolled shaking possessed my body. I couldn't have stopped it if I tried.

Blood escaped my lip where I'd unconsciously bitten down. I smelled it, as well as that within my clenched hands where my nails had broken the skin.

Low words passed between the two men. I didn't hear them. All that carried to me were the desperate sounds of my distress.

"Get the fuck out of here, Matthew."

Fingers folded around my arm. I cowered away, a quiet whimper escaping. Eyes closed, I pushed back against the wall, scrambling away with my feet.

Fingers once again pulled at me. That time, my hands flew out, whipping at anything near, my low guttural growl warning them away.

After a few failed attempts to placate me, Jonathon mumbled an apology and left the room, locking me in. Alone, I wilted to my side, knees curled to my chest, body still shaking as my erupting tears wracked shudders through my body.

NIGHT ARRIVED to coat me in blackness, and I welcomed it. With eyes wide open, I remained forever vigilant. I'd calmed enough for my tears to cease, but the trembling refused to dissipate, as did the rupture within my chest each time Sean's voice returned—an attempt at comfort creating more pain.

Dusk became twilight, then darkness. Through the barred window, the stars twinkled against the midnight backdrop. I scoured the walls, chased shadows cast by night birds in flight. To my hearing came the distinctive whip of bats' wings, flickering from one sanctuary to the next.

As I lay, the gloom lifted. Sky shades altered to deliver the arrival of dawn. Once again, my body began its violent trembling, and every one of Matthew's words that I'd tried so hard to blank out growled through my mind.

With no control over my emotions, the tingling in my limbs came to call. I knew a change was imminent, didn't try to prevent it, or push it away. Instead, I harvested the ripples and the growing spasms as muscles contracted. At my invitation, shards of agony shot through me, as did the licking burns that accompanied my contorting flesh.

Back bowing, clothing tearing, I pushed up, eyes wide through my silent scream.

Each tendon adopted the change, each bone conformed in unison, and all thirty-three of my vertebrae clicked into place. My heart played a rapid tune beneath the weight of my panted breaths, and aware of the advancing end, I pulled back, an attempt to slow it down. After all, with the absence of agony, I'd have no distraction, nothing to chase away the unwanted images playing out inside my mind—but I was too far gone.

Taking control, the change forced through and called my wolf to the surface. I collapsed to the carpet, chest heaving and tongue hanging from my open jaws, with inner thoughts my lone companion.

Long after first light, the key jiggled in the door. In one swift motion, I was on my feet, snapped to a sense of preparedness.

With the rattle of the key came the twist of metal upon metal, the mechanical workings clicking into place. Backing away and to the side, I faced the door, head down. Ears back, I exposed my teeth.

The door nudged across the carpet.

A low thrum vibrated in my chest.

The door widened.

I listened for the first step upon the soft pile.

A steady heart beat thudded. Whoever they were, they held no fear. Well, more fool them.

I watched, listened, waited.

The toe of a foot appeared before the body emerged.

I crouched, tensed for attack—lunging, the instant I knew they had no time for retreat.

As though sensing my flight, they turned. Brown eyes widened in shock.

I hit the body hard. Fur slammed on flesh. Together, we dropped. My jaws located their neck. Teeth breaking the surface, I gripped, ripped, yanked, until a jerk of my head took his throat. The body landed with a quiet *thunk*.

His warm exhalations bristled my muzzle, while blood pumped from his artery to spray my face. He grabbed for his wound—made a weak effort to cry out. No sound arrived, only bubbles of red as death crept forth to stake its claim. Blood soaked the carpet around his neck, and the thick wool absorbed it until saturated in a wide circle of crimson.

No time to look at his face, to take in his scent. No hesitation. Out, onto the landing, my race for freedom took me to the end without interjection. I collided with the wall. A rebound knocked me the way I needed to go.

They'd be alerted, I expected, would have heard their pack mate hitting the deck. If not that, then my thuds, my accident-induced yelp, surely.

Throwing myself on, I tumbled, almost bounced down the stairs. Confusion masked awareness as I skidded into the kitchen. *Where the hell is the front door?* Across the tiled floor, I slid until cupboards blocked my path.

Three werewolves sat at the table. At my intrusion, they thrust to their feet.

I stumbled upright. My eyes glanced about for an exit.

At the click of a catch, my head whirled, tracing it out, alongside the stairs—to the front door that pushed open as I watched.

I scrambled, almost comically, feet slipping on the spot for seconds before I found enough grip to propel me toward the outside scents.

"Shut that *fucking* door!"

The roar at my rear faltered my step for only a split second. I ploughed forward, but the shouts alerted the man ahead to the crazed wolf bounding toward him.

As he turned to me, his mouth formed the words, '*oh, shit*'. He had no chance to respond, to run, or trap me again, before I sailed toward his face. Snarls flying freely, my maws opened for attack.

We barrelled out the door, hit the driveway. His arms lifted in defence, but I snapped at them, tearing, tossing bites of skin left and right. When he attempted to grab me, my teeth lurched for him. I bit, tore, shredded his arms, hands, face, legs as he tried to anchor me down. Every wound drove me insane—each spray, each fleck of blood.

Kicks and shoves pummelled my chest, my flank. Screams penetrated the air.

"The fucking gates!"

My eyes swung to the source of the cry, and I tracked Jonathon's gaze to my right—to gates that had begun to move. My exit was narrowing.

I dismissed the writhing man and threw myself down the driveway. My head pushed forward in determination, desperation. I neared, yet it looked hopeless. I ran faster. Almost there, I leaped, flung myself through. Metal scraped my rump as I dove out the other side.

Unable to stop, my legs carried me into the road—into the path of an oncoming car. It skidded as it braked. Horror froze me to the spot. With its final decline of speed, it nudged me over. My hind leg gave way on impact, and I let out a loud yelp.

The driver stepped out onto the road. Gates rattled beneath the demands of the pursuing werewolves.

Pausing would see me dead, so ignoring the throb at my rear, I forced myself up. Across the road, I pushed through bushes, branches, thorns, sharp twigs scratching at my face. I closed my eyes against them, opening only once on the other side. A field stretched before me, and I ran, as fast as I could, faster than ever before. Even when my throbbing injury requested a break, I ran —wild, out of control.

The field wasn't large—rural landscape didn't continue for long, and I found myself on house-lined streets. People paused to glance at me, yet none attempted approach. They probably rationalised what they thought they'd just seen.

Realising how straight a run I'd travelled, I altered course to veer left and right, to dart around corners and duck behind walls.

With no concept of time, I eventually paused beside water, where I took stock of my surroundings: some kind of recreational park. My throat burned from my panicked plight, and I teetered on the bank, trying desperately to reach the rippling pool below. I managed a few licks before backing off.

Through the park, I kept my padding paws to the bushes, or beneath the shelter of trees. Another pause, another look around showed a whole row of gardens to the left, backed onto the park, some enclosed, some exposed.

Continuing as wolf was no longer an option. I had no idea where I was, which way to go. If I found a way to enter one of the properties, then maybe, just maybe, I could call for help.

Bushes invaded by dense bramble clusters made good cover. Safe from prying eyes, I pressed into a niche within the bush and prepared to change back.

I rushed through, despite the agony, afraid of being caught in the act. To be discovered mid-change would've been catastrophic. I'd probably have ended up bludgeoned, or with the emergency services contacted. Neither outcome appealed.

Once completed, I stayed in position and checked for an approach, breathing out a sigh when I detected none. A naked woman in the local park was not a usual occurrence, either. Even that would have earned me a highlight spot on the news.

As I crept across to a garden with a low fence, I couldn't contain my sigh. The house beyond had wide patio doors—probably to take advantage of the view. I willed myself to see past the reflective glare, until the open-plan setting of downstairs became clear.

I watched for minutes, and when there was no apparent sign of activity, I mounted the fence and scurried toward the house in a crouch, despite the screaming ache in my hip.

At the windows, I pressed my face to the glass, checked for occupants. Nobody. I tried the handle. Locked. *Not so lucky.* Hoping to snap it, I tugged at the locking catch, but my energy had already evaporated, my nerves were frayed, my entire body still shook from my ordeal. I couldn't do it. I'd have to break the glass—not ideal, but I had no choice.

I reached for the first boulder I spotted, sliding my hand over to get a grip, yet paused. The texture seemed *wrong*. Studying it, I realised it wasn't even made of stone. Stupid thing was plastic. I swung my arm to toss it back down, but halted at a jangle from within. Shaking it created another tinkled clatter, and I located an opening, slid off a tiny panel. Upon finding a set of concealed keys, my lips spread into a smile.

Stepping into a kitchen, I inhaled, detecting the stale odour of breakfast dishes left dirty in the sink. A deeper intake brought lingering hints of body odour but nothing else. Across the kitchen, I came to a lounge, where a far table supported a telephone. I took one step toward it, two, but at running footsteps descending the stairs, I froze. I'd dealt with too much over the space of two days. My reflexes had had enough.

A young man, or boy, jumped into the living room. Spotting

me, he halted, as his eyes skimmed my body. A smile appeared on his lips, and he glanced around as though expecting someone to announce the joke.

I watched him, waiting to see what he'd do.

He spoke. "Shit, I got some naked bird in the lounge."

The subtle tightening of my hands and the tiny alteration to my stance in preparation for the worst were my only movements.

"'The fuck you doin' in 'ere?" Laughter bubbled beneath the words.

"I'm sorry," I murmured, "but I really need to make a phone call."

"You in some kinda trouble, lady?"

I nodded, not once removing my attention from him.

His eyes, as though unable to resist, roamed back over me, and I tensed. "I thought it was only the stags they did this to." His entire face participated in his frown.

I shrugged.

"Your friends do this to you?"

Another shrug.

"So, if you've been on a hen night, or summat, how come you got blood all over you?"

Think! "It was themed. Zombies." *Pathetic.* I held my pose.

He didn't look convinced. "That blood looks real to me."

Definitely not convinced. "It's supposed to. Special effects stuff." I tried a smile with my shrug. Not with teeth, though— that I couldn't do, not without scaring him.

"And your face, the bruises?"

Obviously, I hadn't fooled him one bit. I shrugged again. I must have looked pretty desperate, though—even I felt the pleading in my eyes.

He nodded. "'Kay, you can use the phone."

"Thanks." I stepped over, lifted the receiver—and realised I had no idea of anyone's number. I knew Jess's, but calling her would lead to questioning. Even if I did call, and she contacted Sean, would he answer, knowing he'd be unable to tell her where I was? Not an option—and Poppy was way out of the running for someone to involve.

"Whassup?"

My trembles restarted. "I ... I don't know any numbers." My lips quivered and tears sprang to my eyes.

"Shit, what you cryin' for?"

"I really need to get home. He'll be so worried ..."

"Your fiancé?"

Rather than correct him, I nodded as a tear tracked over my face.

"Shit!" He went to pat me on the shoulder, some kind of comfort gesture, but pulled away like he remembered it would mean contacting bare flesh. Perhaps my defensive body language made him back off, also.

More tears erupted as I replaced the receiver. "I don't know what to do."

"You really *are* in trouble?"

I guessed boys didn't usually find naked women, covered in blood and bruises, breaking and entering. Swiping at my face, I nodded

"Dammit!" He paced the room, faced the far wall, turned back to me. "Do you want me to call the police?"

"No!" My whispered plea screamed of distress.

"Shit!" He paced again, mumbling under his breath. "I think you should."

I shook my head hard enough to hurt, more tears escaping.

"Shit!" He strode the length of the room again, incoherently mumbling to the wall for seconds before he turned to face me. "You know where you live?"

I nodded.

"I'll give you a lift."

"You drive?" He didn't look old enough.

"Coupla weeks. Got myself a little run around outside. You wanna ride, or not?"

Forcing the tears back, I nodded.

"Let me ... you can't ..." He gestured to my body. "Hang on." He shot upstairs. When he re-emerged, he carried a bedcover. "You can use this."

I took the child's duvet cover, which sported spaceships and planets, and wrapped it around myself.

"Right, let me just lock up. Me mum's got a Sat-nav—we'll use that." He darted into the kitchen, secured the patio doors, found the Sat-nav in a drawer, then turned back to me. "Okay, nekked bird. Let's get you home."

Chapter 41

The kid frowned at the Sat-nav. "Shit! It's about forty miles."

I stiffened for a second, terrified he'd change his mind about taking me. Instead, he stuck the car in gear, and although he mumbled about being late, having to use all his fuel, and something like 'if Lauren hears about this, I'll probably be dumped,' he pulled off.

Snuggled inside the thin cotton, I kept my head down. The boy tried talking to me, mostly stuff like asking my name. I answered *Marie.* He tried to find out what had happened, but I shrugged. Once he'd accepted my unwillingness to talk, he asked if I liked music and put a CD in the stereo, singing along in a quiet murmur.

During the ride, the heat of my hip injury deepened until I could think of nothing else. I closed my eyes, breathing deeply. When sleep attempted to sneak in, I snapped my lids back open.

A further twenty minutes passed, and as my surroundings became familiar, hope built within me. Another ten minutes, and I directed him through the gates, my lip quivering at the sight of home.

The kid peered up through the windscreen. "Lady, your house is sweet."

Nodding, I asked him to write down his name and address, with the promise to send fuel money. Being a teenager, he agreed. Clutching the sheet bearing the name of my saviour, I forced my seized-up hip to get me out of the car and offered profuse thanks.

Once he'd driven away, I turned to the house. Lack of a greeting suggested no one was home. To be certain, I banged on the door and the windows, peering through. Nothing. Round to the back of the house, I did the same. Even the conservatory was locked tight.

Turning toward the forest, I glanced farther in my mind, to Connor's house. I couldn't enter the forest, though. Not alone. Not in my condition. Overwhelmed by exhaustion, I wedged myself deep into the corner between the house and conservatory walls, where I had a clear view of all approaching angles.

With each passing minute, my distress heightened. In my mind, every second added to the chance that Jonathon or Matthew would show up to take me back. As the day plodded forever onward, I also began to believe Sean wouldn't come— that I'd be there all night. Waiting. My body trembled, and I chewed my bottom lip to a pulp when panic pushed its way through. Blood coated my palms from relentless clenching and unclenching of my hands, and the pain of my damaged body intensified with each passing hour, the hard paving a brutal discomfort. As the sun submitted to the looming night, my tears resurfaced.

At some point, too emotionally burned out to fight any longer, I must have fallen under into a fitful sleep. When my eyes snapped back open, my entire body tensed. I listened, inhaled, listened, peering hard into the darkness.

Voices drifted from inside the house. At the sound of keys, I tried to push up, jump to my feet, to call out, yet couldn't.

Please, whoever's there, please know I'm here.

"... telling you, I could smell her ..."

"... do this to yourself, Sean, you'll ..."

I strained my ears. Could I really hear them? *It's all in your head, Jem.*

"... I *know* what I smelled. I could ..."

"... You said that yesterday, too ... if you ... she's not there ..."

The back door opened. Shadows shifted across the conservatory to the glass. Only my eyes held the ability to function, and I strained to see who was there, what they were doing.

Keys twisted in the door beside me before it swung inward. As a dark outline filled the space, an inhalation brought me his scent and my sob burst out.

"Jem? Oh, Jem." Sean dropped to his knees and pulled me forward by my shoulders. I tried to push up to him, to reach out, to hold him, but my wasted body refused. "I *told* you I could smell her," he growled over his shoulder.

I sensed Ethan in the doorway, but my eyes refused to leave Sean. An arm slid around my back, another beneath me. As he lifted me, the warmth of his body offered instant comfort, his scent a gift. Drawn close, face pressed to his chest, I started to cry.

I moved as though weightless, floating on the wind, but my eyes scrunched against the kitchen's brightness.

"What the hell did they do to her?" Ethan asked.

New footsteps arrived. "Jem?" Nathan's voice held disbelief.

My mind refused a look up while my face nuzzled into Sean. I didn't want to leave there, not when it felt as though I'd waited an eternity to return. Something scraped across the tiles, and as Sean lowered himself, my rear hit something solid, my legs and arms dangling either side. Palms warm yet rough, his hands swept over my back, up into my hair, over my back again. Finding will power from somewhere, I lifted my arms until I clasped tight to his shirt, my knuckles aching with fear of letting go. When Sean's lips nuzzled into my hair, his soothing whispers seeping into my ears, I broke down. As though overtaken by a fit of convulsions, my body shook, and I sobbed—until I no longer had control, no longer even sounded human.

Secure in his arms, Sean's murmurs continued. Although the flow of saltiness slowed to a stop, my body continued to judder, each shock of movement jarring my teeth. His hands took my face, tilted it up. When he came into view, I averted my eyes and stared to the side—I felt unworthy of his caresses and comfort, unworthy of him.

"Jem?"

I breathed through my mouth, my stuffed nose no longer available for use, and hiccupped on a tremor. My stare darted to the other side. Face soaked by fallen tears, lids swollen and puffy, they dashed back again.

"Jem, will you look at me?"

His clothing tightened in my twisting hands.

"Jem, please look at me."

I dragged my gaze to his.

He sighed as he looked at me, his eyes so full of emotion they would surely brim over.

"She's covered in blood," said Nathan.

"I don't think it's hers," Sean whispered, still staring into me.

In my periphery, Ethan moved to the sink. Splashes and swishes followed. When he walked over, he had something in his hands, which he placed on the table behind me. More splashing, then, "Jem, I'm just going to ..." His hand neared.

Flinching, I jerked away.

He halted, and whatever he held, he handed to his brother.

Sean released my face to take the flannel and wiped soft fabric across my mouth, cheeks and neck. I watched his face throughout, even as the white towelling turned red. He leaned forward, rinsed the flannel, and repeated the process before dismissing the cloth. Retaking my face, he rubbed at my sore cheek, fury darkening his eyes. "It wasn't her blood."

Although I heard Ethan over in the corner again, I paid him little attention. Clattering, cupboards opening, and the pouring of water arose before he walked back over and passed something to Sean.

A mug materialised beneath my nose. "Drink this, Jem."

My eyes closed as an inhalation caught the warm scent of hot chocolate floating up on a spiral of steam. My hands released his T-shirt, and I forced my fingers to slide around the receptacle in front of me, but kept my lids lowered. After days with little fluid and zero food, I savoured the touch of liquid over my taste buds.

Sean caressed and soothed as I drank. If the others spoke, I didn't hear—wasn't listening. Only the beautiful liquid sliding down my throat held my attention. Sighs escaped between sips, each pause shortening in my desperation to fill myself with more, and my stomach rejoiced at the offering. Once finished, as though encouraged by their success, another mug appeared. I drank that one, also.

"You should get her to bed," Nathan said behind me.

I shook my head.

"She's frozen, Sean," he continued. "Take her up, get her warm, then she can come down and eat."

I gave another headshake.

Nodding, Sean braced his body and shuffled forward in the seat.

Eyes widening, my head shook again, but he slid us to the edge, and as he went to stand, I shoved back against him. "No. We need to stay here."

"Jem, you need to get warm."

"No." My head shook until my brain thumped the inside of my skull. I pushed at him again. "If they come back, we won't hear them from upstairs."

"Ethan and I will stay awake," Nathan said. "You don't need to worry."

Sean pushed up, his arms tightening, and my arms flew out, almost knocking me from his grasp, as my body jerked to rigidity. "No!" My voice sounded ragged.

"Okay." Attempting to keep hold, he lowered us back down. "Okay, if it makes you feel better, we can stay here." He returned to our position on the seat. Calmness arrived with his arms smoothing around my back, his hands rubbing in small circles, before his fingers brushed into my hair and he drew me to him.

My tension drained when I found a new hold in his clothing. My breathing steadied once I accepted he'd allow me to remain. Lids lowering, I tried to control the trembling.

After a few minutes, a heavy quilt covered me. Thick socks were worked over my feet, their warm softness like a silk caress. I didn't move or listen, as tiredness laid its claim to an already weary mind. Each whispered word washed over my mushy brain. Held close by Sean—the warmth of his body so wondrous, the scent of him a luxury I never expected to regain, the beat of his heart reassurance that I wasn't dreaming, and his deep, velvety voice bringing me peace—I allowed myself to sleep.

. . .

Creams and blues danced before me. Even a few rapid blinks didn't bring clarity to them. I rubbed at my lids, tried again—same result. I was pretty certain I was home, in our bed ... but how?

A heavy weight pinned my stomach. Great warmth spread across my back. When I tried to turn, the weight grew heavier, pulling me backward, until the heat at my rear rose and soft breaths fell against the nape of my neck.

I inhaled and sighed. Either I was dreaming—another good one—or I was actually in bed with Sean. Another inhalation drew his heady muskiness into my nostrils, and I knew I had to be awake. He'd never smelled so strong in my subconscious.

To check, I whispered, "Sean?"

An exhalation followed a low grunt.

Definitely Sean, but he sounded as though still under. Teeth gritted against my injured hip, I made an effort to roll without waking him until we faced.

Dark lashes rested over his cheekbones, and his lips vibrated softly with each of his breaths. Placing a palm against his chest, I became hypnotised by the rise and fall, by the pattern of rhythm within. With my other hand against my own chest, I followed my beat, just to be certain of our connection. As always, we matched. Eyes closing, I listened to our mingling breaths, our hearts drumming their tune—a perfect moment that tempted me to stay, to never again move.

The second his breathing altered, my lids lifted to his dark eyes. I didn't speak. Neither did he. He studied me, staring into rather than at me.

Unable to resist any longer, I stretched forward, watching him as my lips brushed against his. "Baby, I missed you so much."

"I missed you, too, Jem," he whispered.

We didn't pull away by more than an inch, and probably

would've remained in silence if the low rumble of my stomach didn't break into our thoughts.

"You're hungry," he whispered.

"It can wait."

Another rumble, more insistent, yet I didn't want to move. Maybe if I just stayed there, where nobody would dare come searching for answers, I could pretend the last few days hadn't happened. Except, more ill-tempered growls echoed from my stomach.

"When was the last time you ate?"

"Before ..." I trailed off. He'd know what I meant.

"You need to eat."

"Later," I said. "I don't want to move."

"You won't have to. I'll fix breakfast, and you can eat up here."

My hand slid around his back to hold him. "I don't want you to go. I can eat later."

He sighed. "Okay, we'll both stay." Lifting his head, he turned toward the door. "Ethan!"

The door swung open and his brother appeared in the frame.

"Can you fix Jem some food?" Sean seemed to communicate something with his eyes. "She's not ready to get up yet, and she needs to eat."

"Sure. What do you fancy? Eggs, bacon, toast ... sound okay?"

I nodded. "And coffee. I need coffee."

He didn't re-close the door when he left. Shuffles and clanks came from the kitchen, and in no time, the sweet, tempting aroma of bacon wafted up.

"Is that just for you?" Nathan said from the hallway.

I thought I'd heard the soft tread of his feet but had been concentrating too hard on the scents.

"No, it's for Jem," Ethan answered.

"Is she awake?"

"I don't think she's eaten in days."

"Is she coming down for it?"

"Dad, do you really expect her to leave that room today?"

"She will," Nathan said. "She's strong."

At the clatter of plates, Sean reached his arm down to the floor. On its return, his hand bore his dirty T-shirt. He kissed my nose before easing his T-shirt over my head. When footsteps hit the first step, I was decent enough to sit up.

The higher up the stairs Ethan came, the busier my nose twitched, the more my stomach called out. By the time he rounded the door, I'd progressed to the foot of the bed with my hand outstretched.

He chuckled at my eagerness.

Sean fit himself at my back, his thighs coming either side of me for support, as Ethan tugged my legs into a sitting position and lowered the tray. It didn't even reach my lap before I grabbed the fork, scooped up egg, and snatched toast in my other hand.

I shovelled in as much egg as my mouth could hold and bit down on toast. As I chewed, I leaned back against Sean's chest, my lids lowering. Once I'd finished that mouthful, I went in search of a second, eating the whole meal in that fashion. At some point, I opened my eyes to find Sean and I alone again.

"Thanks, Ethan," I called around bacon.

"No problem," his voice called from the hall.

"You want some, baby?" I mumbled over my shoulder.

"You eat it. I'll get something later."

By the time I finished eating, I'd almost run out of breath for my coffee, yet I still gulped at it between sighs.

Sean lifted my tray aside. "Better?"

His murmur hit my ear, and I tilted my head to catch it.

"Much better." His lips hovered there as his arms came around to tug me back against him, and I slid my hands over his arms in search of his strong fingers, gripping them before I spoke. "You'll want to know what happened."

"Not until you're ready."

I shook my head. "The sooner I tell you, the quicker we can decide what to do, because something will have to be done. This won't stop unless we end it. Jonathon's already put dibs on me as his."

He stiffened. "Are you ready to talk about it?"

I drew in a breath and nodded. Starting at the beginning, I told him how Matthew had been waiting for me at work, the dust mask, the smell and my inability to function.

"Sounds like ether," he mumbled, his voice deep.

He didn't interrupt, while I explained about waking, them all greeting me like a long lost friend, and the sniffing, but I heard the rumble of frustration buried in his chest. When he asked who'd hit my face, I told him about Hugh. At my belief that Jonathon had his own plans for me and locked me in of an evening, his suppressed growl pushed forth.

I remained calm until I reached the part about Matthew visiting my room. As though aware something worse was coming, Sean's hold tightened. His cheek came to rest against my shoulder, and he listened to me so intently there could have been nobody else in the house with us. The surrounding air seemed to fill with static silence, muting any sounds other than my quietly spoken narrative. I mumbled on, our hands ringing together, about Matthew telling me what he wanted to do to me, how he told me to be ready for him. Unsure of how Sean would respond, I paused to prepare myself to tell him the rest. I was afraid of how he'd feel about my behaviour, that he'd think differently of me, at the same time knowing it wasn't a secret I could keep from him.

He told me it could wait—I didn't have to go on. I argued that I did. The sooner I told him, the faster I'd know his reaction.

After taking a deep breath, I described how Matthew's words terrified me enough to induce a change, how I'd feared his return. Reaching the part when I heard the key in the door, I faltered again, but despite a brewing headache, the tightening of my jaw, and my deepening frown, I pushed forward. "I knew exactly what I was going to do before the door even opened. I wanted to do it, Sean. As soon as I knew he wasn't getting back up, I made a run for it." I skimmed over details, knowing he'd fill in the gaps. "I hurt myself running. I was so frightened, looking like crazy ... but somebody must have been looking down on me" —a tear leaked out—"because one of them came through the front door at that exact moment ... I had to knock him out of the way, they were all yelling at him, but I was too fast. I had to be. He tried grabbing at me ... I think I hurt him pretty bad. There was so much blood, it drove me crazy. But then one of them shouted, and I snapped out of it ..."

My lucid memory played out the scene, as I described my leap for freedom, my hand removing from his to rub across my hip. He tugged at the T-shirt hem, leaned to take a closer look, and caressed it with tenderness.

"And then I could see the driver getting out of his car, could hear them trying to get through the gates. So, I ran. I don't know how long for. All I could think about was getting away, about coming home, but ... where were you, Sean? I came home to nobody ..."

"Jem, I'm so sorry."

"I waited for ages. I waited and waited. I thought ..."

"We were searching for you. We've spent the last three days searching for you ... I've been going out of my mind. We located where they work, but none of them turned up, so we couldn't even follow them. We didn't know where you were, what was happening. I ... thought I'd lost you, Jem. Then, when we came back and your scent was here ... I told them I could smell you, *told* them. God, when I saw you there, I was so relieved, Jem, *so* relieved. I thought I'd lost you, and you came home ..." He gave a long shuddering breath. "You came home to me."

Chapter 42

An hour later, Sean had excused himself to go and talk to his dad, while I took a shower. I didn't object—not if it meant I didn't have to repeat the story.

Water pummelled my hair to rinse away the soap, the spray stinging if I faced one way, but paining even more facing another. Cleaned, refreshed, and unburdened, I lowered my head, braced my hands against the tiles and tried to clear my mind. Only once certain I was ready did I force myself out and go in search of something to pull on.

Dressed in a super-long T-shirt of Sean's and teamed with nothing more than a pair of knickers, I deemed myself equipped to face the others. It took time to descend the stairs in my semi-hobbling state, though, and I sighed upon reaching the bottom.

As soon as I rounded the corner, my inhalations alerted me that Connor and his sons had arrived. When making the bargain with myself, convincing myself I was ready to emerge, it had been with the understanding it was only to face Ethan and Nathan, not everyone else. Stalled in the hallway, my gaze stared toward the door, until the decision was taken out of my hands. Just as my senses alerted me to their presence, theirs must have alerted them to mine, because Josh appeared in the open doorway, a tentative smile on his face.

Despite my inhibitions, my lips curved at the sight of him, and I shifted forward a step. "Josh," I whispered.

I needn't have worried about being unsure, unable to make the move to greet them. Josh made sure of that. At his name leaving my lips, he crossed the space between us and threw his arms around me. My feet left the ground, his face pressed into my hair, and as he *sniffed* me, my concerns vanished.

I wasn't afraid of Josh—or any of them. They'd never judged me, never questioned who I was, anything I'd ever done. Why would I believe my absence would make them behave any differently toward me? They'd shown nothing but understanding, adoration and total acceptance. Why would I even consider that might change?

"It's so good to have you home, Jem," he murmured.

"It's great to *be* home."

The hug lasted longer than necessary before Josh set me back on my feet. He didn't let go of me, though. Keeping a hold of my hand, he encouraged me into the kitchen.

Once in the sights of the others, I endured the same welcome from each of them. Strange, how being sniffed like crazy didn't bother me in the slightest when it came from people I'd begun to consider as family.

Embraces concluded and tension dissipated. I limped across to put on the kettle. It was already early afternoon, and one shot of caffeine nowhere near fuelled me. Although they all jumped up to do it for me, I waved them away. It seemed easier to be on my feet.

"I found this on the ground outside," Ethan said, as I spooned sugar into mugs. "Piece of paper with a name and address on it. Lee Collins?"

I'd completely forgotten—what with my breakdown. "I have

to send him money. He's how I got home." I turned to them. "I promised to repay him."

"Someone gave you a ride home, Jem?" Nathan asked, and I nodded. "But you were naked."

Again, I nodded. They all stared at me, obviously awaiting some sort of explanation, so I recounted about ending up in the park and changing back, about my grand idea to break in somewhere and my luck in finding the house keys.

They didn't interrupt, and I continued on, telling them about the supposedly empty house having one of its occupants come downstairs to find a naked woman in his living room.

"And he didn't find this strange?" Sean asked.

"Of course he did, but he's a teenager. Once he'd got over the initial shock, he thought all his Christmas's had come at once."

Connor chuckled—Ethan, too.

Sean only frowned. "Wasn't he even concerned about the condition you were in? Didn't he question that?"

"Well, he sort of tried coming up with his own theories for it."

Nathan raised an eyebrow. "Which were?"

I told them about the boy's suggestions for my nakedness, enlightening them on the concept of stag and hen nights.

"And he bought all of this?" Nathan asked.

"Not for a minute."

"Yet, he drove you home? Just like that?"

On the verge of explaining my near hysteria over forgetting everyone's numbers, I changed course and gave a nod and shrug instead.

"If you didn't know where you were, how did you find your way back?" Nathan asked.

"He used his mum's Sat-nav. According to that, I was forty miles away—hence the fuel repayment."

Nathan rubbed his fingers across his chin. "So, he just brought you home, no questions asked?"

"Of course he asked questions, but I didn't answer them." I shrugged again. "I think he accepted my reluctance to talk about what happened. He was a nice kid."

"Then, I'll ensure he's repaid."

I gave a small smile of appreciation. "Oh," I said, remembering, "it will need to be signed *Marie*."

"You told him your name was Marie?"

"Of course." I frowned. "I wasn't too far gone to give him my real name." That earned me nods of approval and a couple of smiles.

I finished making the drinks, and Daniel stood to pass them for me. I let out a growl at the burn in my hip as I padded across to join them.

Ethan told me he'd fetch me something for it, disappearing upstairs. He came back down with a tube of cream and looked to my hip, as though wondering how it would get on me, before tossing it to Sean.

"What is it?" I asked as he rubbed it in.

"Arnica cream," he said. "It will bring out the bruising sooner, help it heal faster."

I nodded, teeth gritted while his fingers applied pressure in their appliance of the ointment.

"I'm really sorry about everything that's happened to you," Nathan said.

I glanced over my shoulder at him.

"I should have taken better precautions. I should have kept you safer, been more aware when the other pack spotted you—"

"Actually, Nate, the only one to blame is me."

"You can't shoulder the responsibility for everything, Jem."

I hobbled over to the table to sit. When Sean took the seat

beside mine, I turned to face him. "Sean, do you remember the day we met in the restaurant?"

He toyed with a strand of my hair. "Of course."

"And do you remember what I was doing when you came over and spoke to me?"

"Writing about your dreams." He sat straighter in his seat, as did Josh and Daniel.

I saw in his eyes that he understood there was relevance to my words but hadn't quite made the connection. At the confusion in the others' faces, I quickly explained about logging my dreams.

"When I drove away from Sean that day," I continued, "my writing book was on the rear seat of my car. I haven't written in it since. I forgot all about it when I left Peter." I paused to glance round at them all, returning to Sean. "Peter found my record. Bloody idiot took it to work and left it on his desk ..."

As the dots began to join, the guys either sat up straighter or leaned forward, but all eyes trained on me. Groaning, Sean rubbed his hands over his hair.

"Jonathon found it. He took it home, read it—showed his dad and the pack. Then he and Matthew grilled Peter and the workers about me. They gathered enough details to put two and two together." I shrugged. "That day I turned up to confront Peter, they were there. They already knew who I was and followed me. I know that, because Hugh told me. I never stood a chance of avoiding them. But they still have those records, and I really ..." I paused. "*We* really need to get them back."

"So, they've known all along." Nathan looked thoughtful. "No wonder—I never understood how your existence was discovered so soon."

I nodded at him. "Plus, I think Jonathon finding and reading them first is the reason he took me. I got the impression he's slightly infatuated with me." When they all frowned at me, I explained my assumption. "I think he holds my writings for himself. When I was there, the ones who bothered me most were Jonathon and ... Matthew." I glanced at Sean, spotting the tightening of his jaw. "I felt as though I was their pet project, or something. Matthew, I think, was only interested in repaying me for Sean killing his brother—"

"So, it was his brother, then?" Daniel asked.

I nodded. "But, with Jonathon, I got the impression it was more than that. He wanted me to sit with him. I think the meals were provided at his insistence. He apologised when his dad hit me. He was mad as hell when he walked in to find Matthew threatening me ..." I paused, took a deep breath. "I truly believe Jonathon took me for himself. I think they were telling the truth, when they said they weren't trying to kill me that day in the forest. I think their intention was to bite me themselves, to tie me *to them* before Sean had the chance to do it. Unfortunately for them, it backfired. All they did was push my life in the direction it was always meant to go. So, based on this,"—I ignored Nathan's smile at my new acceptance of his bedtime story—"I think Jonathon is the one we need to watch because I'm certain taking me was his idea from the beginning. The others need taking out because they hold the threat of knowledge, but Jonathon cannot be left standing because he won't give in. As long as he's alive, he'll keep coming back. I'm certain of it."

AT NATHAN'S INSISTENCE, we reconvened in the lounge. Sean settled me beside Ethan on one of the large sofas before fixing me more food—the rumbling in my stomach had made itself heard again. When he returned, I straightened, my lips curving at the bowl of stew and thick wedges of crusty bread. Billowing steam carried the flavours to my senses and had me salivating before I'd even picked up my spoon.

Sean sat beside me, and they were all respectfully quiet while I ate. Hungry as ever, I chomped on bread with one hand, used my other to spoon in the hot comforting liquid. A groan of pleasure erupted on tasting the stew, followed by a second when it headed south to land in my stomach, filling the expanded void within.

"Nathan, I've been thinking," I mumbled around stew-soaked bread.

"About?"

"Your bedtime story."

"What did you want to know?"

"Well, according to you, the original Sean made sure he taught his Jem how to fight, to defend herself. If I'm who you say, then surely this should apply to me, also." I glanced from Nathan to Sean, then back again. "But nobody even mentioned training me."

Nathan allowed me his special, smug smile he seemed to reserve purely for me. "Well, that's where you're wrong."

"Huh?" I could manage no bigger response with my mouth full of food.

"We've been training you all along. We just didn't tell you."

"When, exactly?"

"Within thirty-six hours of meeting you, I had you in training."

My brow creased.

"The ball games, Jem. Every ball game you played helped you develop skills which you'd allowed to lie dormant."

"How can playing ball help me with defending myself? What good is that to me in a fight?"

"When you came to us, you were afraid of your own shadow. Within hours, we had you answering back, sticking up for yourself. The ball games simply helped you progress. They taught you to move faster, dodge others, heightened your reflexes, to hone your response and reactive times, to get you in shape and develop your agility. Are you following me? They also taught you to work as part of a team. You gave your trust over to Ethan on your first day. Within a day of being here, your inner wolf, your place within the pack, showed its face. All of these things, and more, are what you got out of playing ball."

"Okay, I get all of that, but I still don't understand how it helps with self-defence or fighting."

Smiling, he shook his head, as though I'd exasperated him a little.

"What?" I glanced from him to Sean, back to Nathan. "What are you shaking your head at?"

"How can you say you haven't learnt anything when you escaped from a pack who had no intention of letting you go?"

"My escape was just dumb luck."

"No, Jem. You escaped because you kept your head."

"I didn't—I panicked."

"That's not true. Whether your change was controlled, or not, is irrelevant. What's important is that you used it to your advantage. You didn't stand worrying over some werewolf whose throat you'd torn out ..."

I winced, but didn't interrupt.

"... you kept focused enough to move your arse in the right direction—which you knew because you'd spent the time figuring out the layout of the house, I add. Even when you were downstairs, you didn't panic, you got yourself out of—"

"No," I said. "I wasn't in control of the door opening. That was just a fluke."

"The second you saw an opening, you moved, didn't you, Jem?"

"I—"

"You saw an escape route, and you were on your feet."

"Yes, but it wasn't as easy as that ... my exit was blocked, and—"

"You unblocked it. No hesitation, you just did it. Even while attacking, you held enough control to be instantly aware about the open gates—another immediate response. You even ignored your quarry to plough on. Do you have any idea the level of control it takes to snap out of an attack?"

I shook my head, lowering my tray to the floor. Sean's hand warmed my back where it moved in small circles.

"It takes immense control," Nathan continued. "There aren't many werewolves who can switch off mid-attack and walk away. Usually once started, they can't stop."

"You say *they*. Does that mean you all hold that level of control?"

"No, Jem. Only Sean and I have that level of control. And now you. Which makes me believe you could also achieve other higher levels of control."

"Such as ... ?"

"A running change."

"What's that?"

"It's when you can change while mobile. You don't have to stop for it but can do it on your feet. You'd have a great advantage over anyone in pursuit, because they'd need time out for their change. You wouldn't."

"And this is something only you and Sean can do?"

"You, too, Jem."

I shook my head. "I doubt that."

"Of course you can. You've done it before, you just don't remember. Last time, it took a bit to learn that level of control. This time you're stronger."

"How can I possibly change that quick? I've only had three changes."

"Yes, I know. But on only your second change, you matched Sean for speed. I know because he told me."

The others all sat up straighter at the new information.

"And you caught your prey on your first attempt."

My eyebrow lifted.

"Nobody succeeds in their first hunt."

"I didn't do it alone. Sean helped me."

"Because it's natural for the two of you to work as a team. Everything you know is already in there." He tapped the side of his head. "You just need to relight your knowledge. That's what you'll be doing once your hip has healed enough to change. Sean will teach you everything you already know, show you what you can do. Then, if you come face to face with these mongrels before we deal with them, you'll be better prepared. By the time we've finished with you, you'll be more than capable of defending yourself against any pack."

I didn't believe it for one minute, but arguing would be worthless. Once he'd got an idea in his head concerning me, Nathan was too stubborn to see anyone else's point of view. Besides, it couldn't hurt to try and learn the stuff he wanted me to, even if only to prove him wrong.

THE REST of the afternoon was spent coming up with as much of a plan as we could. I'd suggested that, much to his disgust, Sean would be their next target, and Nathan agreed. They hadn't succeeded in keeping me, would know we'd have extra precautions in place, so using him as a bartering tool would make it impossible for me to refuse to go back. It was more than belief, though. If they got him, I *would* lose him. Because if their ploy worked, and I waltzed right back to them in exchange for Sean's release, I'd be as good as signing his death warrant. If they had me, they'd no longer need Sean. If Sean no longer existed, I'd have no reason to leave. So, despite his growls of protest, Nathan and I wholeheartedly agreed that Sean—more so than me—needed to be kept safe. With that in mind, and considering the boldness of their previous abduction, both Sean and I were on house arrest.

It should have sounded like bliss—the house to ourselves, time to catch up—but there was no way Nathan would risk leaving the two of us alone. Ethan's expression told me the job of chaperone had already been allocated to him.

Thankfully, I only had one day to endure before the week-end. Nathan and Connor were convinced I'd be ready to begin training by then. One day stuck indoors didn't sound too bad when I'd be permitted back into the forest on Saturday.

Our next topic lent itself to finding the location of the other pack. With no way to trace them, we had to hope they'd return to the construction site and lead us to their abode. It would take patience I didn't think I had, but unless they turned up on our doorstep, we had no choice. For hours, Nathan questioned me on anything I remembered about the area where the other pack lived, around which, enthusiastic descriptions were tossed around about what they'd all like to do to the other pack once found.

After being plied with more food, the house filled with a darkness that warranted illumination. When my body slumped and I took over the sofa—Sean's and Ethan's legs, too—Nathan insisted I get more rest. I didn't argue, though I'd no intention of going anywhere without Sean, so I grabbed his hand, dragging him off like my favourite toy.

My semi-invalid condition carried me just beyond the door before Sean lifted me, and I smiled at him as he mounted the stairs. "A girl could get used to this kind of treatment."

"Get used to it as much as you like. I'll happily carry you to bed every night of the week, if it means you'll be with me when

I close my eyes." He paused when we reached the landing. "Bathroom or bedroom?"

"Bathroom," I murmured, my head resting against his shoulder.

A few more steps, and he lowered me to my feet. My senses drank him in for minutes before I pulled away and stepped over to the sink.

Sean stood beside me while we brushed our teeth. When I leaned down to wash my face, he moved behind me, his warm hands sliding over my thighs, sweeping up beneath his T-shirt. When they ran across my stomach, inner flutters sent tremors through me, and hygiene dismissed, I turned, fingers stretching for his hair to bring him to me.

Our lips parted as they met, tongues darting out to taste. My body responded to his caressing fingers, pressed into his erection. We each reached for the other's clothing. I tugged off his T-shirt, he mine. I found his buttons, shoved down his jeans, and his fingers removed my underwear.

Our heavy breaths filled the bathroom, and ignorant to my pain, I leaped into his arms, crushed my mouth to his. My limbs enfolded him, and his arms swept around to support my frantic clinging. We bumped the wall, my back pressing against it, and his fingers traced a path across my flesh, inducing a sigh.

Almost twenty-four hours since reuniting, and we'd scarcely touched each other. Whether through caution or uncertainty about how the other felt, I didn't know or care, but I needed him. My fingers sought to guide him into me. Frustration kicked in when my success wasn't immediate, and my growl earned a chuckled response.

I gasped when he did fill me, and as he moved inside me, I clutched at his shoulders. His lips toured my throat. My hands found his hair, encouraging him. Shivers swept through me at the rough scrape of his canines, and a low moan escaped on my breath.

As though spurred on by my response or unable to wait any longer, his thrusts grew urgent, his quiet snarls of passion matching his pace. With his tongue sampling my neck and shoulders, his nostrils inhaled as though drinking in my taste and scent all at the same time. In return, my lips and teeth nuzzled Sean's throat, tasting, inhaling, teasing as he did to me, until vibrations ran through his rippling body.

As our heat built, he brought my face to his. Our breaths infused, glazed eyes locked, and the rhythm of his motions rocked us closer to climax. I watched him with each pant, each snarl, just as he watched me with each cry that gasped from my lips. He stared into me when I caught his lower lip and nipped. Meeting his gaze with equal intensity, I contracted around him, my legs clenching, fingers flexing, before my back arched into the fire weaving its way upward. With the peaking of orgasms came the darkening of eyes, the tightening of grasps, the unified pounding of our hearts. His name sighed from me on a cry of ecstasy as I went blind with passion.

Chapter 43

Friday passed without incident. Ethan and Kyle stayed home with us, and at Nathan's orders, we spent the day indoors. Yet, each time I stepped to the kitchen window, saw the basketball in the garden, and studied the forest beyond the arches, I wanted to go out.

Thanks to copious quantities of arnica cream, my bruising had begun its first alteration to an interesting shade of yellow. With my limp reduced, making my way around the house came easier, and I seemed to be on the mend—emotionally and physically. Though, that could have been because, once Sean and I had worn ourselves out before bed, I'd fallen into a deep sleep. When Nathan returned from work, he even gave me an approving glance, as though pleased with what he saw.

SATURDAY BROUGHT with it the chance to get outdoors, brightening my mood. Connor and the boys arrived early, on Nathan's orders, to play 'lookout'. No doubt, it would be an exciting day for them.

As it turned out, they didn't mind. Especially Josh, once he was told I'd spend a good portion of the day running naked through the forest and he realised he might earn himself a sneak peek at me.

Nathan pushed everyone straight out into a game of ball. A little slower on my feet, I found the game harder than usual. I still loved it, though. Even aware that the ball games held a higher purpose than just a bout of playful frolicking, I still had a barrel of fun.

After an hour of laughter, sweat spraying, and body jostling, we broke for food. I ate in silence. For some reason, the closer it got to my training, the more my nerves kicked in. The pack all seemed to have such high expectations of what I'd be able to achieve. I didn't know why they thought I'd be capable of what they proposed when I didn't believe it myself.

After lunch, we headed to the trees. Finding a spot not too far in, Nathan and Sean explained exactly what I'd be learning: they wanted me to run and change without stopping. They assured me I could do it, that I already knew how—I just needed to remind my brain of the process. A vision involving the act would have been handy right about then. Unfortunately, they couldn't be summoned on demand.

"You can feel my changes, Jem," Sean said. "That's how we push through at the same time. When you change, it can incite one in me, and vice versa. So, if I begin a change, you should be able to join me." When I just stared at him, his crooked smile appeared. "You'll be fine."

I glanced round at the others. "I can't do it with everyone watching."

An incline of Nathan's head sent them off to the sidelines, leaving the three of us in the clearing, and he turned to me. "To begin, Jem, I want you to tune into Sean's change. Then you can draw off it, to bring forth your own."

"Simple," I mumbled. Too simple.

Once Sean and I were undressed, Nathan positioned us back to back. "If you can't see him, you'll have to sense his change. Ready?"

Taking a deep breath, I nodded.

I expected Sean to lower when Nathan stepped away, but he didn't. As he stayed on two legs, I remained standing, also—awaiting command. On the verge of believing I wouldn't feel anything, pain shot through me. I gasped, my hands balling into fists, as the falter of my legs almost sent me to the ground.

Sensing Sean still upright, I forced myself to remain, and as the pain subsided, I glanced up to see Nathan watching with a small smile on his lips.

"Again," he ordered.

Hands still clenched, I closed my eyes, prepared that time—I hoped.

Splintering agony darted through my limbs. Teeth gritted, I stumbled, unbalanced for a moment. Nathan stood before me when my lids snapped open, and I focused on him, relaxed my body. With deep breaths, I allowed Sean control.

Nostrils flared, my flesh pulsating, the beginnings of contortion entered my limbs. My chest heaved in an energetic rise and fall against the assault, until, no longer able to retain eye contact, my lids lowered.

The moment they did, my brain took over with its insistent chant—*Not my command. Not my change*—and my reversal pushed through in protest.

"Relax, Jem," Sean murmured. "Go to your meadow. Raise your shutters. Let me in."

As always, the mere sound of his voice calmed me, and my reversal slowly stepped aside. A backward shuffle brought contact, the heat of his body, and when the throbbing once again invaded, I stifled any cries I wanted to give.

I knew the connective change was happening, felt it within

every part of me. Even though I gave no encouragement, each stage of the change arrived. Opening my eyes to glance down, I half-expected to see brown hairs protruding, as I had in my vision, but the lengthening hairs were light. Only seeing their shade, rather than colour, told me my vision had already altered.

My skull split. The agony pierced me like talons. I toppled, biting back the snarl deep in my throat as I righted myself. My hind legs shifted to accommodate their new shape, already preparing for flight. Holding back, I took deep breaths, and awaited Sean's release of me.

Like a tie had been severed, my legs thrust me forward, and I flew through the air to land inches from Nathan. Growls ripping from me, my paws skidded to a stop as I glanced around. I was wolf, I knew I was. But ... how?

My body didn't care—it would take being wolf, however it occurred.

Sean crossed to me. His body brushed mine, the vibrations running through him sending trembles along us both. Successful or not, he seemed pleased with my achievement—Nathan, too, judging by his broad smile.

With Nathan's permission, we loped off for a five minute rough and tumble—Sean in the lead. Through the forest, we darted, leaped, ducked. At one point, I led and Sean gave chase.

As we veered off after rabbits to the north, Nathan's whistle summoned us back. I whined, my nose stretching forward, twitching toward the flavours of proffered delicacy. Sean prodded me to about turn, and I snorted at him, took a testing step. The scents floating on the light breeze were too good to ignore, but his low warning growl drew me back to follow— though not before giving another whine of complaint.

In the clearing, we changed back, had a recess, and started over. Five times, Nathan made us do it—until my upright change time matched that of a regular one and exhaustion bled through my brain.

As we fell into bed on Saturday night, I wondered how much more demanding Sunday's training would be.

Sean and I overslept the following morning—though, not for long. The nine thirty, rough shoulder shaking by Ethan gave the ogre far too much pleasure, in my opinion. Swatting hands and grumbles responded to him, until his laughter, firmer grips and more shakes brought us round.

Our objections were still verbal when we dragged our rears, stretching and yawning, into the kitchen. Although disgruntled at being woken, it was a pleasant surprise to find the others already there, and to arrive to the mouth-watering aroma of gammon and eggs, courtesy of Daniel and Kyle.

Leaving Sean to provide me with a shot of caffeine, I collapsed into a chair. Josh leaned across to kiss my cheek, and I allowed him a smile—my natural reaction to his affections.

A steaming mug appeared beneath my nose. Before it hit wood, my fingers slid around it, and I sighed with the first sip, closing my eyes as the satisfying liquid flowed over my tongue.

Connor chuckled. "Did you need that, Jem?"

Eyes still closed, I nodded, and I stayed that way until gammon-scented steam wafted into my nostrils. A quick lid fluttering revealed a plate of food waving below my chin, and I couldn't help but laugh. Thanking Kyle, I ate myself awake, shifting forward to allow Sean to wriggle behind. His arm enclosed my waist while he leaned round to fork up mouthfuls of his breakfast.

"How's the hip today?" Nathan asked.

I shovelled in a gammon chunk. "Better than it was."

"Do you think you'll be up for a spot of running today?"

"I managed some yesterday in between changing." I swallowed before looking at him. "It should be okay so long as we get longer breaks in between." What I really wanted was longer time to chase wafting scents, instead of being called back and having to remain disciplined.

Nathan gave a small smile. "We'll see."

We headed straight for the forest after breakfast, with an air of enthusiasm buzzing through everyone. The previous day's training and my achievement had been a hot topic. Apparently, nobody but Sean and Nathan expected me to pull it off, so I'd shocked the hell out of them—myself, too.

Uncomfortable with an audience while naked, I sent everyone who didn't need to be in the clearing packing. They'd never be so disrespectful as to openly ogle, but it had been bad enough with just Nathan.

Sucking in a few deep breaths, I kicked out my legs. Standing still and allowing Sean to bring forth a change was one thing—but running full out with a gammy hip, while concentrating on everything happening to my exhausted body, would be something else entirely.

I relaxed to allow the sensations of Sean's change to bring forth my own. Although not fully in control, my brain had learned to accept the process. Of course, if I didn't trust Sean with my life, it wouldn't have been remotely possible.

The transition was successful—our fastest time, at three minutes forty-seven seconds—and Nathan sent us on our five-minute break with a beaming smile. Once back at the clearing, and changed again, Nathan informed us that he wanted me to induce the next change—to draw Sean in with me. I didn't have a clue how to do it, but according to Sean, he felt every part of my changes, just as I did his. All I had to do was control my own change while vertical, and he would automatically connect.

The hardest part was concentrating on supporting myself rather than relying on Sean's mental strength to do it for me. However, after a few growls and enough teeth grinding to earn me a dentist trip, I burst from my change and spun to face Sean with excitement dancing through me. His eyes sparkled as they connected with mine. I bound over to him, leaped playfully onto his back, and pinned him to the ground. With my mental giggle arriving as a loud snort, I raced away.

Highly amused by myself, I didn't care when I spotted the others just outside the clearing, where they'd crept closer to watch. I pranced past with another snort, caught their looks of wonderment. Ethan's expression surprised me most—I'd only ever seen Ethan look impressed with himself.

FOLLOWING A SECOND SUCCESSFUL CHANGE—INDUCED by me—and an hour's break for lunch, we headed back for the forest. I'd spent the hour's reprieve preparing for the next stage—that one sounded impossible, too.

Taking my hand, Sean smiled at me. "You'll be fine, Jem."

I tilted my head to look at him. He'd scarcely spoken above a whisper, his lips didn't appear to have moved, yet I'd heard him clearly.

His eyebrow lifted. "You heard me?" His voice arrived barely audible again.

"Yes." My eyes widened when I acknowledged the volume of my response matched that of Sean's.

He chuckled—even that, lower than the softest of sighs—and I halted.

"Is this what your dad was talking about?" It felt strange to communicate that way—lips almost motionless, words too quiet for anyone other than the two of us to hear.

He grinned. "Yes, it is."

The others stopped walking, turning to watch us. Nathan appeared smug—as always.

"Can nobody else hear us when we talk like this?"

"No."

"It's ... weird."

Nodding, he shrugged, his fingers tracing my knuckles.

"How are we doing it?"

Another shrug. "We've always done it."

"But ... how?"

"It's just something we can do. I don't know how it works. For some reason, it doesn't matter how low we speak, we still hear each other."

"Like the connection when changing?"

"Yes, like that."

"That's odd, too, isn't it?"

He shrugged. "I've never asked any other bitten werewolves to test the theory."

"If they'd succeeded, if Jonathon or one of the other's had bitten me, would I have been connected to them instead?"

"I don't know, Jem."

I shuddered. "I'm lucky things turned out the way they did."

An unreadable expression settled into his features, but I caught it before staring away across the garden. Who knew what could have happened if Sean hadn't come home in time?

Having been spied on for my last couple of changes, it seemed pointless to keep ordering the others away. At least they showed enough decency to turn away while I undressed.

"Okay, Jem, what you need to do is engage with the change

in here,"—Nathan pointed to his head—"hold fast to it, and then take off."

I raised my eyebrow. He made it sound easy. It probably was —to him.

"If you struggle, use your connection with Sean to keep focused. It's no different to what you've learnt over the weekend, except you'll be moving. Okay?"

"Sure," I mumbled. "A walk in the park."

It didn't register that I'd mumbled too low for anyone else to hear, not until I saw Nathan's face, still awaiting reply, and heard Sean's chuckle at my rear. When I nodded to Nathan, he stepped away, while the others hung back, the circle of trees our only privacy.

"Ready, Jem?" Sean murmured.

I blew out a breath. "Ready."

My hands clenched at my sides as I closed down my mind to everything but the change. Deep inhalations, slow exhalations, I lowered my lids to concentrate and control the pace at which it arrived.

"Hold it," Sean whispered.

My breaths deepened, my fists tightening until painful. Tingling built in waves until ripples washed over me.

"Hold it, Jem."

A small bubble of a snarl built within my chest against the effort to remain in control. Ignoring everything around me, I focused solely on the beat of our hearts, the sounds of our breaths, the escalating pain.

A gasp burst out. "I can't."

"You can." Sean's voice had already begun to deepen. I knew he pulsated, also—his own pain pushed through.

The rumbling in my chest expanded. The contortion of my muscles grew excruciating when the change attempted to be the one in control.

I bounced on the balls of my feet.

"*Wait*," he growled.

"*Sean!*" My reply came out a low warning snarl. I didn't want to wait.

As intense agony thumped through me, my legs considered giving out. I could almost envisage my prominently strained tendons in the battle to remain.

"Okay, Jem."

I whipped my head up and round, and my eyes shot open. On dancing toes, my body leaned forward, my nostril flaring in search of what lay ahead.

"*Go!*"

We spun and flew in the same direction, a rumbling roar ripping from our throats.

I didn't need to look at Sean as I sprinted. Somehow, we both knew which turns the other would take, as trees, brush, and fallen branches entered our path. With every obstacle, we took the same route, bodies close enough to touch, heat radiating from one to the other. It seemed magical, otherworldly—despite the pain.

As we ran, our changes progressed, each stage showing its face. Muscles completed their transformation, bones shifted.

I'd thought it difficult to remain upright and innate. It was something else expecting my legs to function at the same time.

My body dipped. A jerk to one side, then to the other, white hot agony licking through me. As my contorting legs gave up, I threw out my half-formed paws to break my fall.

Still racing, still changing, Sean lessened his steps.

I didn't want—couldn't afford—to hinder him. To do so could place him in peril. "Keep going." My voice arrived as a deep guttural whisper.

With a growl of determination, I surged back up, urged myself after him. I blanked my cramping legs as they altered in structure, didn't look down to see how much of my coat had pushed through. At the splitting pain of my skull, I bit back my cry.

Like a signal had been received from Sean, I flung my body through the air, and the final stages completed my change.

Paws hit dirt. The forest filled with the snarls tearing from us, yet we carried on running, leaping, as though my brain hadn't quite registered the accomplishment. Finally skidding to a stop, I gave a vigorous body shake, head to tail, to be certain everything was as it should be.

I'd done it.

Sean stopped running a few feet ahead and turned to look at me, questions in his eyes.

Excitement, arousal, exhilaration—they all filled me. I couldn't believe my success. In celebration, I danced on the spot and threw my head back in an ear-splitting howl.

At Sean's echoed cry, I took off.

My muscles held stiffness to begin with, as though overindulged on a workout, yet they soon loosened. As I ran, I heard and smelled Sean at my heels. He kept pace so closely, his breaths hit my flank, their warmth ruffling my fur.

I raced through the forest like crazy, each turn a sharp veer. Sean seemed to know every direction I'd take as fast as the notion entered my head—just as he was aware the precise moment that rabbit scent caught me by surprise.

Too elated to consider the consequences, I followed my nose.

WE RETURNED TO THE CLEARING, each of us carrying our quarry, to find Nathan pacing in irritation. He turned on us, looked about to let rip at our prolonged absence. When he caught sight of our meal, he blew out a breath, ran his fingers through his hair. "I suppose I asked a bit much of you to keep ignoring the hunt."

Agreeing wholeheartedly, I tucked into the fresh meat, warm blood tricking across my tongue—Sean, too. Once we'd finished and cleaned each other up, we were allowed a little longer for digestion.

"Okay, change back." Nathan continued to mumble as we obeyed, along the lines of, "I told you, you could do it, Jem. I had every faith. You just needed to believe."

By the fifth successful attempt, darkness had arrived, the others had grown edgy, and Sean and I had snuck off for further nourishment provided by the forest. When we finally made it back to the house that evening, we couldn't even sit upright. After snaring food, we took it to bed with us, falling straight to sleep on a full stomach.

Chapter 44

Monday brought torrential rain and confined us indoors—with Nathan. We couldn't even hide in the bedroom and make love because I'd have considered it rude where Nathan was concerned, and it didn't take long for frustration to creep in like a stealth hunter.

If put to Nathan, he'd have argued that we should make use of the time for regeneration and rest. According to him, resting did not involve sexual exercise.

After lunch, I could sit still no longer and set off in search of stuff to clean, with vacuum and dusting cloths in hand. I started in our bedroom—even got carried away and stripped the bedding off. Checking that it was okay, I did the same in Nathan's room, followed by Ethan's—and just as holed in as me, Sean trailed behind.

From there, I tackled the laundry—none had been done in my absence. Sean stood behind me, while I loaded the washing machine with a dark bundle, distracting me with his nimble fingers. He almost tempted me to forget my task, ignore that we had company, and drag him upstairs to bed. Instead, I pulled out a load from the dryer and passed it to him, discouraging him with an earful of promises and order to 'fold'.

We weren't the only ones bored. Within minutes, Nathan joined us in the kitchen and poked amongst the dwindling grocery supplies.

I glanced over as he placed a handful of food items on the counter. "What are you making?"

"Goulash."

"Need help?"

He shook his head. "Can't you kids find something else to do, besides housework and peering over my shoulder?"

I shrugged, my lips threatening to smile as I took a step back, caught Sean's eye. "Well, I could do with a shower." It seemed a legitimate reason for disappearing.

Nathan, being Nathan, saw right through me, raising his eyebrow. "Hmm-mm."

"Actually, I could do with getting cleaned up as well," Sean said, smothering his laugh.

"Hmm-mm." Nathan didn't even bother to turn.

After racing up the stairs, Sean and I stripped off and jumped in the shower. With too much free time on our hands, we could hardly be blamed.

We returned downstairs to Nathan watching the news headlines for the second time that day. After suggesting a film instead, Sean went off to make drinks and find snacks. Within no time, we were staring bog eyed at the screen, a drink in one hand, food in the other, adeptly coordinating the alternations of fingers to mouths. The film wasn't bad—as far as aliens and world domination went—even if the U.S.A. was going to save the entire world from total annihilation, yet again. The President had just ordered the airstrike of an alien aircraft, when the sound of swinging gates reached us, followed by heavy footsteps and the rolling of wheels across paving.

Our heads tilted at the same time. Recognising the engine as Connor's and the footsteps as Ethan's, I relaxed back into my seat—until the front door hauled open fast enough to rebound off the wall.

Nathan glanced up as Ethan's harried strides shot him past the living room doorway. "What on earth?"

We all jumped up, ducking into the kitchen, as Ethan swung a body from over his shoulder and onto one of the dining room chairs. It slumped against the backrest, head lolled to the side. Swelling and bruising had already begun to form around the right eye.

I moved in for a closer look. "Thomas," I murmured.

Ethan turned to me. "You recognise him?"

I nodded. "Jonathon's brother. Where ... ?"

"Spotted him cruising back and forth past the gates. We boxed him in,"—he smiled—"then persuaded him to come inside and join us."

Nudging Sean to switch on the light, I studied Thomas more closely, my eyes widening. He had chunks missing from one of his ears and fingers missing from both hands. "What the hell did you do to him, Ethan?"

He frowned. "That wasn't me."

I stared at him.

"Well, obviously, *that* was." He indicated the black eye already escalating in size and colour. "But the rest?" He shrugged. "He was already like that."

I believed him. Ethan didn't seem the type to lie about injuries he'd caused to an adversary. "So, you knocked him out cold ... with one punch?"

He smirked as if to say, '*Of course I did.*'

"Bloody hell, Ethan, how hard did you hit him?"

Folding his arms across his chest, he merely smirked.

Nathan patted him on the shoulder. "Good job, Son."

"What are we supposed to do with him?" I asked.

"He'll come round soon enough," Sean said, "and we'll convince him to hand over his address."

Fifteen minutes later, Connor and his sons showed up. Apparently, they'd disposed of Thomas's car, which only confirmed the dimness of his future. They all appeared as pleased with themselves as Ethan.

Uncaring of the unconscious body at the table, Nathan dished up dinner. With my seat occupied, I took mine into the living room. I didn't particularly want to stare at Thomas across the table, anyway—he'd put me off my food. Once I'd finished eating, I tuned in to the conversation in the next room, picking up their humming anticipation at the idea that they may actually get somewhere with their new lead.

When all went quiet, tension seeming to seep through the dividing walls, I knew the werewolf had stirred.

"What the—" Thomas's panicked words cut off as his chair scraped across the tiles, and a growl turned into a low gasp.

I imagined Ethan's strong hand on his shoulder, a warning to stay in his place.

Nobody else spoke, probably an intimidation technique: allow the silence to build while he wondered where he was, as his brain kicked into gear to replay his capture, and his demise sank in. I understood how he felt. My only advantage was I didn't believe they intended to kill me—if the alternative fear of rape and degradation could be termed an advantage.

An urge to see how he liked being the one on the wrong side of the fence compelled my feet into the kitchen.

He sat, not particularly straight, with his face twisted to the side, ignoring everybody—almost as I'd behaved in his position.

Sean watched my every move, and I gave a nod, confirming I

was okay, before looking back to the young werewolf. "Thomas?"

His head snapped up. The widening of his eyes caught me by surprise. He raised a hand, went to point, groaning as his missing finger inhibited the action. "Keep that crazy bitch away from me." He tried to straighten, to wriggle free of Ethan's hold.

The entire pack turned to me, their eyebrows raised in a gesture that said, '*What did you do?*'

I shrugged and raised my palms, but it took only seconds to sink in. "You were the one blocking the door."

"Blocking? All I did was walk in, and you fucking attacked me."

My hands fisted at the memory. "You tried to stop me from leaving." I growled as I took a step forward.

Ethan studied me closely. "You did this to him, Jem?"

"Yes, she did," said Thomas. "She's off her fucking head. First, Luke checks on her and she kills him for it, and then she tears at me just for being there."

I blinked. "Luke?"

"Yes, Luke. You know? The one whose throat you ripped out?"

"It wasn't Matthew?"

"No, it wasn't Matthew, you stupid—" He gasped. Whatever Ethan had done caused him pain, though to me, Ethan didn't appear to have moved.

I glanced at Sean with a shrug. So, it hadn't been Matthew who'd come to my room on Wednesday morning. Would it have made a difference had I realised? No—I saw the opening, and I took it. I turned back to Thomas. "What exactly did you all expect me to do, Thomas? Sit and wait while you decided which of you were worthy of me?"

Glaring, he lifted his hands. "But you fucking mauled me."

"Then, you shouldn't have stepped in my way. Ethan, he's all yours." I strode from the room.

In the living room, where I didn't have to look at Thomas's pathetic face, I paced.

He'd been quite happy for me to be under their care, within their grasp, and he was doing nothing but feeling sorry for himself because I'd retaliated. My soul refused to find pity for him.

No sounds carried from the kitchen for minutes. Thomas had obviously gone back to giving them the silent treatment.

When footsteps came my way, I knew they'd be Sean's before he even appeared. "Jem?" A silent mumble, intended purely for my ears.

I paused in my tracks and inhaled, allowing the scent of him to calm me. Unclenching my fists, I turned to face him. "I'm okay." I glanced toward the door. "What now?"

"They'll ... *we'll* take him outside,"—evidently Sean needed to be a part of it—"see what we can get out of him. Ethan usually gets people to talk, though."

"Outside? What if the others are hanging around some-where? They'll hear."

He shrugged. "Where else are we supposed to take him?"

I returned the shrug. "Why not take him down to the cellar?"

He shook his head. "No, Jem."

"Why not? Surely it's made for this kind of thing."

"At Connor's, yes." I raised my brows in question, but, glancing away, he tugged his hands through his hair. They came to rest on his hips, and he shook his head again. "You're wrong about what's down there."

"So, what *is* down there, Sean?"

He took a step forward and placed his hands on my cheeks. "I promise I will show you, Jem, when this is over."

My brow creased again, my brain working on overdrive with relit curiosity. "What is it? What's so important down there?"

"I will show you, I swear. But, please, let's get everything else over with first."

He looked so earnest, held such pleading in his eyes, I found myself nodding. If he hoped I'd forget about it, though, he'd be doomed to disappointment.

I SAT ALONE in the kitchen. Sean had followed them all outside. I knew he needed to be there. Whether to see harm come to those who dared take me or through eagerness to gather the information required to finish what needed finishing, I didn't know—I just understood he needed to participate in some way.

My ears twitched as they demanded Thomas tell them what they wanted. Each non-answer preceded a thud, followed by a grunt, a gasp, a cry. I should have flinched, felt distaste or disgust as a result of what I knew to be happening outside, yet I felt nothing. To defend my life, to protect my and Sean's future, it was a means to an end and unavoidable. Already, in my mind, it was as simple as that.

Ten minutes later, I found myself standing in the conservatory. Although the rain had ceased, the ground was still sodden. Each step sent a spray of moisture to soak the legs of the men's jeans. Connor and Kyle held Thomas. Ethan poised before him with his top off. His impressive upper body strength appeared intimidating beneath its coating of sweat. Any doubts I'd ever held regarding Ethan's might dissipated—I'd never before seen anyone look so powerful, so dangerous, as his movements hypnotised me.

The repetition of the question became almost a mantra in my head. Even once Sean took over speaking, the monotony didn't alter. Each time Thomas replied with anything other than the answer, he was struck.

It became clear, as I watched him, that Ethan knew exactly what he was doing. Cause as much pain as possible while keeping Thomas fully conscious. Ensure he didn't go too far before answers arrived. Without an address, he'd be no good to us dead.

My hands pressed against the cool glass of the dim conservatory, while outside grew darker with the moon's ascension to the approaching night sky, and as I mentally willed him to give us what we wanted so it could be over sooner, my head filled with the outside sounds. "Tell us where you live." Sean's warning snarl followed with a thump, chased by a grunt, a gasp or cry, at one point a scream. They all ended with the doubling over of Thomas's body, the spraying of blood.

They'd removed his T-shirt. Torso bruising suggested fractured ribs. Deformation of his nose confirmed bone breakage there. His right arm was definitely busted.

With each strike, I didn't avert my eyes. The only indication of my distress showed as the barest of twitches just below my left eye, which arrived with each impact.

Almost seventy-five long minutes of torture later, the words we'd been waiting to hear, the address we so desperately needed, spilled from his lips on a spray of bloodied phlegm.

I marched into the kitchen, snatched up the first writing implement I saw, and jotted down the address he'd given. Back in the conservatory, I waved the paper at the others to let them know I had it.

Nathan approached, pulled open the door. "Come on, Jem." He took my arm. "We're going for a little drive." He called over his shoulder, "Stay with him until we get back."

He grabbed the laptop on our way to the door, handing it to me as he picked up his truck keys. We left the house at a run.

No hesitation. Within seconds, the engine roared to life. He pointed to the laptop as he pulled out the gates. "Find the address."

I opened the computer and booted it up. Nathan told me the name of the website to enter, and I followed his command, keyed in the address I'd noted down. "Okay, got it." Keying in further instructions produced directions, and I navigated as Nathan drove.

We turned onto a hedge-lined lane thirty minutes later. "This is the road, according to the map," I said. Before we even reached the property, I nodded. Beyond the hedgerow to our left stretched a field. Even though I hadn't paid much attention at the time, I was certain that was the way I'd fled.

"This look familiar to you, Jem?"

"Yes."

Nathan carried on driving for another half mile or so, until the gates to the property came into view—as did Jonathon's black Range Rover. He barely slowed as we passed, didn't pause to look, but pulled into a turn a little farther along. "Well?"

I nodded.

"Definitely?"

"Without a doubt."

He spun the truck back the way we'd come. As we passed the property a second time, he craned his neck, appearing to take in every detail, before blinking as though the image of information had already been processed and stored.

Reminded of my experience there, I swallowed, goose bumps dotting my arms.

He didn't require my directions on the drive home. We scarcely spoke. He asked a few times if I was okay. I responded with a mumbled yes, and he reached over, patted my knee. Eventually, I leaned back in the seat, lifted my feet to rest on the dashboard, and closed my eyes.

On returning, we climbed from the truck and marched around the house. When we rounded the corner, the others looked toward us, expectant. With a dual nod, we continued across the paving stones.

Ethan stepped over Thomas, where he slouched on the ground, and hauled him to his feet. I made the mistake of looking, my left eye twitching again when Thomas stared straight at me with contempt in his eyes. With that one look, I knew, if allowed to live, he'd come after me.

I broke eye contact, as a crack as loud as a gunshot rang through the air, faltering my step before Nathan took my elbow to right me. I didn't look back, just kept going—through the conservatory, the kitchen, into the living room. Nathan followed, his contact warm against my skin. As soon as I halted, he turned me to face him and held me tight.

I hadn't realised I'd been holding my breath until I gasped in air, hadn't realised my hands shook until the trembling spread to my arms, my shoulders. As I tried to find control, Nathan's arms offered support, as his large hands swept over my back, his murmured words floating into my mind. Even when soft footsteps reached us, he didn't let go. At the light shake of his head, the footsteps receded.

All, except one set. Sean's. Through Nathan's soothing, Sean's presence and the comforting words he whispered, I eventually calmed.

Josh, Daniel and Ethan disappeared in the pickup soon after. I had no idea where they went, didn't ask, but I knew Thomas's body was no longer on Nathan's property.

On their return, once armed with coffee, the argument kicked in over our plan of action: attack immediately or wait until the next day.

Exhilarated and pumped up, Ethan wanted to go then—he was already primed for a fight. Sean was also ready for battle.

A much calmer Nathan debated whether the other pack would be expecting that, as Thomas hadn't returned home. He wanted to wait at least twenty-four hours and give them time to sweat.

I agreed with Nathan. At least twenty-four hours to plot meant I'd have time to try and convince Sean I needed him with me, and Nathan would easily back me wholeheartedly.

After a couple of hours of irritated growls from the ones not getting their own way, and a lot of good points raised by the more mature pack members, the order was ruled to wait.

With Nathan as Alpha, what he said went.

＿＿＿＿＿＿＿＿＿＿＿＿＿＿＿＿＿＿＿＿

Chapter 45

＿＿＿＿＿＿＿＿＿＿＿＿＿＿＿＿＿＿＿＿

The following day dragged on and on, enhanced by the torrent of liquid bestowed upon the earth by the gods. As much as I wanted everything to be over, the closer it got to the end, the edgier I grew. By five in the evening, both Sean and I—and Daniel, our reinforcement—paced the floor, climbed the walls, or squinted through the window. Once impatience got the better of me, I headed into the kitchen to rustle up a chilli for dinner. The action calmed me a little, as though my subconscious believed the pack would be home the second their meal was prepared, like I could spur my desired events to take place.

Sean and Daniel remained in the living room, their feet swishing across the carpet in their continued pacing.

At ten minutes to six, the low rumble of the pickup's engine carried through, followed by a second, and their shuffling feet ceased. A step back from the cooker brought the front door into my sights. Sean appeared from the living room, glanced at me, and went to open the door to them.

The returnees nodded at Sean as they brushed past him, then at me.

"Go and clean up for dinner," I told them.

With a smile, Nathan led the way upstairs. As the ancient faucets kicked into action, I threw rice in to steam. By the time they trudged back downstairs, I had dinner on the table and plates and cutlery set out.

Without speaking, we sat to eat. Besides a handful of smiles in acknowledgement of their meal, silence continued. Though, their lack of words couldn't disguise the buzz of excitement—as energetic as a jolt of electricity—thrumming through them all. It was evident they'd all been waiting for the moment, at *least* since the other pack trespassed upon Nathan's land. Just as it was evident they didn't want to—couldn't—wait any longer.

Fuelled and ready, they still didn't speak as they filed back upstairs to change from their work clothes. None of them bothered to shower. What would be the point?

Although I didn't want him to go, I knew Sean hoped for a chance at the takedown, so I made sure I was ready. If he'd insist on going, so would I.

The others took their time upstairs. I could imagine the low murmur of words passing between Nathan and Connor in private. Ethan would be called in—as the pack's best fighter, he'd play a prominent role. Once the key players had their parts established, the others would be informed of their expected participation, which meant Daniel would be called soon.

Not Sean and I, though. Nathan wouldn't want me there. To achieve that, he'd need to get Sean to stay behind.

My gaze never left Sean. I knew his options: go up to his dad and demand to be taken, or make a break for the truck and be there waiting for them when they left.

He didn't go the truck route. After fifteen minutes of standing at the bottom of the stairs, arms folded and glaring up at nobody in particular, he climbed them, and I moved into his vacated spot. On the landing, he tapped on Nathan's door before entering. "So, what's the plan?"

"We're all going. Except for Josh. He'll stay to keep you and Jem company."

Sean's growl carried down. "No."

"This isn't up for discussion."

"Let someone else stay behind with Jem," Sean said. "She won't be in any danger."

"Jem will need you here."

"No, Dad. *You* will need me."

A sigh of exasperation—Nathan, I presumed. "How do you think Jem will cope if we take you along? How do you think this will affect her? We've already discussed, and agreed, that you're a target. You'll be the first one they attack. I know this, Jem knows this, and if you weren't being so bloody minded about wanting to take out Matthew and Jonathon, you'd see it, too."

"This is bullshit, Dad!"

I padded from my position at the foot of the stairs, grabbed every set of vehicle keys, and snuck out the back door. Three trucks sat dormant on the driveway. Which to choose? Picking Nathan's, I climbed in and settled down to wait.

The debate ended sooner than expected—well, not ended, exactly. Ten minutes later, as dusk introduced dimness to the day's light, the front door flew in a wide arc.

Sean filled the opening. "I am coming!" he yelled before storming out.

Nathan emerged. "Think of Jem."

"Sean, get your arse back inside," Ethan shouted, coming up the rear.

Sean snarled over his shoulder at them as he strode away. He didn't even spot me until he yanked open the truck door. Halting, he blinked before reaching in to pull me from the cab.

I dug in my heels, tugged my hand back, pushed out with my feet to prevent him.

"What the hell are you doing here, Jem?"

"Same as you, no doubt," I snapped with a kick.

"Like hell you are!"

I shoved him in the chest. "If you go, I go."

"No! No fucking way!"

He grabbed at me again. I shoved back. We must have looked like a couple of teenagers squabbling over who got to ride up front.

"If you think I'm going to sit here, twiddling my bloody thumbs and worrying sick over whether or not you're okay, you can think again, Sean. I am not—"

"Get *out* of the truck, Jem."

"No!"

"Get out of the truck, and get back in the house! Now!" His voice deepened by the second.

"No!"

He made another grab for me. "You are *not* going! Get back in the fucking house!"

"*Make* me!" I snarled. The kick I aimed thwacked his chest hard enough to send him back a step.

Before his head could snap up, I darted out a hand, slammed the door closed, and engaged the locks. As I met his glare through the window, his eyes darkened.

"Open the door, Jem."

My chest rose and fell with each breath intake, matching my rising temper.

"Fine! Stay in there, then! We'll take Ethan's truck." He whirled to leave.

I tapped on the glass until he gave his attention back to me. His dark, furious eyes burned when he stared over his shoulder, and I jangled the keys at him. "You won't get very far without these."

He turned to face me, his expression wild—made even more effective by the constant shower plastering his hair to his forehead. The reddening of his face united with the tightening of his jaw, a split second before his fist pounded the front bumper with enough force to dent and set my body shaking with the rocking of the truck. He spun away, kicked out at a garden planter. Leaving the compost to spill over the paving blocks, he stomped toward the garage.

Toward the Porsche.

"Shit!" I unlocked the door, scrambled out, tossed the keys to Nathan. "Go! I'll take care of this." Without awaiting a response, I jogged to the garage.

Loud clanking rang out from within, the echoes of metal on metal. I took a deep breath, released it on a slow exhale, and nudged the door ajar. As engines fired up behind me, I paused to nod to the others as they left in Nathan's pickup. Only Josh remained, staring after his disappearing brothers. I sent him a nod, also, before going in.

Sean ceased to smack the tool in his hand and turned to me, his chest heaving. A throb drummed his temple, fluttering the artery in his neck. The rumbling of his chest carried with the depth of thunder. Ripples flew through his body, as he stood with his fists at his sides, eyes aflame, at the far end of the building.

My own hands clenched, as I braced myself to stare him out. The pulse at each of my wrists beat a tune as the blood pumped through. So close to him, both of us wound up, his barely controlled body began to affect mine, and within seconds I tingled, my flesh pulsing like mad. Teeth gritted, I readied myself for the worst.

Sean's glower could have ignited an iceberg. "Why, Jem?"

I didn't answer—couldn't, with my concentration focused on retaining control rather than giving in to Sean.

He roared, swung his arm out, and the wrench he held crashed into a shelf. Tools flew into the air before descending, clubbing Sean on their way down. If he noticed, it didn't show. "Why did you stop me from going?"

My left shoulder dipped, the muscles pierced by a sharp twinge. Grunting, I righted myself.

"Why?" he asked. "Why fucking stop me? You *knew* I needed this. You *knew* I—"

"What about what *I* need?" I bit back. "Doesn't that matter?"

Footsteps approached the garage. My head twitched, but my eyes never left Sean's, and an inhalation identified Josh. I willed him to stay out of it. Sean would restrain himself while in front of me. I couldn't vouch for anyone else's safety.

Sean's sharp breaths snorting from his nostrils misted the air like an unbroken horse—he looked no tamer than that, either.

"I couldn't allow you to go there," I said. "You know what your dad said is true. You know as well as anyone you'd be the first they'd hit on."

"You think they could take me, Jem?" His voice arrived low, dangerous.

"I know you can't fight them all."

He bared his teeth and snarled, as though outraged by my lack of faith.

"If they took you as a team, if your family weren't fast enough to back you—you wouldn't even wait for their backup, Sean. I know you wouldn't. You're so hell bent on revenge you can't even think straight. Look at you. You're out of control."

"No ... I ... am not!" His face contorted. He tightened and released his hold on his weapon and it clattered to the ground. He grimaced.

So did I as his pain passed to me. My knees gave out, and I landed hard, solid concrete scraping my skin. Eyes still connected, I gave a low growl.

He exposed more teeth, and his neck stretched up, his head

twisted to the side. Only when I gasped in pain at the needle-like stabbing to my skull did he reel himself in and glance back at me.

"What was the point of it all, Sean?"

He took a step forward. Even through his shifting flesh, confusion at my question showed in his features.

"What was the point of bringing me here, convincing me to stay?"

Another step. Although still dark, his eyes softened a little, the fire cooling.

"If you went and they killed you, then all of this would have been for nothing. Why the hell would I take that risk when I gave up *everything* to be with you?"

He took a step closer but halted, and palms out in front of me, I closed my eyes. The dissipating stabbing in my head had become a throb, my eyes hurt, my jaw couldn't relax, and my fingernails had bloodied my hands—in fact, my whole body ached.

Push forward or bring myself back were my options—because I couldn't remain stuck mid-change. If I pushed forward, the connection would drag Sean along—not a good idea with the mood we'd adopted. Taking long, slow breaths, I tucked my head down and threw every scrap of concentration into controlling us both.

Instinct encouraged Sean to fight my dominance. I gave a low growl, perspiration beading my brow and shoulders as I tried harder. With immense effort, I pushed back the pain, aching, and throbbing, until my body tried to relax. My regulated breathing brought the natural rhythm back to my heartbeat, and with my body ceasing to heave from the weight of greedily drunk oxygen, success showed its face.

Opening my lids, I raised my head.

Anguish and distress lent a high shine to Sean's eyes and

forced tightness to his jaw. His flesh, his body, had stilled. His muscles no longer pumped, and his hands were no longer clenched but within his thick hair. He lowered to his knees. "Jem, I'm … sorry." His hands took my shoulders, lifting me to face him.

"I'm sorry, baby," I whispered. "I'm sorry for stopping you from doing what you so badly wanted to … but I couldn't take the risk. I'm not prepared to lose you over this, Sean. If I lose you, my life is pointless, don't you see?"

I reached out, stroked his cheek, and he pulled me to him until my face pressed against his shoulder. Arms tight around him, bodies once again harmonised, I closed my eyes. I just hoped not all our fights ended up so intense and exhausting.

"Are you guys okay in there?"

The tentativeness of Josh's voice from outside brought a smile to my lips.

"We're fine," Sean answered.

Disentangling ourselves, we pushed to our feet and went out. I bit back a laugh when I saw Josh braced as though prepared in case he had to jump in at any point. He was also as wet as a soggy sheet, killing his aura of toughness. His clothes clung to him, and his shaggy hair hung in his eyes, the rain running over his cheeks. He was so adorable—like the little brother I'd never had—if I ignored that he liked to sniff my butt.

"Come on." I tugged at his hand. "Let's get you out of those wet clothes."

Relaxing his stance, he wiggled his eyebrows. "That's the best offer I've had all year."

I swatted his arm with my free hand. He dodged me but not quickly enough to avoid the curling of Sean's arm around his neck, as he took him in a headlock. He rubbed his knuckles across Josh's scalp, flicking wetness over the three of us. They tussled across the paving and into the kitchen.

I disappeared upstairs in search of dry clothing for Josh, hoping to relieve him of his soaked items before too big a puddle developed on the floor. After hopping down with jogging bottoms for him, I went back up to find clean items for myself.

Nathan and the others had been gone a while. If they weren't already at the house, deciding their plan of penetration, I figured they soon would be. The gradually darkening sky had taken on a navy hue, almost grey due to the rain clouds covering most of its expanse. I tugged on one of Sean's larger T-shirts with a pair of knickers and grabbed similar attire for him, minus the frilly underwear.

In the kitchen, Sean stood over the kettle as it came to a boil. I handed him his lounging clothes, before padding into the living room to loaf with Josh while Sean finished making the drinks.

Five minutes ticked slowly by with the three of us sprawled on the largest sofa, sipping hot chocolate. We must have looked like a pile of lazy cats, despite the underlying tension we expelled. When the phone rang out, our nerves pulled tight as guitar strings, we all started.

Sean leaped up and hit the connect button as he snatched up his mobile. "Dad?"

"You've calmed down?" Nathan's voice carried through the earpiece.

Sean glanced at me. "Yes. Did you finish it?"

"They're not here, Son. The house is empty."

Sean gave a low growl before checking himself.

"I'm not sure if they've fled, or if they're just out," Nathan continued. "My guess is the latter because there are still a lot of belongings here."

"Did he find my dream record?" I asked.

"Tell Jem we've got it," Nathan said, obviously hearing me. "She was right. I found it in Jonathon's room."

"So, you're coming back?" Sean's un-tensing shoulders portrayed his relief. If the other pack weren't there, but hadn't fled, he'd get another chance to state his case, to persuade us to let him join in the next time.

"We're just digging to make sure there are no details of a second property. Then we'll be home."

Sean nodded before telling his dad he'd see him soon. His eyes remained on mine as he hung up—but while he appeared pleased about the turn of events, I wasn't.

Leaving him in the living room, I headed into the kitchen without bothering to switch on the light. Dread twisted in the pit of my stomach. I'd expected the problem to be over. Maybe if I stayed in the dark, they'd understand I needed a moment alone.

Five minutes past, with deep mumbles of encouragement carrying along the hall. I moved to the window, eyes adjusting to the blackness of the poorly lit night. Although a partial moon hovered, it provided no illumination, thanks to ever-moving clouds obscuring its view of the earth.

The outline of the ball stood proud in the centre of the lawn. Farther out, I traced the curves of the arches, the spectral shapes of the forest beyond. Small tremors ran through me at the sight of my sanctuary under the cover of night. A group hunt was due for certain.

I turned away from what I couldn't have. Only one step taken, my head whipped back at a howl from beyond the garden.

Sean and Josh were behind me in seconds.

A second call arrived, followed by a third and fourth—four individual howls.

"It's them." My eyes remained on the garden. "All four of them are here."

Sean strode over to the doors, pulled them open, and stepped into the conservatory.

"What do we do?" Josh asked beside me. "Should we call Nate?"

"If we call him, he'll tell us to wait, forbid us to go out there," Sean said—as the only member of his family present, the rank of command would fall on his shoulders. "If we wait, they'll assume we're afraid, maybe come and search for us. They could know there's only the three of us here. I don't know about you two, but I'm not thrilled about the idea of hiding out and waiting to see their intentions."

"You want us to go out there, Sean?" I needed to be clear about his words.

"The others won't be back in time, even if we call them. Josh and I can handle it. You—"

I stormed out to him. "No way."

"I'm not leading you out there to them—"

"You don't have a choice. I'm coming."

Josh stepped through the doors. "Maybe you should stay here, Jem."

I glared at him before turning back to Sean. "If you go out there, and I'm not with you, they'll come looking for me. I'm not sitting here, waiting for them to find me."

"We'll hide you."

"I'm not *hiding* from these mongrels like a coward. I refuse to. If you go, I go. Besides, I may be the best protection you have."

"I can watch his back for you," Josh said.

"No, Josh, you can't. If they see you two, they won't hesitate to strike. And how will one of you cover the other's change against so many? I'll be okay. I'm pretty certain they still want me alive—at least, Jonathon does. I can cover you."

"We're not going to hide behind you," Sean snapped.

"That's macho bullshit, and you know it."

"I don't *need* you to protect me. I will not—"

"Will you quit with your small-minded, arrogant way of thinking?"

"I won't allow—"

"Well, then, *you're* not going out there." His eyes darkened again, but I continued before I had a change to argue more. "If you don't agree to allow me to protect you, when I'm probably your only chance against the *four* of them, then I *will* use every ounce of strength I have, whatever it entails, to prevent you from going."

He groaned, evidently unhappy with my stubbornness—I'd learned from the best—and brushed his hands over his hair. We were wasting time, and he knew it. Because I wouldn't cave— something else he knew.

A look from me to Josh, then he nodded. "We go out. Josh, I want you to branch off, find somewhere to change. Jem and I will approach them, find out what the hell they're doing here, and then you can cover us while we change. Then we take them out. No hesitation. If you see a window, take it. Even if they're vulnerable." He meant if they were mid-change. "I'm not taking any chances with Jem out there. Do you understand?"

Josh smiled. "Sure, Sean, whatever you say." Fists formed, already poised for action, his body hummed.

"Ready, Jem?" Sean asked.

Despite feeling far from it, I nodded. "Ready."

Chapter 46

I'd lied about being ready. I sensed the shifting of Sean's eyes as we headed for the danger awaiting us, knew he searched for a sign that I wasn't happy, an excuse to send me back. I'd no intention of giving him one. With my resolute expression plastered on, I kept pace.

Entering the forest to unyielding darkness brought disorientation. "Where's the damn moon when you need it?"

"You'll be okay in a few minutes," Sean whispered.

He lifted his chin to Josh, indicated he should head to the right. Without speaking, Josh obeyed. A few metres in, he was no more than a vague outline. Only his skin reflecting the glistening rain gave him away.

Both Sean and I tilted our heads—on alert for sounds that didn't belong. Detecting a crack of a twig ahead in the distance, our faces pushed forward. Side by side, necks stretched, shoulders tensed, we inhaled. Nothing. We knew Josh hadn't caused the sound, so we chanced it and set off.

As the breeze didn't bring their scents to us, there was a good chance it took ours to them. They would know of our approach, so we didn't rush. If they wanted us badly enough, they'd wait.

Our shoulders brushed as we walked. Sean's tension tightened with every step he took. He wouldn't be afraid of the werewolves ahead, though. I knew the only fear seizing Sean's heart would be having me there.

On the other hand, I was petrified. I knew my presence would distract Sean. Distraction could cause hesitation. Hesitation could lead to harm. The thought of seeing Matthew again scared me, also. I was unsure how I—or Sean—would respond to that. But mostly ... I was terrified I might not be up to the job if Sean required my protection. I had strength when it came to my changes, but in other ways, I was still newly bitten, young and inexperienced—the weak link. He could protect *me* without a shadow of a doubt. I didn't hold the same confidence in myself, if the roles were to be reversed.

This is no time to question yourself, Jem. Giving myself a mental shake, I tried to focus on who was out there and where they were.

The farther we walked, the clearer my vision became. After fifteen minutes, I detected the trespassing scents on the altered course of the breeze.

"Ahead," Sean mumbled so only I could hear.

I nodded, my eyes trained on the expanse of trees before me. With each step, I swept my sights in an arc—until I saw them.

Surprisingly, they'd taken their human forms. I counted them, checked their position left to right: Hugh, Jonathon, Stuart, Matthew. The quartet waited in the largest clearing the forest had to offer.

On a second inhalation, the scents of nature travelled in, awash with freshness thanks to the rain. Under different circumstances, it would have been a delight to my senses.

Sean and I halted before the naked wall of muscle. Their

bodies stiffened, and they leaned toward us for a second or two before they realised we had no further company. The relaxation of their shoulders and the scornful attitude in their twisted smiles suggested they hadn't known the others weren't around.

I positioned my body half in front of Sean. He didn't argue. We could show no signs of weakness within our relationship, not to the group before us. From Hugh, to Jonathon, to Stuart, my gaze swept their row until it met with Matthew's, lingering there a little too long.

He leered at me, hatred within his stare. The stiffening of my shoulders was enough for Sean to know which of them dared threaten me, and a low rumble brewed within his chest.

Freeing my eyes of the invisible force holding them to the huge, blond werewolf, I swung left until they were back on Jonathon.

His grin greeted me. "Jem, you came."

I didn't respond.

"Did you miss me?"

'*Don't flatter yourself, moron,*' I wanted to say. Instead, I scowled.

"Of course, we'd have preferred you to come alone. Then we wouldn't have to kill anyone. You didn't think this through very well, did you?"

Sean gave a low warning growl. My hand reached behind, grasped at his T-shirt, willing him to be patient.

"The infamous Sean, I presume," Jonathon said, shifting his gaze to my right. "Apparently the greatest influential leader ever, yet he brings his mate out to meet us ... alone. Surely you don't believe you can protect her against so many?"

Sean's knees flexed against the back of mine.

"He's goading you," I mumbled. "He wants you to make the first move." I returned my attention to Jonathon, bringing his back to me. Two could play that game. "You know your brother came calling yesterday. We invited him in, introduced him to the family ..."

They bit faster than I expected. Jonathon's chin dipped as he took a step forward. Despite his low growl, Hugh kept his composure, placing a restraining hand on his son's elbow. They weren't the only ones affected. Thunder entered all four sets of eyes, and their knees bent as though preparing to pounce.

"Of course," I continued with a small smile, "I did invite him to hang out a while, but ... he'd already outstayed his welcome."

They all took a step forward.

I'd no idea what I expected to achieve. Maybe I hoped drawing their focus onto revenge and them into a wild enough rage would affect their concentration and rationality.

"I'm going to bring forth the initial stage." Sean's words arrived so low, so deep, I barely heard them myself. He'd have known, as well as I did, it could be only seconds before they charged.

I clenched my fists, inhaled, and nodded. With his temper already fired up, the tingling hit with immediate effect. My jaw tightened. "Of course, he was full of conversation before he went." I forced my eyes to remain on the threat in front of us.

Heads lowering, their shoulders hunched.

Pain shot through me. I tried to control the gasp, almost stifled it, and thought it had gone undetected until I saw the tilting of Stuart's head as he studied me.

"Hold it," Sean mumbled.

"He begged for it to end." My voice had become hoarse. "How long did he last, baby?" I cocked my head. "Ten minutes? Fifteen, maybe? Still, he was stronger than I expected."

The rumbling growls in the chests of the four werewolves accelerated with each word, until the forest sounded as though consumed by the hum of static bouncing off the surrounding timber.

Sean nudged me a little further. At the sensation darting through me, I couldn't stifle my gasp, almost stumbled, but Sean's hands took my waist. *"Hold it."*

I studied the four before us, all poised and ready, glanced over their physiques—deciding who could be the most agile, move the fastest. Definitely the largest, Hugh should be the slowest, I thought. His bulging muscles, his additional body weight would more likely hinder than help his speed. "We should go left," I whispered.

Sean nodded, leaned over my shoulder, his warm flesh swishing against my cheek.

After remaining speechless throughout, Hugh's furious eyes met Sean's. "You killed my son?"

Too busy concealing the rippling of our bodies, the pulsating beneath our flesh, neither of us answered.

Stuart had seen it, though. More than aware of our intention, he took a step back and lowered to his knees. The others didn't seem to notice as he braced himself for his change.

"We need to move," I whispered, and Sean nodded.

At Stuart's bark of, "They're changing," Sean almost knocked me off my feet in a left-turn propulsion.

Hugh and Jonathon lunged for us a fraction too late, the collision missing us by a hairsbreadth.

The second we'd passed them, the race began. At our rears, three individual sets of feet pounded the soil, telling me Stuart must have remained to complete his change.

We concentrated on picking up speed before calling forward our own wolves. Distance needed to be created for us to succeed.

Sean ran so close at my rear, his breaths bursting against my shoulder, I wondered how we didn't trip over each other. At a ripping sound, I almost looked back, until I registered Sean's tossing away of his clothes. His own done, he grasped mine. My T-shirt tore down between my shoulder blades. I tugged it forward, yanked it away, threw it aside. He'd removed my underwear before the top even hit the floor.

"Do it," Sean ordered when the gap hadn't widened. "You don't need me, you can do it. I'll watch your back and then follow."

"But—"

"Now, Jem!" Do it!"

The running change was hard without Sean to lead me— harder still because I sensed him behind in his timing, holding back to separate our connection long enough for me to progress without him.

Even though racing ahead, through agony strong enough to disable if I lost focus, I was aware the instant heavy footfalls ceased to follow, just as I was aware the exact second running paws took their place. I hoped for Josh. A sharp inhalation told me otherwise.

Stuart.

Almost complete in my change, the realisation that Sean had stopped faltered my step. I went to brake, thought about turning, but Sean's growled demand of, "*Go,*" spurred me forth again. My legs trembled as I left him to watch my back.

Shoulders dipping under pressure, teeth bared against the pain, my change reached its excruciating conclusion. The thrust of my hind legs sent me sailing through the air, and I slid through mud on my landing. No time to waste, my snarls echoed as I spun.

I slammed to a halt.

Something had altered.

My body told me—felt—Sean was changing. Yet, my brain screamed out, pleaded with my scrabbling paws to find purchase and carry me to him. One desperate shove off with my claws had me mobile, and I raced back, faster than ever.

He couldn't be far—I hadn't gone far without him—yet the route I'd taken lay deserted. Had he turned off? Led them away?

In my panic, my head bobbed left, whipped right—until I growled at myself to gain control and stop for a second. Catching my breath, I inhaled. His unmistakable scent drifted in from the south. I took off again. With each thudded bound forward, his scent grew stronger—amongst others—and the closer I got, the louder the snarls, roars, and growls infiltrated past the surge of my blood.

A blow against my body sent me sprawling. I rolled over and flicked upright, hunched for attack—but uncoiled at Sean's dark eyes staring down at me. Seeking reassurance, I pushed my muzzle into his fur, shuddering in relief. It hadn't been him I'd heard fighting.

Whirling, I caught the flash of dark blond. *Josh!*

Josh must have arrived in time to cover Sean, and the raging battle sounds emanated from him and Stuart.

Sean joined me, and we circled to watch the snarling wolves, heads low, waiting. I passed him in my anticlockwise path around the two fighters, as he trod a clockwise one. We wouldn't interfere, not while Josh held his own. He wouldn't thank us for it.

At howls piercing the darkness, our heads shot up—Josh's, too. The instant Josh's attention had diverted, Stuart dived for him.

With a snarl, Sean and I leaped toward Stuart.

Josh turned, but too late, and Stuart struck his flank. A loud yelp burst from Josh as he bowled across the dirt. Before he could recover, Stuart's open jaw made a beeline for his throat.

Sean's impact with Stuart mirrored my own, crushing the wolf between the weight of our blows.

Air whooshed from Stuart as his eyes glazed, and I grabbed him by the throat.

Sean matched my move on the opposite side, his short, hot breaths breezing my face.

Our eyes locked. *'You want him?'* his expression seemed to say.

Releasing my hold, I backed off, and my earlier terror converted to excitement as I watched Sean whip his head to the side with a vicious snarl.

As the dying wolf twitched, blood pumped from the gaping hole and spilled across the earth, pooling in a wide circle.

I stepped to Josh, nudged him to his feet, whimpering my concerns. He gave a long lick across my snout, but at Sean's snort, we spun.

We may have taken one down, but there were still three to go, and they were approaching.

With a growl, Sean took off—not in the direction of the nearing wolves, though, but to the side, circling around on them. Josh and I chased his disappearing hind. Unlike them, we knew where we were going.

Once out of their path, we slowed to minimise our noise and enhance the chance of taking them by surprise. With deft steps, we stuck to the shadows, ears pricked.

The other pack made no effort to conceal their trampling as they blazed through the trees, and I followed their route with ease. Stepping onto their course, I lowered my nose, sniffed the ground. When I lifted to the stares of Sean and Josh, communication somehow passed between us, and we resumed the path toward our foe.

Roars rebounded off bark, telling us they'd come across Stuart's body, and allowed us to pinpoint their location. With the racket muffling the landing of our paws, we picked up speed.

Once close, Sean loped left, Josh right—leaving me in the centre.

I pressed my stomach flat to the dirt and shuffled forward. My muzzle poked through the thickness of my covering bush until the three wolves came into view.

Their nostrils flared with their deep inhalations. Spiralling around Stuart's body, they bobbed their noses in an attempt to locate us.

Jonathon tensed before swinging to face the bush I lay behind.

I hadn't even considered I may be on the wrong side of the breeze.

Aware that Sean would give me the verbal beating of my life if I didn't wait for them to be in position, I stayed in place and braced, just in case. Ready, and waiting for the nod, I could barely contain myself.

Jonathon took a slow step toward me, seemed to struggle to connect his sight to my form. His uncertainty, as he questioned his senses, showed in the knit of his brows.

A glint distracted me for a split second—the shine of Josh's eyes, glazed with the thrill of the hunt—before I returned my attention to Jonathon.

He'd padded closer. His head hung low, his shoulders high. He inhaled and no longer looked unsure.

I attempted a backward wriggle out of the bush, and his head tilted. Something akin to triumph glistened in his eyes. Did he think I had come to him?

A shadow of dark fur passed between the opposite cover of foliage. Sean. When he ducked back behind cover, I breathed out a sigh—until he reappeared. He'd obviously spotted Jonathon's proximity to me. If the two wolves turned, they'd see him. I had to do something, or he'd try to take on Jonathon, as well as Matthew or Hugh.

I scraped back, flexed my legs, and pounced.

Jonathon's head snapped up, his eyes widened. My heavy slam into his side knocked him flying. His breath wheezed on landing.

I forced myself to my feet and faced the attention of the other two.

Their lips vibrated, their teeth exposed in a hostile snarl, and they lunged.

I froze, as the two huge airborne wolves soared toward me. My pulse raced. A gulp lodged in my throat, my eyes refusing to budge from the missiles.

In my periphery, Jonathon pushed to his feet and whirled to face me.

I thought my breaths would cease ... until every surrounding sound silenced.

Like my brain had filled with cogs, forcing it to perform, I heard only ticking within my skull, my mind whirring like a suped-up engine.

I acknowledged the two leaping wolves, who'd be upon me before Jonathon, as well as the protective actions of Sean and Josh, both already counterattacking.

My brain clicked, assessing.

Matthew and Hugh would be intercepted in time, if only I moved. Even then, Jonathon would be upon me, especially since he knew I wouldn't play nice.

Click! Click! Click! Click! Click!

Hugh, Matthew, Josh, Sean, Jonathon. I took them all in.

My calmness shocked me. Where had the ability to analyse the situation come from?

I even recognised what the outcome of everyone's actions would be, could break down each individual body and the speed at which they travelled. Although they all appeared to shift at the same rate, they hadn't. Josh changed slower but could run fast. Sean changed fast and ran slower but was stronger than Josh. Despite Matthew's and Hugh's bodies leaving the ground at the exact same moment, Hugh's power, evident in his strong hind legs, had propelled him a greater distance. In a millisecond, I'd processed the whole scene before me.

Click! Click! Click! Click! Click!

My thoughts spun with great velocity, breaking down every single millimetre of alteration to the picture playing out before my eyes.

Click! Click! Click! Click! Click!

I had no idea how I did it. Like a video played on freeze-frame, I paused on each image just long enough to take in every detail, before forwarding to the next.

Click! Click! Click! Click! Click!

Matthew, Sean, Hugh, Josh, Jonathon.

Already recovered, Jonathon advanced. I knew they expected me to bolt. If I fled backward, the two leaping wolves would hold more chance of reaching me before Sean and Josh. If Sean and Josh accomplished their aim first—which they would—there was the strong possibility I'd be in their flight path.

Click! Jonathon. Click! Hugh. Click! Josh. Click! Matthew. Click! Sean.

I needed to go forward. It would place me out of the way, I could surprise Jonathon again, and I'd be doing something constructive—because I didn't *want* to run away.

I flung myself at Jonathon. With my movement, the illusion of time slowing vanished, and battle sounds once again filled the air.

Sean and Josh impacted with the other two, taking them down, a fraction before I reached my goal.

Jonathon pounced as though predicting my intent. Our

bodies hit midair. Air whooshed from us both—me, more so than him—and we fell to the ground.

We flipped to our feet, wheezing for oxygen. Our lips drew back, and we each sent warnings. Eyes locked, fur puffed up—like he needed it against me—and vibrations ran the length of our bodies as we trod a slow circle.

He jumped, catching me off guard, and as he slammed against my tail end, his teeth snapped at my flesh. When he punctured my hind leg, I let out a loud yelp—followed by one from Jonathon as his canines ripped from my skin.

I whipped round and saw Jonathon on his side, Sean growling down at him. With a roar, Sean swung down, his jaws wide.

A tackle from Matthew knocked Sean sideways, and he flew into the air.

I sprung at Matthew, but my paws landed short. I wrapped my teeth around his leg, tugged backwards.

Whirling on me, Matthew didn't even seem to recognise Sean's recovered advance until he landed on his back to send them both rolling through mud.

A yelp followed by a whimper had me spinning. Josh lay on his back. His legs tried to flick him out the way as Hugh descended on him with jaws snapping.

I drove forth, ploughed into Hugh's side. Despite my insubstantial weight, I shoved him far enough for Josh to right himself, and I whined at him, urging him to his feet.

Hugh barrelled into me. The slam of his body sent me soaring, and I landed with a thud, pain jolting through every inch of my body. My responding yelp escaped loud enough to cut through all other noise. With the intensity of a lightning bolt, deep burning throbbed through my muscles, as Hugh stepped over my body.

I whipped my head to the left in search of escape and

caught Sean raging toward me. A twist to the right showed Josh bolting my way, too. Back on my left, Matthew tackled Sean, dragging him away by his scruff.

Sean's jaws clashed. His head whipped like crazy. The snarls that ripped from him warned of his fury.

I turned again to Josh. He'd have reached me—if Hugh didn't surge from me to smash into him head on.

Josh staggered for a second, gave a sharp headshake. With a launch back at Hugh, their fight resumed, and I forced myself upright.

The agony at my rear suggested I'd landed hard on my recently recovered hip. At a growl, I glanced back, as Jonathon bore down on me. Feral wildness possessed his features as snarls rolled from his throat. I needed to move, yet knew I couldn't—not in time. At an attempted step, my injury pleaded with me to stop.

Lowering my head, shoulders bunched high and muscles drawn taut, I braced myself for the inevitable.

An inch from impact, Jonathon soared sideways. I followed his flight, my confused brain trying to take it in. At a quiet chuff, my attention darted back to Jonathon's vacated spot.

Nathan.

Jonathon didn't jump back up. His limbs twitched, but the power behind Nathan's blow seemed to have done something to him.

Nathan padded to him and snorted as he looked into his eyes. With a growl, he tore out his throat.

I spun in search of Sean. Still up against Matthew, he vied for dominance. Each snatched at the loose flesh above the others ruff. Their heads whipped left and right, their paws scrabbling to hold the other in place. My heart thudded at the roars flying from them.

My eyes averted to Josh, holding his own against Hugh.

Nathan circled them—he'd remain distanced unless assistance was required.

Taking his example, I hobbled over to Sean. At the crushing of underbrush, I swung back round to the entrance of new arrivals, as the rest of our pack jammed to a halt. They glanced from Sean to Josh, from Josh to Sean, before settling to wait in the wings.

I went back to circling, limping around them as I observed Matthew's movements. As he spotted me over Sean's shoulder, making eye contact, hatred oozed from his expression. Ceasing in my looping, I lowered my head and growled at him.

His stare blazed through his evasion of Sean's jaws, but I continued to stare him down, lips quivering against my deepening growls.

His eyes flashed his wrath. Even rapid reaches for Sean's throat couldn't distract him from me, until a twist of his body removed him from my sights.

I darted to the left, brought him back. He no longer attempted control of Sean. His interest shifted to me—and with his back to me, Sean was unprepared when Matthew barged around him and pushed off.

Sean spun, followed Matthew's aim, and kicked back to dive forward, but I stood my ground as Matthew accelerated toward me.

Calm, assessing, evaluating.

Click!

My brain went into overdrive again, as he grew nearer. I didn't move.

Click!

The hush behind me indicated Josh's triumph, or one of the others had interceded and finished Hugh. Only Matthew remained standing.

Click!

Within my line of sight, Sean came closer to Matthew. Prepared for action, my mind, my nerves, my body prepared to compensate for my injury.

Click!

With Sean's flight, he reached Matthew's left, his jaws wide, straining, so near.

Matthew's face came within inches of mine.

Click!

At the last second, I feinted left. A pivot twisted my body, and my head shot back to come in at an angle.

Click!

Matthew didn't have chance to acknowledge my shift. As his throat slid past my muzzle, I snapped forward, clamped down and tore.

So close, so frenzied, the connection between Sean and me heightened.

I knew he'd mirrored my action on the other side of Matthew, knew we both ripped on the flesh at the same moment.

Matthew thudded to the ground, and standing opposite, Sean's chest rumbled as his eyes sought mine.

In that last second, every instinct within me flooded back. As though created purely as protection for the other, we'd fought side by side, to the death, each defending what was ours —connected, as we were meant to be, as we always had been.

A shudder ran through us both. The silence, after the crashes of violence, almost pained my ears. Eyes glazed, breaths deep, our chests rose and fell in unison. With a lift of our faces, the vibrations built in our chests, and we filled the night with our favourite music.

Chapter 47

With our victory song over, quiet descended. Sean and I stepped around Matthew's form. He let out a whine as his warm tongue stung the bite on my leg. From there, his nose pressed to my injured hip. His sniff preceded a nudge, and he led me somewhere more private.

The swelling and yet-to-arrive bruising hurt like hell as my body pushed back through the change. In my crouched position, chest heaving, my eyes opened to Sean's, mere inches away. For seconds, we stared into one another before he drew me into his embrace.

His hands swept over my back, my face, my hair, as his lips gave their own style of healing to my body and tender hip. I, in turn, showered him with the same level of devotion, discovering Sean had been bitten, clawed, and battered, also.

Ethan interrupted our silent meeting. He came bearing clothes for me—the T-shirt he'd worn prior to changing.

I fed my head in, followed by my arms, and gave a muffled, "Thanks," through the fabric. My face popped out at eye level with Ethan's crotch—lucky for me, he'd pulled his jeans back on.

Ethan chuckled before swinging me up to my feet and enfolding me in his arms. His rough cheek squished against mine, and he surprised me with a kiss. "I'm so proud of you," he murmured.

Between Sean and Ethan, my hands in theirs, I went back to the others. Josh had changed, too, and he hobbled over to greet me. Despite the pain his eyes revealed, he grabbed hold of me, and his arms squeezed hard enough to cut off my oxygen supply as he whirled me round. "You were amazing, Jem."

I held his young face and leaned in to kiss his cheek, but he whipped his head round, caught me on the mouth instead. I giggled as his chuckle vibrated against my lips.

"Put her down, Josh." Sean's voice held only amusement.

When we pulled away, I placed his hands over his privates —they'd enlarged somewhat during our exchange—while I made a good inspection of his injuries. I limped around him, my fingers sweeping over the parts seeping blood. He appeared the most battered of us all—no doubt a result of dealing with the largest adversary.

Body checks over, we stood in silence for a few minutes, taking in the carnage we'd created. I had the impression it wasn't the first time the pack had dealt with a problem of that nature, and it was obviously normal post-battle behaviour for them, so I joined in. After all, I'd become one of them when I accepted my place beside Sean.

Once a respectful length of time had passed, Nathan turned to me. "You want to go back to the house, Jem?"

I considered the offer before shaking my head. Though I didn't want to pick up dead bodies, I had helped create the mess. I couldn't expect the others to clean up after me while I hid.

Settling on the ground with a broad trunk at my back, and

pulling Josh down with the ruse of needing his company, I watched the others in their cleanup duty.

I'd no idea where they put the bodies, hadn't the energy to investigate, but digging scrapes rang out, and the strong odour of accelerant, followed by wisps of smoke, wafted across.

With everybody suitably sweaty, we made our way back, and I sighed when the illuminated house came into view. The walk had seemed centuries long.

In the kitchen, my gaze fell to the table, to the book responsible for causing so much trouble. My hands ran across the laminated cover, before I picked it up and pressed it to my chest, my eyes meeting Nathan's. "Did you read it?"

"Of course not," he said. "Dreams are private."

BY THE TIME we came down from our high and found time to shower, morning had arrived. We bustled about in the kitchen, cooking, eating, and chatting. Once we'd satisfied our hunger, creating an air of laziness, we found places to crash. Lunchtime peeked around the corner, but even the option of further food couldn't prevent us from sleeping until evening.

With our second overindulgent meal of the day eaten, the Larsens reluctantly went home. The rest of us settled in the living room, watching the repeat of an action film showing for the twenty-billionth time. I was positive Sean only came up with the idea to keep me away from the cellar door.

My eyes had strayed constantly to the kitchen corner, to the opening that held some kind of secret, or so I believed. Sean's enthusiasm about loafing and distracting ourselves with the screen seemed a little over the top.

· · ·

THE FOLLOWING MORNING, I woke to Sean watching me. From his expression, he looked like he'd been awaiting the opening of my lids. I studied the beauty of him, but the longer I watched him, the more I thought I'd read him wrong. He appeared excited, yet apprehensive, all at the same time.

My eyes narrowed.

"Breakfast!" Ethan's voice boomed from the kitchen.

"Come on." Sean smiled. "Let's go eat."

We found Nathan and Ethan downstairs, already tucking in. They glanced up as we entered, and they, too, both looked as though they knew something I didn't. Rather than look excited, though, they appeared ... nervous.

In silence, I watched them all through my meal, pondering the situation. My wariness kicked up a notch when Nathan got up to clear the table as soon as he finished eating.

He wiped the last of the dishes, rubbed his hand over his hair. "I'm taking a walk."

A walk? Rain pummelled the paving like a jet wash outdoors.

He glanced at Sean before sending Ethan a meaningful stare. "You coming?"

Nodding, Ethan scraped back his chair.

My head lowered, my eyes hooded as I followed their movements. With one backward glance my way, they stepped toward the back door, the two of them patting Sean on the shoulder on passing.

As soon as the door closed behind them, I turned to Sean. "What's going on?"

He took a shuddering breath, and my pulse accelerated.

"Has something happened to Josh?" I knew his injuries had been nasty, but healing had already begun when he left the night before.

Sean shook his head, sucking in another deep breath before

pushing to his feet. Joining me on my side of the table, he took my hand. "Come on." He drew me to my feet.

I didn't know where I expected him to take me, and stared hard at him when he swung open the cellar door and reached in for the light switch. Only his quickened breaths competed with the tension pumping off him. He was obviously giving me what I'd asked for, but with his behaviour, I wasn't sure I wanted to see, after all.

At the bottom, he released my hand and stepped to the far corner—to the right of what I'd always been certain was a false wall. He felt along until he seemed to find what he was looking for. With his palm flat against the surface, he pressed, hard.

At a quiet click, my head tilted. The wall depressed slightly before springing ajar. "I knew it," I mumbled. "It's a door."

I didn't know who'd fabricated the doorway, but they had been an amazing craftsman. As Sean swung the door wider, I looked for hinges yet found none. If someone didn't know it was there, they'd never have found it.

I waited with bated breath for the inside to come into view. The door opened to capacity—I had to step back to allow it— and a frown crept across my brow.

Only two low-based rectangular, stone structures, with lids of the same fashion, greeted my eyes. They appeared to be sunk into the ground beneath the cellar. I glanced around the rest of the space, with Sean watching me like he awaited my reaction. As my eyes located two stone plaques attached to the wall, one at each head of the concrete rectangles, I stepped forward for a closer look.

Words had been carved into the plaques. I read the nearest one: *Sean Holloway*. Beneath the name were two sets of dates— the first from the eighteenth to the nineteenth century, the second from the nineteenth to the twentieth.

My eyes widened. "Holy shit!" I whispered.

I already knew what I'd find when I turned to the inscription on the left, but I looked, anyway. I read the words there a few times, my brows rising a little higher with each intake.

The matching years hadn't been what snared my attention. The name had.

It didn't read Jem *Stonehouse*. Jem *Holloway* stared back at me.

Spinning to Sean, I forced my dropped jaw back up. "We were *married?*" Another whisper—for some reason, it seemed disrespectful to speak any louder when we were in someone's— no, *our*—final resting place.

Sean nodded, his hands sifting through his hair, before he brought them to rest on his hips.

"And you didn't think to tell me this?"

"I was waiting ... for the ... right moment."

I wiped at a tear trailing over my cheek, one I hadn't even noticed the shedding of. Still unable to believe, yet knowing it to be the truth, I turned back to reread the plaques. "This is our third time together?"

He didn't speak, but I caught his nod. I glanced down, ran my fingers over the stone structures each side of me, tracing the indentations. A closer look at what lay beneath my hands revealed another inscription. My eyes flickered from one structure to the other.

Both held the same words.

My voice murmured as I read them. "'Fate and destiny go hand in hand. It is impossible to change our destiny. Only the path upon which we walk to reach our destination alters. If we should stray from that path, fate will take control and guide us in the right direction.'"

Tears welled in my eyes. I'd already spoken those exact words as though heard somewhere before. Obviously, I had.

"The words were a part of your mother's binding, Jem,"

Sean said. "They meant a lot to us, so ..." Shrugging, he pointed to the tombs before lowering his hand again.

I gave a huge sigh and swiped beneath my eyes as I closed them, regulating my breathing to a gentler pace until calm washed over me. "The dream," I whispered, without opening my eyes. "The one in the barn. I'm wearing white ..."

"The eve of our wedding," he said.

I took a shuddering breath, nodded to myself and him. Although I'd sensed that particular dream held a special meaning for us, I'd never pinpointed why.

I stayed there for a long time. When I opened my eyes, I stood alone.

With my welcomed privacy, I walked around the small space, ran my hands over both containers again, bringing myself to terms with it all. I guessed whoever I was—whoever *we* were —must have been pretty special for someone to go to such lengths to protect us in death.

But then, Sean *had* been the 'greatest influential leader', hadn't he?

When I ventured back upstairs, Connor's lot shared the kitchen with the Holloway's. I didn't give them more than a slight nod as I passed them. After all, I had an important job to do.

In the bedroom, I pulled open my bedside drawer, took out my writing book. I also grabbed pillows and a pen before re-submerging in the cellar. I stayed there for hours—maybe longer than a day. Settled down between the two of us, I prepared to finish what I'd started.

I completed my dream recording—what few I'd had. In great detail, I also logged my initial meeting with Sean in the restaurant, a smile forming at the memory. I didn't have to think about what to write; it all flooded into me. Once started, I couldn't stop.

My hand cramped, my hip burned, my leg throbbed. I ignored it all. I was a girl on a mission.

Descriptions of the house—omitting the location of the burial site—and the garden, about the adding of the perimeter wall in nineteen fifty-seven to null any confusion, all went in. So, too, did the forest—how it looked to me, smelled to me, how it felt to be in there. I also explained how to run beside my mate, as wolf, made me feel. Anything I believed would help my understanding and help me accept the path I was destined to take, I put in—before ending it with a note to myself.

Sean sat with me a lot during my time down there, seemed to know when to offer comfort and when to allow me space. Throughout the hours, I was checked on by Nathan and Ethan, under the pretence of providing food. Josh visited once, but I told him he could have some of me when I was done.

Approximately twenty-seven hours later, I emerged. Nathan grabbed a box from the table before leading me downstairs again with Sean trailing behind. Back in the cellar, Nathan deposited my book inside the container. It was airtight and would keep my book safe, he assured me.

After placing it in sight for self-discovery purposes, we left. The door was resealed, the light turned off, and I re-entered the real world—as real a world as it gets for a family of werewolves.

I didn't think about the book again. It was no longer intended for my eyes—not the current one of me, anyway. I couldn't help but wonder, though, if I'd done the right thing. It was, after all, a vitally important document in my new life. I didn't want anything to happen as a result.

Hopefully, when—I say when, and not if—I returned, it would be there, waiting for me.

If not, if someone should read it at any time, a book whose title page looked like:

FOR THE ATTENTION OF JEM STONEHOUSE

– TWICE WAS HOLLOWAY –
WILDLY IN LOVE WITH, AND DEVOTED MATE TO, SEAN HOLLOWAY,
AND BEARER, AND ANIMATOR OF WEIRD AND WONDERFUL DREAMS
... then I'd have to assume it had fallen into the wrong hands—again.

Epilogue

Almost six weeks since being shown the secrets within the depths of the house, I humbly accept who, and what, I am.

I refuse to alert Nathan to this fact, though.

If I have questions, I start with: *Suppose your bedtime story is true ...*

I only do so because I know it amuses him and use any excuse to encourage the blueness of his eyes to lighten, the laughter lines to surface, and that smug smile of his to show its face.

Besides, he *knows* I believe.

I used to think my life was so easily categorised into darkness and light, night and day, awake and asleep. How wrong I was.

Of course, I realise with hindsight, so many of my brightest periods came while under the cover of darkness, in the form of my dreams—just as I had plenty of my blackest periods during times I thought would provide only light.

Fortunately, with the precautions taken to ensure my existence stays undetected, my life finally holds only light.

. . .

THANK YOU FOR READING

Reviews are like gold dust to authors.
If you enjoyed CALLED, please consider leaving a review.
♥

Do you love supporting authors?
Would you love to be in the know before everyone else?
How would you like to read everything J.A. Belfield as part of a
package deal?
If your answers to the above are Yes, Yes, and Hell, yes, then
come join us over on Ream, and exclusive community just for
fans of J.A. Belfield.
Find us here: https://reamstories.com/jabelfield
Or scan the QR code before for easy access.

We look forward to seeing you there.

Acknowledgements

First, because he's the most important, I have to thank Mr B. Not only has he suffered my blank expressions each time my brain is in novel-land, he has done so with little complaint. Love ya, babe.

Next up, I offer huge thanks to The Boy and Boop, because whatever the outcome, they always 'get' that writing is something I just have to do.

To my friend, Carla Huxley, who reads every single word I ever write and tells me it's brilliant, who sings my praises, and who puts up with my ignorance when I pay more attention to the conversations I hold with my muse when I should be listening to her.

A massive thanks to Aimee Laine, for being the first person I didn't know to believe in me and tell me I had 'something' in this novel, for thanking me because I allowed her to read it when I should have been the one thanking her. And another thank you for this beautiful cover.

Street Team: Belfield's Book Babes. You have no freaking fracking idea how much your support helps. From looking at countless images of the same darn cover with all different-yet-horribly-similar fonts, just to help me feel as though I was getting the 'new look' right, to Hollering about the Pack, and reading my work and ... pretty much making me feel like I have something worth sharing in my writing.

Keri Lake—although I've already group-thanked you above with the Street Team, I *must* thank you again. For all the emails

I've sent you about self-publishing, my countless questions, my ignorance, my dumba$$ness (it's a WORD, dammit!) .... For each of these, you emailed me back without complaint—from messages convincing me I can DO THIS, to answers about publishing itself and necessary computer programs I have pretty much zero patience with. So, cheers.

I thank my sister, Jenny, for reading the original at first draft and loving it enough for me to write on to the end. And my original beta readers: Dawn Whipps, Elaine Hart, Carol White and Helen Parker—for begging me to get this book published the first time round, which has led the Holloway Pack to where it is today.

ABOUT J.A. BELFIELD

Best known for her Holloway Pack Stories and The Therapist,
J.A. Belfield lives in Solihull, England, with her family, a spoiled
dog, and a cat who likes to vomit in unfortunate places.

Once upon a time, she was a little girl with a vivid imagination.
Not much has changed in the last forty years.

J.A. Belfield writes paranormal romance, with a second love for
urban fantasy. And now she writes saucy romance, too. Because
she can. ;)

Scan the QR code to discover more: